£4

D1631400

The Unicorn Never Dies

To David and Toni McMurray
With very best wishes
from

[signature]

July 1998

The Unicorn Never Dies

Robin Mackenzie

The Pentland Press Limited
Edinburgh • Cambridge • Durham • USA

First published in 1998 by
The Pentland Press Ltd.
1 Hutton Close
South Church
Bishop Auckland
Durham

British Library Cataloguing in Publication Data.
A Catalogue record for this book is available
from the British Library.

ISBN 1 85821 582 X

Typeset by CBS, Felixstowe, Suffolk
Printed and bound by Bookcraft Ltd., Bath

For Jean
whose first love is Scotland

Author's Note

The characters in this story are entirely imaginary but I believe they are representative of the politicians, soldiers and people of Scotland in the nineteen fifties and sixties. The events described are also entirely imaginary, but I believe it would not have been impossible for them, or something very like them, to have happened at that time.

I have used real names for most of the places described. However I have taken certain liberties with the geography of Ardgour and Morvern in order to keep the events at Altachonich and Glenlochan in a reasonable framework of both time and space. In the case of the events described in the second half of the book, they take place in the Moray Firth area as I remember it at that time, although I have invented, renamed or transposed certain houses, farms, hotels and other locations.

I hope that the Army, the Royal Air Force and the Highland Constabulary will forgive me for the liberties I have taken with certain establishments under their control.

Finally I would like to make clear that I finished writing this book in the autumn of 1996, well before the current position on devolution was established.

Robin Mackenzie
25 March 1998

Foreword

By Major General JCOR Hopkinson CB

A thriller with a touch of romance, this book brings out the passions and loyalties; the connections with the past and insights into the future which are so much a part of the Scottish Highlands, a country of outstanding natural beauty, steeped in history and well described in this ancient Gaelic toast.

The Land of Hills, Glens and Heroes;
Where the ptarmigan thrives
And where the red deer finds shelter.
As long as the mist hangs o'er the mountains
And water runs in the glens,
The Deeds of the Brave will be remembered.
Health and Success for ever
To the lads of Cabar Feidh

CABAR FEIDH GU BRATH!
(The Deer's Horns for Ever)

This toast was first used by the Clan Mackenzie and because the Earl of Seaforth was Chief of the clan, it was adopted by the 78th or Earl of Seaforth's Highland Regiment and is still used by the successor regiments down to the present day. The author of *The Unicorn Never Dies*, Robin Mackenzie, served in the Territorial Battalion of the Seaforth Highlanders and lived in the Regimental Area, hence his understanding of and feel for the country and its traditions.

The forces of law and order and their ability to work together, so well portrayed in this book, would have been practised during the author's service, and their traditions of expertise and co-operation have not changed. A visit to Fort George near Inverness, scene of some of the action in the book, will give the reader a feel for the Highland soldier and the part he has played in the history of his own country and of the United Kingdom.

As for Scottish Nationalism – Scots will always be Scots and Highlanders will always be Highlanders – and without the talents and traditions of the people of Scotland the United Kingdom would be the poorer.

Chapter 1

To travel north from Euston to Inverness on the overnight train, The Royal Highlander, is to make one of the world's great train journeys. So thought the tall man in the grey check suit who was walking up platform 11, glancing at the reservation lists in the windows of the sleeping cars.

Over the years Duncan Forsyth had made the journey often enough, and in the course of an adventurous life, had travelled the world using many different means of transport, including several trains even more romantic than the Inverness sleeper. For all that, as his taxi drove through the arch into the station on that early spring evening in 1962, he felt again the thrill that always came with a journey to Scotland.

Tall and athletic, with dark brown hair and the sort of looks that instinctively inspire confidence, he also had, when he chose to use it, very considerable charm. This was much in evidence when, a few moments later, an attendant stepped down from one of the cars and greeted him warmly.

'Good evening, Colonel. Good to see you again. You're in here tonight; number eight it will be.'

Duncan followed him down the narrow corridor to his berth while the attendant regaled him with all the news on who was travelling that night. Then having given up his ticket and arranged his call for the next morning, he walked up the platform to the dining car and secured a seat for dinner. Finally, to complete the routine he had followed since his schooldays, he went to look at the engine, hoping against hope that they might be taken on the first part of the journey by steam.

'No such luck,' he said to himself, 'diesel-electric again!'

Somewhat disappointed, he returned to the dining car and sat down to watch the train crawl slowly past the high blank walls, topped by the backs of dingy houses, that line the northern outskirts of Euston Station. Then, as they gathered speed, he leaned back and opened his evening paper.

Some two or three minutes later he became aware of someone standing by the table and saying, 'Is this seat taken? If not, do you mind if I join you?'

He looked up and saw an attractive dark haired woman smiling at him. He noted that she was smartly dressed in a light coloured coat and skirt which admirably set off her slim figure. He reckoned she was about forty and was in business, holding a fairly responsible post. 'By all means do,' he

1

replied, 'as far as I know, no-one else is intending to sit there.'

He then returned to his perusal of the paper, while the woman settled herself in the seat opposite and proceeded to study a small notebook which she took from her handbag. A few minutes later the steward appeared at their table and asked about drinks. The woman ordered dry sherry and Forsyth asked for a large whisky and soda. Having noted their orders, the steward then enquired if they would like any wine.

Forsyth looked across at his companion and asked, 'Would you share a bottle of wine with me?' and smiling both at her and at the steward, added, 'Andy here will confirm that British Railways really can produce quite a decent bottle.'

'I would be delighted,' she replied, 'and what does Andy recommend?' Andy's suggestion, it appeared, was to have a bottle of the Medoc, and this was greeted with general approval.

'Right then, Andy,' he said. 'Medoc it is.'

Having settled the question of what they would drink, they returned to their respective papers. Even after the drinks arrived, they continued either reading or staring out of the window, first at dreary industrial suburbs and then, in the gathering darkness, at the villages and fields of Hertfordshire. When the soup arrived Forsyth folded his paper and looking across the table, decided the time had come to break the ice.

'I'm sorry,' he said, 'you must think me very rude. But I thought I ought to try and find out what has happened in the world to-day, although with this paper the world tends to mean London! I'm Duncan Forsyth and as you will have gathered, I'm a pretty regular user of this train.'

'I don't think you are in the least bit rude,' she said, adding with a smile, 'I rather think that I should be apologising for interrupting your reading.'

Then, looking up from her grapefruit, she went on, 'My name is Jane Parsons and I'm visiting my sister near Inverness; a rare event I'm afraid, which means I am not a regular on this train. So thank you for dealing with the question of the wine. I'm sure I would not have had the nerve to order a bottle of wine with a railway dinner.'

'You know, you should never make fun of railway meals. People do, but they are usually quite wrong.' Forsyth was a frequent traveller, both nationally and internationally, by road, rail, sea and air. He tended therefore to hold stronger, and perhaps more accurate, views on the competence of the various organisations with which he travelled than did less frequent travellers. 'Railway food and railway wine are both much better than you get on the majority of airlines. They are also far better served and can be eaten in civilised comfort. Look at us – we left Euston just before half-past seven and now, here we are – at eight o'clock – starting dinner; and we're sitting at a proper table with proper plates and cutlery – no plastic for us. What's more, we don't have to hurry. No need to move until we reach Crewe.'

'I defer to your experience and certainly I agree about the discomfort of eating in aeroplanes,' Jane replied and then added, 'Now it is my turn to be inquisitive. May I ask what you do and where you are going? Are you also going the whole way – to Inverness I mean?'

Duncan hated the first part of the question. It always occurred early in a conversation with a stranger and he had a very good reason for finding it difficult to answer. He paused for a few moments and gave himself a bit of time by buttering the remains of his roll before replying. 'I suppose you could say I'm a consultant. I work for a rather odd body. It is responsible to the Government but not to any particular Ministry. It's called The Trade and Technical Training Agency – TATTA for short. Those with a facetious turn of mind call us 'The Goodbye Boys'! And where am I going?' He paused again for a moment.

Then he went on: 'I'm on my way to Inverness. And then on further north for a few days' holiday and I hope some fishing with friends on the Brora.'

He hoped that this reply would do for the time being, for saying what he really did was not normally possible. He was in fact a fairly important member of MI6, or the SIS as it should more properly be called, and his evasiveness in any conversation involving his work had driven his friends and relations mad ever since he had left the army more than ten years before. On this occasion he decided to fall back on TATTA, one of the SIS cover organisations, and a very useful one too. Almost anything could be dreamed up to describe the work of TATTA. He also decided that it was time to put the ball back in her court.

'I think you said you were going to see your sister, so are you too on holiday? And when you are not on holiday, what do you do? Are you a London working girl?'

It transpired that Jane Parsons was a widow, that she had been left comfortably off and that she had no children. She worked as senior secretary in a firm of importers and distributors of fine fabrics for the fashion trade. From the way she described her job, he decided that she was rather more than a secretary, for she appeared to be in charge of all the female staff and was also personal assistant to the managing director.

'As to what am I doing now,' she continued, 'yes – like you I am having a bit of holiday. My brother-in-law has a yacht, so we are going down the canal to Fort William, and then on to Oban. If the weather is good we may then do some serious sailing, at least as far as Crinan, and possibly round some of the inner islands. It's years since I sailed down Loch Ness and so I'm really looking forward to it.'

By the time they had finished their main course, Jane was admitting that there was quite a lot to be said for railway food, and that the wine was indeed passable. The conversation then became more general, covering such things as the problems of managing secretaries, the inability of customers to make up their minds and the difficulties of dealing with the Customs and Excise. This latter subject caused Forsyth to smile to himself. When the coffee, the least good part of the meal, arrived, he offered her a liqueur, which she declined saying she had never acquired a taste for the sweet and sticky, a sentiment with which he wholeheartedly agreed.

The train was now passing Stafford and the architecturally sterile factories of the heavy electrical industry. Jane turned her gaze from this unromantic view to look at the man sitting opposite her and said, 'Tell me – and I hope you don't mind my asking – are you married? I've told you quite a bit about myself, but apart from the fact that you work for a Government Agency of some sort, we have said little about you.'

This was the other question that he hated but, unlike the question of his work, about his personal life he could be truthful.

'Yes,' he said, 'I am married but I don't often see my wife, for we lead completely separate lives. She lives in the South of France and rarely comes to England. We have a daughter of fourteen who is at a boarding school in Hampshire. Seeing her at school is virtually our only meeting now. She – my daughter that is – spends most of her holidays with her mother but she does come over for at least a week to stay with my parents.'

'You are not divorced then?' she asked.

'No. Not even officially separated. It seemed an awful expense and I suppose neither of us wanted or needed to make the ultimate break.'

Feeling that personal histories had gone far enough, and knowing that they would be in Crewe in under half an hour, Duncan suggested that he might buy her a drink. She accepted a whisky and soda and he ordered for them both. She turned out to be remarkably knowledgeable about whisky and for the next five minutes they discussed the relative merits of various malts and blends.

From whisky the talk turned to the problems of the Highlands, the lack of opportunities for the young and the difficulties not only of creating new local industries, but also of attracting outside investment to the area. Their conversation was helped along by another drink and lasted until, with a squealing of brakes, the train lurched over the points into the gloomy glass cavern that is Crewe station.

When it finally came to a halt, Duncan stood up and said, 'I usually walk down the platform. It's much easier than trying to squeeze oneself down the corridor and negotiating the dogs and bicycles in the guard's van.'

After leaving the dining car, they stood for a moment on the platform before walking back down the train. As he reached the door of his sleeper, Duncan Forsyth turned and said, 'This is where I get in, so I'll say good night and thankyou for a most enjoyable dinner. I hope your holiday goes well.'

'Hold on,' came the unexpected reply, 'don't say all your farewells yet. I too live in this carriage and it's still quite early.'

With that she climbed into the carriage and set off down the passage in search of the attendant. Before following her, Duncan turned and glanced towards the front of the train just as, with a hiss of escaping steam, the massive Duchess Class locomotive that was to take them on to Perth came to rest against the first carriage. As it stood there panting gently, the fireman jumped down from the footplate and, having made the coupling, remained on the platform talking to the guard and the driver and wiping the grease from his hands with a bunch of cotton waste.

Smiling to himself, for he loved steam, Duncan climbed into the sleeper and made his way down to his berth, to find his passage blocked by Jane and the attendant exchanging tickets and morning call details. The attendant moved aside and he entered his compartment, shut the door and sat down on the bed. 'So she's in next door,' he said to himself and wondered idly how the night might develop.

Thinking about it, he had to admit that he viewed the forthcoming hours with somewhat mixed feelings. Jane was undoubtedly an attractive and interesting woman, but a little niggle was forming in his mind and experience told him that when that happened, something was usually wrong. In this case he did not know quite what and he needed to find out. He was to do so sooner than he expected. There was a gentle tap on the communicating door and Jane's voice said: 'Is it unlocked and can I come in?' Duncan reached over and turned the catch and she pushed the door open saying, 'I think I owe you a drink. And since I have a bottle of whisky and I have managed to raise some soda water, will you come and join me?'

With that she stepped back, sat down on her bed and wriggled along towards the window, adding, 'and don't forget to bring your glass!'

Knowing how hot and stuffy a first class sleeper can get, he had already taken off his jacket and tie, and, as he stepped through into her compartment, he found himself apologising for his informal appearance. Taking no notice of this remark, she looked up and patted the bed beside her. Accepting the invitation, he sat down and watched while she poured a generous measure into his glass and gestured towards the soda.

'Don't you find life rather boring, living mainly on your own?'

Duncan, who was looking at the pale golden liquid in his glass, took a sip and thought for a moment before answering.

'Not really,' he said, 'You see I spend a good deal of time travelling and even when I am at home, my work entails quite a bit of social life.' He could not tell her the full truth, which was that the travelling, and sometimes the social life, both involved a degree of excitement, and sometimes danger, which was not conducive to boredom.

'You are lucky,' she said. 'For me life is rather different. Now and again

I meet interesting people as part of my job but by and large my life is work, home and then work again. And not much in the way of comfort and support. But I suppose that is true of a lot of people.' She looked at him with a little twisted smile, and he felt that tears – crocodile or genuine he wondered? – were not far away.

She sat up and pouring herself another drink, sipped it morosely for a few minutes. Then, leaning over towards him, she rested her head on his shoulder.

'Do you mind?' she asked. And then after a pause, 'turn out the light please.'

He reached up and clicked the switch, leaving them in that soft purple glow which the railway authorities feel is more appropriate for their passengers than total darkness. He also quietly turned the key in the passage door.

Jane was standing up and he could sense rather than see that she was undressing. 'You too,' she whispered, and then he felt her warm body wriggle down beside him. Her arm reached up and pulled his head towards hers and she kissed him full on the lips. He could feel her breasts pressing against his body and, with her arms locked behind his neck, he surrendered himself to her.

As they lay together in the warm blue darkness, they slept, lulled by the insistent whisper of the wheels as the train roared on towards the Scottish border. It was, as always, Carlisle, with its clatter of milk churns and biscuit tins, that woke him. He rolled quietly off the bed and slipped into his own compartment.

'Please don't shut the door,' he heard a sleepy voice say as he got into his own bed. He lay there dozing and thinking until sleep once more overcame him.

Chapter 2

It was probably the change in the noise of the wheels as they started the ascent of Beattock Summit that woke him and in seconds he was alert, although still appearing to be asleep. He heard a faint scraping noise and through half closed eyes he could just make out a hand reaching for his brief case. A minute or two later he saw the case returned and heard soft creaking noises as his neighbour went back to her bed.

The doubts about Jane which had worried him earlier returned, and he began to think that she might have something to do with the real reason for his journey to Scotland.

Then as he lay listening to the sound of the wheels, he saw again a paragraph in his evening paper about a blonde woman, a Miss Janet Priestley, whom the police wished to interview in connection with some missing property. No details were given and he had thought nothing of it at the time he read it. But now he wondered if certain people in whom he had an interest had moved faster than expected and that he might have discovered this by pure chance. Whether this was true or not, he was quite sure that Jane Parsons, or whatever her name might be, had no idea of his true identity.

Assuming that he was correct, it was now urgent that he make a telephone call to warn his organisation that they might have been taken by surprise. He realised that he must make this call before they reached Perth, or better still, before Stirling. Carstairs Junction, the next stop, seemed the obvious place but he would need to hurry. They would be there in twenty minutes and would be unlikely to stop for very long.

Duncan's first problem was to get out and back without waking the girl. As far as he could tell from her heavy breathing, she was now fast asleep. Considering the amount of whisky she had drunk and also their earlier bedtime activity, he reckoned that she would remain so for another hour or more. He got up and gently shut and locked the communicating door. Then having dressed, he went out into the passage and stood there listening. Hearing nothing but Jane's steady breathing, he closed his door and made his way down to the attendant's pantry.

He told the attendant, who was quite used to Duncan's unusual behaviour, that he would have to get out at Carstairs but would definitely be back on board before they left. He then walked to the far end of the next carriage and, as the train slowed to a crawl, he jumped on to the platform offering silent thanks for the fact that the sleeper windows were on the other side.

In a moment he was across the platform, through a gate and round the back of the station buildings to the booking office. There, as he hoped, he found Jimmie Macleod, the station foreman, who, before he joined the railway, had been a Sergeant in Duncan's regiment, and on several previous occasions had been very helpful. Making a sign for silence he whispered,

'Any chance of holding the train for long enough for me to make a phone call, Jimmie?'

'Up to your old tricks again are you? Aye well, I'll see what can be done,' Jimmie replied, 'but mind you, I dinna like it. Forbye there's a deal o' mail and parcels to be shifted and maybe the lads will be a bit slow. You'd best make the call from the cottage. The wife's up and will let you in.'

A couple of minutes later Duncan was tapping on the cottage door, which opened an inch or two. Finger to lips, he pushed gently. The door opened and then shut as soon as he was inside.

'I'm sorry to disturb you, Agnes,' said Duncan, looking at the questioning eyes of Mrs Jimmie Macleod, 'but I must telephone. Jimmie is holding the train, but not for long.'

'Och, no bother, I was up anyway.' Agnes gestured to the back of the room. 'In there an' ye'll be quite safe. I canna hear you when I'm in the kitchen.' Duncan vanished into the back regions, returning in a few minutes.

'Man, but you were quick,' exclaimed Agnes, 'you canna have been saying much. '

'Enough, Agnes, enough. And now I must run. Many thanks!' Agnes held open the door for him. On the platform, doors were banging and two porters and a postman were pulling back the trolleys.

'In here!' said Jimmie. 'I've squared the guard, and guid luck to you whatever ye're at.' Duncan jumped for the guard's van, whistles blew and they were on their way north again.

After a short conversation with the guard and the exchange of a suitable banknote, he made his way back to his sleeper. The corridor was empty and, as he slipped into his berth, he could hear no sound from next door.

Feeling that there was nothing more he could do, he climbed into bed and slept so soundly that he missed the noise and bustle of Perth and did not wake until they were pulling into Aviemore and his tea and biscuits arrived. There was still no sign of life from next door, but he thought it advisable to give breakfast a miss. Apart from the possibility of meeting Jane, he was not particularly keen to find the breakfast car full of other people he might know. So he dressed in leisurely fashion and, as the train pulled into Inverness, he was waiting by the door, briefcase in hand. When it stopped, he jumped down and was walking towards the Station Hotel when he felt a hand on his shoulder and a voice with a gentle west coast accent said, 'Excuse me, sir, but would you mind giving me your case and coming with us to the Police Station.' Looking more than a little surprised, but realising that protest would merely attract attention and would be better left until later, Forsyth did as he was asked.

'I can't imagine how I can help you,' he said, 'but if that is what you want, of course I agree. But are you sure it is me that you want? And what about my luggage?'

'Aye, I'm quite sure it's you that we are wanting. You are Mr Duncan Forsyth, are you not?' said the tall man in the dark suit who stood beside him. 'I'm Inspector Nicholson of the Inverness CID and I think it would be best if we go straight to the car. Your luggage will be looked after. This way, please sir, it's less public than the main entrance.'

With that, the Inspector took him by the arm and steered him towards a flight of steps leading to a narrow side street where a plain black car was waiting. As they went, Duncan took a quick look back at the train and was pleased to see that Jane Parsons was standing by the carriage door and must have watched all that had taken place, although he thought that she was doing her best to hide her interest.

When they reached the car, the Inspector pointed to the back seat and Duncan got in with Nicholson beside him. Another plain clothes man got in beside the driver and they moved off towards the town centre. To his surprise they did not go to the main Police Station, but headed down to the river.

'The Chief said that we should take you straight to his office,' Nicholson explained and added, 'I hope that the arrest was convincing. I am believing that the young lady was watching .'

'I think so,' said Duncan, 'she certainly appeared to be taking a surreptitious interest.'

The rest of the short journey was completed in silence and when they reached the headquarters of the Inverness Constabulary, they were taken at once to the Chief Constable's office. John Marshall, Chief Constable of Inverness-shire, was a big, heavily built man, a professional policeman to his fingertips. He had joined the police some thirty years ago in Edinburgh and had worked his way up to his present rank through a wide variety of jobs including senior appointments in both England and Scotland.

He rose when they entered and shook hands saying, as Nicholson made to introduce Duncan, 'Fine I ken Duncan Forsyth. How are you, man? Now sit down and I'll tell you what has happened here, what we know so far and what we think we may have to do. And then, sir, I'd be very obliged if you would let me know just exactly what is going on.'

The Chief Constable sat back and waved his visitors to the two chairs in front of his desk. Then leaning forward on his elbows, he looked straight at Forsyth.

'It would have been about four this morning when the Duty Officer here got a call from your people asking for help in support of one of their agents,' he said.

'They told the officer that it was a matter of great importance and highly confidential and that full information was on its way to me personally via the secure teleprinter. The Duty Officer at once got in touch with the Superintendent in charge of the CID, who alerted myself. We both came straight here and just as we arrived, the stuff started coming over the line. Aye, and pretty strange it was too. Have a look at it. And then perhaps you would tell us what it is all about.'

Duncan took the two flimsy sheets which the Chief Constable held out and, leaning back in his chair, read them through. As he had already guessed, the information they contained came from the Director of the SIS. It gave a brief outline of the background to Duncan's arrival in Scotland and the reason for thinking that a possible international crisis, of a kind which must be averted at all costs, might occur sooner than expected. It further indicated that police forces in both Scotland and England already had some involvement and asked the Chief Constable of Inverness-shire to coordinate police support for any action that might be required. Finally it stated that a full explanation would be given by the SIS agent, and that the whole operation had been authorised personally by the Prime Minister.

Duncan leaned forward and gave the papers back to Marshall and then got up and walking to the window, looked down at the wide brown stream of the Ness as he waited for the Chief Constable to speak.

'Mr Forsyth, I have to say that that is all we know. Of course, over the past ten years we have had some involvement in Nationalist outrages. Pillar box bombs, Drill Hall break-ins. Aye, and of course disruption of meetings. But nothing of the kind implied here; of the kind that would involve agencies such as yourselves. And why you? Man, I would have thought this would be for the Special Branch, or MI5 at the worst. If I'm to help you – and it would appear that the highest in the land are ordering me to – I'm still going to need some very good explanations.'

Forsyth turned to face the room. 'Chief Constable,' he said, 'I will do my best to tell you the whole story. But before I do, do you think it would be an idea to have one of your Deputies or the head of the CID in as well? It's entirely up to you of course.'

Marshall thought for a moment, then picked up the telephone and told his secretary to find Mr Maclay and ask him to come to the office at once. Then he said, "Jock Maclay is the Deputy Chief Constable with responsibility for all security matters. He's a good man, you'll like him and, assuming we have to mount a support operation, he'll be in charge.'

As the Chief Constable finished speaking, a broad-shouldered man with a massive face and a well trimmed grey moustache came into the room. A real

Highlander, thought Duncan.

'Jock, this is Mr Duncan Forsyth of M16, the cause of our current problems,' said Marshall as the two men shook hands. 'Find yourself a seat, for he is now going to tell us what's going on; what he is doing in Scotland and what he wants from us.'

Duncan Forsyth remained standing with his back to the window. 'I'm sure I don't need to tell you, gentlemen, that what I am now going to say is in the highest degree confidential. It involves the security of the United Kingdom and probably the security of other countries. The telex you received authorises me to give you this information, but I must still point out that what I say is covered by the Official Secrets Act.' Having issued his warning, Duncan then proceeded to tell them the history of Unicorn and what the Government believed it intended to do.

As early as 1950 the Scottish Office, and also some police forces in Scotland, began to hear rumours of an organisation which would be dedicated to using violence to support the cause of Scottish independence. For the next ten years it remained very much in the background and the authorities could find out little about it. However by 1960, with the increasing strength of the independence movement, certain highly placed persons concerned with national security decided to investigate whether there might be a real possibility of violent action occurring in Scotland.

The early results of these investigations were both surprising and serious. There was indeed a body, associated with, but not part of, the political side of the Nationalists. It had started as a group of people with a common belief that political ends could be achieved more rapidly by the use of force, and who had acquired a knowledge of guerrilla operations during and just after the War. In their early days they had had no formal title, referring to themselves simply as freedom fighters, but now they were becoming more organised. They had acquired a name and it was becoming obvious that they had access to substantial funds.

Some twelve months ago those who moved on the fringes of the independence movement started to hear of two names – 'The American Sons of the Clearances' and 'The Unicorn'. Attempts were made to find out more about these organisations and some information had been forthcoming. But recently the mention of either name in anything approaching polite society had met with an embarrassed silence. A decision was therefore taken to mount a full-scale investigation to find out if there was indeed a secret, and possibly violent, side to Scottish Nationalism.

Very little was discovered about The Unicorn except that a well-known Nationalist firebrand, Fergus Crawford by name, was involved in it. While he would undoubtedly have an important role in any such organisation, he would be unlikely to be the brains behind it. To find out who was had so far proved impossible, as had any attempt to discover where it was based. What had been established though, was that Unicorn intended to make use of those standard weapons of terrorism, blackmail and the destruction of property and life.

Rather more had been discovered about The American Sons of the Clearances. As they were based outside the United Kingdom, investigating them had been the responsibility of the SIS, and this was how Duncan Forsyth had become involved. The American Sons of the Clearances had been in existence for many years, but in the past the body had restricted itself to such things as organising Highland Games and helping with family research. Like most American societies it had, over the years, accumulated considerable wealth and during the Depression had used this to assist descendants of Scottish families who had fallen on hard times. However it had recently come under the control of certain people who had an interest in the Nationalist movement in Scotland and were using the Society's money to further this interest. It appeared that they had made contact with Unicorn and had promised to finance some of its activities. Whether they knew that these activities involved violence was not clear. What was clear was that attempts would be made to smuggle money into Scotland, possibly through the textile industry.

In view of the difficulties that could arise through this involvement of foreign countries, it had been decided by the Government, and agreed by all concerned, that the operation should continue to be run by the SIS. The police, MI5 and the Customs and Excise would be required to give their support, as would the armed forces, should this become necessary. Duncan Forsyth had come up to Scotland, ostensibly on a fishing holiday, because information had been received that Unicorn was expecting an imminent transfer of funds from overseas and was likely to use the money to obtain the explosives and other weapons necessary for their first operation. If it could only be discovered how the money was to be brought in, this could give the best chance so far of locating those in charge of Unicorn.

When he had finished his account of the events leading up to the current Unicorn operation, Duncan returned to his chair and waited for comments from his audience. The Chief Constable, who had been gazing at the ceiling, now swivelled his chair round and looked straight at Forsyth.

'Aye, that's all very fine,' he said, 'but before I can help, I'll need some authority. I can just see the Convener's face when I tell him I'm spending the police budget supporting the Secret Service! Lord Darrochy has a verra uncertain temper and an intense dislike of government authority – aye, of any authority, come to that! You say that we will all be required to give support. But where are the orders coming from and when? That telex is not enough. I'll listen to your plans but I canna promise any support at present, other than for what could be said to be normal police work.'

'Before I left London I was told that all those likely to be involved in these operations would receive official confirmation of the information I have just given you, replied Duncan. 'I also understood that a request for help, endorsed by Downing Street, would be coming from my Chief. I cannot say when or how this will reach you or any of the others involved.'

Before continuing Duncan stood up and resuming his stand by the window, turned to face the room and said: 'Look, you must have realised that on the train last night I had what may turn out to be a major stroke of luck.' Then he looked straight at John Marshall.

'Chief Constable,' he said, 'I presume your people have already looked at my brief case. May I ask what they found in it?'

'Twenty thousand dollars in hundred dollar bills,' replied the Chief Constable, and then continued, 'you have probably guessed that as well as your Chief's telex, we had an anonymous tip-off about your brief case.

'I suspected as much,' said Forsyth, 'and I think what happened is this. Rather than use a bank transaction which could be traced, the money was brought into England as cash via the company that my travelling companion works for, and she was to take it up to Scotland. I noticed, incidentally, that she had two large suitcases. Some sort of problem arose in London, I don't know what, and the police became interested. There was a paragraph in the evening paper about a Janet Priestley, and the similarity of the name to Jane Parsons caught my eye.'

He paused and thought for a moment before continuing. 'I think what happened in London worried her and to divert suspicion, she decided to transfer some of the money to another passenger and inform the police. Her misfortune was that she chose me, not realising that I saw her take my case. So I then called my people from Carstairs and she probably rang you from Perth. Incidentally, whose request resulted in my arrest? Anyway the result of all this is that if I am right in thinking Unicorn is involved, we now have a very real chance of finding their whereabouts.'

'Fine,' said Marshall, 'but bearing in mind my present limited capacity to help you, what do you propose to do?'

'Well I know what the Parsons woman looks like. I assume that she was telling the truth when she said she was joining a yacht. If they are going down the canal, I assume it will be in Muirtown Basin, so I think the next step is for me to sit down with Mr Maclay and the Inspector and see if we can come up with a plan which would be within your current resources.'

'Aye, I'll agree to that,' said the Chief Constable and turning to his Deputy added, 'Jock, see what you can do for Mr Forsyth. But report to me before any action is taken.'

Chapter 3

Altachonich Castle stands at the head of the small sea loch of the same name. It is surrounded by well wooded policies and the garden is famous for the variety and excellence of its shrubs. Behind the castle the ground rises steeply, and to the west merges into the cliffs that form the major part of the loch's coastline. Further to the north lies the rocky wilderness of Altachonich Forest rising to the two peaks of Meall Garbh and Beinn Buidhe. To the east however, the ground slopes gently down to the loch shore and it is from this direction that the castle is normally approached by road, either the main road from Fort William, or a minor road which runs north over the hill to the village of Glenlochan.

However the traditional approach to Altachonich has always been by sea, and to the front of the castle, below the garden, lies a private pier and boathouse. There is also another pier and a small harbour below the cliffs to the west of the castle. This was originally built to serve a quarry but neither quarry nor harbour have been used for many years.

The lands and castle of Altachonich have, for the past four hundred years, been in the possession of the Macleans of Glenlochan. The present owner, Sir Torquhil Drumcairn of Glenlochan, who inherited the estate from his mother, could hardly be called a typical Highland laird, having spent his entire working life with Drumcairn Lines, mainly in the Far East.

At the age of fifty-five, having retired with a considerable fortune and a knighthood, he entered Parliament as a member for a Glasgow constituency. But he soon became disenchanted with the parliamentary type of politics, concluding that the House of Commons would never understand all the things that he believed needed doing in Scotland, and would certainly be unable to persuade any Government to act on them. On the death of his mother he therefore quit Parliament and went to live at Altachonich, determined to use his estate to bring employment and prosperity to the surrounding area.

Sir Torquhil's view of how this might be done was very different to that of the majority of his peers, something which troubled him not at all – in fact rather pleased him, since it meant that he was left alone by most of his neighbours. For, like many Scotsmen before him who had spent much of their lives overseas, on his return he determined to use his fortune, in his own way, to further what he believed to be the best interests of his native country.

With all the ability and energy that had made him a power in world shipping he set about improving the estate, first in the traditional areas of farming and forestry and then by the creation of new enterprises, which he hoped would provide much needed employment. The first of these enterprises was the re-opening of the quarry. This was followed by the improvement of the harbour. In the past, the area in which he lived had always depended on the sea for transport and Sir Torquhil was determined that it should do so again. He was firmly of the opinion that reliance on an inadequate road system made development in isolated communities almost impossible. However the desire to bring new sources of employment to such communities was not his only interest.

Like many of those who have achieved success in life, Sir Torquhil Drumcairn was both a visionary and a romantic. He had always had a fascination with Scottish history and the idea of Scottish nationhood and his experience as an MP had convinced him that what he thought of as an English parliament would never do anything significant for the benefit of Scotland. It was not surprising therefore, that since taking up permanent residence at Altachonich he had drifted gradually, not only towards Nationalism, but also towards support for the Gaelic language and, with a natural ability to learn new languages, he soon acquired a reasonable fluency in Gaelic. This interest in the old language on the part of a man such as Sir Torquhil eventually came to the notice of those who felt that an independent Scotland could not be achieved through the ballot box alone.

On this particular April morning, the laird, usually a man who knew exactly how he was going to fill every minute of every day, appeared nervous and uncertain.

Even a walk round the garden, during which he shouted at a somewhat surprised head gardener, failed to calm him. Returning to the castle, he went straight to his study and standing by the window gazed out over the loch. Sir Torquhil was a tall grey haired man with a natural air of command, a man used to knowing his own mind and getting his own way. Now, for the first time for many years, he found himself confronted by a situation in which he was unsure of his correct course of action. It was this uncertainty of mind that was the cause of his current irritation.

A short while later, still gazing out of the window, he heard a tap on the door and turned to find his daughter looking at him with unaccustomed severity.

'Father, what on earth is the matter with you to-day?' she said, 'you have succeeded in upsetting nearly everybody on the place.'

'I know, my dear, and I'm sorry,' he replied, 'You know I don't like any situation where I cannot see the obvious way forward. Well there's one confronting me now. Come and sit down and I'll tell you a bit about it. And I'd also better tell you about the plans for today.'

Her father moved over to his desk and swivelled the chair round so that he could look at the girl, who had perched herself on a stool by the fireplace. Daphne Drumcairn was an extremely good looking woman and it was a mystery to her father why she was not yet married. He also admitted to himself that he was very glad she was not. For ever since his wife had died, which had been shortly after they returned to Scotland, his daughter had kept house for him and not only did she run the household at the castle with extreme efficiency, even allowing for her constant absences either skiing or sailing, but she was an entertaining and often useful companion. She possessed a natural common sense which he had found helpful on many occasions, and this was one of the reasons why he had decided to tell her something of his present trouble.

'As you know,' he said in his quiet, deliberate voice, 'I am now totally committed to working for Scottish independence, but I have always considered that this should be achieved by normal political means. You also probably realise that this is not the view of many in the movement, even of some of those who are quite respectable. Recently I was approached to see if I could use my influence to facilitate the transfer of funds from sympathisers in America to a part of our movement, a part I know little about, but I believe to be intending to use illegal means to speed the achievement of independence. What their exact plans are I do not yet know, and I'm not sure that I want to.'

'I should think not,' the girl replied and continued, looking straight at her father, 'You are a well known and respected person who has done much for his country and who is in a position to do a great deal more. You know my views on the question of Nationalism. While it may be the ultimate answer, we are not ready for it yet and we certainly do not want it rushed. However if you want to continue your support, that is your affair. But father, for heaven's sake do not get involved in anything illegal. Yours should always be a moderating influence.'

'I know, my dear,' Sir Torquhil replied, 'but the trouble is that I agreed to help over the finances, and the first lot of money from our American friends should already be in Scotland. Later to-day I have two people coming here to discuss plans for its use. You have probably heard of one of them, Fergus Crawford. He is well known in hard-line Nationalist circles. The other is a woman called Jane Parsons, about whom I know nothing. Incidentally they will both be here for dinner and will be staying the night.'

'Fergus Crawford!' Daphne, who was not given to displays of anger, almost shouted the name. 'Father, you're mad! You know perfectly well he's a criminal and that he was involved in that break-in at the Oban Drill Hall and the attempt to steal rifles – and that he was also suspected of derailing that train outside Glasgow. You should have nothing to do with him and if you do, you will be on your way to losing my respect.'

'I thought you would say that, and I expect you are probably right. But I've got to go through with the present meeting. It's all arranged.'

'Well, I think you're a damn fool,' said his daughter, 'and all I can say is, please be careful. This time I will make the arrangements for your guests, but not again. And now I must leave . As I told you earlier, I'm lunching at Kildrum.'

Her father got to his feet saying, 'I'd better move too and get organised for the arrival of these people. Have a nice lunch and my regards to the Kildrums, and see you later. By the way, I'd rather you did not say anything to anybody about what I have just told you.'

When Daphne left the room, her father leaned back in his chair and wondered whether he had been sensible to tell her as much as he had. But he felt he had to give some reason for the arrival of Crawford and the woman and he also suspected that she was beginning to get worried about the activity at the quarry. But this activity he was not yet prepared to discuss with her. For he knew what the result would be if he told her that his new enterprise was actually the cover for the training base and supplies depot of The Unicorn.

It was this fact that was now causing him so much concern. Agreeing to help with financing was one thing; allowing the use of the quarry for undercover operations was quite another. And now he suspected that the two who were coming to see him would use this somewhat unwise agreement to get him even more deeply involved.

'So what?' he thought, 'I'm already almost certainly guilty of treachery, possibly even treason. That being the case, whatever I do to support the cause can hardly make my position worse.'

Having made his decision, the doubts of the morning vanished and Sir Torquhil felt once again his normal confident self. He turned his chair round to face the desk and picking up the telephone, summoned the quarry manager to come and discuss their tactics for the forthcoming meeting.

Chapter 4

Jane Parsons watched the removal of Duncan Forsyth by the police and then, having summoned a porter and seen her two large suitcases loaded on to a trolley, she looked down the platform to see her brother-in-law walking towards her. They greeted each other suitably, then followed the porter towards the exit.

'It's grand to see you Jane. The car's in the yard and Mary's waiting in the hotel but if you don't mind I'd like to leave at once, for I'll be happier when this lot is safely on the boat,' he said, pointing at the luggage. Then he added, 'the *Firefly* is not in the Basin. I've moved her to below the bridge and the locks, so we ought not to be held up. Now, go you and find Mary and I'll get the cases in the car.'

Jane turned and went into the hotel by the side entrance and down the passage to the main hall, where she found her sister just finishing her coffee.

'Let me get you a coffee now, and you can tell me about your journey,' began Mary, but Jane shook her head.

'Roddy said we should go straight to the boat. He's anxious to get the luggage safely stowed,' she said, 'and we'll have plenty of time for coffee and gossip once we're on board. Also, for reasons you will hear, I too will be happier when we are well out into the loch.'

When they got to the car they found the cases already loaded and ten minutes later they drew up beside a nice looking Bermuda-rigged cruiser. Roddy took the cases from the back of the car and lowering them to the deck of the yacht, jumped down after them and stowed them in the main cabin. Then he looked up at the two women and shouted to them to come on board.

'I'll just take the car down to Mackay's,' he said, 'they've agreed to keep her until we return and we'll set off as soon as I get back.'

Roderick Urquhart was a native of the Black Isle. After a brief spell in the army at the end of the war, he had gone to Edinburgh University on a scholarship and had become active in the Nationalist side of student politics. Leaving the University with a good degree, he qualified as an accountant and then joined one of the well known Edinburgh investment houses. After some ten years he left Edinburgh and set up his own business in Inverness. Outside his business he had two interests – sailing and politics – and he appeared to have enough money to indulge both.

His politics were those of his days at University, strictly Nationalist. His support for the cause of Scottish independence had been strengthened by his marriage to Mary Crawford, who was the daughter of an early leader of the cause and the sister of Fergus Crawford. His marriage had brought him into contact with Fergus and, through him, with The Unicorn. Unlike Sir Torquhil Drumcairn, Roddy Urquhart had no qualms about Unicorn. He knew well what their intentions were and, over the past eighteen months, he and Mary had used their yacht *Firefly* in support of a number of Unicorn missions. Mary's sister Jane, who normally used her married name of Parsons but was sometimes known as Janet Priestley, was also a dedicated supporter of the cause and had become involved with Unicorn, which body had found her contacts in the textile importing business to be extremely valuable.

'Roddy will no' be long,' said Mary when they were both safely on board, 'and I'm thinking he will want to get under way at once. I hope I've got everything we need. I had to do it all in a wee bit of a hurry yesterday. Anyway, tell me how you are and what's this about your journey?'

'That can wait until we're out in the loch, for I want Roddy to hear it too,' her sister replied. 'Why don't you make some coffee while I just change into trousers?'

A few minutes later a series of noises on deck heralded the return of the skipper. Shortly afterwards the engine started and he shouted, 'Everything secure? If so, would one of you cast off and we'll be away.' Jane emerged from the cabin and scrambled on to the quay. She unhitched the bow rope and threw it onto the deck, then walked back, picked up the stern warp and jumped down with it into the cockpit; the noise of the engine increased and Roddy headed out into the stream

As they motored slowly down the canal, Jane went forward to sort out the ropes on the foredeck, and then returning to the cockpit, neatly coiled the stern warp and sat down beside her brother-in-law. At that moment Mary emerged from the cabin with two mugs of coffee, then fetching another for herself, joined them in the cockpit.

'Now let's hear what Jane has to say,' said Roddy Urquhart, then without raising his eyes from the boat's course added, 'I think we'll motor rather than sail even when we get to the loch. It's easier for talking and we've a lot to discuss. Now then Janie, what happened last night?'

'It's not only last night that is the problem. It's the whole of yesterday. We very nearly had a real cock-up! The shipment came in from the States on time two days ago. Fifteen rolls of really lovely silk, all to be delivered yesterday morning to Harrods. As far as I could tell, it was on the correct roll boards and they appeared to have the agreed marks on them. Unfortunately I had to go out that afternoon. Needless to say I got held up, so by the time I arrived back at the office it was shut, and although I have a key to the office, I do not have one to the warehouse. I had planned to stay late, saying I needed to check things in the warehouse, and if I could please have a key, I would lock up and return the key in the morning.'

'But why did you not get a key before you went out?' asked Roddy. 'OK, don't bother, I suppose that would have looked a bit suspicious. So – what did you do then?'

'You may well ask!' she said. 'I decided that whatever happened I was going to need help. I therefore rang Sandy and asked him if he was free the next day, which he was. So I told him to stay by the phone all morning until I rang again, and then to bring his van as quickly as possible to wherever I told him. I then prepared some things which I thought might be useful the next day. When I finally got to bed, you can imagine I had a rather sleepless night. Well, I got to the office early and went down to the warehouse to find that the rolls for Harrods were already loaded for delivery. I asked the driver whether he was going to Harrods first and if not where he was going. I said I was particularly concerned to see that the Harrods delivery arrived safely and I had promised them I would be there when it did. The young man was not in the least suspicious and gave me his full morning route.'

'Are you sure it was safe to involve Sandy?' Mary asked. 'You know I have never been convinced of his commitment; and with his brother being a policeman.'

'I had no alternative,' replied Jane, 'I had to have help and, as you'll see, I think I gave him enough of a fright to make him keep his mouth shut. Anyway, when I had finished talking to the driver, I went up to the office, rang Sandy and asked him to meet me, with the van, in a side street near where one of our deliveries was to be made. Then, telling the boss I had an important meeting, I took a taxi to Kensington High Street and in the ladies at Barkers I changed from Jane Parsons to Janet Priestley, with blond hair and a bright red jacket in place of the one that matched my skirt. I then nipped round the corner, found Sandy and told him what I wanted. Then we waited for the van to appear.

'I let the driver make the delivery and just as he was getting back into his cab, I came rushing up brandishing some papers. "I am very sorry, I said, but there has been a mistake about the delivery to Harrods. Mrs Parsons has sent me to collect what you have and take it back to the warehouse." I showed him a new delivery note which I had prepared the previous evening and asked him to back round the corner to Sandy's van. I'm sure he had no idea who I was, but there was a nasty pause while I could see him debating whether he should obey this complete stranger. But he did and the transhipment to the other van was accomplished successfully. Sandy and I then beat it like hell back to his garage.'

'What about the other driver?' Roddy asked.

'I told him to continue his round and then go back to the warehouse and report what had happened.'

'But what did you do?' her audience persisted.

'When we got to Sandy's place,' continued Jane, 'I told him to unload the rolls. I, meanwhile, opened the ends and got out the money. It was not as difficult as I expected. It had been very cunningly packed. Closing the ends again proved slightly more difficult, but I think we did a pretty good job. It all took time though, and I was in a fever that the driver might have become suspicious and rung the office before he returned.'

'Any moment I expected to hear a police car. However all was well. When we had packed the money in the two cases which Sandy had collected from my flat in his own car, I suggested that he took the Harrods delivery to some place where he could unload it without being seen and then ring the police from a call box, report having found what he thought were stolen goods, and leave them to get on with it. Finally I took off the wig and red jacket, put them back in my brief case and set off for Harrods, having told Sandy that after he had dealt with the rolls he should take the cases back to my flat by car and wait for me there. I also made clear to him that any mention of what he had seen and done that morning, even to those he knew to be safe, would result in a visit from some of Fergus's friends. He got the message!'

By this time they were just clearing the canal entrance and when they were in the open waters of the loch, Jane paused and looked around, saying that she was in need of a break and a drink. This prompted a general agreement that lunch might be a good idea. The girls therefore retired to the galley to produce sandwiches, while Roddy had a good spy of the loch and the surrounding country through his binoculars. The loch was remarkably empty; just one small motor boat going south and a fishing boat on its way back to Kessock. Looking north he could only see two cars and a lorry on the main road and nothing at all on the south bank road.

When Jane returned with two glasses of beer, she found him still scanning the main road and asked if he had seen anything suspicious. He shook his head and she said she thought it unlikely that she was being followed as she had taken steps to allay any suspicions that might have been aroused in London and further steps that morning in Inverness. Mary then appeared with the sandwiches, which they ate in silence, while admiring the magnificent scenery that is Loch Ness.

It was a glorious early spring afternoon. There was not a ripple on the surface of the loch, and although they were too far north for there yet to be much sign of leaves on the trees, the grass was beginning to show a shimmer of green, while to the far southwest the hills showed up purple against the pale blue of the sky.

Roddy looked up at the sky and sniffed. 'I smell rain,' he said, 'it will be a fine afternoon, but after dark it will rain. Aye, and I believe we could be in for a stormy couple of days. Now Janie, let's hear the finish of your story.'

'Right. You will remember that I was now Jane Parsons again,' she said, continuing from where she had finished previously, 'and that I had an appointment with Harrods. So I went there by tube, and of course found that the material had not arrived. I made a great play of apologising and at once rang the office. They said the van driver had just got back with some story of a strange woman and transferring the Harrods delivery to another vehicle. They told me they were in touch with the police and to calm the customer as best I could. About fifteen minutes later the office rang back to say that the police had found the missing goods and that they were being picked up and would be delivered shortly.'

'What happened then?'

'Having dealt with Harrods, who said they could not think why any one should try to steal that particular batch of material, and were only too pleased to have it arrive safely, I went back to the office.' Jane paused before continuing. 'They told me again what had happened and asked me what I had been doing that morning and whether I could think of any reason for the apparent attempt at robbery. I said I could not and neither could the customer, who was now quite happy, and I imagined it was a matter for the police, who, I thought, were unlikely to discover anything except possibly a case of mistaken identity! With that I pointed out that it was now five o'clock, I was on holiday and had a train to catch, and that I would see them in ten days' time.'

Roddy looked across at her and asked if she thought any suspicion attached to her and she said that it seemed unlikely. Her disguise was good, Sandy had used false number plates, and the fact that she had gone to Harrods as arranged seemed to have convinced everyone that neither she nor the firm were responsible for the incident. Furthermore, Sandy had reported that no one had seen him dump the stuff. However there had been a paragraph in the evening paper saying that the police were looking for a woman called Janet Priestley in connection with an attempted robbery. So just in case they did associate this woman with Jane Parsons or found some clue to the real contents of the rolls of material, she had done one further thing to divert suspicion from herself.

Jane then described her train journey north and her meeting with the man called Duncan Forsyth.

'He had the berth next to mine and after we had our nightcap, I noticed that he did not lock the door; so once I was sure he was asleep, I managed to get hold of his brief case, put twenty thousand dollars in it and return it. It added quite a bit of weight but I had to hope he would not notice this until too late.'

'Then what?' asked her brother-in-law, and looking straight at her added, 'I just hope you have not tried to be too clever. And I'll tell you why in a moment.'

Jane looked a bit puzzled but went on with her story. 'The rest was easy. I knew I would have time to telephone from Perth, so I rang Sandy, who was not very pleased at being woken at five in the morning, and told him to make an anonymous call to the police and alert them about a suspicious character arriving at Inverness off the London train. This I managed without disturbing the man, whose blind was drawn, or the attendant who was not around. It all worked perfectly, and just before I met you, I saw Mr Forsyth carted off by the police.'

'Well, I hope you're right,' Roddy said, 'my worry is that I believe I've heard the name Forsyth before – I think Fergus mentioned it. What did he tell you about himself?'

'Oh, nothing much,' Jane replied, 'he said that he worked for some training agency, that he did a lot of travelling all over the world and that he was going up to fish somewhere in Sutherland. He was rather nice. I'm sure he is quite harmless.'

'I hope so. But I think we'd be best telling Fergus about him all the same,' said Roddy Urquhart with a distinctly worried look. However, after a short pause he went on. 'Aye, it's no good worrying over burnt porridge. We've got to think what happens next. We're over halfway down the loch, but for all that we're a wee bit behind schedule.' Then turning to Jane he asked, 'what time are you due at Altachonich?'

'I said sometime late afternoon. Deliberately vague. As long as I get there tonight, I don't suppose it matters too much,' she replied.

'Uh uh! that's what I thought,' said Roddy, 'well, it's now three o'clock and by any road it will be three hours to the castle. So we must have a think about the best thing to do. There's a man called Colin Vass who I used to know on the Black Isle. He now lives in Fort Augustus and is a fervent Nationalist. I arranged for him to meet us at Invergarry and he should be there now. My idea was that he should take the money to a place where the people from the castle could collect it tomorrow. We would then go on, at least to the end of Loch Lochy, where someone could pick you up and take you to Altachonich. But we've not anywhere near enough time for that now.'

'We'll be at Invergarry in an hour and a half if we're not held up,' said Mary after a quick glance at her watch, 'we can then discuss with this Vass man how we might get Jane to the castle.'

After further discussion it was agreed that this was the best plan. Luck was with them and shortly after four-thirty they were anchored in Loch Oich. Roddy went ashore immediately and found Vass in the forecourt of the hotel, leaning on the bonnet of an elderly Land Rover and talking to someone who looked like a local garage hand. Vass broke off his conversation and walked over to Roddy, who asked him if he had seen anyone who might be on the look out for them – police or otherwise.

The answer was that, far from anyone suspicious, there were very few people about at all. Even allowing for it being early in the season, there was very little traffic around and the hotel was almost empty. Roddy then asked him if he had any ideas for getting Jane to Altachonich that evening, and here they had another piece of luck.

'You saw yon laddie I was talking to when you arrived,' said Colin Vass, 'he has a girl bides in Glenlochan and he's wanting to see her, so he'll be driving over just now wi' a package from the garage in Fort Augustus. It's a spare part of some sort to be left somewhere for collection. I'm sure he could drop your young woman on the way.'

It transpired that in fact the package was for Altachonich Castle, so the young man said he would take both Jane and the package there before going on to see his girl and added that he had one or two things to do before leaving, so could Jane be ready in about forty-five minutes. Colin meanwhile said he would like to have a word with Jane and agree a place where he could leave whatever it was they wanted him to take for the castle.

'Good idea,' said Roddy, 'come out to the boat in about ten minutes.'

When Urquhart got back on board, he explained to Jane what they proposed and then went to the little for'ard cabin and came back with a tea chest.

'I think we'll put the money in this, it will be more secure than the suitcases,' he said. 'Now Colin doesn't know what it is he's carrying, and I think it best if it's left that way, even if he's guessed – which he probably has! Have you, Jane, any suggestions as to where the handover might take place?'

'Have you got any maps on board?' she asked, 'Not charts, ordinary one-inch maps or the equivalent.'

'Sure – hold on a moment.' He opened a drawer under one of the bunks and dropped a bundle of maps on the chart table. 'Have a look at those while I pack this chest.'

Roddy had just finished knotting the last rope round the chest when they heard the dinghy come alongside and Colin Vass heaved himself into the cockpit.

Having introduced the two women, Roddy said, 'Well Colin, here's your cargo. Now Jane, where's he to take it?'

Jane beckoned them over to the chart table and pointing at one of the maps, said to Colin Vass, "do you know this road – well it's more of a track really?' After a moment's study Colin said he thought he did. Jane then turned to her sister and said, 'when we used to come over here on holiday, Father sometimes took us to this old croft here for a picnic.' Then to Colin, 'do you see where I mean?'

'I ken the track. I can't say I ken the croft but I'll find it. Uh uh, yes, I've got a map. So what time do you want me there?'

It was agreed that he should be at the place not later than eight the next morning and wait there. Whoever came to collect the box, Jane said she would come with them, so there would be no problem with recognition.

'Fine then, I'll see you tomorrow morning,' concluded Colin, 'Roddy, can you give me a hand wi' the box? I need to get away now as I've a meeting in Spean Bridge and I'll spend the night there. Just help me get it in the dinghy. I'll manage it myself then.'

With that Vass departed for the shore and shortly afterwards they heard the Land Rover drive off in the direction of Spean Bridge. Roddy looked at his watch and told Jane to be ready to go ashore in about ten minutes.

Up in the woods above the Glen Garry road, Duncan Forsyth lowered his binoculars and turning to the Inspector who was lying beside him said, 'I'm going to follow the Land Rover. You stay here and watch the yacht. Report anything interesting to Inverness. I'll ring Mr Maclay some time tomorrow morning.'

Chapter 5

On leaving the Chief Constable, Maclay took Forsyth and the Inspector to his office, waved them towards chairs and ordered three cups of tea.

'And now, Mr Forsyth,' he said, 'I wonder if you'd like to tell us how we might proceed. Despite what the old man said, I think I could mebbe manage to spare you a wee bit of support, for I certainly do not want Nationalist problems starting in this area.'

'The main thing, obviously, that we have to do is to find and shadow this yacht,' replied Duncan. 'Do we have any idea what it might be called or who it might belong to?'

The others shook their heads. Nicholson, however, said that he had a constable who was a keen sailor and it might be an idea to send him down to the basin to see if he could find out anything.

'Right,' said Maclay, 'send for him at once, even if we have to get him from his home. And while we're waiting, tell us what you'll do when we find this boat.'

'The first thing for me to do is to hire a car.' Maclay was about to interrupt but Forsyth held up his hand, and then continued, 'No, you are very kind but I think it best if I do it myself and in my name. I'll get something robust but inconspicuous. Then assuming that your man finds the yacht – and I'll tell him what he should be looking for – I suggest he follows it down the canal. I assume he's well known around the waterside, so if he wears plain clothes he should not arouse any suspicion. As soon as I have the car, I will drive down to the start of the loch. He can meet me there and, I hope, will be able to point out the boat. Finally, would you be able to lend me Inspector Nicholson? Preferably for the rest of today.'

Maclay thought this would be possible providing, of course, that the Chief Constable agreed. Once it was decided to go ahead with this plan, Duncan left the two policemen to work out the details, saying that he would brief the constable when he got back from collecting the car.

Possibly because it was essential to his work, Duncan Forsyth was one of those fortunate people who always seem to have friends in the right places. As a result of this, acquiring a suitable car presented no problem and in forty minutes he was back with an inconspicuous Hillman saloon. He found Nicholson talking to an intelligent looking young man whose weather-beaten complexion showed clearly how he spent his spare time.

'This is PC Thomson,' the Inspector said, 'He reckons there should be no difficulty in finding the yacht you want, provided you can give an indication of what to look for.'

Duncan shook hands with the constable and asked him how well he knew the canal and the loch. His father, it appeared, was a fisherman and Thomson himself, before joining the police, had worked for a bit with the boats. Now he had to content himself spending what time he could with a small dinghy, although occasionally his duties took him on board larger boats. He knew the canal from Kessock to Fort William and was known by most of the regular users.

Nicholson then explained to him what he had to do once he had identified the yacht and told him that he should treat Duncan as though he were a senior police officer, although he gave no reason for this. He did however tell the constable that the task he had been given fell within the terms of the Official Secrets Act and he was not to discuss it with anyone other than the two of them. Duncan then took over and explained how he thought the yacht might be identified.

'I'm afraid I have not much to go on,' he said, 'except the appearance of the woman on the train. She is medium height, slim build, dark hair and well dressed, although by now she is probably in sailing clothes. She told me the boat is her brother-in-law's and I got the impression that her sister would also be on board, so you are looking for a crew of two women and a man. As to the yacht itself, I don't know. She spoke of sailing and going round the inner islands. That probably means more to you than to me. I think it will be either in the basin or below the road bridge.'

'Och, that's fine, sir,' said the young man, 'there'll no' be many yachts about yet. It's ower early in the year. Aye, it'll likely be a small cruiser – sails and an inboard. If they've any sense they will have left it below the locks. I've an idea already that it'll be one of two boats that I know. So if that's all, sir, I'll be away about the job and I'll see you later somewhere around Lochend. Oh aye, and what's your motor, sir? A bronze Hillman – good, then I'll look out for it.'

As soon as Thomson had left to start his search for the yacht, the other two sat down to discuss how they should proceed once it had been identified.

'It seems to me, Inspector, that for the time being at least, you and I should avoid being seen together,' said Duncan, 'and we should also avoid any sort of procession of vehicles which might arouse suspicion. I shall wait for Thomson somewhere around the start of the loch proper. I think you should drive to somewhere about halfway down the loch, park the car out of sight and find a place which allows you to watch both the road and the traffic on the water.'

'That was my idea too,' said Nicholson. Then he produced a map and pointed to the area south of Fort Augustus. 'I've been giving a wee bit of thought to the likely actions of our friends in the boat. Now unless they are heading for somewhere beyond Fort William, possibly even beyond Oban, which just does not seem probable as it would take them at least three days, they are likely going to stop for tonight at some place round here. Now if I was in their position, I would be unloading the cargo, and possibly some of the passengers, and sending them on by road this evening. Quicker and maybe safer too.'

'Good reasoning,' replied Duncan, 'but I don't think we can decide on anything further now. We'll have another think when we meet on the lochside.'

'Right,' said Nicholson getting to his feet, 'I'll get a car organised and then I'll be off. Oh, and I should just tell you, the car will be one of the old unmarked Wolseleys, and I think I'll take a driver. Could be useful to have a third man with us.'

After a few minutes discussing final details, Duncan too prepared to leave, and as they headed towards the door, it opened and Jock Maclay entered the room.

'Hold on a moment, boys,' he said, 'I've some good news for you. The Chief has heard from London and has got the authority to mount whatever operation is needed. He said he would like to see you, Mr Forsyth, before you go.'

Saying that he would leave them to it, Nick Nicholson set off in search of his car and driver while the others went across to the Chief Constable's office. They found him studying a single sheet of paper with the War Office crest at the top, and on the desk was a buff envelope stamped TOP SECRET. He waved them towards the two chairs in front of his desk and continued his study of the document for two or three minutes before looking up.

'Aye, I've got all the authority I need now,' he said, pushing the paper across to Duncan, 'too much almost! MI6 and Downing Street. What the hell I'm going to tell the Convener, I can't think. As you can see, that document swears everyone to absolute secrecy and yon Lord Darrochy canna keep his mouth shut. I'll have to show him the letter though. Fortunately it only authorises the use of the police in support of an intelligence operation, no details of what or why. I think I will have to tell him it's to do with drugs. But I'm afraid something will soon get out to the press.'

'Can't be helped,' Duncan said, 'if this operation develops the way I think it will, it will be all over the papers in a week's time.'

'Uh uh! Well, you could be right. Now give me a quick run down on your plans and anything special that you may want me to do.'

Duncan handed the paper back to John Marshall and then gave him a brief account of how he and Nicholson had arranged to identify and follow the yacht. If their deductions were correct about its crew and cargo, they should surely be able to get closer to the centre of Unicorn.

'How we do that we won't know until they stop somewhere tonight,' he said, 'that is assuming they do stop. And I do not think we will know what support we may want until after that event. There is just one thing, though – would you alert the Perth and Argyll police about what's going on?'

'I'll do that,' replied the Chief Constable, 'but check with Jock here before your first contact with any other force. One other thing, and I realise that this may be difficult. I would like a progress report tonight or tomorrow morning, and an indication of your future plans. Now Duncan, I'll not hold you up any more. I just wish you good luck.'

After leaving Marshall's office, Duncan asked where he might find his luggage and was told it was with the Desk Sergeant downstairs. Then he shook hands with Maclay and said he'd be in touch as soon as there was something to report.

Sure enough he found his two cases down in the reception area, and seeing that the small waiting room was empty, he took them in there. He reckoned that everything he might need for the next few days was in the smaller of the two, except for one item. So he pulled over the larger case, one of the old-fashioned hard leather kind, unlocked it and pushed a hidden catch. The inside of the lid dropped down revealing another compartment. This had been cunningly designed and was almost impossible to detect by measuring, tapping or any other means, and had defeated Customs Inspectors all over the world. Over the years he had used it for many purposes, but to-day it housed a 9 mm. automatic, three spare magazines and a rather special holster of his own design.

He transferred these items to the smaller case, closed the secret compartment, locked the big case and handed it back to the care of the Sergeant, saying that he or one of the officers would collect it later. Then, picking up the small case and his brief case, he made his way out to the car and drove off in the direction of Loch Ness.

Twenty minutes later, just beyond the gates of a large house, he found a track on the right which led up into some woods. He backed the car a short way up the track, hoping that no one else would want to use it, and sat there looking out over the road at the loch some two hundred yards away

There was very little traffic either on the road or the canal, and he was just beginning to wonder if he had sent everyone off on a wild goose chase, when he saw a mast through the trees and a medium sized yacht with neatly furled sails appeared, motoring slowly down towards the loch.

As it passed him, Duncan had a good look at it through his field glasses. He could see the name *'Firefly'* on the stern, and a man and a woman in the cockpit. The woman looked remarkably like his companion of the previous evening, and if it was she, then he assumed the man was the brother-in-law. A minute or two later, just as the boat vanished from his sight behind another lot of trees, he heard the sound of an engine and an untidy figure riding a rusty looking moped turned up the track and drew up beside him.

'Aye, I'm sure yon's the boat you're after,' said Constable Thomson, '*Firefly* she's called, I ken her fine. She belongs to a man named Roddy Urquhart. He sails her all over the west coast and down to England too. I don't know much about him, for ye'll realise he moves in a bit grander circles than I do, but I have spoken to him in the yard and he knows his stuff about sailing. They do say, too, that he's awfu' keen on the Nationalists. But the main thing is that there are two ladies on board, and one of them, the one sitting in the stern there, exactly fits your description. As you guessed, the other woman with them is Urquhart's wife. I've seen her before.'

'Well done, Thomson, you've done an excellent job. There's no doubt that they are the lot we're looking for,' said Duncan, relieved that his assumptions were proving correct, 'I had a pretty good look at them with the glasses and I'm sure that she is the same woman. You don't think you aroused their suspicions, do you? Would Urquhart know that you are a policeman?'

'Sure, he kens I am in the force,' the young man replied. 'They were tied up below the locks and he would likely have seen me talking to one of the lock keepers. But he'd not have thought anything of that, for I'm often down there when I'm off duty. After they moved off he'd not have seen anything of me. I let them get well ahead and I'm sure they never looked back. They were too busy talking.'

'Good. Now you had better go back and report that we have found the yacht and will be following it down the loch. Say that we will be in touch again this evening if anything interesting happens.'

Thomson gave a salute of acknowledgement, swung his moped round and headed back towards Inverness. Duncan watched him for a few moments, then started the car and drove slowly down the track and out on to the main road.

After about three miles he stopped again and, leaving the car out of sight of the loch, clambered down the bank to a place where he could have a good spy without himself being seen. He had another long look at the *Firefly* through his binoculars and made sure that he would always be able to recognise her. He also scanned as much of the loch as was visible to him, but he could see no other craft that he might confuse with his quarry. Returning to the car, he drove slowly on until he came to a garage. Suspecting that he might soon find himself on roads where petrol stations were few and far between, he stopped and filled the car.

The problem now was to drive down the lochside without getting too far ahead of the *Firefly* and without stopping so often that it might be noticed. A stop at a village shop to buy chocolate and oatcakes, and another at Castle Urquhart, helped to slow his progress. At the castle, posing as an ordinary tourist, he was able to have another look at the *Firefly*. She was still motoring on towards Fort Augustus, and he reckoned that she was not likely to stop before getting there. He therefore decided to press on and meet Inspector Nicholson.

Beyond Castle Urquhart the character of the road changes. To the east a bank, thick with scrub and bracken, descends to the shore of the loch. To the west, however, are the steep, tree-covered slopes and rocky cliffs of a considerable range of hills. The road itself runs between the loch and the cliffs in an endless series of sharp bends and steep climbs, which make any sort of speed and any attempt at overtaking almost impossible. It is also a road with few possibilities for concealing a car, and so Duncan Forsyth was finding it difficult to drive with reasonable safety and at the same time to keep a look-out for Inspector Nicholson. At last, on a stretch of road where the bank of the loch was at its steepest, he rounded a bend and saw on his right the entrance to a track. Nearby a man with a shovel was engaged in repairing the roadside verge.

As the car approached, the man walked towards the middle of the road and waved to him to stop. Not sure whether this was a genuine road mender or the police driver, Duncan thought it best to obey, so he pulled in to the side and wound down his window.

The man with the shovel bent down and said, 'Mr Forsyth?' When Duncan nodded, he pointed to the opening across the road. 'Yon's the start of a track that's just wide enough for a car. I'm about twenty yards in, so run you up behind me.'

The track was indeed narrow and as Duncan drove in, the car was scraping the undergrowth on either side. So thick was it, that by the time he stopped behind the other car, he was completely hidden from the road. Then as he got out of the car, he saw the police driver walking up the track towards him.

'This is a fine spot,' he said, 'the cars are out of sight and Mr Nicholson has a grand spying place down the bank opposite. He canna be seen from the road or the loch. The only problem is for me to keep a lookout on the road without people wondering what I'm at. I believe I'd make a verra guid roadman!'

'You would indeed! And now, where will I find Mr Nicholson?' asked Duncan.

'Right. Just come over the road and I'll show you. Then I'll stay up here and watch the cars and the road.' As he said this, the driver led the way back down the track and across the road. When they reached the opposite verge, he continued on into the undergrowth and pushing aside the lower branches of a birch, he pointed down the hill.

'You see yon fallen tree?' he asked, 'aye, well, go round that to the left and you'll see a wee knoll with a rock at the bottom. Below that there's a flat grassy bit wi' some bracken in front. That's where you'll find him.'

Going down to the place indicated, Duncan found the Inspector scanning the loch through his binoculars. There were just three craft in sight – two motor boats and a yacht. A quick glance with his glasses confirmed that the yacht was the *Firefly*.

'Yes, that's her,' he said to Nicholson, 'she's making good speed now and it won't be long before she's at Fort Augustus. The question is what will they do then?'

'As I said earlier, I believe they will move on down the canal,' replied the Inspector, 'I've seen little other traffic, so they have a clear run and will want to get away from the locks and on to a quieter spot if they are going to do any unloading. My guess is that they are aiming to stop in Loch Oich. It's quiet and sheltered. Aye, and it's a good meeting place too, with the hotel and a road to the west.'

'Yes, I'm sure they'll want to get the money off the boat as soon as possible, particularly if they are going on to Fort William, for they just might get stopped by Customs. Anyway it's as good an assumption as any other, so let's work on it,' agreed Duncan. 'And now you've seen the *Firefly*, I suggest you follow them and if they stop, find an observation place and leave your driver on the road, as you did last time, and he can pick me up. I'm going to stop for a short time in Fort Augustus. There's something I need to do before nightfall.'

As the yacht disappeared behind a shoulder of the hill, Nicholson picked up his glasses and groundsheet and led the way up to the road. There they found the driver, whose name was Smith, still working industriously at the verge. He said there was very little traffic on the road and nothing that looked as if it might have an interest in the loch. Then, having backed his car down the track to let the others out, and seen them on their way, Duncan again drove a little way off the road.

Making sure he could not be seen, he took the automatic and holster out of his case, lowered his trousers and strapped the holster to his right thigh. Then, having checked the magazine and action, he dropped the pistol into the holster and did up his trousers. He had long had a dislike of shoulder or waist holsters and, although his colleagues thought his present arrangement eccentric, he found it both convenient and effective. His right trouser leg was specially cut to allow for the extra bulk and the bottom of the side pocket could be zipped open. He found that the natural gesture of putting his hand in his pocket raised less suspicion than reaching to his armpit, something that had saved his life on two occasions. He had also proved, although only on the range, that in certain attitudes he could actually fire through his trouser leg.

He took a quick walk up and down the path to check that the holster was correctly positioned and secure. Then, having repacked his case, he backed out on to the road and drove off in the direction of Fort Augustus.

His reason for stopping there was to find a telephone, for he had come to the conclusion that before going any further, he needed to know a lot more about Roderick Urquhart and Jane Parsons. To do this he had to find an inconspicuous telephone box from which he could ring his open line contact. Here again he was lucky and found just what he needed in a side street above the abbey. He dialled the number and a man's voice answered.

'Trainers here,' it said, 'can I help?'

'It's D here,' Duncan replied, 'I wondered if my sister was there . . . Oh I see – well, could you give her a message? . . . Fine. Tell her I've met someone I think she may know. His name is Urquhart – a keen sailor I believe – and I think he has a sister-in-law called Jane. I'd like to know more about them before we meet again . . . No, I'll be difficult to contact for the next couple of days, so it would probably be safer to tell our uncle in Inverness. I'm sure to see him before long . . . Yes. Thanks and good-bye.'

Not the most secure means of communication, but it was all he could do. The important thing was that the information he wanted would come by confidential line to the police in Inverness, and could be brought out to him by Nick Nicholson.

As he drove south towards Invergarry, he noticed with some dismay that the sky was clouding over, for a prolonged period of bad weather would add considerably to the difficulties of his job. Hoping that the weather would hold, at least for the next hour or two, he drove on and had just reached the tree-lined section of road at the head of Loch Oich when a figure emerged from the side of the road and waved him down. As he slowed, the nearside door was opened and the police driver, Smith, jumped in.

'Keep going for another two hundred yards,' he said, 'and then you'll need to turn right. It's a private drive but I ken the keeper there, so we're OK. But the main thing is there's a place in the woods where we'll have a grand view of the loch, the hotel and the road to the west. Aye, the Inspector is up there now keeping a lookout. Slow now, sir – right, there's the turning.'

Duncan swung the car to the right and into the gravelled road. This climbed up steeply through the woods until they came to a fork. To the right Duncan could see a house and outbuildings, but Smith indicated that he should bear to the left and they continued up until they reached a small clearing. Leaving the car under some trees, they walked over towards the left side of the clearing and there, on the edge of a sheer cliff, they found Nicholson well hidden behind a heather-covered mound. Down below them was the road to the west, and ahead was a perfect view of the loch and the hotel.

Duncan got out his glasses and saw that there were two men in the hotel yard leaning against the bonnet of a Land Rover and deep in conversation. After a few minutes a third man walked over from the direction of the loch and joined them.

'I think the one who has just arrived is the man whom we saw in the yacht,' said Nicholson, 'that'll likely be the brother-in-law, Urquhart. I don't know the other two. Any idea, Smith, who they are?'

'Not much, sir,' the driver replied, 'I believe one might be a man from the town. I dinna ken his name. The other's probably local. I could mebbe find out from the keeper.'

Smith was accordingly sent off to see what he could discover, while the other two resumed their vigil. The three men in the hotel yard remained talking for about ten minutes and then seemed to reach some conclusion, for one of them, after a quick glance at his watch, made a gesture of agreement and turned and walked off in the direction of some cottages. The other two, after a few more words, also departed, one in the direction of the loch, the other into the hotel.

Thereafter nothing much happened until Smith returned and knelt down beside them. As he did so, the man from the hotel re-emerged and walked off in the direction of the loch.

'Ye see him? – that's a man Vass, from Fort Augustus,' said Smith, 'they couldna tell me what he did, but he's believed to be keen on the Nationalists. The other one you didna ken, he's a local boy, one of the mechanics at the garage. They say he has a girl in Glenlochan – that's over Morvern way.'

Duncan pulled a map from his pocket and got them to point out Glenlochan. After a few minutes study of the surrounding area, he looked up with an exclamation of surprise and pointed to Altachonich Castle.

'Aye, that's Sir Torquhil Drumcairn's place. Do you know him?' asked the Inspector. 'He's another that they say has links with the Nationalists. He used to be a Unionist MP but he fell out with them.'

'No, I don't exactly know him, although my Department is quite interested in him,' replied Duncan, 'but what is more important is that I know his daughter. Met her skiing. I've never been to the castle and I had no idea it was not that far from here.' Duncan paused, then went on; 'You know, I believe we're getting somewhere at last. I wonder what the next move will be.'

They were not left long in doubt for just as Duncan finished speaking, Vass emerged from the trees by the roadside pushing a wheelbarrow containing a small crate. With considerable effort he heaved the crate into the back of the Land Rover, then got into the driving seat, turned the vehicle round and set off in the direction of Spean Bridge.

With a quick 'I'm going to follow him,' Duncan ran back to his car, leaving Nicholson to report on any further happenings at the hotel.

Chapter 6

On the yacht, Jane, having packed what she needed for the next two or three days into a lightweight case, was standing waiting for her brother-in-law to row her ashore.

'Ready?' he asked. Jane nodded, kissed her sister and stepped into the dinghy. When they got to the shore, they found the young mechanic waiting there in a very smart new pick-up truck. He took Jane's case and put it behind the driving seat, and then ushered her into the passenger seat.

'It's the boss's truck. It'll be more comfortable, aye and drier too, than my old banger,' he said with a grin. Then looking up at the sky he added, 'I fear it will rain before we get to the castle. So now, if you're ready, we'll be off.'

'We'll ring you tomorrow as soon as anything's fixed,' said Jane, leaning out of her window and waving to Urquhart.

The young man, whose name turned out to be Alec, was a good and careful driver. He needed to be, for they were not far down the road to Fort William when the heavens opened. The rain, together with the gathering darkness, made driving difficult and looking at the scenery impossible. However Alec turned out to be an entertaining companion and the next two hours passed pleasantly enough. Yes, he said, he went to Altachonich and Glenlochan quite often. They were always needing parts for the new machinery they had installed at the quarry. No, he'd never actually seen the quarry, but there were now quite a few men working there. A great thing for Morvern it was, for there were not many jobs to be had there. A pity though, that they had to bring in so many men from further south, but he understood they needed the specialist skills.

At Fort William they turned west and then, quite soon, south again. The weather got steadily worse and so did the road, a winding, single-track, pot-holed horror. Alec said that the Council would do nothing to it as it was going to be improved, but there never seemed to be much progress towards that happening.

By now it was quite dark, and to dodging the holes in the road was added a further hazard, that of avoiding deer. They had one very close encounter with a hind and calf. Then, at last, after a very uncomfortable ten miles, they descended a hill, crossed a bridge and drew up by some impressive lodge gates.

'I'll be taking my package to the steading,' said Alec, 'but it's a terrible night so I'd best take you to the front door.'

With that he drove through the gates and up the short drive to the gravel sweep in front of the white-harled castle, and pulled up by the massive double doors with the Maclean coat of arms over the lintel.

Almost as soon as they stopped, a man in conventional butler's dress emerged from the castle carrying an umbrella, walked up to the truck and opened the door for Jane. Alec, meanwhile, had brought out her case and handed it to the butler. Then with a quick wave, he drove off to complete his errand. The butler turned and led the way into the castle.

'Welcome to Altachonich, madam,' he said, 'and I hope you did not have too bad a drive. It's a pity that it's such a dirty night, for you will not have been able to see the scenery.'

'Thank you, it might have been a lot worse,' replied Jane, 'and that young man is an entertaining companion. I learned a lot about the neighbourhood, even if I could not see it.'

'Yes, he's a good lad, is Alec,' agreed the butler. Then he stopped in the middle of the great entrance hall, put down the case and turning to Jane said: 'Sir Torquhil said I was to take you straight to the library when you arrived, madam. I will see that your luggage is taken to your room – and now if you will follow me, please. And if you should need me, my name is Charles.'

He led Jane up a flight of stairs, for, as is the case with most Scottish castles, at Altachonich the principal reception rooms were on the first floor. He knocked on a door in the centre of the landing, opened it and ushered her in.

'Mrs Parsons, Sir Torquhil,' he announced, then turned and left the room, closing the door behind him.

Jane found herself in a large, high-ceilinged room with walls that were a mixture of panelling, bookcases and bare, plastered stonework. At one end was a large open fire, on which, Jane thought, it would be perfectly possible to roast an ox and at the other end were two small doors which she guessed led into turret stairs. For all its starkness, the room was comfortably furnished and the rows of books, ancient and modern, gave it a welcoming feel.

As she entered, a tall distinguished looking man in a tweed suit walked towards her and shook her hand.

'How do you do Mrs Parsons, I am Torquhil Drumcairn. I must say I'm glad to see you safely here, for I'm afraid it is a really shocking night.' Then turning towards the fireplace, he added with a smile, 'I don't think I need to introduce you to Fergus, do I?'.

Although she knew that her brother was going to be at the castle, she had been so occupied with Sir Torquhil's greeting that she had not noticed the man sitting in a chair by the side of the fireplace. He now got up and she walked over to him, took his hands in hers and kissed him warmly on both cheeks.

'Fergus! It's too long since I've seen you. How are you?' she exclaimed. Then she stood back and looked him up and down; 'You are looking well enough anyway. And I'm glad to see you've shaved off that terrible beard.'

Fergus Crawford was a thin, wiry man of medium height, and he had that same air of self possession and determination to succeed as had his sister But while she was dark, neat and outwardly calm, he had red hair, rather longer than is usual for a man, and piercing grey eyes, all of which gave him a somewhat wild appearance. This was enhanced by his stained corduroy trousers and patched seaman's jersey. He looked at his sister and thought, as he always did, what an attractive woman she was. It amazed him that a body so precise and businesslike should hide such a fiery nature and such dedication to the cause of Scottish independence.

'Yes, I'm fine,' he said, 'and we're all wanting to know how you've got on and whether we're on track for the big day. I'll tell you, dear sister, we were getting worried when you were so late. I feared that something had happened to you and the money. Aye, but here you are and looking your usual bonny self. Now tell us what has been happening – where's the money and what are Roddy, Mary and the *Firefly* doing? Are they still on course for their meeting?'

'Yes they are,' Jane said, 'they'll be in Fort William by midday tomorrow and they pick up a message there about the rendezvous from some friend of Roddy's. Provided all goes well, I think Roddy hopes to be back here, with the goods, late on Friday – the day after tomorrow. Now about the money. That's on its way here with another friend of Roddy's called Vass. We transhipped it from the yacht to his Land Rover at a place on Loch Oich. We reckoned it would be safer for the payment to take place here. Less chance of a hijack!' Looking at Sir Torquhil, she added, 'do you know a croft called Kettlehole, it's out beyond Glenlochan? I've arranged to meet Vass there at eight o'clock tomorrow morning and collect the money. I thought Fergus could come with me. I've only been to it from the other end, but I'm sure I remember there being a road up from Glenlochan.'

'There certainly is,' said Sir Torquhil, 'although I'd hardly dignify it with the title of road – more of a track, I'd say. But you'll get a car up there all right, unless it rains all night, in which case I'll lend you a Land Rover. Now, I suggest we don't talk any more for the moment. Dinner will be in forty minutes and I'm sure, Mrs Parsons, you'd like the chance of a bath and change. We can talk again after dinner. I'd like to hear how you got on with collecting the money and getting it up here. Tomorrow I shall leave you both to go to Kettlehole in the morning. Then in the afternoon we'll have a full meeting to discuss plans. By the way, my daughter will be at dinner. We do not talk about Unicorn in front of her.'

37

When the other two had gone off to their rooms, Sir Torquhil remained in his chair gazing into the fire. It was there, five minutes later, that Daphne found him.

'Father, I've got to talk to you,' she said, 'Dougie came up to me when I was feeding the ponies. He's very worried about what's going on at the quarry. All those strange men and no proper quarrying work. He says explosives have been delivered, but we've heard no blasting. Then there's that manager. I don't like him and nor do most of the people on the estate. What's more, he does not like Dougie or anyone else going near the place. I know it's all to do with your Nationalist friends and I've promised not to interfere, but you must tell me something. For your own good I must have a story for the neighbourhood.'

'My dear, I know you are right,' Sir Torquhil acknowledged with a sigh. 'Look, we must go up now and get ready for dinner. The others have arrived and Jane Parsons has gone to have a bath. I want to have a word with them after dinner, so could you leave us here for an hour? Then come along to the study about ten and I'll try and put you in the picture.'

Daphne looked at her father and agreed, somewhat reluctantly, with his proposal. Upstairs in her room, as she changed her skirt and jersey for a woollen dress, she thought again about what Dougie Fletcher had told her that afternoon. Dougie was the head stalker, a man of about fifty who had been with the estate all his working life except for six years with the Argylls in the war, during which he had won the Military Medal and risen to the rank of Company Sergeant Major. Daphne had known him since she was a child and she had the highest respect for his opinion. Like all people who spend their lives among the men and animals of the wild places, he had great powers of observation and the ability to draw conclusions, which were usually correct, from what he saw.

'I tell you, Daphne, yon's no' a working quarry,' he'd said to her. 'I know, for ye must ken that my grandfather worked in the old quarry before the estate closed it, and I saw what went on there. This is like a military camp. Aye, and there's the men. Two yanks, a frenchie and the rest all from Glasgow. And the manager, as they call him. He's no manager. He hasna' recognised me but I ken him fine. He was an officer – in the HLI, if I mind right. There was some trouble at the Rhine crossing and he was court martialled. I dinna ken what happened then, but I did hear that after the War he became an accountant or some such in Edinburgh. But keep that to yersel'. It's best no one kens I recognised him. Now, you must speak to your father and try to find out what's goin' on. You must warn him that he's in a fair way to losing the respect of the estate, and I dinna like that.'

She had told Dougie that she would do her best, but that her father was not easy to deal with at the moment. She just hoped that when they met later that evening she would find out something worth reporting. In the hope that she would, she had arranged to meet the stalker early the next morning, ostensibly to check that a peregrine's nest was still undisturbed and to talk to one of the shepherds who was having fox trouble.

When she got down to the library, she found the others already there and when her father had performed the introductions, he suggested that they went straight in to dinner. The dining room, which was also on the first floor and in the oldest part of the castle, was dark and gloomy at the best of times. Tonight, with the heavy green velvet curtains drawn and only the candles on the table and the dimly lit rows of Maclean ancestors for light, it appeared more sinister than ever. The only redeeming point, as far as Daphne could see, was that they were using the small round table rather than the massive oak dining table with its high-backed Jacobean chairs.

As always at Altachonich, the food and wine were excellent – salmon with a perfectly made hollandaise sauce and a delightful Chablis – but Daphne could not help feeling that it was wasted on the company. Her father seemed preoccupied and spoke little; Fergus, never a great talker, seemed bored by the whole thing. It was therefore left to the two women to try to make conversation. Daphne found that talking to Jane was not difficult, although the subjects discussed remained at a comparatively trivial level until near the end of the meal, when the question arose of how the clearances had affected Altachonich and Glenlochan.

'At first, not as badly as the rest of Morvern,' Daphne explained. 'There has always been quarrying around this area and then there used to be lead mined in the hills above Glenlochan, so there was always some employment. But in the end, as was happening everywhere in the Highlands, the local lairds cleared many of the townships and brought in sheep and shepherds from the Borders as well as starting to develop the sporting potential.'

'Don't you think that was wrong?' cried Jane, 'Wrong and wicked to remove people from their homes – to drive them away? And then replace them with sheep!'

'No I don't,' Daphne replied. 'The '45 only hurried on something that was going to happen anyway. A subsistence agriculture – and that's all there ever was in the West Highlands – could never support a growing population, certainly not in the late eighteenth and early nineteenth centuries. It was, I'm afraid, move or starve and the actions of the lairds, distasteful as they may be to modern thinking, almost certainly saved many hundreds of lives.'

'But what about the industries? The quarry and the mines? They gave employment and were allowed to fall into disuse. They were replaced by sheep and deer, giving little or no employment. The land was all in the ownership of anglicized lairds and the government in London knew nothing of Scotland and even less of the Highlands! And it's still the same. Scotland must be free if we are ever to improve conditions for our people.'

'Yes, perhaps in the future,' Daphne replied, 'although I would take a lot of convincing that, for those in the countryside, rule from Edinburgh would be much different to rule from London. You cannot change geographic facts by political decree. Nor, come to that, can you change people's perception of how and where they want to live. Would an independent Scotland really do anything for its people, other than satisfy the ambitions of some power-hungry politicians?'

Sir Torquhil, who had been jerked out of his reverie by his daughter's unexpected eloquence, decided that the discussion was getting dangerously near forbidden topics and should be brought to a close. He looked at his watch, pushed back his chair and stood up.

'Very interesting, my dear,' he said, 'but now I have things I want to discuss with Fergus and his sister, so we'll go to the library. We won't be more than an hour, so don't you go to bed. I want to discuss a couple of estate matters with you.'

When the others had left, Daphne rang the bell and then started to clear the table. Her little argument with Jane had made her more than ever determined to find out just what was happening at Altachonich. When the butler arrived with the trolley, she asked him what instructions had been given for the morning.

'Sir Torquhil asked for breakfast at six-thirty for Mrs Parsons and Mr Crawford. I understand they are going out at seven but I do not know where. Lunch is to be at one and then, I understand, there's a meeting in the Estate Office. What will you be doing, Miss Daphne?'

'I'm really not sure,' she replied, 'except that I will be on the move early. Probably soon after six. We've got fox problems again and Dougie and I are going out with the shepherd from the Craggan hirsel. Don't worry about breakfast, I'll get it with Mrs Fletcher. Lunch I'm not sure about, so I think you should assume I'll be out. Now I'm just going over to the stables and then I'll be with my father in the study. Don't wait up. We will lock up and do the lights. Good night, Charles.'

Over in the stables, she let out her father's two labradors and her own Jack Russell and checked that they and the two riding ponies had water. While she was doing this, the stalker appeared and she told him that she would be seeing her father later. She also said that she understood that the other two guests would be going out at about seven.

'I think, Dougie, we should be on the road above the Home Plantation about then. I'm curious to see where they go.'

'Aye, I'm thinking we should do that, so I'll see you at the cottage soon after six. Now, dinna you worry about they dogs. I'll see to them.'

After saying good night to the stalker, Daphne made her way back to the castle and up to the study. Her father was not yet there, so she picked up *The Scotsman* and a paragraph caught her eye. It was headed 'US Secretary of Defense to visit Inverness'. Little did she realise then the part that headline was to play in all their lives during the next two weeks.

While Daphne was over in the stables, up in the library Jane was telling Sir Torquhil and Fergus the same story that she had earlier told those on the yacht. Apart from Sir Torquhil's pleasure at the success of the currency smuggling, the part of her doings that caused the most interest was her mention of Duncan Forsyth.

'Oh hell!' Fergus cried, 'Duncan Forsyth, you say? It must be the same one. I just wonder what he is doing in Scotland.'

'Why, what's the problem?' said his sister. 'Funnily enough Roddy showed the same concern as you when I mentioned the name of Forsyth.'

'I'll tell you just what the problem is. Duncan Forsyth is a top man in MI6. I've not met him but I've heard of him often. It may just be coincidence, but I think he was over in the Washington Embassy when they were enquiring about the Sons of the Clearances. I could wish you had chosen someone else to plant the money on.'

Despite a momentary stab of fear caused by these revelations about her travelling companion, Jane could hardly suppress a smile at her brother's concern. Her problem was that planting the money had not been her only connection with this Mr Forsyth. Perhaps she had been stupid to get involved with a stranger – time would tell – but it had been fun seducing him.

'Well, what's done is done,' said Sir Torquhil, 'we must hope that his current interest in Scotland really is purely recreational. You did not see him again after you left the station, did you?'

Jane shook her head. 'No. And I'm sure he did not see Mary or Roddy. Anyway, by the time he'd have sorted himself out with the police, we would have been well down the canal.'

'I still don't like it,' said her brother, 'it's too much of a coincidence. We must discuss it with the leader tomorrow.'

Sir Torquhil got to his feet and looking down at the other two, said, 'I'll tell you a curious thing. I don't know this man and I can't say I have ever heard of him in an official capacity, but there is one thing I do know about him and that is that he's a friend of my daughter! No, she hasn't said anything to me about his being in Scotland, so I don't think she knows. And now, if you don't mind, I shall leave you. I have business to discuss with Daphne – family business, that is. But I do not think I will mention Mr Forsyth.'

In the study Sir Torquhil found his daughter staring moodily at the unlit fire, but as he entered she looked up.

'Father, just what is going on here? We have two people staying, one a known Nationalist trouble-maker, and the other – well, she's not much better. That is, if her conversation at dinner is anything to go by. Then we've got your new development at the quarry. Dougie says what's going on there is a poor pretence of quarrying. And the men! Even I can see that half of them have never seen a quarry in their lives. And do you realise that nobody on the estate can stand that manager man, the one called Simpson? Just tell me, Father, are you planning something illegal? I must know.'

'Daphne, my dear, I'm sorry. I think I owe you an apology for not having told you earlier what I'm now going to tell you.' Sir Torquhil got up from his chair and stood with his back to the fireplace. Then looking across at his daughter, he continued in a quiet, deliberate tone. 'Yes, you are perfectly right, I am planning something. You are well aware of my involvement in the independence movement. Well, I have decided that the time has come for me to make use of what prestige and influence I possess for the benefit of the cause.'

'Come off it, Father. You are talking exactly like one of those politicians you always profess to despise. What comic little plan are you and your agitator friends hatching?' Daphne was finding it hard not to smile, but she knew that would only upset her father.

'That is precisely what I am trying to tell you. So please listen and don't interrupt,' shouted Sir Torquhil. Then, realising that if what he was about to say was to be believable he must remain calm, he reverted to his earlier measured tones. 'It was put to me by the leaders of the movement that we need a higher profile, and that this was something that I could provide. I have therefore agreed to organise and lead a grand rally in Stirling in the summer and we do not want word of this to get out before we are ready. We are therefore doing all the planning and preparation here. The people at the quarry are mostly area representatives who will be responsible for mustering and controlling what we hope will be very large crowds. Fergus, Jane Parsons and Simpson are all part of the leadership of the party, and tomorrow the four of us have our first major planning meeting.'

Here Sir Torquhil paused and looked down at his daughter, but neither by word or gesture did she give any indication of what she was thinking. He therefore continued.

'Now I propose to hold several more such meetings here, and since you have little interest in this side of my life, the whole thing will be very boring for you. I wondered therefore, if you were likely to be away. I'm not pressing you in any way, but I believe it would be a good idea, if it suited you.'

'Let me just ask one question,' said Daphne, 'If the quarry is a cover for you and your friends to play at politics, what about its main purpose – the creation of jobs on the west coast of Scotland? Surely that would be more attractive to Scotsmen than all the grand rallies in the kingdom!'

'Yes, yes! Of course it will become a genuine operation in due time,' Sir Torquhil replied. 'The eventual manager is already there. He's one of the stewards and once the rally is out of the way, he'll recruit a proper work force and the venture will be under way. But now, Daphne, what about my question – are you likely to be going away?'

'You seem in an awful hurry to get rid of me. But yes, I was proposing to go south next week. First to Edinburgh and then on to look at a new boat that's building at Cowes. It's for the Richards and they have asked me to crew later in the year, when they take her down to the Mediterranean. But now, Father, if we have finished, I am going to bed. I have to be up early, for Dougie and I are away out to Craggan. Mrs Dougie will give me breakfast, so I don't know when I'll see you. As you have your meeting, I thought I'd probably be out to lunch. Good night, Father, and will you do the lights and lock up?'

Despite all her doubts about the truth of her father's story and the wisdom of his actions, she was fond of him and so he found, rather to his surprise, that he merited a daughter's good night kiss.

Chapter 7

By the time Duncan Forsyth had driven down from the spying point above the hotel and out on to the main road, the light was failing and it was starting to rain; none of which was going to make it easy to follow the Land Rover, for by now it was some three or four miles ahead him. There was still very little traffic on the road and, despite the worsening weather, Duncan was able to make good progress. There was one nasty moment when he was stuck behind first a pre-war Austin and then a heavy lorry, but he finally managed to overtake both and as he passed the lorry, he could see, in the far distance, the lights of another vehicle.

But he soon lost sight of it and then found himself on a very winding part of the road. This presented him with another problem, for he did not want to let the other car get too far ahead in case he could not see what happened should it stop somewhere, or worse, turn off the main road. On the other hand, with the weather and the gathering dark, he did not want to risk rounding a corner and finding himself right up with his quarry. But then he had a further stroke of luck.

He had just emerged from a wood on to a short straight, when he saw a Land Rover parked by some cottages about three hundred yards ahead. The driver was leaning out and talking to a woman in the doorway of one of the houses. The darkness and the weather made identification impossible, but to be on the safe side Duncan slowed to a crawl and prayed that no other car would come along.

He need not have worried, for while he was still a hundred yards away, the woman stepped back into the cottage and the Land Rover drove off. After that he again kept well behind until, as he descended the hill into Spean Bridge, he saw the vehicle parked just beyond the hotel and the driver walking towards the bar entrance. As he stood for a moment in the lighted doorway, Duncan could see that he was indeed the man Vass from Invergarry.

Was he just going in for a drink? Or was he planning to stay the night? On the whole the former seemed the more likely. And anyway, if his guess as to the contents of the case in the back was correct, Duncan reckoned he would hardly leave his vehicle parked in the street. There was nothing to do but wait and see, so he backed up a narrow gravel lane and found a place from which he could watch the front of the hotel without, he hoped, arousing suspicion.

After about twenty minutes, two men came out of the hotel and got into the Land Rover, which then vanished into the driveway of a house opposite. Flinging himself from his car, Duncan ran to the end of the lane and was just in time to see Vass lock the door of a shed and vanish into the house next door.

From Duncan's point of view, this arrangement had one great advantage. The building could be seen from the upstairs windows of the hotel. Returning to his car, he drove round to the car park, took out his bag and went in and up to the reception desk, where he got himself a front bedroom and also found that they were still serving dinner.

Telling the girl behind the desk that he would be down directly, he went up to his room and washed; then he took a quick look out of the window and was just in time to see another two men enter the house opposite.

'Good,' he thought, 'that probably means some sort of party or meeting and therefore our friend is likely to be there for the night.'

Dinner proved to be completely unremarkable and when it was over, Duncan retired to the bar with the intention of doing a little quiet questioning. There appeared to be only one other couple staying and they were whispering to each other in a corner of the lounge. A honeymoon tour of the Highlands, he thought! The bar room was empty and seating himself on one of the high stools, Duncan asked the girl for a large whisky, into which he poured some water from a jug on the bar. The water was real West Highland – light brown and ice cold. He took an appreciative sip and looked at the girl. She too was real West Highland. Dark haired and pretty, with that clear, freckled complexion so often seen in the women of the west coast.

'It's a pleasure to drink water from the hills after the disgusting stuff I usually get,' he said with a smile, 'and it's good to be up in Lochaber again, even though it is a dirty night.'

'Aye, it is that,' the girl replied, 'and the forecast is bad for the morn, so I hope it's not views of the Ben that ye're after. You'll be from the south then – up for the fishing maybe? That's what the gentlemen mostly come here for.'

'No, unfortunately not. This time it's business that brings me here. I have a meeting tomorrow at the works at Kinlochleven. I'll need to be away early so as to be there soon after seven.' Duncan looked round at the empty bar room and the turned back to the girl. 'Talking about fishing,' he said, 'you don't seem to have many people here tonight.'

'Well, it's early in the season yet. I believe there's a party coming next week and then, of course, we'll get the tourists starting at Easter.' She looked at him with a smile, 'it's nice talking to you though. The wee couple next door have never been near the bar. They had champagne sent up to their room when they arrived, and I'm sure drinking it was not all they were doing up there. Then there was Macneil and his friend in earlier, but they didna stay long and they'll no' be back the night. They have some sort of meeting at his house. Aye, that Macneil, he's always on about Home Rule or some such. A load of blether, if you ask me. Now will I get you another drink, sir?'

Duncan nodded, and while he drank, the girl went on chatting but nothing further that was useful came out, other than that the unloved Macneil's friend was off Morvern way early the next day. So, with apologies for deserting her, he paid for his drinks and went to see the receptionist. There he explained that he would need to leave about six the next morning and would he be able to get out? He was told that Willy would be in by then and could let him out by the back door. He therefore paid his bill and, saying he hoped Willy would not be late, he retired to his room.

He woke next morning to the sound of the wind rattling the window frame and the rain drumming on the corrugated iron roof of the shed across the road. He dressed quickly, not in the suit of yesterday but in corduroys, sweater and waterproof jacket. He checked his automatic, made sure it was loaded and clipped it into the thigh holster. He then repacked his suitcase, turned out the light and had a quick look out of the window. It was still pitch dark and the rain made visibility even worse, but as far as he could see there was no sign of movement in the house opposite or anywhere else in the village.

Fifteen minutes later a light came on across the road. Duncan had already decided that at the first sign of movement he would go straight to the car. So picking up his case, he went quietly down the stairs and found Willy setting the lounge fire.

'Ye're wanting away now, are ye?' Willy asked, 'They left me a note saying ye'd be off early. Well I wish you luck. 'Tis a terrible morning.'

With that encouraging remark, Willy unlocked the door. Duncan turned up the collar of his coat and with a quick farewell wave ran over to his car, unlocked the door and got in, throwing his case on to the back seat. Then, having made sure that Willy was back in the hotel, he drove slowly out on to the main road without turning on his lights. Having been told by the barmaid that the man with Macneil had said he was making for Morvern, Duncan reckoned that it was safe to assume that Vass, when he left, would take the Fort William road. He therefore turned in that direction and, about a hundred yards from the hotel, stopped in the shadow of some trees. From this position he could watch the exit from the garage without himself being visible, and if by any chance he was wrong and the Land Rover went north, he would be able to turn and follow it.

He did not have long to wait before he saw a gleam of light from the garage lane, and a couple of minutes later the Land Rover emerged and turned in the direction of Fort William. Then, as soon as it was out of sight, Duncan switched on his lights and drove slowly after it.

Following was by no means easy, for the road they were on was straight and the weather made it necessary to use lights, and also meant that there was very little other traffic. To start with he hung right back and depended on getting the occasional glimpse of the Land Rover's rear lights. But the nearer they got to the town, the more difficult this became, for it was essential that Duncan did not lose his quarry in the increasing traffic and that at Inverlochy he saw whether Vass kept on south or turned west on to the Mallaig road. There were now two other cars between him and the Land Rover so he closed right up and prayed that nothing bigger, which might block his view, would appear. What did happen was that another Land Rover drove out of a side turning and in behind Vass. He had to watch carefully that the two did not change places, and in the driving rain this was not easy. In fact at the turning both cars and both Land Rovers took the west coast road.

Once clear of the town, they drove for some miles along the side of a loch, at the end of which Duncan saw Vass's Land Rover turn left on to a narrow side road.

So checking that there was nothing immediately behind him, he pulled on to the verge and watched. Vass continued on the side road for about four hundred yards and then turned right down a track that led on to open moorland. Seeing no way that he could follow across the hill without being visible, Duncan stayed on the main road and found that he could keep sight of Vass without difficulty.

As the rain had eased somewhat and the light had improved, Duncan stopped again and taking his binoculars and map, scrambled up a bank and lay down behind a clump of whins, from where he had a good view of the surrounding country.

Below him was a narrow haugh, beyond which the land rose steeply. Looking at the map, he saw that the track bent round to the left and continued south west between another loch and the high ground. Once there, it would be possible to follow the Land Rover without being seen, even if he had to stop.

He waited until it turned on to the lochside track and once it was out of sight, he returned to his car and headed west; after two miles, he turned left directly on to the track he wanted. Now it is one thing for a man in a Land Rover to drive along a mountain track, it is quite another for someone in an Hillman saloon to attempt the same feat. So with a silent prayer that all would be well, he drove on.

Apart from a few potholes and a grassy ridge down the middle, the track was not too bad and the overnight rain had not left it that muddy so, as caution rather than speed was the order of the day, he had no problems. His main worry was the possibility of suddenly coming on the Land Rover parked by the side of the track, or that Vass might decide to go up the hill for a spy.

Being a great believer in getting in first, Duncan decided that perhaps that was what he should do and so looked for a convenient hiding place for the car. Then, as he came to the crest of a small rise, he saw the Land Rover about a mile ahead, vanishing round a spur of the hill while below him, at the bottom of the next dip, was a fank and beside it an old shed which would serve to hide the car.

The ground around it looked firm enough, and so moments later the car was safely out of sight inside the ruin. The fank was at the end of a long corrie, the right side of which was formed by a shoulder of one of the peaks that he had seen from the road. At the upper end of the corrie was a near vertical wall of rock with patches of treacherous looking scree, culminating in a boulder-strewn crest. At the lower end of the corrie was a steep grass slope with halfway up a cluster of rocks which seemed to offer a good look-out point.

It took Duncan half an hour of hard scrambling to reach the rocks, for the slope was intersected by deep burns and the surface was all tussocks and hidden boulders. But at length he got there and crawled forward to a gap in the rocks, from where he had an excellent view of all the ground to the north and west.

The track continued for some distance before turning left into a broad corrie, which the map showed led to a low pass and eventually down to Glenlochan. To the east the ground sloped sharply down to the edge of the loch. Turning his glasses to follow the line of the track, Duncan saw that before it branched away from the loch, there was a ruined cottage and steading and also a wooden shed, which seemed in better condition than the other buildings. What was much more interesting though was a Land Rover parked in front of the cottage. There did not seem to be anyone in the vehicle, but after a few minutes Duncan saw a face at one of the cottage windows and then Vass emerged, appearing somewhat agitated. He looked anxiously up the track towards the Glenlochan pass; then he checked his watch and again turned his gaze in the direction of the pass. Finally he walked over to the shed and opened the door.

Back at the Land Rover, he rolled up the rear cover and reaching in, dragged out a tea chest. With this he staggered over to the shed and disappeared inside. He emerged a minute or two later, closed the door and returned to his vehicle. Then, with a final glance towards Glenlochan, he drove off in the direction of the Mallaig road.

It seemed fairly clear to Duncan what had happened. Having collected the crate from the yacht, Vass was supposed to deliver it personally to someone at the ruined croft. They were obviously late for the meeting, and for some reason Vass had felt unable to wait any longer. He had therefore taken the risk of leaving the crate hidden in the shed in the hope that it would be recovered later.

Duncan would dearly have loved to have had a look at the crate, but felt that would be impossible. To get to the croft unseen would take a good half hour, and he would risk being caught by whoever was to collect the crate. He therefore decided to wait and see who made the collection, but to try to get a bit nearer, which he thought he could do without the risk of being seen.

After a good look at the ground through the glasses, he was able, by judicious use of a couple of steep-sided burns, to work his way down to another corrie, where he was out of sight of the croft. When he reached the far side of this corrie, he turned downhill towards the track, which he crossed, before scrambling down the bank to the loch shore. Here again he was out of sight of the croft and he made good speed until he was level with a small wood on a knoll above the track. He was now only four hundred yards away, with an excellent view of the croft.

He had another look at the buildings and the track to Glenlochan, but for the moment could see nothing. He then turned his glasses to the shore of the loch and noticed that, just short of the croft, there was a small burn which passed under the track in a culvert. He decided to try to reach it. It would be risky but he reckoned that on the shore he would be in dead ground even to someone at the top of the pass.

He was half way to the burn when he thought he heard the sound of an engine, and so risked a look over the top of the bank. Sure enough there was another Land Rover, a rather smart looking one, coming down the brae from the pass. Dropping back, Duncan ran for the shelter of the burn and worked his way up it until he found a clump of bracken which afforded cover. He reached it just as the Land Rover pulled up.

The wind had now dropped, so from his new position he could hear as well as see what was happening. First the passenger door opened and a woman got out.

'He's obviously not here,' said Jane Parsons, 'but then we are over an hour late. I told you we should have started earlier. What are we going to do?'

By this time a man had walked round from the driver's side and joined Jane. Duncan thought his face looked vaguely familiar, but for the moment he could not put a name to it.

'Well, the first thing to do is to have a look around,' the man replied, 'he may just have been here and left it.'

'He could not have been that stupid surely.'

'I don't know,' said the man. 'You said Roddy hadna' told him what was in the chest. Anyway we must have a look. Come on, for we canna hang around too long. There doesn't appear to be anyone around at the moment, but you say people do use this road and I would rather not be seen. There's a lot of money in that box. Aye, and suppose there has been a leak, what a grand place for an ambush this would be!'

Jane looked round nervously, but the man told her not to be stupid and himself walked over to the cottage. Duncan wriggled back a little and buried his face in the bracken, hoping they would restrict their searching to the buildings. Not daring to raise his head, he heard the noise of shoes on stone as they moved around the cottage and byre. Then silence until a door creaked and he guessed they had moved on to the shed.

'Aha, look you here, Jane. Is this the tea chest that Roddy gave him?' Duncan heard the man shout.

'Yes, that's it,' Jane's voice replied, 'can you manage to get it into the car? I want to get away from here and back to the castle.'

Duncan heard the man tell her to stop worrying and just to hold the rear door open. This was followed by the noise of something being pushed across the floor of the vehicle. Then doors slammed and the engine started. Raising himself cautiously, he saw the Land Rover swing round and jolt off back the way it had come.

As soon as they had vanished over the crest of the pass, Duncan left his hiding place and started to walk back to his car. Now at last he knew two things with reasonable certainty. First a lot of money was, as he had suspected, on its way to the Unicorn, and secondly the headquarters of that organisation, at least for the time being, was at Altachonich Castle. So the castle, he said to himself, must be the next port of call.

Chapter 8

Daphne woke that morning to the same driving rain that had greeted Duncan in Spean Bridge. A quick look at her watch told her it was just after half-past five and time to get up if she was to be at Dougie's cottage by six. She dressed quickly in trousers and jersey and went out into the passage. There was no sign of movement from any of the other rooms, so she went quietly down to the gun room door, where she collected hat, boots and waterproof and let herself out. The rain was coming down in torrents and that, with the noise of the gale, would certainly deaden any sound she might make; for, although the guests might be told that she had left the castle early, she did not want anyone to see where she went.

A quick glance back showed no light in any of the bedrooms, so turning up the collar of her coat against the storm, she walked over to the stables and up the gravel road to the plantation, on the edge of which was the head stalker's cottage. There was a light in the kitchen and as she reached it, the back door opened and Dougie beckoned to her.

'Come on in out o' the rain,' said the stalker, ''Tis a real dirty morning and you'd best have a cup of tea before we go.'

'Here you are dear, that'll warm you up,' said Mrs Fletcher, thrusting a steaming mug into her hands, while the water dripped off her and made pools on the kitchen floor.

'Thank you, Mrs Dougie. I'm afraid I'm making an awful mess of your floor.' And then to Dougie she added, 'I don't think we should be too long. They are supposed to be leaving the castle at seven.'

'That's fine,' Dougie replied, 'you just finish your tea and I'll bring the truck round to the door. It's only just after six. We've plenty time to get out to Craggan and be back above the road by then.'

Turning back to Mrs Fletcher, Daphne thanked her for the tea and when asked about breakfast, said she had no idea when they might be back.

'Aye, I thought ye might say that, so I made pieces for both of you and a flask. Here tak' these. And you'd be better of a spare coat too. It's no' good for young ladies to be sitting around in wet clothes.' With this admonition ringing in her ears, she was ushered out and into the Land Rover. Then with shouted thanks, they drove off through the plantation and out on to the rocky hill track that led to Craggan.

51

About a mile before they reached the shepherd's cottage, they met him standing by the side of the path with a dead lamb beside him.

'Aye, that's the fourth this week,' he said, 'and it surely is a fox, for there's the teeth marks where it carried it down from those rocks. It canna go on, Dougie, you must try to get him. That's right, is it not, Miss Daphne?'

'Yes it is. So Dougie what are we going to do about it?' said Daphne.

'It's the old bitch from the den below Bheinn Buidhe,' said the keeper, pointing towards the jagged peak towering above the far end of the glen. 'Sure, Donnie, I'll get her for you in the next couple of days. She'll be feeding cubs, so it shouldn't be any bother.'

Then, after some further discussion about the state of the Craggan hirsel, Daphne and the stalker drove on up the glen. As they topped a small rise, the keeper suddenly pulled up and pointed.

'Look there, Miss Daphne. There she is. I know it's one of our grouse she's after, but it's a great sight to see a peregrine stoop. There she goes, back up to the nest. It's two pairs we have now on the estate.' Dougie Fletcher was a keen naturalist and, contrary to the public's view of his profession, he would never have killed a peregrine or any other bird of prey.

They watched the falcon for a few more minutes and also spied a small party of hinds grazing out on the flats.

'Come on, Dougie. We can't stay here all day. We've other things to do,' said Daphne with a glance at her watch. 'I want to get back above the Glenlochan road. I must find out what it is those others are up to.' The keeper nodded, turned the Land Rover and headed back down the glen.

It was just on seven when they stopped in the shelter of the plantation above the main road. While they had been on the hill, the storm had abated somewhat and was now only a light drizzle, although there was still a stiff wind blowing. The light was good but they could see no activity from the castle.

'We'd best eat our piece now, while we have the chance,' said Dougie, reaching behind his seat and producing the packets of sandwiches and the flask. The hot tea and the bread and jam were more than welcome after the cold wet drive across the hill and as they ate, they watched the antics of a small flock of long tailed tits.

'Bonnie wee birds,' said Dougie, then looking down at the castle added, 'now where's our party? They seem to be a bit behind time.'

It was nearly seven-thirty when they saw Jane and Fergus emerge from the castle and walking across to the stable, stand outside one of the garages, apparently engaged in a violent argument. A few minutes later Sir Torquhil appeared, opened the garage and backed out a smart looking Land Rover. Fergus then produced a map, and through her binoculars Daphne could see her father tracing a line with his finger, then looking up and pointing towards Glenlochan. The Land Rover, with Fergus at the wheel, then set off in that direction and Sir Torquhil returned to the castle.

Following was not difficult, for the plantation track ran parallel to the road and was largely invisible from it. Dougie let the other two get well ahead before emerging from the track and following them along the road. About half a mile short of the village, he pulled into a lay-by so that they could watch without being seen.

To Daphne's surprise, the Land Rover did not drive into the village but turned up a track towards the open hill.

'That's odd,' she said to Dougie, 'surely that track only goes to the old croft at Kettlehole. I've not been there more than a couple of times. Can you go on beyond the croft?'

'Aye. It goes on along the loch to the Mallaig road. Och, but it's only used by stalkers going to the back corries of Brackla. Aye, and mebbe by hikers or a picnic party. They canna do much damage there!'

'In that case the Land Rover must be going to the croft. A meeting place perhaps? Can we follow?' asked Daphne.

'It would be verra difficult without being seen,' the keeper replied, 'we'd be better waiting in Glenlochan until they return, for I'm not thinking they'd be going on to the main road.' Dougie added that to do that would suit him fine as he had a number of jobs to do in the village.

Daphne said that she would do a couple of messages and then go and visit an old lady who used to work at the castle and that Dougie could meet her there in an hour's time. The advantage of this plan was that Daphne knew she could watch the Kettlehole track from the cottage she was to visit.

Old Mrs Crombie was delighted to see Miss Daphne. Tea and biscuits were produced and the Crombie family's doings for the past year were recounted in great detail. Then, just as she was about to leave, Daphne saw the Land Rover come over the top of the beallach. Thankyou's and hopes for the future exchanged, and with final warnings to take care ringing in her ears, Daphne left in search of Dougie.

She found him deep in conversation with the blacksmith, and without altering the rhythm of his discussion, he turned to her and threw in, 'Yes, they are back on the way to the castle and in an awfu' hurry, it seems.'

Daphne was about to ask what he thought they should do when, looking again towards the beallach, she saw a small saloon car. 'What on earth is that doing there?' she said to Dougie.

'God knows. Let's see where it goes,' replied the keeper.

'Damned towrists. Ye canna get away from them these days,' added the smith with a gloomy look at the hill.

When it reached the road, the car turned towards the village and as it drew level with them, the driver looked in their direction and immediately pulling in to the side of the road, wound down the window and said somewhat hesitantly: 'Daphne?'

Surprised at hearing her name, she looked across at the man, who had got out of the car and was walking towards them. To see him there was so unexpected that it took her a moment to collect her wits and reply.

'Duncan! What on earth are you doing here? And why have you come by that very unusual route?'

'That's a rather long story,' he replied, 'but amongst the reasons is the fact that someone mentioned you lived near here, and I had in mind to look you up.' Then he added with a smile, 'I have to admit though, I had not expected to find you by the side of the road.'

'Well, I have to admit that I had not expected you to leap out of a car in the middle of Glenlochan. But it's an ill wind as they say, and since you are here, you might be just the person to help with a little problem that we have.' Then turning to the keeper she said, 'Dougie, this is Mr Forsyth. He works for the Government and I would like to tell him about my father and the quarry. We'll go along to the hotel. Come and join us when you're ready.'

Duncan, who had been up since five without breakfast and who was still feeling the effects of having been out in the storm, thought this sounded an excellent idea. So he drove Daphne down to the little hotel, where she organised coffee and toast while he had a quick wash and brush up.

When he got back to the lounge, she was sitting in the window staring out over the loch. He sat himself down beside her, looked at her and said:

'Now, what's the trouble? I always understood your father was someone about whom one did not worry.'

'Yes,' she said, 'so did I. But odd things are happening at Altachonich and I don't like it. And Dougie Fletcher, that's the stalker whom you just met, is dead worried and that's not like him.' Then with a sudden flash of inspiration she added, 'Duncan, tell me honestly – has your being in Morvern anything to do with my father?'

'Look,' he replied, 'why don't you tell me what the problem is. Then we'll have a think about what is to be done.' He had to admit to himself that he was in something of a quandary as to how to proceed. On the one hand he needed access to the castle to find out just what Sir Torquhil was doing and also who was involved with him. On the other hand he did not want to say too much to Daphne until he knew more about her attitude to her father's Nationalist leanings – and indeed how she felt about him after what had happened at their last meeting.

'Right,' she agreed, 'but if I tell you what is happening, I want you to be honest with me and tell me if my father is, or could be, in trouble with the law. I know all about his involvement with the independence people, and I know what your job is. Therefore to see you arrive in Glenlochan by a route most people don't even know exists, and then show an enthusiasm at meeting me that may not be entirely due to my charm and beauty, makes me a little suspicious.'

'Fair enough,' replied Duncan, 'tell me what is going on at the castle and if this seems to be in any way concerned with anything I may or may not be doing, I will let you know. Now fire away.'

Daphne told him about her father's intention to revive the old quarry workings and the odd way he seemed to be going about this.

'They've got a manager there called Simpson,' she went on, 'and Dougie, whose grandfather worked at the old quarry, says he's no more a quarrymaster than the others there are quarrymen. A collection of international thugs, if you ask me. Then there are the curious people who come and go at the castle – and all the meetings. I asked my father about it yesterday, for we have two Nationalist people staying at the moment and more expected this evening. He said it was all to do with a rally they are planning. I don't believe a word of it. You don't rehearse stewards for a political rally in a quarry from which others on the estate are excluded!'

When Duncan asked who the current visitors were, she told him about Fergus Crawford and his sister Jane Parsons, adding that Crawford was a well known agitator.

'There are others coming tonight and tomorrow, at least that's what father has asked me to cater for,' she told him. 'He said they have a series of planning meetings for the rally. The first meeting is this afternoon.'

'Crawford, of course! That's who I saw at the croft just now, but I couldn't remember his name. Yes I know a lot about Fergus Crawford,' Duncan replied, 'and he will know who I am although we have never met. Strangely enough I met Jane Parsons on the train coming up. She had no idea who I was and I certainly did not know she was Crawford's sister. That is interesting news, although I would have found it out later today from another source. However, as I will tell you, I did become suspicious of her for other reasons, not least because she tried to have me arrested.'

He then went on to tell her about his night on the train, including the planting of the money, his phone call from Carstairs and his specially staged arrest. However he did leave out certain events which he thought were irrelevant.

He gave her some information about Unicorn and her father's suspected involvement and then went on to describe his meetings with the police and the subsequent tracking of *Firefly*, and how that had led him to the croft behind Glenlochan.

'I managed to get a good view of Crawford and his sister retrieving the tea chest and taking it off in the Land Rover,' he concluded, 'now I want to know where they have gone. I'm sure it contains the money and I must find out why they need that amount of hard cash. It must be three hundred thousand dollars or more.'

'I can tell you where they have gone. Straight back to Altachonich,' said

Daphne. 'We saw the Land Rover come back over the beallach and then take the main road towards the castle.'

'Good. That confirms what I thought I heard them say back at the croft.' Duncan paused and appeared to be thinking. Then he turned to Daphne and said, 'Now I have told you what I have been doing, I would like to know how you came to be following those two.'

At that moment Dougie Fletcher came into the room and Daphne beckoned him to a chair.

'Dougie, Mr Forsyth wants to know why we followed the Land Rover to Glenlochan this morning,' she said. 'I have told him about your worries over the quarry and my worries about my father. All I can add, I think, is that when I heard that they were leaving the castle early, I wanted to know where they were going and why. As you and I were also out early, visiting Craggan, I thought we might just do a little quiet spying. So Duncan, what happens next?'

Duncan walked over to the window and looked out over the loch. He realised he had a difficult decision to make. He was now convinced that the answer to what Unicorn was planning would be found at Altachonich Castle, but to find it he needed the cooperation of Daphne and probably some help from the keeper. The trouble was that his investigations could well result in criminal proceedings against Sir Torquhil Drumcairn and he was uncertain how Daphne, or indeed the keeper, might react to such an eventuality. He decided it had to be risked and turned to face the other two.

'I have got to find out what is going on at the castle,' he said, 'in particular, I must know what happens in the quarry, why they need all that money, and what the *Firefly* is doing now. To do this I need your help. That may involve you in some danger. It may also involve Sir Torquhil in serious difficulties with the police. Are you willing to help? I don't want to sound hard-hearted, but perhaps I should add that without your help our country could be in considerable danger.'

Daphne looked at the keeper, who said: 'Ye ken, Miss Daphne, that I will do anything for the family and the estate, but I would not be wanting to harm your father.'

'Thank you, Dougie,' she replied. Then turning to Duncan she said, 'What my father does is his business, but I will not be a party to him damaging Scotland or her people. So how can we help?'

There then ensued considerable discussion, at the end of which it was agreed that Dougie should take Daphne back to the castle and that she should endeavour to find out what went on at the afternoon meeting. Duncan meanwhile would go to Fort William, where he hoped to find Inspector Nicholson. This should provide him with additional information on the *Firefly* and her owner, and on the Crawford family. He would also make arrangements for further support from the police. On his return they would all meet at Dougie's cottage to exchange information and to organise a reconnaissance of the quarry.

Having seen the others depart for Altachonich, Duncan got into his car and drove slowly towards Fort William. At the top of the hill beyond the castle he stopped and had a good look at the area through his binoculars, paying special attention to the gardens and foreshore and also to the approaches to the quarry. He then turned his attention to the buildings but could see no sign of any activity. He got out his map and studied the road, memorising the principal landmarks between Altachonich and Fort William and then checking them as he drove along. Duncan Forsyth was a man who did not like leaving things to chance, and he had a feeling that a time would come fairly soon when an intimate knowledge of the local topography might be essential to survival.

When he got to the town, he went straight to the Police Station. Here he found Inspector Nicholson with the Superintendent for the Lochaber District and another officer, who was introduced as Inspector Gray of the Argyll Constabulary.

'I just got here,' said Nicholson, 'and I've brought you a lot of stuff that came over the line from your HQ. Also when I spoke to the Super earlier today and told him you would likely be here this afternoon, and probably be asking for help, he thought we should get Mr Gray along. Altachonich and Glenlochan are in Argyll, you know.'

Duncan took the envelope and said he would read the contents later, but what he wanted to know now was what had happened to the yacht. The Superintendent said that it had come into the harbour early that morning and that a woman had gone into the town and done some shopping. Roddy Urquhart, who was a familiar figure around the waterside, had also come ashore and had been seen at the house of a local councillor, well known for his Nationalist sympathies. Subsequently the councillor's son, skipper of a fishing boat, had gone on board *Firefly*, which was last seen sailing down the loch towards the Sound.

'We'll keep an eye on her,' said the Super, 'or rather Mr Gray's boys will.'

'Aye, we'll do that,' Gray agreed, 'if she goes up the Sound, which seems likely, she'll be watched all the way. Our poacher look-out scheme will take care o' that. It's verra efficient and will no' rouse suspicion in the watchers or the watched. But now tell me Mr Forsyth, what other assistance might you need?'

'None immediately,' replied Duncan, 'but I'm sure that some time in the future we will need full-time observation of the castle. But for now all we need do is fix a rendezvous for this evening. After the Unicorn meeting and a recce of the quarry, we should know enough of their intentions to make more definite plans.'

Gray then produced a map and pointed to a farm on the coast road about five miles east of Altachonich. The farm, which was owned by a retired colonel, was frequently used by the police and mountain rescue people as an assembly point, so the appearance of police cars there would not arouse suspicion amongst the locals. It was therefore agreed that Gray and Nicholson would be at the farm, which was called Ord, from one-thirty the next morning and would wait for Duncan to appear.

'We'll not want to disturb the Colonel,' said Gray, 'so come in by the steading. Ye'll see the car and a light on in a wee room that he lets us use.'

With these plans agreed, Duncan, refusing an offer of lunch, took his leave and drove down to the hotel, where, not without difficulty, he persuaded reception to let him have a room for the afternoon. He then took his case upstairs and, having bathed and changed, he sat down to read his papers.

As regards Roderick Urquhart, these were very enlightening. It appeared that while working in Edinburgh he had been involved in raising money for a company that imported fruit from the Mediterranean and had spent some time in Cyprus.

Although nothing was ever proved, it was suspected that his Nationalist sympathies had led him into contact with EOKA, and from them he had gained a knowledge of the terrorist arms trade. Again, though there was nothing definite against him, his business in Inverness had extensive contacts with French arms manufacturers, ostensibly on the sporting side.

He had been involved in the independence movement since his student days. His marriage had strengthened these links and had brought him into contact with some of the more extreme elements. About his sister-in-law, Jane Parsons, little was known. Unlike the rest of her family, there was no evidence that she played an active part in Nationalist politics. The memo finished by saying that he was already briefed on Fergus Crawford and there was no further information on him available, other than that he seemed to be involved with the financier, Sir Torquhil Drumcairn, and a man called Simpson in the plans for a major rally. Was this a cover? Information please, particularly on Simpson, who could be a danger.

Duncan put down the file and gazed at the ceiling for a few minutes, thinking to himself: 'Headquarters are in for something of a shock if my reading of the situation is correct. For the moment though, everything is falling nicely into place.' With which comforting thought he went downstairs, paid his bill and drove off in the direction of Altachonich.

Chapter 9

When they got back to the castle, Daphne asked to be dropped at the stables, and from there she made her way to the pantry, where she found the butler.

'Where are my father and the others?' she asked, 'and has anyone else arrived?'

'Sir Torquhil is in the library with Mrs Parsons and Mr Crawford,' the butler replied, 'and Mr Simpson from the quarry is on his way over to join them. No one else has arrived, but Sir Torquhil told me they are expecting a Mr Jenkinson, a politician I believe, for dinner and to stay the night. Your father said he had already told you.'

'He said there might be someone but he didn't say who. I think I've heard of Mr Jenkinson; he has some junior position in the Scottish Office. Put him in Lady May's Room. She might give him a fright! You have told Annie, I assume?'

'Yes indeed, Miss Daphne, Cook is aware and I will arrange about the room.'

Now the fact that the meeting was in the library was a bit of luck, for one corner of that room was formed by the northeast tower, a part of the castle no longer in use. However in her younger days, when staying with her grandmother, Daphne had often climbed the crumbling stone stairs to the lookout at the top. In the course of these explorations, she had discovered that in the wall of a little closet on the same level as the library, there was a cleverly concealed spyhole. Indeed, on a visit during the War, she received an early introduction to the facts of life through watching one of her aunts with a young officer. It was to that cubby hole, known only to her, that she now made her way.

As she reached her place, the meeting in the library was just starting and, although her view was somewhat restricted, she could hear Fergus reporting on the successful collection of the money that morning.

'It's now locked away in the quarry safe,' he said, 'and I understand that no one except Davie Simpson knows it's there. But now what we need to know is, where is the yacht and what is happening about the cargo?'

'Yes, Crawford, I agree with that. Before we get down to plans, we'd better know that we are going to have the wherewithal to carry them out. So what can you tell us, Simpson?' Daphne heard her father speaking in what she called his chairman's voice, and it was obvious that Simpson did not like being addressed in that way, even by Sir Torquhil.

David Simpson was an unpleasant man with a criminal record and Dougie was correct in saying that he had been court martialled following the discovery that rations were finding their way illegally to the local population. Shortly after the discovery, there had been a serious accident during a river crossing at a point defended by Simpson's company. Among those killed in the accident had been the officer investigating the disappearance of the rations. Simpson had been arrested and tried for gross dereliction of duty, found guilty and sentenced to dishonourable discharge. Many thought he had been lucky not to have been tried for more serious offences.

His wartime experience had left him an embittered man. It was not altogether surprising therefore, that when he was thrown out of the army, he moved into black market operations. He was involved in the hijacking of whisky intended for export and also dealt in surplus government equipment, including weapons. He and his accomplices were not too particular about how they treated those who got in their way, and it was said that they were involved in some ugly incidents in shipyard strikes on the Clyde. He had always been interested in Home Rule, believing there was money to be made out of it, and when direct action was being discussed, he and his gang had been recruited by Fergus.

'Very well,' he said in his thin hard voice, laying a map on the table. 'We have had a message from Urquhart to say that he has picked up his pilot and is heading for the Sound of Mull. He hopes to meet the French boat some ten miles off the Point, about here I think, and they will tranship the cargo tonight. He hopes to be at the quarry with it and the expert soon after lunch tomorrow. Does that satisfy you?'

'It'll do for the moment,' said Sir Torquhil, 'and now I'm much more interested in what we are going to do with this lethal weapon once we have it ashore. Remember, I have gone to considerable trouble – and risk – to get the money. I want results, but I don't want a blood bath.'

Simpson leant forward and looked hard at Sir Torquhil. 'All in good time,' he snapped. 'First I want to know what has happened to that man from the SIS, Duncan Forsyth.' Then turning to Jane and fixing her with his pale eyes, he said coldly, 'I could wish you would be more careful about whom you choose to talk to on trains. Duncan Forsyth is a very shrewd and dangerous operator. We must find out where he is.'

'How was I to know who he was?' retorted Jane, who had taken an immediate dislike to David Simpson and now found herself the target of his anger. 'And just bear in mind, all of you, that I had a difficult and dangerous time last Thursday. If it had not been for my quick thinking, you might now be wondering not about where Forsyth might be, but about where the money had gone.'

'Aye, calm down Davie,' said Fergus, quick to defend his sister, 'for all we ken, he may still be in police custody. Or, realising who he was, they may have let him go with apologies and he may be fishing happily in Sutherland.'

'Be your age, man,' growled Simpson, 'Forsyth has come to Scotland for a purpose and that purpose is to find Unicorn. It's all too much of a coincidence for it to be anything else. He must be found. I heard, Sir Torquhil, that he knows your daughter – if you ask me he knows too many bloody people round here. Is she likely to know where he might be?'

'I have no idea,' replied the laird, 'she has certainly not mentioned his name recently. That he should come here, where he has never been, to see me, whom he has never met, does really seem a trifle far fetched. I suggest that all we can do for the moment is be on our guard and wait and see. Now could we please move on to the main business of the meeting – what are we going to do to hasten the day of Scottish independence?'

'It's got to be something sensational, something that will make the headlines worldwide and rouse the blood of the Scottish people,' replied Fergus, 'and violence cannot be ruled out. You know, Davie, as I do, that the Council has agreed to this.'

He rose to his feet, his eyes shining with the fervour of the fanatic and his voice rising. 'Tomorrow, with the arrival of the yacht and its cargo,' he cried, 'we become true terrorists! I was not at the last Council. Tell us, Davie, did they agree how we should start our campaign?'

'Calm down, Fergus,' said Simpson, waving him to sit down, 'all in good time. Yes, there is a plan but before we can discuss it, I am going to need some information. That, Jane, is where you come in.'

Crouched in the cramped confines of the room in the tower, Daphne could not see her father. The way they had placed the table had left him just out of her sight and she could not risk too much movement in case they heard something. She would like to have seen his reaction to all Fergus' ranting and talk of violence. As it was, she had to be content with hearing it, and it was not long in coming.

'Now steady on, everyone,' she heard Sir Torquhil say. 'Before we start talking of violence and terrorism, hadn't we better consider what we are trying to achieve? To gain independence, we need to carry the people of Scotland with us. The new Scotland we create must be acceptable to all the people and must be created in a way that is acceptable; that is by political means. Scotland does not want terrorism. You cannot build a stable nation using instability as a weapon. I am prepared to use threats to reinforce persuasion but I do not want to see killing of any sort.'

'Good for you, father,' thought Daphne. But she wondered if he would be allowed to get away with it. They wanted instant results – power through force. 'But he's right,' she said to herself, 'force can be slower than the ballot.

It just seems quicker.'

'Sure, Sir Torquhil,' said Simpson, realising he must slow things down. The tough talking could come tomorrow with full disclosure of the proposed action. For the present he needed information to complete his planning. Looking hard at the laird, he continued, 'our aim must be to get the people to persuade the Government to grant independence by democratic means. We are only going to help supply the persuasion.'

Sir Torquhil grunted. Daphne had heard that grunt before and felt they were going to have a hard time with her father at tomorrow's meeting, whenever that might be.

In response to Sir Torquhil's demand to get a move on and say what he wanted, Simpson told them that the United States Secretary of Defense would be joining the NATO fleet in the Cromarty Firth in the next couple of days, and would attend a parade in Inverness the following Saturday.

'You will all know that he is a rabid anti-colonialist and a supporter of every sort of Nationalist movement,' Simpson continued. 'What you may not know is why an American called Norman Jacobsen should be so keen to see Scotland freed from the yoke of English domination – you remember his speech in Glasgow last year? Well I will tell you. His great-grandfather was a Highland officer who became a general and who, after retiring, spent all his money trying to alleviate the terrible suffering of the unemployed in and around his estate. His son emigrated to the States, was successful, and endowed his family with three things: wealth, a love of his father's regiment (which is why Jacobsen has been invited to Saturday's ceremony) and a hatred of the established Government of the United Kingdom.'

'Very interesting,' said Sir Torquhil, 'but how does that help us? Get to the point, man. We haven't got all day.'

'I give it by way of background,' replied Simpson airily, and then went on in more serious vein. 'In order to establish the feasibility of a certain idea, I need to know how Jacobsen is to travel from Invergordon, where the fleet is anchored, to Inverness.'

'That might be very difficult,' said the laird, 'you know how security conscious the Americans are.' Then in a rather sharper tone, 'Anyway, why do you need to know? Are you planning to kidnap him?'

'It's been discussed. But I am not going to say any more until I have the rest of the information I need.' Then, turning to Sir Torquhil, Simpson continued: 'you have been good enough to ask that silly little man Paddy Jenkinson to stay tonight. He is the Scottish Secretary's PPS and I am told that he knows the details of Jacobsen's visit.'

'Aye, Davie, but surely you're not thinking he'll tell us just for the asking,' Fergus interjected.

'He can be made to,' said Simpson with an air of contempt, 'for as well as being a silly little man, Jenkinson fancies himself with ladies.' Then turning to Jane, he asked her, 'Do you think you could persuade him?'

Daphne was watching Jane, who showed no sign of emotion and gave no immediate reply. It was her father who gasped and then growled.

'Are you suggesting she should seduce him? Because I will not have that happen in my house.' And turning to Crawford he asked, 'will you allow your sister to be treated like this?'

'Och, in support of the cause, Janie can be a bonny wee whore!' her brother replied.

Daphne heard her father get to his feet but before he could say anything, Jane, her face now white with fury, turned on Crawford.

'I'll thank you to keep a civil tongue in your head. You may be my brother and think that you can say what you like about me, but I'm a respectable and successful business woman and I will not be insulted in public.' Then turning to Sir Torquhil, she said, 'please sit down. I'm afraid Fergus tends to get carried away. I'm sure I can find out what we want from Mr Jenkinson; and I assure you, Sir Torquhil, that I will not do anything of which you would disapprove.'

'Very well. But bear in mind, young lady, that scandal never helped any cause,' and then to David Simpson he said, 'when you have this information, are you going to tell us what is proposed?'

'Sir Torquhil, I think we have talked enough for the moment,' replied Simpson, who was beginning to feel things were getting out of hand. 'Jenkinson will be here shortly. I suggest we break off now and meet again tomorrow morning. Assuming we have obtained the information we need, I will then outline the plan and, in the afternoon, provided all has gone well with *Firefly*, we can have a look at the equipment. By then the American from the Sons of the Clearances will have arrived. Isn't that right, Sir Torquhil?'

'Yes, Cyrus P. Groat. He should be here for lunch,' answered the laird.

From her spyhole in the tower Daphne saw that the meeting was about to end and, not wishing it to be known that she had been in the castle during the afternoon, she left her hiding place and went out past the kitchen, warning the butler not to mention having seen her. From there she made her way to the stalker's cottage for her meeting with Duncan.

Sir Torquhil meanwhile had left the library, saying he was going to his study and would arrange for Paddy Jenkinson to be taken there when he arrived.

'He thinks I am going to tell him about a grand Nationalist rally, so I had better do that!' he remarked, and to Jane and Fergus he added, 'and you two had better back me up at dinner. As for you, Simpson, I think it would be best if you were not seen.'

'Thank you for that. I've got better things to do than to waste my time on the likes of him,' he replied, 'and now, if no one minds, I'm going back to the quarry.'

With that Sir Torquhil and Simpson went off, leaving the other two alone in the library.

Jane rounded on her brother and said, 'You're a shit, Fergus, and a pretty stupid one. Surely to God you've learned by now that you don't make that sort of remark about a woman in front of someone like Sir Torquhil? Yes, of course I shall have to use what I think the old man would call feminine wiles on this MP. That should get the information we want. But I think we must also ensure his silence about such an indiscreet affair. Have you got your tape recorder and that fancy camera with you?'

'You mean the one using infra-red film? Aye, I've got them both,' he replied, 'what are you after?'

'If I give you the film tomorrow morning early, can you develop it here before the little man leaves?'

'Uh huh. It'll be tricky and the result will not be magazine quality.'

'I don't want what will be on that film in any magazine, thank you. And avert your eyes when you develop it. I don't want you studying my night-time activities – not with your nasty incestuous mind,' she said with a smile, while Fergus had the decency to blush at the implied accusation. 'We're going to set up the camera and recorder in my room, so that we have a record of Mr Jenkinson baring both his soul and his body to me, and we'll let him have a copy. I'm sure his wife will love to see it!'

'I always said you were a great girl, Janie. Although I don't know what Mary or our mother would think. Mother was always a wee thing straight-laced, even when support for the cause was involved.' Then he added with a laugh, 'I'll no' peep and I'll no' tell on you. But for God's sake be careful. You can never trust a politician!'

'I will, brother. Now I'm going up to my room. Run along and get your stuff and meet me upstairs in half an hour,' she said as she turned and left the room.

Chapter 10

When Daphne reached Dougie's cottage, she found Mrs Fletcher alone in the kitchen.

'Come away in, dear,' that good lady said, 'sit ye down and I'll get a cup o' tea. Dougie will be back shortly. He's away out to the Black Ditch. The wee foot bridge was washed away in last night's storm. And then he was going to find Johnnie and see what damage there's been on the Meall Garbh beat. But my, you do look awfu' dusty. What have you been about? Come, you'd best have a wash before we have tea.'

Daphne was ushered into the bathroom and one look in the mirror showed her that two hours crouched in the northeast tower had played havoc with her appearance. When she emerged some five minutes later, Mrs Fletcher looked at her.

'Aye, that's a wee bitty better,' she said, 'now here's your tea and some scones I just baked this morning.'

'I'm sorry, Mrs Dougie, I was a bit of a mess. I've been sorting out the kennels. Now I hope you don't mind, but I've agreed with Dougie that we can use the cottage for a meeting this evening. Mr Duncan Forsyth, who works for the Government, wants to take a look at the quarry without being seen by anyone, and Dougie has promised to help.'

'Aye, Dougie mentioned something about it. It needs taking a look at. I canna stand yon Simpson.' Mrs Fletcher paused and listened. 'Now there's a car. It will be your man, for it doesna sound like the Land Rover.'

When Daphne opened the door, Duncan, who was searching through his brief case, looked up and said:

'Hang on a moment while I find the map and the right papers.' And then in answer to Daphne's query he added, 'No, I don't think anyone saw me arrive. I certainly saw no other car once I left the main road.'

'Come on in and meet Mrs Fletcher,' said Daphne. Then as she was doing the introductions, they heard the Land Rover draw up outside.

'That'll be Dougie,' Mrs Fletcher announced somewhat superfluously, 'now come on into the front room. It will be fine and quiet for your meeting in there.'

They found themselves bustled down the passage and into a room filled with an amazing mixture of military relics, framed religious texts and some

65

seventy years of family photographs. There they were joined by Dougie, who invited them to sit down and apologised for being late.

'I had to find out if there was any bad damage from last night's storm,' he said, 'and I also had a quick look along the cliffs above the quarry. Yon Simpson, he's a suspicious man. As I was thinking, they have a man watching the path along the shore. But if you're wanting to visit tonight, I can bring you down by the long gully on the east side. They think that's impassable. Now, Miss Daphne, what's it you're wanting?'

'I think we had better let Mr Forsyth decide that.'

Duncan turned to Daphne and said, 'I think the best thing is for you to tell us what, if anything, you found out this afternoon. I will then tell you about my meeting with the police and also some interesting facts about the Crawfords and Urquharts. We can then decide what to do next.'

Daphne started by telling them about the northeast tower and the ancient spy-hole, and went on to say who was at the meeting.

'The quarry manager, Simpson, is a nasty bit of work. I can see why nobody on the estate likes him, and I got the impression that his colleagues, including my father, not only don't trust him but are actually afraid of him.'

'Right,' Duncan said, 'I'll get a search on him. I should have done it earlier. Carry on, Daphne.'

In her cramped position in the tower, she had not been able to take any notes of what she had heard. But now, relying solely on her memory, she gave them a detailed account of everything that took place. It seemed that the yacht was due to pick up a cargo, apparently some kind of weapon, that evening and deliver it to the quarry at lunchtime the next day.

'We must watch that,' interjected Duncan.

Then she went on to describe how Simpson had told Jane off for having got mixed up with Duncan.

'He's worried about you,' she said. 'The others seemed happy to hope you were fishing, but he said you must be found. Then he upset Father by saying he understood that I knew you and might even know where you were. Anyway they then got on with what I took to be the main purpose of the meeting. Rally my foot! Any talk of a rally is just a cover for some major action they are planning. I'm afraid terrorism is not out of the question.'

Her reason for thinking this was the time they had spent discussing the visit of the United States Secretary of Defense to a NATO fleet and a parade in Inverness, particularly how he was to get from one to the other.

'Simpson wants to know how the Secretary, who is called Jacobsen I think, will travel from the Cromarty Firth to Inverness. Now Father has asked Paddy Jenkinson, the Scottish Secretary's PPS, to stay the night and he knows Jacobsen's movements. Paddy is known to be one for the girls – and I can tell you that's true – so Simpson told Jane that she had to get this information from him. Father hit the ceiling! "No seduction in my house!"

The Unicorn Never Dies

he roared. Jane managed to calm him down, but then her brother called her a whore, and so they had a row. Great stuff it was!'

Dougie looked faintly shocked that the laird's daughter should describe these goings on with such enthusiasm. Duncan smiled and thought to himself that he had perhaps had a lucky escape. All Jane had done to him, as a reward for his seduction, was to try and get him arrested!

'At that point,' Daphne continued, 'Simpson thought things were getting out of hand and, as I could see the meeting was about to end, I thought it advisable to remove myself. The last thing I heard was them discussing the arrival tomorrow of an American, a Mr Cyrus P. Groat, who is something to do with some society or other.'

'Yes, he's the President of the American Sons of the Clearances,' said Duncan. 'they are the body that produced the money that's now in the quarry safe. We know several things about Cyrus P., one being that he is a sworn enemy of Norman Jacobsen. All of which is very interesting, particularly in view of what I have learned about Roderick Urquhart. Roderick Urquhart probably has connections with the illegal arms trade. He is known to have been friendly with EOKA in Cyprus and his Inverness company does business with French arms manufacturers, ostensibly on the sporting side. My people have nothing specific on this, nor on Mary Urquhart. Unlike her brother, there is no evidence of her involvement in anything other than normal political activity. On Jane we have nothing at all. It is possible however that Jane Parsons and a certain Janet Priestley, about whose activities we'd like to know more, are one and the same person. Furthermore, although they did not say so specifically, I think the police and Customs have had *Firefly* under observation for some time.'

'Do you think they really are planning a terrorist outrage?' Daphne asked, 'I know my father has been very evasive about what's going on, but would he really countenance something like that?'

'I think he may have to,' Duncan replied. 'He helped with the smuggling of the money and he is allowing them to use the quarry. Yes, I think he may be in so deep that they won't let him out.'

'But can't we do anything to help?' she cried, 'I warned him the other day that these men wanted more than rallies – they wanted action. He pooh-poohed the idea, but it seems I was right.'

'We'll do what we can, but the first thing I have to do is to try to prevent an international incident.' Duncan looked at his two listeners, trying to make up his mind how much of his suspicions he should tell them. They are going to find out in the end, he thought, and I need their help now.

'Listen,' he said, 'what I am going to tell you now must go no further than the three of us.' When they nodded their agreement, he continued. 'Now, what do we know? There is a gang who want to bring closer the day of Scottish independence. To achieve this they want to perpetuate some

outrage, probably one that will embarrass the Government and win sympathy
for their cause. They are expecting a yacht to make a clandestine delivery of
a cargo, apparently a weapon of some sort. There is an international statesman
who is to attend a parade in Inverness and probably make a speech. Finally
we know that they want to find out how he is to get to Inverness from
Invergordon, where he is visiting the fleet. Now what does all that suggest?'

'That the incident, or whatever it is they are planning, involves something
happening to Mr Jacobsen while he is between Invergordon and Inverness.
My father asked if Simpson wanted to kidnap him. How's that for an idea?'
Daphne questioned Duncan.

'Aye, it sounds probable,' said Dougie, 'and they'll likely be looking at
the Black Isle. I ken it fine and there are grand places for an ambush in the
middle of it.'

'Yes, and Roderick Urquhart comes from the Black Isle,' Duncan added.
'I think it will be something along those lines that they are planning. We'll
know more when we see what the yacht's cargo is and that means finding a
place from which we can watch its arrival and then later, trying to get a look
at the cargo itself. But the first item, I think, is for me to visit the quarry
tonight.'

'Well, I'm going to leave you and Dougie to deal with that,' said Daphne,
'I must get back to the castle and change, for I'm expected at dinner and I
don't want to be late and have to explain what I've been doing.'

'No, you certainly don't,' Duncan replied, 'for I think you are already
under suspicion. So be very careful for the next two days; in fact I think it
would be wise to arrange to go away for a bit, if that is possible.'

As Daphne rose to go, Duncan said, 'Hang on a moment, for I think
you'd better know my movements for the rest of the night. After I've had a
look at the quarry I'm going to Ord, where I've arranged to meet the police,
and I think I'll spend the night there. Can we meet here again tomorrow
morning early – say seven o'clock?'

'Is that all right, Dougie, about meeting tomorrow?' Daphne asked and
the keeper nodded. 'Fine then, I'll see you all at seven. And Duncan, I've
already told my father I shall be away for a couple of weeks.'

As soon as Daphne left them, Duncan spread his map on the table and
Dougie described the nature of the ground in and around the area of the
quarry.

To the west of the castle, he explained, there was an almost unbroken line
of cliffs which continued to the end of the loch and beyond. These cliffs
varied in height from two hundred and fifty to four hundred feet. Nowhere
were they sheer rock, but steep, sometimes near vertical, slopes covered in
grass and scrub and a few larger trees. The cliffs were intersected by many
burns, some cascading down as spectacular waterfalls, others being steep-
sided clefts in the rock.

The quarry was about a mile to the west of the castle and formed a deep bowl in the cliff face, going back some two hundred yards from the shore, and about four hundred yards across at its widest. The pier and buildings were to the east or castle side of the quarry. Behind, the land rose from the edge of the cliff in a series of ridges, which were the foothills of the distant mountains.

Having described the ground, Dougie looked again at the map and pointed to a spot above the west edge of the quarry.

'There's a place here we can go to tomorrow and watch for the yacht to arrive,' he said, 'it will suit us fine for we'll be in cover the whole time. But now, if you want to get down into the quarry tonight, ye'll have to go by this burn,' and he pointed to the east edge of the quarry. 'We can get into it here without being seen and if you follow the way I'll point out, it'll take you in cover the whole way to the back of the sheds. I canna understand why they didna block it off. They seem to think it canna be climbed. But it's quite easy going, although you must just be carefu' o' loose stanes.'

'That sounds fine,' said Duncan, 'what time should we start?'

'We will be leavin' here about nine-thirty,' replied Dougie, 'there's no' a moon, so it'll be fine and dark when we get to the top o' the burn just after ten. Now when you get down to the quarry there'll likely still be people aboot, so ye should get a chance to see what like they are.' Then, getting to his feet, the keeper added, 'and now I think the wife has tea ready for us. Are you fond o' ham and eggs?'

Chapter 11

When Paddy Jenkinson arrived at Altachonich, the butler took him straight to the study, where Sir Torquhil greeted him warmly, sat him in a comfortable chair and gave him a large whisky and soda.

'So, Paddy,' he said looking down at his guest, 'if what I hear is correct, you are coming more and more to support our aims, even to the extent that you might attend the forthcoming rally. But tell me, how are you going to square that with your boss? Our Secretary of State is not conspicuous for his support of a separate Scottish nation.'

'Look, Torquhil,' Jenkinson replied, 'you and I have been friends for quite a few years so I'm going to tell you something now which I want you to treat in the strictest confidence. In the near future I intend to go back to being a plain back-bencher. More than that, if your lot could only convince me that you are a serious political party, and that the people of Scotland believe in you and what you stand for, I would happily consider joining you. That's why I want to attend the rally.'

'Splendid!' replied Sir Torquhil, 'so now listen and I will tell you a bit about our plans for the rally and for a completely new Scottish political party.'

Sir Torquhil spent the next forty minutes explaining to the MP his vision of a reborn Scotland, and the events that would lead to its realisation. It was a lecture he kept for occasions such as this, its purpose being to raise enthusiasm in potential converts, particularly those whose influence could be useful. It was designed to allay fears of any more of the sort of violence which had been a feature of recent Nationalist activity, and to this end Sir Torquhil took care to explain the presence of his other guests.

'At dinner this evening you will find my daughter, whom you have met before, and also Fergus Crawford and his sister Jane Parsons. I don't think you have met Crawford, although you probably know of him by reputation, and you may wonder why he is here. I know his name has been associated with certain events which I could wish had not taken place, but his father was a founder member of our movement and Fergus has a lot of influence. I need his support for the rally. I know little about his sister. She has been sailing around the islands and has come over from Fort William for a couple of days.'

'Now then, that's enough for the time being,' concluded Sir Torquhil looking at his watch. 'Dinner is at eight, so I suggest we go and change and meet in the library at a quarter to.'

Unlike the others, Jenkinson was already wearing a suit, so apart from a wash, he did not have much changing to do. Soon after seven therefore, he made his way to the library and sat himself down with a copy of *The Field*. He was deep in an article on the damage done by mink in certain rivers, when he heard the door open and a woman's voice wished him good evening.

As he got to his feet, she crossed to the centre of the room and said, 'I'm sorry if I disturbed you. I am Jane Parsons. You must be Paddy Jenkinson.'

'Yes indeed,' he said, taking the proffered hand perhaps a shade too warmly. 'How very nice to meet you. I gather you have been sailing and came ashore just in time to miss last night's storm. Very wise.'

'Yes, we came down the canal and I left the others before we got to Fort William. They were going to shelter there for the night and hope to avoid the worst of the gale,' she said, then seeing him still standing, added with an apologetic smile, 'I'm so sorry, please sit down.'

With that she curled herself on the sofa opposite him so that he had every chance to look closely at her. She was wearing a black dress with a tight bodice and full skirt, which showed off her dark hair and delicate colouring to perfection, and her eyes had a sparkle which attracted immediate friendship – something he was more than willing to give.

'I know you are an MP. Sir Torquhil told us that. But why are you here?' she asked, 'it seems an unlikely place for a politician, even at a weekend. Are you about to make an exciting speech somewhere?'

'No, I'm afraid not. Nothing as interesting as that,' he replied. 'I am on my way further north and Torquhil kindly asked me to stay the night. I'm an old friend from his time as an MP and I wanted to hear about a Nationalist rally that he and others are planning. Although I'm a Unionist, I have always been intrigued by the idea of an independent Scotland. Sounds contradictory, I know, but it's true.'

'And why are you going on north, and when?' she asked.

'Oh, I'm only here for tonight, then I go on to Inverness,' he said. 'Didn't Torquhil tell you? I am the Parliamentary Private Secretary to the Secretary of State for Scotland and he is involved in an important event in Inverness next Saturday.'

'How exciting! Tell me about it,' said Jane with a smile.

'It's very boring really. There is a parade to celebrate the birthday of one of the Highland regiments and it is being attended by the United States Secretary of Defense. I think his great-grandfather was in the regiment. And because he's going to be there, my boss has to be there too. My job is to see that all arrangements have been properly made.'

'It seems a long way for an American to come just for a parade,' said Jane,

'I thought they were always too busy to do anything like that.'

'Ah, but Jacobsen – that's Mr Secretary's name – will already be in Scotland,' Jenkinson replied, 'he's visiting American warships in the Cromarty Firth.'

'Making a week-end of it, is he?' remarked Jane, 'Lucky man! I love parades. Next Saturday, you say? By then I shall be staying with my sister, who lives in Inverness, so I should be able to watch. You must tell me all about it, so I know where to go.'

'Of course,' he replied, 'but it will have to be later this evening. For I think I hear others about to appear.'

Indeed he did, for the door opened and Daphne came in. She had cast off her tweed and twin-set image and was now wearing a close-fitting red silk dress, which made her look every bit the sophisticated girl about town. It was a direct challenge to Jane and was accepted as such.

'You look wonderful,' she said, 'I had no idea you Highland girls ever wore frocks like that. Don't you think she's a real glamour puss?' she added, turning to Paddy.

'Daphne always looks adorable,' he said, clasping her hand in both of his and raising it to his lips, 'that's why it's such a pleasure to come here. But I had no idea that this time I was to find not one, but two beautiful ladies staying!' Then to Daphne, 'My dear, you do indeed look lovely. But then so does Mrs Parsons, I think we must agree.'

'Oh, please call me Jane,' said that lady, including them both in the invitation. However further conversation was curtailed by the sound of someone approaching.

'Have you got the champagne there, Charles?' came the laird's voice from down the passage, followed a moment later by 'Bring it in then.'

Sir Torquhil entered followed by the butler, carrying a silver tray with glasses, which he offered to the two girls and the MP.

Sir Torquhil, who already had a glass, held it up to the light and took a sip, saying: 'As we have Paddy here, I thought we might have a glass of champagne and drink to the future of our country.' Then, looking round, he said to Jane, 'Where's your brother? I don't like people being late.'

'I'm afraid I don't know, Sir Torquhil, he's usually quite a punctual person,' replied Jane, 'I think he must be making a big effort to look tidy!'

Which indeed proved to be the case, for at that moment Fergus entered wearing a kilt and a light green tweed jacket.

'Aye, ye're all surprised to see me so smart,' he said, 'but I heard that Sir Torquhil would be in the kilt and I didna' want to be outdone.'

'You look splendid, and I'm honoured that you followed my example,' said Sir Torquhil. 'Now have a glass of champagne – unless you'd prefer whisky?'

But Fergus accepted the champagne and joined with the others in drinking to the future of Scotland. Sir Torquhil then took him by the arm and leading him over, introduced him to Jenkinson, saying, 'I don't think you two have ever met, but I believe you may have more interests in common than you think.'

'No, we haven't met, but of course I've heard a lot about you,' said Jenkinson as they shook hands, 'and not only the rubbish they say about you in the papers.'

'I'm glad of that,' the other replied, 'for I think Jane here would tell you there are some good things about me.' Then he looked at the MP and added, with one of his rare smiles, 'my trouble is I'm impatient. I'm always wanting action. I canna sit around talking like you boys do in Parliament. You blether away for so long on a subject that by the time you've decided what to do, you've forgotten what the subject was, and so nothing gets done.

'Take Scotland, for example. A politician considering its future, even one with Nationalist leanings, will talk of the benefits of independence. Aye, but then what happens? Someone says to him "ye canna do that, it's too difficult and you'll upset too many people", so nothing happens. Your true Nationalist must be a revolutionary like me. "Storm the barricades" is my motto. But I'll say no more. I promised I would behave this evening!'

'Well, I don't know,' said Jenkinson, 'you could make a better politician than you think. That was a fine speech and storming the barricades requires a leader to tell the troops why they must go forward and what the rewards are. You'd be just the man to make the inspiring speech before the battle or, come to that, before the great debate in the House of Commons!'

Any further discussion on Fergus's suitability as a politician was cut short by Charles appearing and announcing dinner. Then, when everyone was seated to the laird's satisfaction, the conversation became more general and less political. However that could not last long, and sure enough once the main course was served, Daphne turned to Fergus, who seemed to have lost his earlier sociability.

'Tell me, Mr Crawford,' she asked, 'do you really see yourself storming barricades in aid of an independent Scotland? Do you really believe the people of Scotland want to be led to a Promised Land by, if you will forgive my saying so, a rabble? I don't – and, what's more, I don't think they'd follow you. What do you think, Jane, do you believe in your brother's ideas?'

Before she could answer, Fergus replied angrily, 'There will be no question of leading. We shall give a new Scotland to the people and they will live in it; aye, and we will govern them, not as they are governed at present, by a lot of foreigners, but as we, the heirs of Wallace and Bruce, think they should be governed.'

'Oh come now, Fergus, you know you don't really think that,' his sister said, in an attempt to calm things. 'Father believed in creating a Scotland for the Scottish people, not a plaything for dictators.'

'Surely, Mr Crawford, you are not advocating achieving your purpose through violence?' queried Jenkinson with a hint of surprise in his voice. 'Violence never achieved anything for any movement, except perhaps in the last resort. Even then there must be a definite and desirable political objective, which both leaders and followers believe cannot be achieved by any other means. Furthermore, to be successful, violence needs the tacit support of the uncommitted, and that is certainly not the case in Scotland.'

Before Crawford could answer, Sir Torquhil, following Jane's earlier lead, sought to lower the temperature by saying: 'I'm sure we all want to do our best for Scotland and we all have our different ideas about the road to independence – some being, perhaps, more practical than others. But I think we have had enough of argument for the moment.' To reinforce his point, he turned to Jane and said: 'Now tell me, my dear, where do you work in London, and what exactly is your job?'

This had the desired effect on the company and the conversation once more became general, and continued so until after Charles had served the coffee. Then, leaving the others to drink theirs in the dining room, Daphne and her father excused themselves and took their cups through to the study.

Daphne perched herself on the arm of a chair and, looking at her father, said 'You dealt with the warring factions in masterly fashion. But you must be careful. That man Crawford was not joking, and you know he wasn't. I know you are aware that something's brewing and you won't tell. Well, I'm not going to ask again. But I will just warn you – violence is not your scene, and you know it.

'And now to change the subject. You remember that I told you earlier that I would be away for a couple of weeks. Well, I'll be leaving the day after tomorrow, but before I go, I will arrange everything here so you don't have to worry.' Then with a glance at her watch, she got to her feet and said, 'Now father, I'm off to bed, for I've been up since just after five.'

With that she said good night to her father and kissed him on both cheeks. After she had left the room, Sir Torquhil stood gazing at the fire until he was roused from his reverie by the entry of Fergus.

'I thought I should just make a wee bit of an apology,' he said, 'I meant to keep off the politics but your daughter led me on, and yon Jenkinson – he just gets me. I canna stand him. Anyway, I've left him with Jane and I don't think she will have much difficulty getting the information we want.'

'I'm sure she won't,' replied Sir Torquhil, 'she seems a most competent person. Yes, I'm sorry about Daphne. She has a tendency to ask awkward questions, but she means no harm.'

'I'm not so sure about that,' said Fergus. 'She's not one of us, yet I get the feeling she knows more than she's letting on. Aye, I realise that she is your daughter and no, I'm no' saying she has learned anything from you. It's that Forsyth I'm worried about. How do we know she's not in touch with him?'

'We don't. But I don't think we need worry because she has just told me she's going away for a couple of weeks. Now I suggest that we meet in the library tomorrow morning after Jenkinson has gone – say ten-thirty. I'll let Simpson know.'

'Aye well, I hear what you say Sir Torquhil, but I would still like a further discussion about Forsyth. I would like Davie's views.' Then, as he turned to leave, Fergus added, 'a very good night to you, sir, and let us hope young Janie has one too.'

And before Sir Torquhil could think of a reply, he had left the room closing the door behind him.

After Daphne and her father had left the dining room, the other three remained there to drink their coffee and continue arguing about the relative merits of force and democratic agreement as the best means of changing a country's constitution. Jane tried hard to explain to the MP the attitude of those in the Nationalist camp, who had seen terrorism succeed in many countries when other methods had failed. Jenkinson, for his part, responded by pointing out that, whatever they might think to the contrary, the public view was that Scottish Nationalism was in its infancy, and there needed to be a lot of explaining done before people were convinced of its benefits.

'Independence, self rule – call it what you will – may well come one day, but it will only come when the population see a real advantage in it,' he said. And then he went on slowly, emphasising each word: 'It will not happen, and nothing you do will make it happen, if the majority perceive it as an attempt by a romantic-minded minority to gratify an urge for power.'

Fergus, whose desire for action far outweighed his powers of argument, decided that he was never going to convert the politician to his point of view and so rose to go.

'Maybe,' he said, 'but I think you underestimate our power. I'm away now to have a word with himself, and then I'm for my bed, so I'll wish you goodnight and sweet dreams.'

Once they were alone, Jane suggested to Paddy Jenkinson that perhaps they too should leave the dining room and move to the morning room, which their host had said was the most comfortable room in the castle.

This indeed proved to be the case, for it was furnished like a London drawing room. Jane nestled herself into the cushions of a sofa and patted the space beside her.

'Come and sit here, Paddy, if may I call you that,' she said. 'Then I can apologise for my brother's behaviour, and you can tell me about this parade in Inverness and the American bigwig who is going to be there.'

Paddy Jenkinson walked over to the sofa and, looking down at the smiling face of the woman, said: 'Of course you may call me Paddy and I hope I may call you Jane.'

To anyone meeting Jane Parsons for the first time, it would be obvious that she was a very attractive and desirable woman and Paddy Jenkinson was no exception to this view. And now, seeing her sitting there on the sofa, with no light other than the warm glow of the fire, he realised just how much he would like a more intimate relationship with her.

'There is no need to apologise for Fergus,' he said, 'you forget that I am a politician and like a good argument. Having often heard Torquhil on the subject of Home Rule, I was very interested in what the real fanatic thinks. Now let's hear what you think. Are you another rabid Home Ruler?'

'No I'm not! And particularly not at this time of the evening,' Jane replied, 'There are much better things to talk about than that; like telling me what's going to happen in Inverness next Saturday – no, on second thoughts that can wait – just tell me if you think I'm beautiful.'

Jane, who was now on her knees facing him, reached over, put both arms round his neck and pulled him down towards her. He rolled over on to his back and found her face only inches from his own. He put up a hand and brushed the hair back from her forehead.

'You don't need me to tell you that you are beautiful. You know it perfectly well. You're just fishing for compliments.'

'Mm, I know, but I do love compliments and here's one for you.'

She bent over and kissed him and he felt her tongue feeling for his. He ran his hands down her breasts and pushed her gently away saying,

'Not only are you beautiful and kiss divinely, but you are the fastest worker I have ever come across. And that's another compliment!' he added, raising the hem of her dress and running his hand up her leg.

'You're not that slow yourself,' she smiled down at him and kissed him again, while his hand found that exciting gap between stockings and knickers and stroked the smooth skin of her thigh.

After a few minutes she raised her head, reached down for his hand and lifted it to her lips. 'Not here darling,' she said, 'it's a little too public. And anyway beds are more comfortable than sofas. I'll go upstairs now and if you want to say goodnight, I'm in the room at the end of the passage beyond yours.'

Like most men who have achieved a certain position in the political world, Jenkinson had a high opinion of himself and particularly of his power over women. But on this occasion he had to confess he was puzzled by the way Jane had positively thrown herself at him. As they were guests in a friend's house, he would have expected a little more finesse, even allowing for the fact that he was only there for one night. Nevertheless his vanity, and indeed his increasing desire, would not allow him to back down. For all that, as he made his way to his room, his instinct warned him that she must want something, and that he must be careful.

He undressed slowly and put on a silk dressing gown, then crossing to the window, he looked out at the ghostly silhouette of the trees on the opposite hillside. And still he wondered what Jane's motive might be, and why the hurry to get him into bed.

'Very strange,' he said to himself, 'I could almost feel she was trying to get something from me – but what? Help for the Nationalists? But I don't know how I could help, and anyway she doesn't seem that interested in her brother's pet cause. I wonder, should I forget the whole thing? Tomorrow morning I can apologise and say I fell asleep.'

Now whatever risk may be involved, there are very few men who can resist a direct invitation from an attractive woman to visit her bedroom and Paddy Jenkinson was certainly not one of them. So after glancing at his watch, he closed the curtains and crossed to the door. Looking towards the main landing, he could see no sign of life and the only light showing was the big lantern above the stairs. With everything appearing quiet, he walked down the passage to Jane's room, tapped gently on the door and went in, closing it softly behind him.

Apart from a dim bedside light, the only illumination in the room came from a standard lamp on the dressing table where she sat. When he entered, she rose and switched off the light, and as he walked towards her she turned, shook the hair back from her face and allowed her white cotton bath robe to fall open.

''Come over here, I want to show you something,' she said, pointing to a very old tapestry screen, 'don't you think that is one of the most beautiful things you have seen?'

He bent down to look at it and had to agree that it was quite lovely, and he thought again what an extraordinary person she was. Then, as he straightened up, she reached forward and slipped his dressing gown gently down and over his arms, at the same time allowing her own robe to fall to the floor. She pressed her body close to his and whispered in his ear: 'Carry me over and put me on the bed, darling.'

She must have had considerable confidence in his strength, for it required quite an effort to take her in his arms and lay her gently in the middle of the great four-poster bed. She had already turned the bed clothes right back and, as he lowered her on to the soft linen sheets, he felt her arms pulling him down beside her.

It must have been a good half hour later, as he lay dozing in that blissful half world that follows successful love, that he became aware that she was saying something.

'Are you awake, darling?' she whispered, and when he gave a grunt of acknowledgement, she snuggled up close to his back and asked, 'who is this man who is coming to the parade in Inverness?'

Struggling against sleep, he muttered, 'I told you – The American Defense Secretary.'

'How is he getting there? Is he flying from America? I didn't think the airport at Inverness was big enough for that.'

'It isn't,' came the drowsy response, followed by a long sigh. 'I told you that too. He'll be with the ships at Invergordon, so helicopter to Inverness. Now please let me get some sleep.'

'Yes, my sweet. But first, just once more please,' she said, putting her arms round his shoulders and pulling him over.

When he next wakened he found it was three o'clock. The bedside light was out and Jane was sleeping soundly, so he slipped out of the bed, picked up his dressing gown and crept back to his own room and in a few minutes was again asleep.

It was not a quiet sleep though, for he dreamt that there was an old, old lady sitting on the edge of his bed and when he reached out to touch her, she held up her hand and it was icy cold. Then fear gripped him, for he realised it was no dream and that he was fully awake. There was no one on the bed, although he had the impression of a shadowy grey figure gliding towards the door.

Then he was asleep again and the next thing he knew it was daylight and there was a tap on the door. It was the butler saying: 'Good morning, sir.'

Chapter 12

When they had finished their tea, Duncan and the keeper sat back to talk and, as so often happens on such occasions, the talk turned to their wartime experiences. It seemed that in Italy, while Duncan was still an officer in an infantry battalion, they had been in neighbouring brigades.

For an hour and a half they fought again battles, some famous, some little known, and discussed the merits of their regiments, their leaders and also their enemy. Finally Dougie, after a look at the kitchen clock, got up and knocked out his pipe in the grate.

'Man it's been grand to have a crack wi' you, but I'm thinking it's time we were moving,' he said, 'we can go a wee bit in the Land Rover but then we'll have to walk. Aye, and you'll have quite a bit o' a climb down the burn. Have you the right boots now?'

'No, but just give me a couple of minutes and I'll be with you,' he replied. Then he turned to Mrs Fletcher and thanked her for her hospitality. 'You have been most kind, and I'm afraid we are going to disturb you again in the morning. But I'll try to keep it short.'

A few minutes later, having put on light, rubber-soled boots and a thick black jersey, he joined the keeper in the Land Rover and they set off across the road and out on to the hill in the direction of the quarry. They followed a track that led over the high ground behind the castle. It was quite difficult going as Dougie thought it best not to use his lights.

'People are used to seeing me out on the hill at night, but sometimes they just get a bit curious and we're not wanting you to be seen. Aye, and now here's where we leave the vehicle.' At this point he pulled into the side of a thick clump of birch and alder.

'Just stick close to me till we get to the big burn,' said the keeper, and set off round the edge of the clump, then across a shallow burn and into a dip between two ridges.

'This is a grand piece o' dead ground and will take us right to the edge o' the burn we want.' Sure enough, after about four hundred yards, they were on the edge of a deep cleft, at the bottom of which Duncan could hear the sound of fast-flowing water. There was no path, so they made their way down by a series of sheep tracks and tree roots until they were nearly at the level of the stream.

'We'll have to go careful here,' Dougie whispered, 'there's two steep waterfalls and then the goin' gets easier. When we get past the second, I'll leave you to go on. You'll have good cover in the burn for three hundred yards but then it opens out and ye'll have just the side o' the quarry on yer right. If you keep to the heap of rock to the left, you should find cover enough right to the huts.'

Passing the waterfalls required considerable care, for there were few footholds and the only handholds were the scrubby trees clinging to the sides of the gorge. However once past the second, the ground levelled off to make a reasonable path along the side of the water.

'I'll wait for you just up there,' said the keeper, indicating a point above the falls, 'and for God's sake watch for loose stanes.'

'I will, Dougie, and if I'm not back in two hours, you'd better alert the police. You'll find them waiting for me at Ord. Inspector Nicholson or Inspector Gray.'

Without Dougie to guide him, Duncan found negotiating the course of the burn in the dark not at all easy. The relatively flat part of the gorge was not too bad; it was when he reached the open area at the bottom that his problems really started.

For, as the channel of the burn neared the quarry, the gorge flattened and the right bank joined the quarry face in a tumbled mass of rocks, the result of earlier workings. The left bank continued on to the cliffs, thus forming the eastern wall of the quarry. The burn ran down to the loch at the base of this eastern wall, its course protected by heaps of fallen rock. To the west of the burn there were two stone buildings, several modern prefabricated huts, and, scattered about the floor of the quarry, the usual collection of rusting machinery.

None of this could Duncan see, so he had to rely on Dougie's description, which, as far as topography was concerned, was fine. But when it came to security, the keeper had admitted he had no information. However, knowing Simpson, he had suggested that Duncan should look out for both alarms and sentries.

When he reached the end of the gorge, with Dougie's warning in mind, Duncan decided his best plan was to continue along the base of the cliff towards the shore. There was a fitful moon, just enough to show him the nearest buildings, but still leaving his route along the cliff in shadow. There was also some cover to be had from the rocks and clumps of whins along the burn.

When he was level with the last of the buildings, he crossed the stream and lay down behind a convenient heap of sand, and it was as well he did so. For at that moment a man emerged from one of the huts, walked down to the shore and then across the floor of the quarry until he was lost from sight in the darkness. After about ten minutes Duncan heard the rattle of a dislodged stone and the man reappeared, coming down the burn towards the buildings. He walked round looking at all of them, and finally went back into the one from which he had emerged.

'A peripatetic sentry,' said Duncan to himself. 'Must watch out for his next patrol.' He was just about to move forward towards the huts when a glint of moonlight on metal made him pause. He eased back and felt around until his hand encountered a docken. He broke off a dead stem and holding it in front of his face, he inched forward to the right of his sandbank. The precaution was justified, for after he had gone about two yards he felt a light pressure on the wand. A gentle tap to left and right confirmed that there was a wire running across his front about six inches from the ground.

Having checked again that there was nobody in sight, he got to his feet and stepped carefully over the wire. Then, bending down, he searched the ground in front with the wand and finding nothing, took a step forward. After he had repeated the process a further five times he concluded that there could only be one alarm wire, so hoping there were no other invisible detectors, he crept forward to the first of the stone buildings.

There was a single window on his side and as he was well hidden, Duncan risked shining his torch in. The window was so dirty that it was hard to see anything, but it appeared that the building was some sort of store. He could see piles of metal boxes, one of which was open. Hanging out of it, to his astonishment, was a cotton bandolier. Seeing nothing further, he edged round the end of the building and looked down the other side. In the middle were double wooden doors and towards his end a large window.

Then, hoping that the blank wall of the hut opposite would protect him, he crawled to the window and, to his delight, found one of the lower panes broken. He decided to risk his torch again and this time, with no glass in the way, he saw much better. Against the opposite wall was a rack with some ten or twelve rifles and also a number of wooden packing cases, some open, which contained what looked like army battle dress.

As the moon then showed signs of emerging from the clouds, Duncan moved quickly across the quarry floor and took cover in the shadow of a massive stone-crushing machine. What he had seen so far was more than he dared hope, but he still wanted a look at one of the huts, which he could now see had lights showing, and also at the other stone building.

This latter, unlike all the others, was parallel to the face of the quarry and about ten yards from his hiding place. Waiting until the moon had disappeared again, he made his way round behind the building and found three windows in the back wall. Judging by the pipes below it, one was that of a washplace. In another, a dim light showed a barrack room with beds and cupboards. Then, judging it to be too risky to hang about any longer, Duncan returned to the shadow of the crusher, wondering how he could get a look into the hut with the lights.

This was some twenty yards from the bothy he had just left and at right angles to it. Between the crusher and the hut there was no cover at all. However, overlooking one of the lighted windows was another hut, slightly higher than the others, and with a short flight of steps up to the door. Parked between the two huts was a Land Rover. He made a dash for the vehicle and as he crouched by the radiator, the door of the hut opened and a man emerged and looked round.

'If he's coming to the Land Rover, I've had it,' Duncan thought. 'If he's going to the bothy, I'm OK. If he's the sentry on another patrol, I may have to deal with him, which will be a pity.' He remained quiet, but put his hand in his pocket and loosened the gun in its holster. The man looked at the Land Rover then at his watch, and walked quickly to the bothy.

Realising he had no time to lose, Duncan made a crouching run for the steps, which, despite the glow from the window, were in deep shadow. Keeping low, he crawled to the top step and, as he suspected, from there he could see into the room.

There were five men there. Four were seated at a table on which a map was spread, the fifth was standing up and pointing to some large photographs pinned to a board. It was too far and too dark for Duncan to see what they were of, and anyway his position was one of considerable danger. The man from the bothy might come out at any moment and make for the Land Rover. He therefore slipped down the steps and returned to the back of the first stone building.

There was one more thing he wanted to see and that was the pier. This was directly below the huts, where the floor of the quarry shelved steeply to the tideline. To the west of the huts a road, built over the sloping ground, gave access to the pier, to the east of which a small harbour, sheltered from the southwest, had been formed by building out an arm at right angles to the main pier.

For Duncan to go down to the pier was impossible, for there was no cover on the road or the pier. All he could do was to stay where he was and wait for another glimmer of moonlight, which was not long in coming. It showed him that the layout was exactly as Dougie had described it. Then just as he was about to leave, he heard an engine, and a moment later the Land Rover came down the road to the pier.

Short of the pier it turned left on to a rough-looking track and disappeared in the direction of the castle.

Reckoning he had seen as much as was possible and not wishing to chance his luck further, Duncan stepped carefully over the alarm wire, scrambled back up the burn and rejoined Dougie.

'I was just beginning to wonder if you were a' reet,' that worthy said. 'Did you see all ye wanted?'

'I'll tell you when we get back to the car,' replied Duncan, 'for the sooner we're out of here the better. One of the sentries was definitely becoming suspicious. Go on, you lead the way.'

Having spent the better part of two hours motionless in the cold night air, fit though he was, Duncan found the climb up the burn and the passage of the waterfalls hard going. However it was safely accomplished and when they were seated in the Land Rover, Dougie produced a flask of tea.

'This'll warm you. Just drink it while I turn round.'

'Thanks, Dougie, just what I needed,' and then as they headed back towards the cottage, he went on 'that was very useful. I think now that I'm beginning to understand what's going on. I was able to look into three of the buildings and saw some interesting things which I will tell you about tomorrow. I think for the moment, though, the most important thing is for me to get down to the police at Ord. I need them to do several things for me – and quickly. Oh yes, the other thing I found out is that the site is surrounded by a trip wire. There don't seem to be any other warning devices, but there are patrolling sentries.'

On reaching the cottage, Duncan went straight to his car and as he was getting in, he said to the keeper, 'Thanks for all the help. See you in the morning.' Then he paused and added, 'By the way, is there a road from the quarry to the castle? I saw a Land Rover head off along the shore in that direction.'

'Aye, there's a track that goes up from the shore and joins the one we were on. You'll not have seen it in the dark.'

Duncan waved acknowledgement, drove down to the main road and turned in the direction of Fort William. Even in the dark it was impossible to miss the farm, for it stood close to the shore of the loch, separated from it only by the road. The first thing to be seen was the large white house and just beyond it, the entrance to the steading. Duncan drove into the square and saw a light on in a building next to the tractor shed. He parked beside the police car and walked in.

He found both Nicholson and Gray there, seated at a table talking to their driver, a constable who was familiar with the Morvern area and who was pointing out something on a map. Duncan sat himself on the only other item of furniture in the room, a somewhat dilapidated camp bed

'I have found out a lot and I'm going to need a fair amount of assistance in the next few days. Now listen and I'll tell you what I've found out, what I think is going to happen and who will be involved.' He then gave them a full account of what Daphne had heard during the meeting in the castle and what he had discovered on his visit to the quarry.

'There is no doubt now in my mind,' he said, 'that this is the Unicorn base, and that they are planning an act of terrorism which I believe they intend to carry out in a way that will embarrass the Government. I am not yet sure exactly what they intend to do or how, but we should know more when we see what comes in on the yacht. What I do know is that the United States Secretary of Defense, Norman Jacobsen, is probably the target.'

'Aye, that seems likely,' Nicholson agreed. 'Jacobsen is to speak at the parade.' Then he laughed. 'The Government will no' be looking forward to that. Foreign statesmen who make the sort of Nationalist speeches that he does are no' popular! But it's hard for them to stop him. So, what do you want us to do?'

'We have got to avoid causing undue alarm and, at the same time, prevent any international incident. That will not be easy, but here's what I propose. I will watch the arrival of the yacht and the unloading of the cargo. After dark I will try and get a closer look at it. Security will be tight, so I may have to make a hurried exit. If I do, I will come here, so be ready for me any time after midnight. I may have Miss Drumcairn with me, as I think she is in some danger. Now, two other things. First, a shadow on Mr Jenkinson please, and for God's sake be careful – I don't want questions in the House! Secondly I want the castle, and especially the quarry, watched, again without raising suspicion.'

'That's easy,' said Gray nodding at the constable, 'Cameron here can do that. Use the van as if you were after poachers. You can fix it wi' Dougie Fletcher.'

'Fine. But I don't want Dougie too heavily involved from now on. Lastly, if I stay here for the rest of the night and write a report, can someone get it on the wire to my people first thing in the morning?'

'Aye, again that's easy. We keep the van here, so Cameron will have to come back in the morning. Whoever brings him can take your report back to Fort William.' Gray looked at Duncan and added with a smile: 'You'd be as well to call on the Colonel in the morning. His name's Matheson. He's a verra nice man, ye'll like him – and he'll likely gie you breakfast!'

Then with goodnights and handshakes all round, the police left and Duncan sat down to write his report.

Chapter 13

The next morning Daphne was up early, for she had promised Dougie she would look at the ponies, a job which would give her a good excuse for going to his cottage. None of the visitors were as yet up, although as she passed Crawford's door, she heard movement and the sound of water splashing in a basin.

In the field beyond the Mains steading she subjected each of the four Highland ponies to a thorough inspection. Then, having distributed the expected sugar lumps, she made her way up the steep bank behind the farm and through the plantation to the keeper's house, where she found Dougie loading posts, wire and other fencing equipment into the Land Rover.

'Good morning, Dougie! and it looks a much better one, so perhaps we'll have a fine day at last. I've had a look at the ponies. That saddle sore has healed well and I couldn't see any leg problems. Is the smith coming soon? If not, you should ring him; there are several feet needing attention.'

'Aye, her back's done well and I've sorted that deer saddle, so it shouldna' happen again. I'll check wi' the grieve if they're needing the smith, if not I'll ring him.'

'Good. Now tell me,' Daphne said, 'how did it go last night? Did Mr Forsyth find out what he wanted?'

'I believe so,' the keeper replied, 'he seemed well pleased. But he said he'd tell us more this morning.' Then looking down towards the main road, he said, 'that'll be him now.' Sure enough a car appeared over the rise and pulled up beside the Land Rover. Duncan got out and having been greeted warmly by Dougie at the back door, both he and Daphne were led through to the front room. Then after Mrs Fletcher had once again produced the regulation tea and scones, Duncan said:

'Now before I tell you what I found out last night, Daphne, did you find out anything at dinner?'

'Not a great deal,' she replied, 'except that there is another meeting this morning. I don't know when, but I imagine after the Jenkinson man has left. Probably about ten o'clock. The only other thing is that, judging by the way Jane was carrying on with Jenkinson, I would think she got all the information they want about the American's movements!'

'I bet she did!' he said with a grin; and then, seeing Daphne's expression, rather regretted his enthusiasm. 'Sorry, but I have a poor opinion of our Paddy's powers of resistance. Now, can you do one more thing for us? I hate to ask you, but can you go back to your hidey hole and listen to this morning's meeting?'

'Yes. But I'll have to be careful. I'm sure Simpson is suspicious and I did rather tease Fergus Crawford last night. And daughter of the house or not, I don't much fancy falling into their hands.'

'Yes, for God's sake take care. I'd never forgive myself if anything happened to you. Do what you can but don't take risks, and if you don't hear everything, it can't be helped.'

Duncan leaned back in his chair and gazed at a dark brown photograph of Balmoral Castle on the opposite wall, then went on. 'Let me tell you briefly what I saw in the quarry. One of the old buildings is a store. In it, amongst other things, there are rifles and ammunition and also, rather oddly, several suits of battle dress. The other building is a sort of superior bothy. I could see a barrack room with beds and also a wash room. As for the wooden huts, I only had time to look at one. It's an office and meeting room. There were five men in there; four were sitting at a table with a map on it and the fifth, who I took to be Simpson, was standing pointing at some photographs. I could not see what they were.'

'What about the other huts?' Daphne asked.

'There was no sign of life in them. There is probably a mess room and possibly more accommodation and storage. I also had a look at the pier. I hadn't realised that it had road access. That means they can unload and transport quite large items. They would need a big four-wheel drive truck, but there are plenty of them about. So what can we conclude from what we know so far?' Duncan paused and got to his feet.

'We know,' he went on, 'that they intend some sort of mischief to Norman Jacobsen, and it looks as though they may be planning something more drastic than kidnapping. If we can find out what is on the yacht, we may get a better idea of their intention, although I do have my suspicions and have reported them to London, and also asked for any information on David Simpson. And Dougie, I have arranged for the castle to be watched. A constable called Cameron will be in touch with you about this – I think you know him. Now let's get moving. You, Daphne, must get back to the castle. Dougie and I must watch *Firefly* arrive, and how, Dougie, do we do that?'

'Well, I was thinking I might do a bit of fencing, and I just might have a new assistant. That way we can hang about the hill and watch the boat come into the loch and tie up at the pier,' the keeper replied.

While all this had been going on, there had also been quite a lot of activity in certain parts of the castle. What Daphne had heard as she passed Fergus

Crawford's room was himself and Jane dealing with the tape and film of the previous night's activity.

The camera had been positioned so that Jane could operate it remotely and photograph anything happening in front of the tapestry screen. The tape recorder, which looked like a radio, was on the bedside table with a further microphone hidden on the screen. Now, before anyone else was moving, and hoping no one would come to her room, Jane had slipped along to her brother with both camera and recorder.

'OK,' Fergus said, 'leave it all with me. I'll develop the film and I'll copy the tape. It will take me about an hour. Why not go back to your room, dress and come back here, and then we'll make up a wee present for your boy friend.'

When Jane got back to her room, she sat down at the writing table by the window, took a sheet of the castle's headed paper from the holder and composed the following letter to Paddy Jenkinson:

Darling,

Last night was so wonderful that I thought you might like this little memento, which comes to you with my love.

So that I do not forget our happy time together, I too have a keepsake, which I shall always treasure. But however much I value it, should you ever disclose our secret lover's talk, I might be tempted to show it to people who could use it to your disadvantage.

With all my love,

Jane.

When she had read the letter through, she folded it neatly and put it in her handbag. She then had a leisurely bath, dressed and made her way again to her brother's room, noting as she passed that Jenkinson's door was open and the room empty.

When she entered his room, Fergus turned round and, with a broad grin, handed her an envelope. 'There are the prints,' he said, 'two copies as requested. They are as good as can be expected – though of course I've only seen them through closed eyes! And here are two copies of the tape. There are no other copies but I have listened to them, so I can back you up as to the content. Janie girl, you've done a great job. I just hope it was worth it!'

'That's as maybe,' replied Jane, who was looking at the prints. Then she held out her hand and said, 'I think perhaps I will have the negatives too. I would feel happier if they were safely in my possession! The prints look fine. Poor Paddy! I'm afraid he's in for a nasty shock. Anyway, thanks for your help, and now I'll just nip back to my room and put everything in an envelope for him. See you downstairs.'

Once in her room, Jane shut and locked the door, walked to the desk and selecting a suitable envelope, addressed it to Patrick Jenkinson Esq. MP. She then took from her bag the two tapes, together with the prints and the negatives. One tape and one set of prints, together with her letter, she put in the envelope, sealed it and put it in her bag. The other cassette, the set of prints and the negatives she put in a small jewel case, which she locked and placed in the bottom of her suitcase. Then, having made sure she had left nothing lying about, she went down to the dining room.

There she found her brother helping himself to a kipper. Having refused his offer to help her as well, she poured herself a cup of coffee and was about to join Fergus when, looking out of the window, she saw Sir Torquhil and Jenkinson walking along the path towards the front door.

'Aye,' said Fergus, looking up, 'they went out a few minutes ago. I gathered that the politician would be leaving in about a quarter of an hour, for the laird sent for his car to be brought round.'

Apparently as soon as the two of them had finished their breakfast, Jenkinson said that he ought to leave before ten, and so while they waited for the car, the MP suggested that they might take a short walk in the garden.

'I could do with some fresh air, for I won't get much in the Department Building in Inverness,' he said. And then, when they were out of earshot of the door, he stopped and turned to his friend. 'Torquhil, I am not at all convinced that you know what you are doing. What I said yesterday about joining you was quite true. I would like to be involved in seeking a means of reducing our dependence on England, although I'm not sure about attempts to destroy the United Kingdom. I do not like that Fergus Crawford, and I'm not certain that I trust his sister.'

'My dear Paddy, you are being like Daphne,' his host replied. 'What do you think I am going to do, start a revolution? Fergus's bark is loud but his teeth are really quite blunt. About the girl I know little, as I told you yesterday. Now don't you worry, I know what I am doing and I shall keep the whole thing on an even keel. Now, if you want to be in Inverness for lunch, you'd better be off.'

They turned back towards the castle and when they reached the front door, they found the butler putting Jenkinson's case in the boot of the car. Then just he was about to get into the driving seat, Jane came running out saying:

'I didn't realise you were off so soon. Goodbye, safe journey and I did enjoy meeting you.' Then, before he could reply, she gave him a quick peck on the cheek and thrust the envelope into his hands. 'That's the book I promised to lend you.'

All he could do as she ran back into the castle was to shout: 'Goodbye, and thank you so much.'

He threw the package on to the passenger seat and got into the car, saying to Sir Torquhil, 'I don't know what all that was about, but thank you again and will you say goodbye to Daphne for me?'

As he drove out through the main gates and on to the road to Fort William, his thoughts turned again to Jane's behaviour over the past twenty-four hours. 'All very peculiar,' he said to himself, 'definitely not someone to be trusted.' And he determined to investigate Mrs Parsons further when he reached Inverness.

As soon as Jenkinson was safely on his way, Sir Torquhil went to his study, rang Simpson and told him to come to the library in fifteen minutes. On his way back he looked into the dining room and gave the same message to Jane and Fergus. He then went in search of his daughter, whom he found in the kitchen making arrangements for the running of the castle during her forthcoming absence, and told her about the meeting in the library.

'That's fine,' she said, 'I will be out for the rest of the day, but I have arranged lunch for you and I have told them to get a room ready for the American. Have a good meeting and see you this evening.'

When her father left, Daphne finished giving her instructions and then made her way once again to the northeast tower. The first thing she heard when she got there was Simpson asking Jane if she had got the information.

'Yes,' Jane replied, 'next Saturday morning Norman Jacobsen will be taken by helicopter from Invergordon to Inverness so as to be there in time for the parade. I did not find out the route, but from what I remember of the area there is only one way they could go.'

'Aye, that's so,' said the manager. 'Anyway we can leave that to Roddy Urquhart. That's his home ground and his part of the operation.'

'One other thing,' interrupted Jane, 'I thought we should take out some insurance against Jenkinson realising what he'd done and talking out of turn. So I've given him a wee packet, a memento you might say, which I think will keep him quiet.'

'Yes, I think that was wise,' Simpson went on, 'but now I have something serious to report. We have reason to believe that last night someone visited the quarry. No, no one saw anything but there were footprints in the sand by the burn, and when Joe was in the hut getting his coat, before he came up to the castle, he thought he heard footsteps. However he saw nothing when he went to the Land Rover or when he drove down to the shore road.'

'Why are you so worried?' asked Sir Torquhil, 'there is nothing incriminating or even suspicious in the quarry at the moment, is there?'

'No. But there will be from this afternoon, and I think this may have been some sort of reconnaissance,' replied Simpson, 'so from the time the yacht arrives there will be increased security. And I think, Sir Torquhil, we should keep a close watch on your daughter. I'm sure the man Forsyth is around and I'd take a fair bet that she knows this, and also where he is.'

'Well, I hear what you say,' said the laird, 'and I'll certainly watch her. But I don't think you need worry. She's leaving tomorrow morning and will be away for the next two weeks.'

When she heard this, Daphne decided that it was time she removed herself from the castle in case her father came looking for her. So the last she heard of the meeting was Simpson saying, 'Well done Jane. That was a great job. Now, assuming all goes well with the *Firefly* this afternoon, I think we can go ahead with the plan to get him over the Black Isle.'

What she did not hear was her father demurring and saying that creating an international incident would not be in their interest.

'The Americans have made clear that they want to see their money put to a use that will bring quick results,' Fergus told him. 'They are like me. They want action, not words. Wait till you hear what the Groat man has to say.'

'I'm afraid, Sir Torquhil, that you will have to agree,' said Simpson. 'Those are the orders from Unicorn.'

'And what if I don't?' asked Sir Torquhil.

'You have something of a reputation, sir. You also have a great ambition to lead Scotland to her new destiny,' replied Simpson. 'We could destroy the first and make the second impossible for you to achieve.'

Chapter 14

As soon as Daphne left the cottage, Duncan and the keeper loaded the rest of the posts and wire into the Land Rover, drove down to the main road and turned in the direction of Glenlochan.

'We'll go out the far track, not the one we took last night,' said Dougie. It's quite new and was put in when they made the Meall Garbh plantation. There's holes in the deer fence needing mending. We'll do them and then we can go down to the old track and along to the spying rock. It's verra convenient, for we'll be in dead ground the whole way and the rock gives us a grand view of the quarry. I brought the telescope; you'll see more with it than with the binoculars.'

'Fine,' Duncan replied, 'and we'll need to be in position by twelve-thirty at the latest and it's now just after nine.'

'Aye, I was thinking just that,' said the keeper. 'There's about three hours work on the fence needing doing, so that will suit us fine.'

While they were talking, Dougie had turned off the road on to a very rough track which, in places, was only just passable for the Land Rover. Soon they were in the skirts of Meall Garbh and climbing steeply to cross a shoulder of the hill, then dropping down the other side and crossing a burn, swollen by the recent storms. Finally they topped another ridge and below them was a wide corrie, the lower end of which was almost blocked by a massive plantation of spruce.

'Damn silly place to put a plantation. Ruined the stalking. Aye, and just asking to be eaten by the deer!' was the stalker's comment.

It was some years since Duncan Forsyth had done any fencing, and then it was not the sort of professional performance required by Dougie. It was obvious that the fitness required of a secret agent was inadequate for fencing! So the next three hours were a severe bodily trial.

He carried posts and wire over broken, rock strewn ground; he went up and over the eight foot fence half a dozen times; he held posts while Dougie drove them in and he strained wire for him to staple. But he survived and when they had finished and he had sunk exhausted on to a grassy hummock, the stalker turned to him and said:

'Aye man, you'll make a fencer yet. It's a bit more practice and a bit less sitting in that office in London you'll be needing! Now we'll just collect the tools and then we'll be off to the spying rock.'

Not knowing whether to be pleased with the praise or annoyed by the implication that he lacked fitness, Duncan rose reluctantly from his hummock and helped to load the Land Rover. Then he climbed into the passenger seat and Dougie drove off down the track.

Beyond the plantation the track continued in a gentle slope until it joined the one they had been on the previous night. They turned west and drove along until the track petered out on the edge of a steep drop. On their left was a grassy ridge protecting them from the cliffs, and to the right and behind them, the western rim of the corrie sheltered them.

'I told you this was a fine place,' said Dougie, 'we canna be seen from anywhere, except by someone on the hill. I had a good spy and the hill is quite bare. Now our place is just up there,' and here he pointed up to the left, 'I'll just go up and see if there's anything in sight. If there's not, I think we'll eat our piece down here. It would be safer and there's plenty time.'

When he came down from his reconnaissance, Dougie announced that there was a yacht some way up the Sound and that if it was the *Firefly*, it would be a good forty minutes before it was near the quarry. With that he reached behind the seat of the Land Rover and brought out two packets of sandwiches and the inevitable flask of tea. While they ate, Duncan, pointing to the west, asked what the country was like out there.

'About fifteen miles of nothing,' Dougie said, 'it's just hill and more hill, and it's all gie steep and rough. As ye see, this track stops here. You can get down to the shore, but it's just a sheep path. Our march is about five miles on and there's no track or path of any sort goes to it. There is a bit track comes up from the other side, from Dunmore over on the next loch. There's a road round from Glenlochan to Dunmore, but it's in verra poor repair. The path to the shore goes to a wee inlet and there's an old boat house there. And now, if you've finished your piece, we'll just go up to the rock and see what's happening and I can point things out better.'

The spy point was a ledge with a big rock buttress behind, and slightly below and to one side was a boulder-covered mound. Dougie led the way up to this knoll and lay down between two boulders.

'You get a grand all round view from the ledge,' he said, 'but we're better here today. We can see the quarry well and we've good cover if anyone should decide to look up.'

Duncan turned his glasses to the broad waters of the Sound and there, about two miles out from the quarry and heading for the pier, was the yacht. There were three people in the cockpit, though he could not tell who they were, and lashed to the foredeck was a large object covered with a tarpaulin. Duncan turned to point it out to Dougie, but he had his telescope out and was looking in the direction of the pier.

'Now that's verra interesting,' he said. 'Look you at the pier and what do you see?'

'Look's like a truck with something sticking up at the rear.' Duncan replied.

'Aye, it's a truck right enough. It's one of those from the sawmill that they use for carting timber. It can lift and carry a heavy load and, with its four-wheel drive, it'll get up the track from the shore.'

'Presumably they are going to use it to unload this mysterious cargo,' Duncan answered, 'and to move it too, I would imagine. Tell me Dougie, is the lorry suitable for use on long road journeys? And who owns the sawmill?'

'It's part of the estate. It's always been there but the laird has modernised it and made it into a right business,' Dougie told him. 'Aye, that lorry is often used on the road to fetch and carry for the estate.'

'So it would not surprise people to see it around the Highlands, even as far away as Inverness perhaps?'

'No, no. It's often away up there, and over to Aberdeen as well,' Dougie said. Then, after another look at the *Firefly* through his telescope, he handed it to Duncan saying, 'I think you should have a look through this. You'll see the crew much better than with the glasses.'

Duncan took the telescope and focusing it on the three men in the cockpit, he was able to identify Roddy Urquhart. The other two were unknown to him. One looked like a local fisherman but the other, who was wearing a blue reefer jacket and a Breton cap, he guessed was foreign. Then, as the yacht approached the pier, he turned the telescope to the object on the deck, but it was completely covered by the tarpaulin and impossible to identify.

However when Roddy had brought her alongside and the two other members of the crew had secured her, they all went for'ard and removed the tarpaulin to reveal a large wooden crate. The lorry driver, who had brought his vehicle level with the *Firefly*, then went to the controls of the hoist and swung the jib out over the deck. Chains were attached to the crate and it was lifted on to the lorry and secured. The lorry was then driven round to the building Duncan thought of as the weapon store, where the double doors stood open. The crate was lifted on to a waiting fork lift and driven into the shed. A tall man, who had been supervising the operation, nodded to the driver to go and then followed the fork lift, closing the double doors behind him.

'You saw yon man who was watching,' said Dougie, 'well, that's Simpson. So now ye'll know him when ye see him again.'

'Yes, and he's the man I saw in the hut last night pointing out something on the photographs,' said Duncan, lowering his glasses and after a pause adding, 'I don't think we are going to see anything further here for the moment, but I must find out what is in that crate. I've got an idea, but I must be sure and that means another visit to the quarry tonight. It will be much more dangerous than last night, for I must get a good look and security is bound to be much tighter. I may have to make a run for it, so which way do I go? Any suggestions, Dougie?'

'Aye, I was thinking about that,' the keeper replied. 'Now you mind me telling you of the boathouse down there. Well we keep a boat there. It's the only way we can get the beasts back when we're stalking the far end. You can get from the quarry to the boathouse along the shore, but I'm no' thinking there's anyone there knows that. I was thinking maybe the polisman, Cameron, could help. He's a grand boatman.'

'Excellent, Dougie. And now let's get back to the cottage and make plans. I have a feeling we've been here long enough, and also I want to know if Miss Drumcairn has found out anything new.'

When they got back to the cottage, Daphne was already in the front room with Cameron, who had come to discuss with Dougie the best way of keeping watch on the castle without arousing suspicion. Dropping into a chair, Duncan looked across at Daphne and asked if the morning's meeting had produced any new information.

'Yes, two things, at least two main things with one or two minor items attached,' she replied. 'First, Jane Parsons obviously did have a successful night with her MP! Norman Jacobsen will be taken by helicopter from Invergordon to Inverness next Saturday in time for the parade. Then just before I left (and I'll tell you about that later) I heard Simpson say: 'We'll get him over the Black Isle.'

'That is just what I thought was going to happen. It's all falling into place quite neatly,' said Duncan and then, looking at Daphne, he asked: 'And what is your second main item?'

'That, I think, is of more immediate concern,' she said. 'Simpson said he thought they had had a stranger in the quarry last night. Apparently they found footprints in the sand and one of the men thought he heard someone or something suspicious. As a result, security is to be stepped up, particularly in view of what happens today. They apparently acquire some new and valuable property.'

'That is just what I was afraid of,' was Duncan's response. 'Whatever is in the crate that came off the yacht is something they do not intend that anyone should see. I, on the other hand, have every intention of having a look at it.'

'They also think that you are somewhere around,' she said to Duncan, 'although it didn't appear that they had any direct evidence of this. Unfortunately my father had told them that I knew you, so their reasoning seems to be "Daphne knows Duncan. Duncan is in Scotland, therefore he is near Daphne." I'm afraid that both Simpson and Crawford have nasty suspicious minds. Anyway, as a result of hearing this, I thought it wise to remove myself sharpish so I missed the rest of the meeting.'

'Very wise, I would say. And I think that the sooner you are away from the castle the better. But we'll come to that a little later.'

'One other thing,' Daphne added, 'Jane said she had taken out some insurance against Jenkinson confessing that he had given away secrets. " I have given him a wee packet. A memento you might say", were her exact words. My woman's instinct suggests some form of blackmail.'

'Looks a bit like it,' Duncan agreed with a smile, 'and it's just as well to know about it. It could come in useful. Now, what did Dougie and I discover today? The answer, I'm afraid, is not much. We watched the *Firefly* berth at the quarry pier, where a large wooden crate was unloaded. It was taken straight to one of the huts so there was no chance of seeing what was in it. That I have got to do this evening. Incidentally, everything you hear from now on should be treated as secret and confidential, and not to be discussed with anyone else. You, Cameron, may have to talk about it to your superior officer, but please see me first. By the way, I take it you were authorised to help in any way required?'

'Yes sir,' the constable replied, 'Mr Gray said I was to place myself under your orders.' Then he added with a grin, 'but I was just to keep in mind the limits of a policeman's authority. "Ye canna trust these Secret Service bodies, they can get up to awfu' mischief," was what he said.'

'I will do my best to keep you out of trouble,' said Duncan amid general laughter, and then went on to explain what he thought Unicorn were trying to do.

'As I see it,' he said, 'they intend to create an international incident involving the United States Secretary of Defense. To do this they have raised money in America and used it to buy some sort of weapon, probably from France – one of the men on the yacht looked distinctly French. This terrorist attack is likely to happen over the Black Isle. The uniforms I saw in the quarry suggest that they intend to make it look as though the Army, which means the Government, is responsible for the atrocity. The resultant international furore will, they hope, hasten Scotland's chance of independence.'

'They surely can't think people will believe that!' exclaimed Daphne, 'and surely Father would never let them do it.'

'My dear, as I told you yesterday, he may have no option. As to whether people will believe that the British Army is involved – no, they won't; even though it is known that Jacobsen is not the Government's favourite American. Furthermore, it will certainly not encourage Whitehall or Parliament to hasten the break-up of the United Kingdom. That does not alter the fact that whatever it is they are planning must not happen, and the preventive operation starts here.'

'Aye, you could be right, although I canna believe grown men could be so stupid,' said Dougie and then asked, 'What are you proposing for tonight?'

'Most terrorists and all fanatics have never grown up. Like children they believe that a big enough tantrum will get them what they want. When analysing their likely behaviour, never treat them as grown men.'

'Now for tonight's plan,' he said, turning to the table and spreading out a map. 'We will start as we did last night with Dougie taking me as far as he can in the Land Rover. I will then go down to the quarry by the same route, but I will go the whole way alone. You, Dougie, will remain with the vehicle. If all goes well, I will get a look at whatever it is that is in the hut and then come back up the burn and rejoin you. We will then come back to Altachonich, to some suitable place on the main road, where Daphne will be waiting with my car. We will then go on to Ord, where the police will be waiting, and Dougie will return home. But what if things do not go right?'

For the next hour they discussed what to do if Duncan ran into real trouble, and finally agreed on the following plan. As soon as the meeting finished, the keeper and Cameron would go out to the spying rock with an outboard motor and take it down to the boathouse. Cameron would stay there and Dougie would come back to the cottage. Daphne would go down to the castle, pack her bags and take them up to Duncan's car at the cottage, then return to the castle for dinner. After dinner she would take the car down to the ruined keep on the road just beyond the Mains, park it out of sight and wait.

Should anything go wrong while he was in the quarry, Duncan would make for the west end and try to get along the shore to the boathouse. Dougie meanwhile would create a diversion to draw any pursuit towards the hill and away from the shore.

'I'll do that alright,' he said, 'just leave it to me. No, they'll no' suspect me of any involvement in whatever's happening in the quarry.'

Then, assuming Duncan made the boathouse, Cameron would take him round to the keep by sea. Pursuit was unlikely, for Dougie said that there was only a rowing boat at the quarry, the outboard being away for repair.

'That I think is all we can do for now. What actually happens is in the lap of the gods,' was Duncan's summing up. 'There is just one thing though. Once they have discovered that Dougie's operation is a diversion, they are going to be on the telephone to the castle and they are also going to be round themselves in their Land Rover, so even if we get to the keep unharmed, we could face pursuit on the main road. I think we will just have to play that by ear. Finally, remember, Dougie, once you have dropped me, you must have no further involvement. Whatever you do for the diversion must appear to be something in your normal line of duty.'

When the others had all dispersed about their various tasks, Duncan drove over to Glenlochan and used the hotel's telephone for a long conversation with Inspector Nicholson in Fort William. He then retired to the lounge and, after a cup of tea, had an hour's sleep in an armchair.

There was no moon and heavy cloud cover when Duncan left the Land

Rover and made his way to the edge of the burn above the waterfalls. Dougie had offered to guide him part of the way, but he refused as he did not want to risk further involvement by the keeper. The fact that it was so dark would be to his advantage once he reached the quarry, but it made negotiating the falls extremely hazardous and increased the risk of causing a rock fall. Eventually, after a very uncomfortable forty minutes of scrambling and several unpleasant tumbles, he found himself at the entrance to the quarry. He lay there for some time listening for any signs of alarm, but it seemed that so far his presence was undiscovered. He therefore continued on, keeping close to the base of the cliff, where he had good cover from the piles of fallen rock.

When he was level with the building where he had seen them take the crate, he stopped again and listened, but heard nothing. He therefore crossed the burn and lying flat on the ground, felt for the alarm wire. There was a light visible in the window of the shed and he could hear voices and the chink of metal, so he felt it prudent to cross the wire without standing up. He accomplished this without setting off the alarm and crawled forward until he was in the shadow of the building, then edged towards the window and raised himself until he could just see in through the bottom left hand corner.

Some dozen or so men were standing in the middle of the building looking at what Duncan recognised as a French *Hirondelle* surface-to-air missile launcher. The Frenchman from the yacht was pointing out the features of the device to the men, who were then formed into groups to try out the controls, all this under the watchful eye of Davie Simpson. He seemed to be trying to select a missile launcher team, for after each group's session he would discuss their performance with the Frenchman.

After a while Duncan moved back into the shadows and thought about what he had seen. 'A SAM,' he said to himself, 'so it looks as if they are going to shoot him down. But why would American money be used to kill an American, and how on earth could this possibly put pressure on the British Government?'

When he went back to the window, Duncan found that the training session had finished and the men were trying on the battle dress he had seen on his previous visit. One item, however, which had not been there then, but he now saw stacked on a table by the window, was a pile of SAS berets.

Simpson and the Frenchman had moved to the other side of the room and were sitting at a table with a pile of papers in front of them, the contents of which they were discussing. Duncan noticed that they were quite close to the open window, and decided to risk going round and try to hear what they were saying.

To get round to the other side of the building was easy and, as the whole area was in darkness, which surprised Duncan, it was not difficult to crawl to the window. To look in was much more dangerous, for he would be silhouetted against the light and anyone coming out of one of the other huts, or any patrolling sentry, could hardly fail to see him. However he had to take the risk, so he raised himself cautiously to his knees and peered over the sill. He only stayed up for a few seconds for he saw at once that watching was out of the question. The two men were seated not more than four feet from the window and, as Simpson was facing it, he had only to raise his head to be staring straight at anybody looking in.

As he crouched back against the wall, he realised that although he would not be able to see, he could hear every word they said. They were speaking French, a language in which Duncan was fluent, and they were discussing whether the agreement to provide the missile launcher had been completed satisfactorily and how payment would be made. Simpson said that the equipment and documentation appeared complete and the training was going well. The American sponsor would arrive later that evening and could be given a demonstration in the morning. If that proved satisfactory and he, Simpson, considered the training complete, the yacht could leave after lunch with the Frenchman and the money on board.

This arrangement appeared to satisfy the Frenchman, who then went on to remind Simpson that care and accuracy were all important.

'Remember that you have only four missiles and no chance of getting any more,' he said, 'and please, too, be sure to return the equipment to a safe place after use. I do not want it traced back to the makers.'

'It will be brought back here and stored in the old First War ammunition dump at the back of the quarry. Nobody except my men know where the entrance is, so it will be quite safe,' Simpson replied, 'and now, one more thing I need to know . . .'

But Duncan was not to know what that one more thing was, for at that moment and just behind him came a stifled curse and the sound of a falling body. As he swung round two powerful floodlights were switched on and he saw, about two yards away, a man getting to his feet, one hand reaching under his jacket. The man raised his head, and Duncan took a step forward and caught him on the jaw with a crashing left hand. With his gun now in his right hand, he stepped over the unconscious man, reached the corner of the building and turned to see men running from two of the huts, but before they could get near him, he shot out both lights.

The ensuing darkness was absolute and Duncan could hear men cursing as they collided with each other. In the brief moment of light he had noted the position of the stone-crusher that had been so useful earlier in the day, so taking advantage of the confusion, he raced across to it and flung himself to the ground under a projecting piece of machinery. No sooner had he done so, than two shots rang out and he heard the sound of a ricochet from high up the eastern cliff. Then moments later, from the direction of the waterfalls, came the noise of falling rock and this was followed by Simpson's voice shouting:

'Over here everybody and after them! They're moving up the burn. Get the Land Rover, Joe, and drive up to the junction to see if there is anyone on the lower track.'

'Well done, Dougie,' said Duncan to himself. Then, deciding that he was unlikely to get a better opportunity, he made a run for the back wall of the quarry and scrambled along towards the shore at the western end. He was about halfway there when another light came on and a man emerged from the bothy. Caught in the open, he was seen at once and the man started running towards him. Duncan decided that there was nothing for it but to make for the shore as fast as possible and hope that, once he was round the corner of the cliff, he would find some way of baffling his pursuer. At the corner he was still some hundred yards ahead, and once round it he was again in darkness. Suddenly he was conscious of a noise from the cliff above and a rope snaked down, the end landing at his feet. Then he heard Cameron's voice saying:

'Quick, man, grab the rope and up here. I'll give you a pull.' Duncan did as he was told, and by a combination of climbing the rope, scrabbling for footholds and Cameron's considerable strength, he reached a ledge about twenty feet above the shore just as the pursuing footsteps came round the corner. There now appeared to be two or more men, for a voice said:

'Keep in cover Jamie, while I try the torch. Remember he has a gun.' A moment later a powerful beam swept over the beach and searched the face of the cliff but failed to show up the two men crouching at the back of the ledge.

'Can you see anything?'

'No! But he canna be far. We'd best get help, so run you back while I keep watch.' Then came the sound of retreating steps and the torch was switched off.

The two lay absolutely still and about two minutes later the beam again swept over the beach and cliff. Cameron bent over and whispered in Duncan's ear:

'Looks like he's going to have a look every few minutes. If we crawl along the ledge when it's dark, we can get to a grassy gully which will take us to the top of the cliff. It's not that high here; and then it's only five or six hundred yards to the boat. I don't think he can see us, so if we dinna dislodge any stones we should be right enough.'

'I agree,' Duncan whispered, 'we can't stay here. They'd be sure to find us when they return, so you lead on.'

It was not an easy journey in the dark, for every step had to be checked for loose stones or other debris and there was also the danger of slipping off the ledge or down the gully. There was the added problem of having to stop every time the torch was switched on. Eventually however, they reached the cliff top, where they were able to make better progress and Cameron could risk using his torch. Ten minutes later they were in the boat and Cameron was pushing off.

'I'm going to row a wee bit west to start with. When we round yon point which you can just see looming, I'll go out a bit and start the outboard. They'll hear us coming back round the point, but if you flash the torch at the water they'll likely think we're fishermen from Dunmore. OK?'

As he spoke, Cameron took the oars and started rowing towards the point. He was a powerful man and a skilled boatman and it was not more than twenty minutes before he shipped the oars, started the motor and headed round towards Altachonich.

Their course took them diagonally across the loch with the pier some three hundred yards away on the port side. The floodlights were on again, and although they could see no one in the quarry, they could see the flash of torches further up the course of the burn, suggesting that the search was still concentrated in that area. Nobody appeared to be interested in what was happening out on the water and the party that had followed Duncan along the shore seemed to have given up. But not quite. For Cameron suddenly pointed in the direction of the spying rock.

'Look there, sir,' he cried, 'can you see yon glimmer of light? There's a man with a torch moving up that same gully we used to get up the cliff. Aye, and there's a vehicle moving along the lower track. They must think there was more than one of you, and now they are aiming to prevent you joining your friends in the burn!'

'Yes, and that means Dougie's diversion must have worked better than we could have hoped,' Duncan said, 'for the Land Rover's going away from the castle and I don't see any sign of activity there or on the main road. Wait a minute though, what's happening now? Yes look, you can see the torch now up there by the car lights. It's the Land Rover and it's stopped. Now it's turning. And now it's heading back quite fast towards the road to the castle. How long before we get to the rendezvous?'

'Five minutes mebbe,' the policeman replied, 'look, you can just see the keep now. I'll take her in as close as I can, but I'm afraid you will get a bit wet. Then straight through those bushes there, over the road and you are at the keep. There's a place just along where I can hide the boat. I have my jacket and cap, so if there's any pursuit, I'll hold them up. We're badly troubled with nest robbers at the moment, ye ken. Now sir, there's your chance. And good luck to you.'

'Well done, Cameron, and thanks for your help. With that Duncan jumped for the shore and landed at the very edge of the tide. He turned and waved, then plunged through the bushes and out on to the road.

As soon as she saw him emerge from the bushes, Daphne, who had been sitting on a rock at the door of the old keep, jumped up and ran forward.

'Quick, over here,' she shouted, 'the car is round the back and I started her as soon as I heard the outboard.'

She grabbed his arms and almost dragging him round to the car, pushed him into the passenger seat while she herself got into the driving seat.

'I'll drive,' she said, 'you'll be cold and stiff, and anyway I know the road far better than you. We'll have to hurry, for I saw the lights of a car coming down the hill above the castle and heading for the main road.'

'Don't worry about that. Cameron is on the road back there and said he will delay them. We think it's Simpson in the Land Rover. But I'm much more bothered about a car from the castle. He might have some difficulty delaying your father.'

'That is no problem,' she replied, 'there is no one at the castle. There has been some hitch in Cyrus P.'s travel arrangements, so Father has had to go to Fort William to meet him and the Jane woman has gone with him. Her brother went off to the quarry before dinner, so he won't have known that the others have gone to the station. Of course if they rang the castle, Charles will have told them.'

'Sure, and that'll be why they came down off the hill in such a hurry,' Duncan said, 'but I don't think they know about the boat, so they will probably be expecting their intruders to have made for the road on foot and to have a car hidden back towards Glenlochan. They might even search that way, but we can't bank on it.'

'No. And I just hope we don't meet Father on his way back! He tends to treat the road as his private property and the Highway Code counts for nothing!'

As they roared round hairpin bends and shot over blind summits, Duncan was inclined to think that the daughter had the same opinion of the road as her father. However, he had to admit that although she drove fast, Daphne was undoubtedly a very good driver, and that, combined with her local knowledge, meant that they reached Ord without a sign of any pursuer and without meeting Sir Torquhil. When Daphne turned in through the gates, their lights showed Inspector Nicholson standing by a car in the middle of the yard. Daphne pulled up beside him and Duncan wound down his window.

'I think we're being followed,' he said, 'Simpson in the Land Rover. Cameron may have held him up for a bit, but he can't be far off now. Also Sir Torquhil is somewhere ahead on his way back from Fort William and I'd rather we did not meet him.'

'Right then. Tell me now, do they know this car?'

'No,' Duncan replied, 'I'm sure they have never seen it. It's my rental from Inverness.'

'Fine. Now jump out quick, both of you!' directed Nicholson, then turned and shouted to a constable standing by the office door. 'Over here, Kennedy, and take this car to Fort William. Treat it as an unmarked police car. Aye, and you'd better be on an illegal eggs patrol, right? You may be followed by a Land Rover. If they try to stop you, use your head, but firmness, honesty and politeness will be best. And watch out for the laird coming towards you, ye ken his style of driving! OK? Off with you and go straight to the police station.'

With a quick 'Aye sir', the constable got into the car and swung round and out on to the road. His lights had hardly vanished round the first corner when they heard the sound of a car coming from Altachonich and the Land Rover raced past the gates.

The Inspector then turned to Duncan. 'I think it best if you two come into Fort William in my car – the plain one,' he said. 'We'll leave the patrol car here and the driver can go and check that Cameron is OK.'

'And get Cameron to check on Dougie. I'll tell you what he was doing later. And come to that, what I've been doing. And I'll need to get on to London and probably Edinburgh, and I'll need to do it tonight.'

'Sure,' Nicholson replied, 'we can do it all at the station, for if Miss Drumcairn doesn't mind, I suggest you spend tonight as guests of the Inverness Constabulary.'

Chapter 15

It was after midnight when Sir Torquhil and Jane arrived back at Altachonich Castle, having collected Cyrus P. Groat. They were met by a very agitated Charles, who told them that the whole place was in uproar. There had been shooting at the quarry, Miss Daphne was missing, Mr Simpson was in a terrible temper and driving all over the place in a Land Rover, and now Mr Fletcher was outside demanding to see the laird.

'Just calm down, Charles. We'll deal with all this in a minute,' was Sir Torquhil's response to his butler's tale of woe, as he led the way to the library. Always at his best in a crisis, his immediate reaction was to get his new guest out of the way until he knew the facts of the situation. 'First things first. Which room is Mr Groat in?'

'The Prince's, sir.'

Sir Torquhil turned to Jane. 'Do you know where the Prince's Room is?' Jane nodded. 'Splendid! Will you therefore be so kind as to show Mr Groat the way?' Then to the American he said: 'Please excuse me, sir, while I try to find out what exactly has happened. Jane will show you your room and your luggage will come up shortly. Give me half an hour and then we'll have a drink and some sandwiches.'

'Sure, Torquhil,' the American replied, 'you just go right ahead with your business. I'm sure the young lady will look after me.'

When they had left the room, Sir Torquhil turned to the butler, who looked as if he was about to collapse.

'Pull yourself together, man. Here drink this and sit down,' he said, handing him a glass of brandy. 'Now, what's all this about shooting in the quarry?'

'Well, sir,' stammered Charles, 'about half past ten or eleven I heard several shots from the direction of the quarry. I did not think much about it. Mr Fletcher is often out at night and I'd heard them discussing foxes. But then, sir, about forty minutes later the telephone rang. It was Mr Simpson in an awful state, asking for you. When I said you had gone to Fort William, he swore and said something like "the bastards have got away and we'll never catch them now," and rang off.'

'Then what's that you say about Miss Daphne? She's missing?' The laird asked.

'Yes sir,' the butler replied, 'about half an hour ago Mr Simpson appeared in the Land Rover asking for her. I told him she had probably gone to bed, and didn't he realise what time it was. He told me to go and find out if she was in her room. Very rude he was, saying that if I didn't go, then he'd go himself. Well sir, Miss Daphne was not in her room and I could not find her anywhere. Her car's still here though.'

'Well she said she was going away tomorrow. Perhaps she made other arrangements,' Sir Torquhil grunted, and then in a kinder tone he added, 'all right Charles, that'll do for now. I'm sorry you've been kept up, but as we all have, perhaps you would bring a plate of sandwiches. And ask Dougie to come in. Oh, and could you take Mr Groat's luggage up to his room?'

'Of course, Sir Torquhil.'

As the butler left the room, Dougie came in still wearing his cap, a sure sign that he was upset, and started straight in with his complaint.

'What the hell's going on at the quarry? I was up below Meall Garbh after that vixen I told you about when I hear shooting down by the shore. A bittie later up comes that Simpson. "Have you seen them?" he says" "Seen who?" says I. "Them coming up the burn," says he, "and what the devil are you doing here?" "Man, what am I doing here?" I say to him, "That, Mr Simpson, is for me to ask you. But if you must know, I'm at the foxes; and no, I have not seen them, whoever they are. Aye, and now clear off my ground or you'll mebbe follow the vixen," says I, holding her up by the tail.'

'Well, Dougie, I know no more than you and I'm sorry you have had this problem. I have not yet seen Simpson but when I do, maybe I'll find out what it's all about. By the way, do you know where Miss Daphne's gone? She's not in the castle but her car's still here. Did she say anything to you this morning?'

'No, Sir Torquhil, she said nothing to me other than that she was away from tomorrow, and would I see that the dogs and ponies were looked after,' the keeper answered.

'All right Dougie, that will be all. Goodnight and I'll see you in the morning.'

When the keeper had left, Sir Torquhil poured himself a drink and sank back in a chair. He looked old and worn out and he felt it too. But he was not to be left in peace for long, for no sooner had he sat down than there was a knock on the door and Charles appeared with a tray of sandwiches and biscuits.

'Excuse me, Sir Torquhil, but Mr Simpson and Mr Crawford are outside and want to see you urgently. Shall I show them in?'

'Yes Charles, do that,' the laird answered, 'and would you ask Mr Groat and Mrs Parsons if they would join us?'

As the butler left the room, a grim looking Simpson entered, followed by Fergus Crawford. Simpson walked straight over to Sir Torquhil, who got to his feet and, before the manager could say anything, suggested that they go and sit at the table, himself taking the chair at the head.

'Now, Simpson,' he said, 'what exactly happened at the quarry last night? You can start telling me now; the others will be joining us in a few minutes.'

'Yes Sir Torquhil,' he replied in a more subdued tone than he had intended. The older man's prompt action in taking control of the situation had rather taken the wind out of his sails.

'You remember,' he continued, 'that earlier today I told you that last night someone visited the quarry, presumably with the intention of spying on our activities. We saw no one, but to be on the safe side, we increased security after the arrival of the yacht. Then this evening, while we were practising in the storehouse, one of the men on guard thought he saw movement near the hut. The floodlights were switched on and a man was seen by the open window. The guard sprang at him but slipped, and before he could recover or draw his gun, the suspect knocked him out with a single blow and then shot out both lights. I tell you this was no ordinary intruder. This was a highly trained man who knew just what he was doing.'

'And what happened then?' Sir Torquhil asked. But the answer was delayed by the return of Cyrus P. Groat and Jane and the consequent need to introduce Mr Groat. When these formalities had been completed, they all took their places at the table and were given a brief summary of what Simpson had just said.

'Say, do you have any idea who this guy is?' asked Groat.

'Yes, I'm sure he is a man called Forsyth – Duncan Forsyth. He's a well known senior MI6 agent,' Simpson answered. 'I know he was one of the people who went to the States to investigate the Sons.'

Here Simpson paused and looked hard at Sir Torquhil, then continued. 'We know that he is in Scotland and, what's more, Sir Torquhil's daughter knows him. Anyway, sir, to answer your question about what happened next. When the lights came on we all ran out of the hut, but when he shot them out I have to admit there was some confusion. I had just got this sorted and was organising a search, when we heard two shots up from the hill, one of which ricocheted over our heads, and shortly after there was the sound of someone making their way up the burn.'

'I thought I saw a body running from the hut towards the back of the quarry,' put in Fergus, taking up the story, 'so while the others went up the burn, I got a torch and one of the boys and myself made our way to the west end. By this time they'd got another light on, and I just had a wee glimpse of someone going round the corner towards the shore. We followed, but had to be careful as we knew he had a gun, and by the time we reached the corner there was no one to be seen. I then sent the lad back for help and myself stayed watching, but there was no sign of anyone.'

'What about the burn? Did you find anyone there?' asked Sir Torquhil.

'Yeah, and how many do you think they were?' was Groat's question.

'We don't know,' Simpson replied, 'for, in the end, we never found anyone. When Crawford's lad arrived with his message, I told two of the more experienced men, one with a gun, to go back to Fergus and tell him to search the shore and see whether it was possible for the intruder to have got back up the hill. I myself took the Land Rover and drove up to the lower track, where I could cut off anyone who came up the burn, or anyone coming up from the shore at the west end.'

'And what did you find?' Sir Torquhil asked.

'Well, the first person, in fact the only person I saw, was your keeper, Fletcher,' was the reply. 'I asked him if he'd seen anyone – and also what the hell he was doing there – mebbe not very clever of me, for he said it was for him to ask me that. Anyway he said he had seen nobody and that he was after foxes. He held up one he said he had just shot and asked: Had we not heard his shots, and what were we doing shooting down in the quarry?'

'Dougie has already told me about it. He's not too pleased. You know, I've told you before you'd be wise to keep on the right side of him.'

'I know, and I realised immediately that I had not been very tactful!' Simpson gave a wry laugh before continuing. 'I therefore muttered something about rabbits and, before he could reply, drove off down the track to look for Fergus.'

'Aye, and you found me just a wee bit mad,' Fergus said, 'I'd found a way up from the shore and had just reached the track when the Land Rover appeared. We'd had a long walk and a steep climb and seen nothing. God knows where he went. Well then Davie and I went back to the big burn and found one of the men, who had just run up from the quarry to tell us that when they rang the castle, they were told that the laird had gone to the town. Davie swore something awful!'

'I did that,' Simpson agreed. 'Anyway, I decided that the intruders must have got up the burn ahead of us, dodged the keeper and gone off towards the Glenlochan road, where they probably had a car. Fergus and I therefore went back to the castle, I was fairly sure that they would make for Fort William, so I took that road, driving as fast as I dared.'

'Did you find anyone? Did you make any enquiries?' Sir Torquhil asked.

'Aye. About five miles beyond that big farm we found a car parked in a lay-by. A brown looking Hillman – and who do you think was in it? – the police! Looking for nest robbers, they said, and no, no one had been along the road in the last hour. I didn't believe a word of it. That was no police vehicle, and besides they gave me the impression they were expecting us. What did we do then? Well, under the circumstances there did not seem to be much point in going further, so I turned round and came back here.'

'I agree with Davie,' said Fergus, 'that was no police car. They knew all about the goings on in the quarry and where the people we were after had gone. Swapped cars, I wouldn't be surprised. Though how we missed them,

I canna understand.'

'Well,' said the laird, 'they didn't run across the hill, not in the time you are talking about. Did anyone see a boat?'

'I don't know,' answered Simpson, 'but I'll find out.'

Sir Torquhil nodded and glanced at his watch. Seeing that it was already after two, he looked up and said, 'I don't think there is anything further we can do now, so I suggest we all go to bed and reassemble in the morning. Let's say nine o'clock, here.'

The next morning Sir Torquhil walked into the dining room sharp at eight, having already spent an hour trying to find out what had happened to his daughter. He checked again with Dougie Fletcher and also rang the grieve at the Mains, but neither could throw any light on where she might have gone. Her car was still in the garage and the butler confirmed that no one had come to pick her up on the previous afternoon. The housemaid then appeared and said that her bed had not been slept in, and added that a suitcase, some clothes and her dressing case were all missing.

Still puzzling over her strange behaviour, he was helping himself to bacon and eggs and coffee when Cyrus P. Groat arrived. Sir Torquhil greeted him and waved vaguely in the direction of the hotplate.

'Thank you, sir,' the American said, 'but I will just have a slice of this toast and half a cup of coffee – no, no cream thank you. Say now, tell me is there any sign of your daughter?'

'No, I'm afraid not,' answered his host, 'but I'm not particularly worried. She goes away a lot and was due to go this morning. I think she must have changed her mind and arranged for someone to pick her up yesterday. Though why she left no note, I don't know.'

'What do you know about this Secret Service guy?' was the next question, 'It seems your daughter knew him, or so Mr Simpson says. Could it have been him last night and could Miss Drumcairn have been involved? Looks like everyone has been a bit careless, I guess.'

'I really don't know,' Sir Torquhil replied, 'let's talk about it at the meeting. And now, if you will excuse me, I have things to attend to. I will see you in about half an hour.'

When they all assembled in the library, Simpson made it quite clear that this time he was going to run the meeting, for he started straight in attacking the laird.

'We now know for sure that it was Forsyth last night. The man who switched on the lights knows him and had a clear sight of him. He swears it was Forsyth. And what I want to know is what has happened to your daughter?'

'I don't know,' replied Sir Torquhil, 'all I can tell you is she has left the castle taking clothes with her. She was going today anyway and all I can suggest is that she left a day early.'

'She left a day early all right. I don't know about clothes, but it's almost certain she took Forsyth with her. One thing you were right about, sir, there was a boat went across the loch from west to east. No one did anything about it as they thought it was just fishermen.'

'Do you know where that boat went?' Groat asked.

'We made enquiries and it was not seen in the Sound,' answered Simpson, and then continued, 'I believe Forsyth had two accomplices. Somehow he dodged Fergus, was picked up by the boat and taken to somewhere on the Fort William road where a car was waiting, and I think that car was driven by your daughter.'

'Right,' said Sir Torquhil, 'then you tell me where they are now.'

'That I cannot,' was the reply, 'but I'm sure the police could tell us. That car I met on the road was all part of the show. But that's all I have to say on the subject, anyway for the moment, so let's get on with plans for next Saturday. At our last two meetings I promised that as soon as the yacht arrived at the quarry and we had its cargo safely ashore, I would tell you the full details of how we intend to bring Scotland's desire for independence from England to the forefront of the political agenda. We shall do it in such a way it will appear that the Government, by deception and violence, is determined to prevent it. But we will triumph! Just wait and see what happens after next Saturday. As a result of what we do then, such pressure, both national and international, will be brought to bear on the Government that a Bill to repeal of the Act of Union will be before Parliament in weeks rather than months or years.'

David Simpson's eyes were gleaming with the ardour of the true fanatic, although Sir Torquhil wondered whether his fanaticism owed more to a desire to get even with authority than to any feeling for the political future of Scotland.

'OK then, Mr Simpson, let's hear your plan,' said Groat.

Simpson then explained that, thanks to the efforts of Mr Cyrus Groat and the American Sons of the Clearances, sufficient money had been raised to purchase a French *Hirondelle* SAM and to recruit and train a team to operate it.

What was the use of such a weapon? Well, some time ago Unicorn had learned that a NATO fleet would be visiting Invergordon in the spring and, at the same time, a famous Highland regiment would be celebrating its bicentenary with a parade in Inverness. By a curious coincidence, at the time of the parade the American Secretary of Defense, Norman Jacobsen, would be visiting the fleet.

Furthermore, an historically minded Regimental Secretary had discovered that an ancestor of Mr Jacobsen had served in the regiment, and so plans were put in hand to invite him to address the parade. After much negotiation the Secretary of Defense, the United States Government and the United Kingdom Government all agreed to the proposal and the invitation was duly issued and accepted.

However the agreement of the UK government was given somewhat reluctantly, since Jacobsen was a known anti-colonialist and anglophobe, who had in the past spoken in favour of independence for Scotland and, protocol notwithstanding, could well choose the occasion of the parade to do so again.

'So you see,' Simpson continued, 'events have presented us with an ideal opportunity. How? Well, I will tell you. A member of the Government of our principal ally is to speak at an event which will be widely covered in Scotland. He is to go to this event by helicopter. And a lot of people know that the Government would much rather he did not make his speech. So what do we do? We shoot down the helicopter and we make it look as though the Government was responsible.'

'You cannot do it!' exclaimed Sir Torquhil.

'And why not?' asked Crawford.

'I'll tell you why not,' said the laird with some vehemence. 'First, I cannot agree to the assassination of a member of their Government. Secondly, no sane person would really believe that our Government would perpetrate such an act against an ally. Thirdly, I will prevent it. If you do not withdraw this childish plan, I shall get on to the Chief Constable straight away.'

'Say now, wait a minute, Torquhil,' said Cyrus P. Groat, 'You got some of this wrong. Whoever said Americans might not want Norm Jacobsen dead? There sure are plenty back home who would be glad to see the end of him. He's got enemies in the Cabinet and any number on Wall Street and in his home town of Milwaukee. His friendship with the President is all that keeps him in power. The money you got came from friends of Scotland, but the idea that Secretary Jacobsen might become a martyr for the cause sure helped.'

'You are wrong on your second point too,' Fergus put in, 'we have got something here that just might help to convince people of the English Government's part in the loss of the helicopter. Yon Parliamentary Secretary laddie, Jenkinson; well, Jane's tape that you heard about this morning is not his only bit of recent recording. We have a tape of a telephone conversation of his – we don't know who with – but he's saying that his boss would dearly love to prevent Jacobsen's speech in Inverness. We can edit that tape to make it sound as if he is speaking to a reporter.'

'Aye, that's right,' agreed Simpson. Then, laying some sheets of paper on the table, he added with an air of triumph, 'just look at this now. This is a draft of the speech itself, at least we are nearly sure it is. He must have been dictating as he flew in to Prestwick, and despite all their protective gadgetry, it somehow got transmitted. One of our members in Kilmarnock picked it up and recorded it. A lad on a motor bike has just delivered it to me.'

'You boys sure do have some luck,' remarked Groat, 'the US Air Force ain't usually that careless. Here let me see it. Yeah, that's his style all right. And I sure see why your Government wants him shut up!'

'So now you see what we do,' said Simpson with mounting excitement. 'The helicopter will have to cross the Black Isle on its way to Inverness. The SAM will be hidden in the woods there, with the crew in SAS uniform. Helicopter shot down, end of Jacobsen. International incident filmed by the Press – we'll have our own boys there – and then we release the tape and speech. Weapon quickly removed, then returned here and hidden.'

'What happens to the *Firefly* and Roddy? And what about Mary?' Jane asked.

'As soon as we've had a demo of the *Hirondelle*,' Simpson replied, 'Roddy will take the French agent back to his ship, which is somewhere off Mull, and then return to Fort William, leave the yacht on a mooring and you, Jane, will pick him up and bring him here. Mary has already gone back home.'

'That all sounds very fine and easy, but I'm not happy about it,' said Sir Torquhil, 'and I don't believe it is the right way to proceed. You are all being very naive about the likely behaviour of the Governments, and indeed the British people. And I want to know a lot more about the actual procedure for getting to the Black Isle and what happens once there.'

Before Simpson could say more, Cyrus Groat, who realised the importance of Sir Torquhil and the fact that they were in imminent danger of losing him, suggested that they all go down and watch the demonstration. That at least would allow the yacht to sail. Then the next day, when Roddy Urquhart was present, they could get down to the real plans.

'Well I guess if that's agreed,' he added, 'why don't we all go and watch this demonstration.' Then taking his host by the arm he said, 'I think that afterwards, you and I, Torquhil, might go somewhere and have a quiet talk.'

'Yes. Good idea,' replied the laird, 'but before we finish here I have one further question. Part of our plan has been blown. If, as you say, a member of MI6 has discovered we have a guided missile here, he's not going to keep that information to himself. Even now he is probably on to his HQ, and it's not going to be long before people start putting two and two together – they're not stupid you know. So, what are we going to do about it?'

Simpson looked at the worried faces round the table, for the significance of Sir Torquhil's question had obviously struck home, and he realised that an answer was expected from him now. He had hoped to put it off until the next day when he might have more information.

'I'm afraid there is little we can do now except continue with preparations,' he said. 'I have already taken steps to try to find out where Forsyth is, and also to see whether there are any signs of suspicion amongst the authorities. I assure you I will let you know anything we find out before a final decision is taken. So now, if you are ready, we'll go down to the quarry. The two Land Rovers are outside.'

Chapter 16

Having watched the Land Rover pass the gates of Ord in pursuit of Duncan's car, Nicholson thought it best if they waited to see what happened before leaving for Fort William. This proved to be a wise decision, for thirty minutes later the Land Rover was back again heading for Altachonich, followed very shortly after by another car, which Daphne recognised as her father's.

'That's fine,' said Nicholson, 'that's both of them making for the castle. It's not likely they'll be back this way, at least not for some time. So if you like to get in my car, we'll go now. If we see your car, we can find out if they told that laddie anything.'

The drive to Fort William proved uneventful, and they did not even see the Hillman until they arrived at the police station. As soon as they drew up at the door, Nicholson led them into the front office and the Sergeant on duty took them straight to the Superintendent's room, where they found not only the Superintendent himself, but also Inspector Gray.

'Now I'm sure Miss Drumcairn must be tired,' Superintendent Davidson said, at the same time pressing a button on his desk, 'and you're in luck, it'll not be a cell for you tonight, ma'am. We have a wee bedroom upstairs for emergencies and you are very welcome to it.' There was a knock on the door and a woman constable entered. Davidson looked at Daphne and added, 'I'm afraid our accommodation is not just up to the Station Hotel, but if you like to go with this young lady, we'll do our best to make you comfortable.'

Daphne said she was sure everything would be fine, particularly as all she had expected was a cell, or worse still, a night in the car. When Daphne had left with the woman constable, Davidson waved them to chairs and, picking up the telephone, ordered tea and then looked at Duncan.

'Now, Mr Forsyth,' he said, 'when I heard yesterday from these boys what you were preparing to do, I thought there might be problems, so I suggested to Gray that he report what was happening to his superiors and then, if they were agreeable, he should return here.'

'Aye, and I did just that,' Gray told them, 'I went down to Oban and reported to my Superintendent. He got on to the Chief Constable, who confirmed that the Argyllshire force was authorised to give Mr Forsyth all necessary help and I was to continue to see that that happened.'

'And very useful he's been too,' said Davidson, 'he's been on the radio to his people at Ord all night, so we know most of what's been going on.'

'In that case I'll not waste time now telling you more,' Duncan remarked, 'That can wait till the morning. But I would like to know that Cameron and Dougie Fletcher are OK, and that the castle is under observation. Then I'll tell you what I want to do.'

'Aye, I can tell you all that,' Gray answered, 'for I've talked to Cameron. He and Dougie have hidden the boat and the outboard is back with Dougie. Cameron is away off to get some rest, but another man is watching the castle. Cameron said there'd been a gie lot o' coming and going at the castle and that the keeper had been down to see the laird about the goings on at the quarry. The latest information we have is that all seems to be quiet and everyone has either gone to bed or back to the quarry.

'Very good,' Duncan said and then, turning to the senior officer, continued, 'Mr Davidson, here's what I need and I hope you'll be able to help me. I am going to need to make a long call to my HQ, possibly two, for I may have to speak to the Chief and he will have to be got out of bed. Now I believe you can provide a secure line here. Is that so?'

'Aye, we do have just that, Mr Forsyth,' Davidson replied, 'in fact it goes via Oban. There's a special undersea cable. May I ask how you knew about it?'

'Let's just say I was concerned with the reason it was installed,' Duncan said, 'for although we deal mainly with things outside the UK, we do have information on all such facilities in case, as now, we need to use them. So, if I have your permission, I will go ahead and make my calls and then get a bit of sleep in the armchair that I see in the corner over there. I don't think there is any need for the rest of you to hang about. Perhaps we can meet again in the morning.'

'Let's make it ten o'clock then,' suggested the Superintendent, 'and I understand from Nicholson here that Mr Maclay will be coming down from Inverness. Now, if you boys will just leave us, I will get Mr Forsyth's equipment set up.'

When the two Inspectors had left, Davidson selected a key from his key ring, walked over to a cupboard, unlocked it and took from it a dark blue telephone with a red label in the middle of the dial. With another key he unlocked a small door at the bottom of the cupboard disclosing a black metal panel with a socket, two switches and a dial. He plugged the telephone cord into the socket, clicked one of the switches and, with a glance at his watch, adjusted the dial setting.

'There you are. The number for the central exchange is 3KS, then follow your normal procedure; you can also be rung using that number. When you've finished, switch off and unplug, then just lock the wee door – here's the key – I'll lock the cupboard in the morning. And now,' Davidson added,

'I'll say good night. If you need anything, ask the Duty Sergeant.'

As soon as the Superintendent had left, Duncan got busy on the telephone. After a short talk with the officer on duty at his headquarters, he was put through to the Chief of Operations, who was not particularly pleased at being woken at home in the middle of the night and having to struggle downstairs to his secure phone.

After Duncan had described what had occurred over the past four days, and then explained what he thought Unicorn's plans might be, they agreed that the Chief must be informed.

'I'll ring him now,' the Chief of Operations decided. 'I'll tell him what you have just told me. I suspect he will want to talk direct to you and I don't need to warn you, he'll be in one hell of a bad temper! You say you have a meeting at ten tomorrow morning? I'll try and get a telex to you before or during that meeting. It had better go to Oban and they can send a DR up with it. Right? So good night, young man, and stand by for one very irate retired general!'

Looking round the room after his friend had rung off, Duncan noticed that both his suitcase and his briefcase had been brought in and, deciding that a police station was not a place for a too obvious display of firearms, he took off his holster and removed the automatic from it. This he cleaned and oiled, and then returned both pistol and holster to the hidden compartment in his suitcase. He then sat down to think what would be the best thing to do about Daphne, who he considered to be in grave danger. After a moment's reflection it occurred to him that his cousin Geoffrey, who lived miles up an obscure glen west of Beauly, could not be that far away.

He took a map from his briefcase and after a moment's study, he found what he wanted. 'Dalbeg, that's the place,' he said to himself, 'and just about two hours' drive from here. I'll ring Geoffrey in the morning; his number should be in the local directory.'

He was about to check this, when the blue telephone gave a low pitched ring and the red light on the dial glowed.

Duncan picked up the handset and said, 'DF speaking.'

'Yes, DF, and well may you be speaking! It is now nearly three o'clock and, as you are aware, there is nothing I like better than to be got up in the middle of the night. Indeed, for your own satisfaction, you may like to know that I was the guest of the Army Council last evening, that I have an incipient hangover and that I'm in a bloody awful mood!' roared the well known voice at the other end. 'However just this once I will let you off, for you have obviously been more successful than we could have hoped. Just give me the facts again and then tell me what you think should be done.'

Once more Duncan ran through the events of the past three days and described in great detail what he had seen in the quarry.

'You say that they were actually practising operating the *Hirondelle?*' the

Chief asked.

'Yes, sir,' Duncan replied, 'they were working under a French instructor, and after the practise finished, he gave a detailed warning to Simpson about not wasting missiles and observing the strictest security. I suspect the equipment is either stolen from the factory or obtained by other fraudulent means, and the gang concerned are afraid that it might be traced back to one of their members.'

There was a grunt of assent from the other end of the line and then the Chief asked about the involvement of Paddy Jenkinson.

'I believe his appearance at the castle was somewhat fortuitous,' was Duncan's opinion. 'He is a friend of Sir Torquhil's and the daughter, and when it was known that he was coming, Simpson arranged for the Parsons woman to get from him Jacobsen's travel plans for next Saturday. I think, sir, he should be challenged. It will ruin his career but may help his conscience, and he could provide further useful information. Incidentally, I gather from Miss Drumcairn that he is a potential recruit for the Nationalist cause.'

'So you think they are planning to assassinate Jacobsen,' said the Chief at the end of a further thirty minutes' discussion. 'Seems an odd way to popularise Scottish independence!'

'Well sir,' replied Duncan, 'I believe they have some plan to do it in such a way that the Government will appear to be involved. I don't know exactly how this will be done, but the uniforms I saw at the quarry suggest putting the blame on the SAS.'

'All right, DF. You say you have a meeting with the police later this morning? I will see that you have my orders in a telex in time for that meeting. Now you had better get some sleep, while I, thanks to you, spend the rest of the night disturbing the great and good. Good night, DF.' And before Duncan could reply, the great man rang off.

Superintendent Davidson's armchair was not an ideal bed, but such was Duncan's state of exhaustion that the next thing he knew was a tap on the door and the appearance of a constable with a mug of tea.

'It's half past seven, sir,' the young man said, 'and we thought mebbe you'd be better of a cup of tea. Aye, and if ye've no' discovered it already, you'll find washing and other facilities first on the right down the passage. Then, when you're ready, sir, Sergeant was saying that if you come to the desk, we'll take you to the canteen. It's no' verra great, but you'd mebbe like a bite o' breakfast. Maggie will have been calling the young leddy and will bring her down.'

Duncan thanked him and roused himself from the chair. While he drank the tea, he looked out at the grey and cheerless harbour and the distant cloud-covered hills. However a shave, a wash and a gargle served to clear his mind and remove the dregs of the previous twenty-four hours, so that by the time he presented himself at the desk, he felt almost cheerful.

The canteen was one of those somewhat grim eating places common to all public authority buildings. Pale blue walls, flimsy melamine topped tables and a servery backed by a steam-filled kitchen. Duncan was ushered to one of the tables, where he was joined a few minutes later by Daphne and the pretty woman Constable, who brought them cups of tea. Duncan, who suddenly realised that he had not had a proper meal for well over twelve hours, was only too pleased to go and collect a large plate of ham and eggs. Daphne, who had had dinner the night before, contented herself with home-made oatcakes from the local baker and honey which, she was assured, came from the Sergeant's own bees.

Then, just before half past nine, Duncan was told that the Deputy Chief Constable had arrived and was in the Superintendent's office. When Duncan joined him there, Maclay suggested that, as Davidson was otherwise engaged, Duncan should bring him up to date on what had been happening at Altachonich.

'An excellent idea,' said Duncan, 'it will save a lot of time later on, and I suggest that I get Miss Drumcairn herself to tell you what she heard at two Unicorn meetings where she was a fly on the wall.'

So Daphne was sent for and, by the time Davidson and the two Inspectors arrived, Maclay knew as much as everyone else about the happenings at the castle and the quarry. Then before the meeting went any further, Daphne said that as she was in Fort William, there were a couple of people she needed to see, including the Altachonich factor, so if they felt it was safe, the Sergeant had agreed that Maggie should escort her down the town.

Maclay and Davidson looked at Duncan, who, after a moment's thought, said, 'I'm sure that would be OK. You are well enough known in the town so I doubt they would try anything violent. All the same, Maggie should perhaps wear plain clothes. My guess is that they already know that we're here, so any problems are likely to arise after we leave. The open road's the danger, not the town.'

'Aye then, that's fine, Miss Drumcairn,' said Davidson, 'and tell Maggie to bring you back here when you've done with your messages.'

When Daphne had left the room, Maclay turned to Duncan and suggested that, as everyone present knew what had happened over the past two days, perhaps he would like to give his views on what Unicorn was planning and what should be done about it.

'I believe the Unicorn thinking goes something like this,' he said. 'The only way to obtain Scottish independence is by constitutional means. This will never happen unless we make it. How do we do that? By getting the international community to put irresistible pressure on the Government. How? By staging a terrorist act in such a way that it appears that the Government itself was the perpetrator. I think they had already decided to use the money raised in America to buy a missile type weapon, and the purchase was well advanced when they had an unexpected stroke of luck.'

He then went on to explain the visit of the US Secretary of Defense to the NATO fleet, his invitation to address the parade in Inverness and his unpopularity with Whitehall because of his anti-colonialist views.

'As soon as they knew of this plan, they realised he would probably go by helicopter to Inverness,' Duncan explained, 'and in due course this was confirmed by Paddy Jenkinson. Even before that, they had persuaded Sir Torquhil Drumcairn to let them use Altachonich as a base for missile storage and training. They had acquired battle dress and SAS berets, and yesterday their weapon arrived. What I think they intend is to take the *Hirondelle* to a suitable site on the Black Isle, shoot down the helicopter and somehow make it look as if it was done by the SAS.'

'But surely the Americans cannot be planning to allow their money to be used to murder – and murder is what they have in mind – a member of their own Government?' protested Maclay.

'Well,' said Duncan, 'when I explained this to my boss last night, he said it was not an impossible idea. There are, apparently, plenty of people in the States who would not be sorry to see the end of Mr Jacobsen. However the Chief made it quite clear that Mr Jacobsen must not come to any harm whilst he is in the UK, and asked whether I had any ideas. I suggested a possible plan and I'm now waiting for a telex from London which, I hope, will give us instructions.'

'Are there any plans we need to discuss which are not dependent on London's instructions?' Maclay asked.

'Yes indeed,' replied Duncan, 'I would very much appreciate your help in three areas. First we need to continue and, if necessary strengthen, the watch on the castle. I need to know of any comings and goings between the castle and the quarry and also if any truck or other large vehicle leaves the quarry and proceeds out of the area.'

'I'm sure Mr Gray can arrange that,' said Maclay, and the Inspector nodded.

'Next,' Duncan continued, 'I wonder if it would be possible to bug the Urquhart house in Inverness? I would very much like to know if any meetings take place there. I also believe that Jane Parsons is likely to go there in the near future, and I would like to know of any telephone calls she makes or receives. I don't want to bug the phone; that involves too many people.'

'What about it?' said Maclay looking at Nicholson.

'Shouldn't be too difficult,' replied the Inspector, 'but we may have to bend the rules a wee bittie. Where would you want the bug?'

'As near the telephone as you can manage,' was the reply and the Inspector agreed that it should be possible, but no one should ask too many questions about how it was to be done.

'Lastly there is the question of the yacht,' said Duncan. 'I believe it will be leaving this afternoon and will make contact again with whoever brought the missile, so that the Frenchman can return home and the payment be made. *Firefly* will need to be shadowed, and it must be done without them realising it. Once the handover has been made, I am sure the yacht will return to Fort William. Don't board it, but I would like to know what the crew do when they get there. As for the boat they meet, I think that as soon as it is out of sight of *Firefly*, it should be arrested by the Customs. It would be nice to recover the money! Once that is done, I suggest that the crew are sent on their way with a warning. I don't think we will hear any more of them. I expect that the Foreign Office will drop a hint in the appropriate quarter that such behaviour is not very neighbourly!'

Maclay looked across at the Superintendent, who said there should be no difficulty about that; it was the sort of joint operation that took place fairly frequently off the west coast. The only problem might be if the other boat left territorial waters before *Firefly* was out of sight.

Then just as Duncan was about to say what his own plans were, there was a knock on the door and a police motor cyclist came in and handed an envelope to the Superintendent, who signed for it and dismissed the constable with a nod. He gave the envelope to Duncan, who opened it and had a quick look at the contents.

'A lot of it is in code,' he said, 'and it will take me some time to decode, but the bit that is in clear says there will be a meeting at Fort George at ten-thirty tomorrow morning. I would think that Mr Maclay and Inspector Nicholson will need to be there, but we'll know more when I've read the whole message. I will need about an hour.'

'Right. In that case I suggest we break up and reconvene when you are ready,' said Maclay, 'I expect the Super can give you a room.' Davidson nodded and took Duncan to a small office down the passage from his own.

Once in there, and with the door shut, Duncan opened his briefcase and took a thin booklet from a hidden slot in the lining. He then spent the next hour and a half rearranging the groups of figures and letters in the telex and writing out the message which emerged. As this operation took him longer than expected, it was nearly one o'clock when they assembled again in Davidson's office.

'There is nothing in the telex that alters the plans we have just made,' said Duncan. 'That's the first thing. Next, it is confirmed that we meet the Army at the Fort tomorrow and Mr Maclay and Inspector Nicholson will definitely need to be there. There we will discuss my plan for preventing the assassination. That can therefore wait until tomorrow, when I will have it in greater detail. Finally it appears that Jenkinson MP has confessed all and a bit more. Again, I will tell you more about that tomorrow. Now, what are my own plans? Well, the main thing I want to do is to get Miss Drumcairn to a safe place.'

He then explained about Dalbeg and its owner, a retired general, and that he proposed to take her there later that day in his own car. He would stay the night and it would be an easy drive to the Fort the next morning. Maclay was not happy about this and wanted them to go in a police car, but Duncan eventually persuaded him that his own car was safe, and that it was very unlikely that they would have noted its details the previous night.

At that moment Daphne appeared and settled the argument by saying that it sounded an excellent idea, and that they could not possibly waste any more police time.

So, despite Maclay's doubts, and after Duncan had spent a couple of hours with his maps and notes and had telephoned his cousin, he and Daphne left for Dalbeg. In Spean Bridge they stopped at the hotel, and it was there that Alec, the young man with the girl in Glenlochan, recognised Daphne and mentioned the fact to his friend Colin Vass.

Chapter 17

When the two Land Rovers from the castle reached the quarry, Simpson led the party straight into the large stone building.

'I think if you stand over here,' he said, ushering them all to one end of the room, 'you will see and hear everything very well.'

The missile launcher was in the middle of the room with its crew of three men, and standing watching them was the Frenchman.

'Alain here, and the crew, will give a quick demonstration of how the *Hirondelle* is loaded and directed at the target. We shall be using a dummy rocket and of course, we do not have the radar set up. Alain will then tell you a little about the device and answer any questions. If his English fails, I will do my best to translate.' Then, turning to the Frenchman, he added: 'Alors, d'accord, Alain. Vas-y!'

At a sharp command from their instructor, the team loaded a missile and then went through the motions of directing the launcher at an imaginary plane. It was a slick and impressive demonstration and the audience could see that the launcher crew knew exactly what they were doing.

When the demonstration was over, Alain, in remarkably good English, explained how the weapon worked and what its capabilities were, then asked if there were any questions. The American wanted to know just how accurate it was and was told that, once locked on to a target, there was no escape. It was however essential that the missile was launched the moment the radar gave the signal, or the target could be out of range. Sir Torquhil asked about transport and set-up time, and was told by Simpson that he would tell them about that in a few minutes.

'If there are no other questions,' he continued, 'I suggest we go across to the office. There we can watch a short film of *Hirondelle* in action and I will tell you more about the plans for Saturday. Meanwhile Roddy is waiting to take Alain and the money out to the French ship. Are you all satisfied that we now hand over payment in full? That was the agreement.'

After a moment's silence, Sir Torquhil glanced at the American, who said he thought the deal had been completed to his satisfaction. He then looked round the others, all of whom nodded their agreement.

'We agree that payment should be made in accordance with our contract,' he said in French to Alain, 'and we are most grateful for your assistance to our cause. And now Mr Urquhart will take you out to your boat and, when you are on board, will hand over the money. Bon voyage, monsieur.' Then, turning to Simpson he said, 'let's go over to the office and hear your plans.'

The film of the missile in action proved to be the high point of the afternoon and was greeted with enthusiasm by all concerned.

'That sure is a great little toy,' said Cyrus P., 'it should do the trick nicely. I guess you people must be thinking your day is surely coming. Say now, Torquhil, don't you agree?'

'It may all be fine for you, Cyrus,' the laird replied, 'you just want this man out of the way. We want more than that. We want a free Scotland and I still do not believe this is the way to get it.' Then looking round at his audience, he continued in his most commanding voice. 'Now all of you, just come down to earth and listen to me. What you are proposing is to commit murder and that, in Scotland, is a capital offence. Furthermore the whole operation almost certainly constitutes treason, not only against the United Kingdom, but in your case, Cyrus, against the United States as well. So now, how do we all feel about swinging on the end of a rope in a whitewashed shed at Barlinnie?'

They all looked somewhat taken aback by Sir Torquhil's speech, as though this possible outcome of their scheme had not previously occurred to them. However before anyone could reply, they were interrupted by the shrill ringing of the telephone. It was answered by Simpson, who listened for a few minutes with an increasingly grave expression. Then, covering the mouthpiece with his hand, he turned to the others.

'It's a man Vass, a friend of Roddy Urquhart's,' he said, 'he's in Spean Bridge and a few minutes ago, while he was talking to someone in the street, a car drew up opposite and a woman got out and went into the hotel. The lad he was with, who knows Glenlochan, recognised the woman as Miss Drumcairn and when Vass had a closer look at the car, he realised it was the one we saw last night. I had warned various people to be on the lookout for it. I'll bet the driver is Forsyth. They must be stopped and brought back here at all costs, for we must find out what they know. Do you agree, Sir Torquhil?'

The laird's normal self control for once deserted him, and he got to his feet and went over to Simpson, who was still standing by the telephone. Simpson, who was not a small man, found himself looking up at a furious Sir Torquhil.

'Now listen to me, young man,' the latter said in his most formidable voice, at the same time resisting the temptation to lay hands on the man, 'there's no way your going chasing after this man Forsyth while he's with my daughter. For a start, he's a professional at this game and I don't believe you have anyone capable of competing with him. Secondly he's armed, and has shown himself prepared to shoot. I'm not going to have my daughter mixed up in a confrontation between Forsyth and a gang of amateurs. Do you understand me?'

Simpson, by nature a bully and not used to being spoken to like that, realised that he must have time to think, and for the moment he must humour Sir Torquhil.

'All right, all right! Keep your hair on, sir. We'll not harm the lassie. We're not that stupid,' Simpson said, and then went on, 'I think we'd better adjourn for the moment. I must have time to think what we can do. Why don't you all go back to the castle?'

'Well, whatever you arrange, for God's sake man, be careful,' insisted Sir Torquhil, who had recovered some of his composure. 'From all I have heard, Forsyth is not a fool, so the police probably know their movements and may even be following them. And do not commit us to anything until you've consulted me again. If anything happens to my daughter, it will be the worse for you.'

'Damn! damn! and damn again!' shouted Simpson when the others had left. 'Damn the old fool!' Then he thought for a moment and realised there was only one thing he could do, and that was continue with his original plan. 'Aye, sod it, there's nothing else for it,' he said to himself, 'we'll have to take them and keep them somewhere secure for the time being. I'll think of some story to tell the laird.' Then he picked up the telephone and spoke at length to Vass.

Having received his orders from Simpson, Colin Vass went in search of his friend Macneil, leaving the other man, Alec from the garage at Invergarry, to keep an eye on the car in the hotel forecourt.

A few minutes later Daphne came out of the hotel carrying a plastic shopping bag and got into the car. The driver smiled and said something to her which Alec could not hear. She nodded and laughed and then held up the bag and Alec heard her say, 'I don't know about you, Duncan, but I'm starving so I got them to make us some sandwiches.' Again Alec could not hear the reply. Then, after waiting for a lorry to pass, the car drove off in the direction of Fort Augustus.

When Vass returned, he was driving a Ford van with Macneil in the passenger seat. Alec reported that the car had left about five minutes earlier, heading north.

'Did you say the man you were looking for was called Duncan?' he asked Vass.

'Aye, Duncan Forsyth was the name they gave.'

'Well I heard the Drumcairn lassie say to the driver: "I got some sandwiches, Duncan," or something like that, but definitely Duncan was the name,' Alec said.

'That's grand, Alec,' was Vass's comment, then to Macneil he added, 'I tell you boy, we're on the right track. All we need to do now is to get ahead of them, then think of a way to stop them and get them into the van. Let's get going before they get too far ahead. Want a lift to Invergarry, Alec? Right then, hop in.'

When they dropped Alec at Invergarry, Macneil ran into the hotel and came out with a bottle of whisky, getting cursed by Vass for the delay.

'Man, if I'm going to tackle a laddie from the Secret Service, I'm going to need a drink,' was his excuse as he raised the bottle. He was about to offer it to his companion, when he thought better of it. 'Not while you're driving, mebbe. We're no' wanting you off to the jyle!'

It was as they passed a garage just outside Fort Augustus that they spotted the Hillman filling up. Vass drove on slowly, while telling Macneil what he proposed to do. Once he was sure Forsyth and the girl had left the garage and were continuing north out of the town, he increased his speed and drove until he reckoned he was half a mile and two or three bends ahead of them. Then, on a flat, straight bit of road, he stopped in a position that made it impossible for anyone to get past him. They both jumped from the van, and while Vass ran for the cover of some trees, Macneil opened the bonnet and peered at the engine.

They were barely in position before the Hillman came round the corner and pulled up at the side of the road. Duncan got out and walked over to Macneil.

'Can I give you a push?' he asked, 'then at least the road will be clear.'

'Aye, that would be best,' the man replied, 'I canna make out what's wrong. She just stopped on me.'

Together they pushed the van over to the side of the road. Then, as Duncan straightened up he heard a faint shout, something hit him hard on the back of the head and he remembered no more. As he fell, Macneil, who was a well known heavyweight athlete, caught him round the waist and with one heave, pitched him into the back of the van.

While Macneil was dealing with Duncan, Vass chased after Daphne as she tried to run back down the road, and grabbed her by the shoulder. With one hand he held her two wrists and before she could shout, he stuffed a rag into her mouth and held it there with his other hand. A few seconds later, with wrists tied and gag securely in place, she joined Duncan in the back of the Ford.

'Man, that was gie close,' said Vass as a lorry and two cars came over the crest of the hill ahead; but to the occupants there was nothing visible except two vehicles by the roadside, their drivers deep in conversation.

'We've to take them to the croft at Clach. You know it? No – well it's about five miles on,' said Vass, 'then we wait further orders. I'm thinking they'll be going back to the castle. You'd better come along for I'll not manage them alone. We can come back for the car later. Here, let's have a dram from that bottle.'

The van was one of the high-sided sort with a partition behind the driver and an open space between the passenger seat and the load compartment. Duncan was sprawled against the partition with Daphne lying between his feet and the rear doors. Suddenly she felt a gentle kick and realised that he had regained consciousness and was expecting some action from her, so without alerting the two in the front, she wriggled up until she was lying between him and the side of the van.

Whether it was the effect of the whisky or whether he thought that Duncan would be out for longer will never be known, but the fact is that Vass had done no more than tie their hands, and not even behind their backs. This was a mistake on his part, for Duncan, being an old hand and distrusting having all his eggs in one basket, had given Daphne his pocket knife and told her to hide it about her person.

Now she put her mouth against his ear and managed to loosen the gag enough to whisper something, then turned over on to her front, while Duncan managed to reach inside her bra and extract the knife. With some difficulty he got it open without either dropping it or disturbing the other two.

Freeing his hands was even more difficult, as there was the added danger of cutting his wrists as well as the cord. However once this was achieved, and he had found that they had not even bothered to remove his gun, it was the work of a moment to free Daphne and remove her gag. Then, signalling caution, he slid quietly to his right and looked into the front of the van.

It was obvious that the man in the passenger seat was three parts drunk. He was lying back and waving a bottle in time to the tuneless dirge he was trying to sing. Suddenly he sat up.

'Colin, I'm fair bursting,' he shouted above the noise of the engine, 'pull in man, for God's sake.'

Duncan could not hear the reply but he felt the van slow down and swing to the left. As soon as it stopped the passenger got out and staggered to the bushes. Once he was sure the man was suitably engaged, Duncan, who already had his automatic in his hand, slid round the seat and jammed the barrel into the driver's neck.

'Not a sound from you,' he whispered, 'leave the engine running and open the door . . . Quietly now!' He emphasised the point with a jab of the muzzle. Then, as Vass reached for the handle and the door swung open, with one smooth movement Duncan pitched him out on to the verge, slid into the driving seat and hoping the road was clear, swung the van round and headed back the way they had come. When they came in sight of the abandoned Hillman, they saw a police car parked beside it.

'I think we have a reception committee,' he said with a smile; then turning to the girl, he saw she was shivering and near to tears. 'Oh my God,' he cried, 'I am sorry. Are you all right?'

'I think so – yes,' she said, 'it's just suddenly come over me that we have had a rather narrow escape.' And then, trying to laugh, she added, 'What to do when thrown into the back of a van with an unconscious man is not something young ladies are normally taught! Now please go and see if my bag is still in the car. Then just leave me for a little and I'll be OK.'

Duncan, who had pulled up opposite the flashing blue lights of the patrol car, got out and said to Nicholson and the Superintendent that he'd be with them in a moment, but could he first retrieve Miss Drumcairn's handbag. Having got permission, he collected the bag and took it over to the girl. She opened it, smiled at him and then lay back in the passenger seat of the van with a handkerchief over her eyes.

Duncan, realising that she wanted to be left alone, walked across to where the two policemen were studying the Hillman. Davidson looked up and, without showing any surprise, asked what had happened. When Duncan told him they had been ambushed, he nodded his head with an air of satisfaction.

'Aye, I was telling you that Jock Maclay was right; you should have let me send you in a police car. The man Simpson will have noted this car last night and told his men to look out for it. You were recognised back at Spean Bridge. The hotel were telling me that there was a man from Glenlochan there who said something to his companions about a girl. They all got very excited and went off in a van.'

'I'm pretty sure one of them was the man we saw two days ago, sir, the one in the Land Rover who you went after,' added Nicholson.

'It was,' agreed Duncan, 'but unfortunately he was not visible when I stopped to help them.'

'I understand,' Davidson replied, 'now go on. Tell us the rest of what happened.'

Duncan continued his account until ten minutes later Daphne, who with the aid of comb and lipstick had recovered her composure, joined them and in answer to their questions, assured the policemen that she had come to no harm, but asked them to decide quickly what they were going to do as she was cold, tired and hungry. Duncan again apologised profusely and the Superintendent said he would send them on in the police car.

'Just one thing though,' he said, 'we'll need to get these lads. Any idea where they might have gone?'

'I heard them say something about a place called Clach,' Daphne volunteered, 'not far from here, I gathered.'

Davidson turned to the patrol car driver. 'Know it?' he asked.

'Aye sir, it's up the hill, about four or five miles on, I'd say. It's been empty a wee while now.'

At that moment another police car, it's lights flashing and siren blaring, came round the corner and stopped beside them and a Sergeant and two other men got out. The two constables were told to take the van and the Hillman back to Fort William.

Then Davidson turned to Daphne and asked, 'Are you ready to go now, Miss Drumcairn?' Duncan looked enquiringly at the girl and when they both nodded, the Superintendent said, 'Fine then. Nicholson and the driver of the first car will take you and Miss Drumcairn to Dalbeg now. Nick will then arrange for another car to be there at nine-thirty tomorrow morning to take you to the Fort.' Then to the Sergeant he said, 'Macpherson, you and I and your driver will see if we can find this man Vass and his friend. Now let's get moving. Good night, Miss Drumcairn, and I hope we have no more alarms!'

They reached Dalbeg safely, to be greeted by the General's housekeeper with the news that he had been called to a meeting in Inverness.

'He's decided to stay the night at the Highland Club. He's awfu' sorry not to see you and said I was to see you had all you needed. So I've prepared a wee bit dinner. It'll be ready in ten minutes. Now, if you'd just like to see your rooms.'

Duncan offered a meal to Nicholson and the driver, but the Inspector said he must get back to Inverness and report and also check how the other car had got on.

'There will be a car here at nine-thirty and I'll see you at Fort George at ten-thirty.' Then with a quick good night, he jumped into the car and they roared off down the drive.

'Mrs Mack will look after you, Daphne. I must use the telephone and then see you in the drawing room in ten minutes.'

Mrs Mack was as good as her word and twenty minutes after their arrival, they were sitting down to an admirable dinner of scotch broth followed by boiled mutton. Despite his absence, Cousin Geoffrey had also arranged a most generous selection of wines: a pleasant Fino with the soup and then a superb 53 Claret. There was also a little note saying 'I have not got up any port. I fear my 45 might be wasted on you young things so late at night!'

'Tell me about your cousin,' Daphne asked, looking round the dining room. 'He certainly lives in great comfort and I'd give a small fortune to have Mrs Mack look after me.'

'Lieutenant-General Sir Geoffrey Forsyth. Yes, a remarkable man,' Duncan mused. 'He is the eldest son of my father's eldest brother. He joined the Ross-shire Buffs before the Great War and while still a Lieutenant, at Ypres I think, with all the officers in the company dead or wounded, he extricated the remaining men from a very sticky position and led them forward to reach and hold their objective. He was awarded the VC. He also killed a great many of the enemy; history says with the butt of a rifle, although I'm not sure about that! He spent much of the inter-war period in the Balkans, and in 1941 went back there to organise Tito and the Yugoslav resistance. He then returned to normal soldiering, something he hadn't done for quite some time. Being the person he was, that did not prevent him getting a brigade, then a division and finishing the war commanding a corps in north west Europe! He married a rich girl who brought this estate as her dowry and he did pretty well himself out of his books on the two World Wars. Geoffrey has always landed on his feet, but invariably after hair-raising adventures!'

'He is a widower?' asked Daphne, 'And what about children?'

'Cousin Phemie – Lady Euphemia Cullen, she was – died two years ago. There are two sons and a daughter. The eldest son followed his father into the Ross-shire Buffs. I've rather lost track of the others. You'll no doubt find out all about them tomorrow. Now I think Mrs M has put the coffee in the drawing room and then I'm for bed. It's been a long day and tomorrow will be even longer.'

In the drawing room, Daphne sat herself on the sofa in front of the fire, handed Duncan a cup of coffee and indicated that he should sit beside her. Then she turned her direct, uncompromising gaze on him. So like her father, he thought.

'You realise, Duncan,' she said, 'that this is the first time we have been alone since you left me in Vienna, and that's nearly four years ago. Why did you do it? We'd had such a lovely week and then I woke up one morning and you'd gone.' She paused and wiped away a tear, then went on with a catch in her voice, 'I could never get in touch with you – always fobbed off with "he's busy", or "he's in Ulan Bator or Patagonia or some other impossible place". What had I done? That's all I wanted to know. Or was it just your old "I don't want a divorce and I can't ruin this girl's life" syndrome?'

'I suppose it was a bit of everything,' he said, looking at the floor and fiddling with his signet ring. 'Just as he always did,' thought Daphne. Then he looked up and smiled. 'Yes, I was very busy, darling, and I really was always being sent off to somewhere improbable, and usually dangerous. I suppose too, I thought "that sort of thing has mucked up one marriage," and I funked it; I guess I just could not face it happening again.'

He got up and walked over to the fireplace and started picking up and replacing the ornaments. Finally he turned and faced her.

'My dear, I know I should have trusted you. The trouble was I loved you and I thought I was hurting you. I could see it in your eyes when you looked at me – hope and disillusion mixed. Of course I got everything wrong, for it seems I just imagined it. Men do, you know. We're terrified of our pride being damaged.'

He gave a little laugh. 'I never stopped loving you, you know; and when I discovered your father was involved in this operation, I very nearly asked to be taken off. But I thought, "this time I'll go through with it, and if we meet . . ." Well we did meet and here we are.' He walked back to the sofa and took her hands. 'I know you'll say I'm an unromantic old fogey, but I simply must go to bed. Good night my darling.' And he bent over, pulled her up and kissed her gently on the lips.

When they parted at the top of the stairs, Daphne threw her arms round his neck and said: 'You haven't changed a bit. You're still the same silly old person you always were.' And with that she vanished into her room.

It must have been an hour later and Duncan was fast asleep, when Daphne crept into his room. It was a brilliant moonlit night and he had not drawn the curtains, so standing by his bed she could see his face clearly. So different to his daytime appearance; the tousled hair like a small boy's, the hard lines softened by sleep. All the old longing returned. He's really quite a gentle creature, she thought, and he has never lost his looks – probably never will.

She bent over and looked at the firm chin, then gently ran a finger down the fine straight nose and stroked the hair back from his forehead. He turned over, opened his eyes and smiled. With that smile they both knew that the long years of frustration were over. She smiled back, slipped off her dressing gown and pulled down the sheet.

'I'm coming with you,' she said, 'I know you're tired and there is a lot of hard and dangerous work ahead, but now you've come back to me, I can't let you go without having this night together. So please darling, love me. And please, and I promise I won't mention this again, please don't be too hard on my father.' Then putting her hand over his mouth, she whispered: 'No answer required. Just love me. Oh! and what about Mrs M?'

'She won't hear anything, she lives in a cottage by the stables.' He sighed and put his arms round her and felt once again her firm body and wonderfully smooth skin. He pulled her towards him and stroked her face and breasts.

'What a fool I've been. When I think how long I've loved you, darling, and done nothing about it. I know there have been others – and I know you know it. There always are for people like me. But you must believe me – you were the only one who counted – the others were ships in the night. Exercises perhaps!'

'Fool,' she said and rolled over on to her back, pulling his lips down on to hers and gently massaging the back of his neck.

Chapter 18

As soon as the payment for the *Hirondelle* had been agreed and the others had left to see the video, Roddy Urquhart took the Frenchman down to the *Firefly*, ushered him into the cabin and asked him to stay out of sight for the moment. He shut the cabin door behind him, whispered to the crewman to watch that Alain stayed put, then jumped across to the pier and walked over to a Land Rover which had just arrived with Jane Parsons at the wheel.

'There's hell's own panic down at the office,' she cried, 'they've just had a phone call from your friend Colin Vass, who has spotted Daphne Drumcairn and a man, thought to be Forsyth, in Spean Bridge. He's been told to follow them, grab them and take them to some cottage in the hills. Then they'll be brought back to the castle so we can find out what they know. I wouldn't like to be in their shoes. Simpson is in one helluva bad mood!'

'And I don't like it – not one little bit,' Roddy replied with a scowl, 'it'll not be as easy as that. Forsyth's a professional. Colin will have no chance against him. It'll be worse if he's got that drunken wretch Macneil with him. But it's not our worry for the moment. What's more to the point is, are there any special orders for us?'

'No, other than to get off as soon as the money is on board,' Jane told him, 'and then follow the agreed plan. So let's get going.'

'Aye we'll do just that.' Roddy turned to two men who were waiting in the back of the Land Rover with a large wooden box between them. 'OK, boys, let's have it on board,' and to the man in the cockpit he added, 'start her up.'

The box was carried up the gang plank and dumped on deck. The two men returned to the Land Rover and drove off. The crewman pulled up the gangway and Jane, having cast off fore and aft, took a flying leap into the cockpit as, with Roddy at the helm, they nosed out into the loch. Twenty minutes later, as they headed southeast down the Sound, he looked up at the burgee and then across to Mull.

'The wind's gone right round. It's west with even a touch of north,' he said, 'and since we're aiming to meet up somewhere off Loch Buie, we'll be better off sailing. We can run down to the tip of Lismore and then we'll be on a reach until it's dark, when we'll have to motor again. Here Jane, you take the helm while we get the sails up.'

Then followed ten minutes of furious activity, and once Roddy was satisfied that all was well and they were on a steady course with a true wind, he turned to Jane.

'Your French is better than mine. Hand over to Willie and come down with me while we sort out the money with Alain.'

'I'm sorry we've kept you so long,' he said to the Frenchman as he negotiated the companion way to the cabin, 'but we're on our way now. We should meet up with your friends in about five hours. It's fine at the moment, but it may be a wee thing choppy when we turn the corner beyond Craignure.' Then, producing a bunch of keys, he unlocked the wooden box and pointing to the contents said to Jane, 'tell him that there should be a quarter of a million dollars in hundred dollar bills there. He'd better check it, for there'll be no comeback later if it's wrong.'

For the next half hour, under the watchful eyes of Jane and Roddy, the Frenchman laboriously checked each bundle of twenty-five bills, until eventually there were one hundred bundles on the table.

'Oui, c'est bon,' he said, 'and, as I think you say, all present and correct. Merci – and now let us drink a toast.' And he reached into his bag and took out a bottle of brandy. Glasses were produced and a generous measure poured into each, including one which was handed up to Willie in the cockpit. 'A l'Ecosse,' Alain said raising his glass, and then added, 'it is better than whisky, non?'

'A l'Ecosse – to a free and independent Scotland and long live the Auld Alliance,' the others responded. Jane then made a short speech congratulating Alain on what he had achieved for them and asking him to take their thanks to his people in France. She concluded by saying how nice it was to drink a toast in brandy.

'For all my Scots blood, I can easily tire of whisky. So my special thanks to you, Alain,' she said with a smile, and then bending down, kissed him on both cheeks.

'Aye, it's a grand drink, the cognac, but myself, I prefer whisky,' said Roddy. 'And now if you two have quite finished, I think we should have something to eat. Can you manage to find something, Janie?'

'I expect so, but I'm afraid it will only be tinned soup and cheese. Not exactly a gourmet meal, Alain, I'm afraid.' However the Frenchman expressed himself delighted with whatever the enchanting Madamoiselle Jane might produce.

When she had finished cooking, Jane took a mug of soup and said she would relieve Willie at the helm as she needed fresh air after the heat of the galley. Some twenty minutes later Roddy came up and joined her and took over the helm.

'We'll need to come up into the wind a bit and round the point soon,' he said, 'but before we do, tell me, do you think it was Forsyth in the quarry? And do you think it's him they've spotted with Miss Drumcairn?'

'I'm sure it is – in both cases,' Jane replied. 'Senior operatives of the Secret Service, particularly those who know of Unicorn, aren't in Scotland for the fishing at present. His bosses knew we were planning something, and he was sent to find out what. I wish I'd bloody well known who he was before I joined him for dinner. I just thought he looked rather nice and it would be fun to try to seduce him. It was too! Then, of course, I have to be too clever. I was worried about the money and thought it a splendid idea to get the police interested in someone else. I'm almost sure now that he beat me to it, and far from me organising his arrest, he organised his own. Though God knows how. Then somehow he got on to Altachonich, and we had the further bad luck that he knew the Drumcairn bitch.'

'Aye, a chapter of accidents, that's for sure. But how much do you think he knows?'

'Hard to say. If he saw the missile he could guess a lot. If he didn't he may still be in the dark,' Jane said. 'Of course if the girl has told him about Jenkinson, and Jenkinson is made of sterner stuff than I think, they may get hold of him and he may talk. We'll just have to hope that our plan is so improbable that, whatever they learn, no-one will guess the details.'

'I hope you are right. Willie, come up now,' he shouted down to the cabin, then as Willie appeared, 'Jane, you steer while we take in the sheets. Right, now bring her round to starboard. You see that buoy? Steer just to port of it. That's fine. We'll hold this course for the moment, while I work out what we need to do to find the Frenchie. Let's hope they are where they said they'd be.'

An hour later, as the light began to fade, Roddy took over the helm, started the engine and switched on the navigation lights.

'OK, let's have the sails down,' he shouted, 'and you two, keep a sharp look out all round. I don't want our meeting seen. So if there is any other vessel in sight, I'll just go on past until the coast is clear.'

Half an hour later Jane suddenly shouted 'Lights approaching fast on the port bow.' A few minutes later a fair sized launch went past them at speed, its wash setting them rocking violently. Suddenly, when it was about two hundred yards beyond them, it slowed and a searchlight was switched on and the beam swung round on to them. 'Name and port,' a voice shouted through a loud hailer. '*Firefly*, Inverness. Heading for Loch Buie,' Roddy replied. 'OK, goodnight,' the voice came back, the searchlight was switched off and the launch disappeared into the darkness.

'Customs launch. They are often about here,' Roddy said, 'but he seemed quite satisfied. It was a nasty moment though. If he'd asked to board, I'd have had to let him, and we'd have been in the shit. "Yes officer – a quarter of a million dollars it is – what for? Aye, well this French gentleman wondered if Duart Castle was for sale!" Ugh! I could surely have done without that! Anyhows, he's gone off in the right direction. And now, where are our friends, I wonder? They should show to starboard in about three miles.'

Once again it was Jane who first saw what looked like the lights of two vessels dead ahead of them. She shouted to Roddy to slow down and send Willie forward with the glasses. Now a good pair of 7x50 binoculars will show up a surprising amount of detail, even if there is only a faint glimmer of light, and that is just what Jane found when Willie passed her the glasses.

'Yes, I can see two ships,' she shouted to Roddy, 'one looks like a trawler and it's hove to and facing us. The other is much bigger. I can't tell what it is but it's a long way off and I guess heading south at a fairly good speed. Here, Willie, you have a look.'

'Aye, Roddy, the near one is the French trawler right enough. I can just about make out that queer tackle she has at the stern. But I don't know about the other, she's a long way off and she looks gie big. Hold on a moment though, there's the moon. Aye, that's better; now I can just see what looks like a warship number on her side; it'll be the Fishery Protection, that'll be what's in it.'

'I wonder what she's doing here? I don't like it, but we'll have to take the risk,' Roddy decided. 'I can't see anything else, so here Jane take the torch and give the signal – three long, one short and another two long.'

Jane repeated the signal twice, and after the second attempt they saw three short flashes and a long from the trawler.

'That's her. Come on Alain, we'll be with your friends in five minutes,' Roddy shouted down to the cabin, then turning to the others said, 'Willie get that crate up and be ready to heave it on to the trawler. And Jane, be ready with the hook to hold us alongside. Quick, all of you, for I don't want to hang about.'

The trawler had lowered a short folding ladder and, as Roddy brought them up under the steps, a light was switched on. Then, with Jane and one of the French crew holding the two vessels together, Alain stepped across and was pulled up on to the trawler's deck. As soon as he was safe, the derrick arm swung round and a rope dropped to the yacht's deck. Willie secured the crate and it was hoisted on board.

'Warn them about the fishery,' Roddy said to Jane, 'tell them to keep well clear of it, and no radio contact with us please. And wish them goodbye, good luck and bon voyage.'

As soon as the exchange of messages between Jane and the French skipper, who had come to the rail, was complete, Roddy swung the *Firefly* round and with both crews waving, headed north towards Loch Linnhe.

Their journey back to Fort William was uneventful, although just as it was getting light, they saw the Customs launch alongside a luxury motor yacht, the crew of which looked distinctly unhappy.

For the Frenchman, however, things were far from uneventful. Unknown to those on *Firefly*, about an hour after they left, a party from the Fishery Protection vessel, including a Customs officer, had boarded the trawler on suspicion of currency smuggling, and it was now on its way to Oban for investigation.

Ignorant of this event, the crew of *Firefly* continued up the loch and when they reached Fort William, Roddy gave the helm to Willie, who brought the yacht alongside the quay.

'You and Jane go ashore here, for the sooner you are back at Altachonich the better,' he said to Roddy. 'Don't worry about *Firefly*. I'll put her on one of our moorings and she can stay there as long as you like. You can take my car. Mother will give you the keys. Just try and get it back in the next couple of days.'

'Thanks, Willie, that's very helpful and I'm sure Jane can return the car tomorrow. So goodbye for just now and see you sometime.' Having shaken Willie's hand, Roddy picked up the two small kitbags and he and Jane walked quickly up the hill to Willie's father's house. There his mother handed over the keys, as though giving them to comparative strangers was something she did every day.

Then with her 'Mind now that you drive safely,' ringing in their ears, they drove out of the town and on to the road to Altachonich. When they reached the castle, they found a very agitated Charles standing by the front door.

'Thank heavens you're back,' was his greeting, 'Sir Torquhil and the others are in the library and they are in a terrible state. Sir Torquhil said you were to go straight up the moment you arrived. Don't worry, I'll take the bags up.'

In the library they found the laird and the American, Cyrus P. Groat, together with Simpson and Crawford, all sitting round the table in gloomy contemplation of a very different situation from that of the previous afternoon. Sir Torquhil waved towards two vacant chairs.

'Bad news,' he said, then turned to Simpson, 'you tell them what has happened and then let's find out how they got on.'

'Hold on a moment,' Roddy interrupted, 'I can tell you straight away that we had no trouble at all. We met the trawler right on time and Alain and the money are now safely on their way to France. We were hailed by a Customs launch but they seemed to have little interest in us. Then we saw the Naval Fishery Boat but they were away in the far distance.'

'Aye, well I just hope you are right,' said Simpson, 'after what's happened here, I don't like the idea of those Government boats being around your rendezvous and you'll soon see why. You left yesterday just as we heard that Miss Drumcairn and a man had been spotted in Spean Bridge. In fact I think Jane gave you the news. It was your friend Vass, or rather a man he was talking to, who recognised Daphne. I wanted to send Vass and Macneil after them, catch them and hold them somewhere safe.' Then with a scowl he added, 'Sir Torquhil would have none of it, saying no one was to attempt any sort of violence with his daughter there. Anyway I agreed and told Vass to try and follow them and see where they went.'

'Who was the man with Miss Drumcairn?' Roddy asked.

'We don't know for sure,' Simpson replied, 'but we assume it was Forsyth.'

'What was he like? Did they get a good sight of him?' Jane asked.

'No, but Vass said the lad who recognised the girl described him,' Simpson said and gave them Vass's description.

'Yes, that's him all right,' said Jane and then Roddy looked across at Simpson and said with mounting anger:

'You damn fool, even without Jane's confirmation you were pretty sure it was Forsyth – Duncan Forsyth, the most experienced spy in MI6 – and you sent Colin Vass after him! Colin's a great lad, but he's no match for a professional. And you must have been mad to allow him to take that drunken bastard Macneil! So what happened?'

Simpson was not used to being spoken to like that and, somewhat taken aback by the tirade, found himself confessing that they didn't know.

'Something went wrong though, for the next thing that happened was a call from the lad Alec. He was the one who recognised Daphne in Spean Bridge. He was outside the garage where he works when he saw the van that Vass had used go past in the direction of Fort William. It was being driven by a policeman and it was closely followed by another policeman driving Forsyth's car. Realising something must have gone wrong, and although it was getting dark, he remained watching to see what would happen next. Aye, and what does he see? He sees a police car with Vass and Macneil in the back. So he then rings Davie.'

'That was when I consulted Sir Torquhil,' Simpson said, 'and he advised that there did not seem to be much more we could do then, and we'd best meet in the morning; see how you had managed, and whether anything had happened that might give us a clue about the state of the enemy's knowledge. So now, what do we do?'

Sir Torquhil then took charge. Now that the time for action was approaching, he seemed to have dropped his distaste for the operation and to be keen to proceed, whatever the difficulties.

'The first thing we have to do,' he said, 'is to find out two things. First of all, what does Forsyth know and secondly, where is he and what is he doing. The most likely people to have this information are the police in Inverness. Urquhart, do you have any contacts there?'

'Uh uh, I might have,' Roddy replied, 'there's a Sergeant in the headquarters owes me a favour. I could mebbe ask him.'

'Fine,' Sir Torquhil said, 'but we can't spare you, as you will see in a minute. Is there anyone else who could approach him?'

'Aye, Mary, that's the wife – she could. She knows him well. Suppose Jane was to go back to Inverness, then between them, they could do a bit of investigation. I'd be happier if Mary was not alone and also if Jane was away from here.'

'I could take that car back to Fort William,' Jane said, 'and then get the bus.' As the laird started to protest, she held up her hand and went on, 'No! I don't want a car. The fewer chances of cars or names being recognised the better. I like the anonymity of a bus.'

'Well, it's a bit late now but you'd best get to Fort William. Willie'll put you up for the night,' said her brother-in-law, 'and you can get a bus first thing in the morning. Try to find out all you can about Forsyth and also about the parade, particularly whether there is any alteration in Jacobsen's plans. Let us know the moment you find anything out. We'll go ahead on the assumption that all is well, unless we hear from you to the contrary.'

Jane went upstairs to collect the rest of her luggage, which Roddy carried down to the car. Then, as she got in, he took her hand.

'For God's sake be careful,' he said, 'that man Forsyth is dangerous and I don't want any harm coming to you or Mary. If you think there is any danger, let me know at once.'

Having seen his sister-in-law off, Roddy returned to the library to hear Sir Torquhil talking to the American.

'Cyrus, I think you should go back to London and then on to the States as soon as possible. We don't want there to be any possibility of you being mixed up in whatever may happen in Inverness. Also I would like our plans reported to the Sons as soon as possible – and also our thanks for their contribution. The best thing, I think, would be to put you on the train at Crainlarich tonight or tomorrow.'

'Well Torquhil, I don't want to leave you but I guess you are right. Before I go though, I would like to hear a bit more about the final plan of action so let's make it tomorrow.'

'That sounds sense, Sir Torquhil,' said Simpson, 'Fergus, Roddy and myself will go over to the quarry now and work out the final details. Tomorrow we will present our complete plan of operations, and we should also have some input from Jane, so with both of you here, you can give a "go" or "no go" decision.'

'Agreed,' said the laird. 'Now Cyrus, we'll leave them to get on with it, and I'll give you a tour of the estate.'

Chapter 19

Early the next morning Duncan slipped out of bed without disturbing Daphne and retired to the bathroom, where he shaved and bathed. When he returned to the bedroom, he found Daphne struggling into her dressing gown.

'Darling, you should have woken me. Mrs M will have a fit if she finds me not in my bed when she brings my tea. I must fly. See you at breakfast.' With that she reached up, kissed him and was gone.

It being the first time for some days that he had been able to get at his luggage, he took considerable care over dressing. Clean shirt, dark suit and regimental tie, all he thought appropriate for a meeting at the place which to him would always be 'The Fort'. Then as soon as he had finished dressing, he set about preparing for the meeting. Like all good country house bedrooms, his was provided with a desk, and he was just about to sit down and sort out the papers he would need for his meeting when there was a tap on the door and Mrs Mack entered with the early morning tray.

'Aye,' she greeted him, 'as I expected, ye're already up. You always were one for the early rising, just like himself. Well, no doubt it's a good thing, but you'll be better for a cup o' tea and breakfast will be in half an hour. Plenty time before your car comes.' And with that volley of instructions, she bustled out.

Having got his papers and maps in order, Duncan roughed out how he proposed to present his ideas. He had already arranged for a large scale wall map to be available, and had telephoned a friend at the local Brigade Headquarters in Inverness and given him some details which he asked to be put on flip charts. Then deciding there was nothing further to be done for the moment, he went down to the famous Great Hall and out on to the terrace.

The Great Hall at Dalbeg occupies almost the whole of the south front of the house. Outside there is a balustraded terrace with a view of the distant peaks of the west coast, the hills of the upper glen, and far to the east, the shining waters of the Moray Firth. As Duncan looked out on this panorama of mountain, wood and river, Daphne slipped her arm through his and her voice echoed his thoughts.

'This must be one of the most beautiful views in Scotland. What a place to have and how lucky that someone like your cousin owns it! Someone who obviously loves it and is able to maintain it. Fergus and company would say, of course, that the people should own it. So probably would Father – so long, that is, as such ideas did not apply to Altachonich. What curious people fanatics are.'

'Yes indeed, and they are the same the world over,' he replied, then with a glance at his watch, 'Come on, it's breakfast time. My car will be here in ten minutes.'

While he was finishing his coffee, Mrs Mack appeared and announced with an air of disapproval that 'One o' they polis cars is outside and asking for you.'

'Thank you Mrs M,' Duncan said and then, turning to Daphne, he added, 'I'll be back, I hope, in time for tea. I may have to leave again later; we'll just have to see how things go. Meanwhile I'll leave you to Cousin Geoffrey and Mrs Mack.'

'Aye, I'll look after Miss Drumcairn and the General will be back directly. Just you look after yesel' and dinna worry about us.'

Then, as Daphne went out to the car with him, she said, 'I agree with Mrs Mack – just you look after yoursel'! and please remember that I will be thinking of you. Having got you back, I don't want to lose you again.' And she kissed him fondly.

The arrangements at Fort George were excellent. At the main gate the Provost Sergeant and the Guard Commander were waiting and, as the police car drew up, the Sergeant got in beside the driver and escorted them through the famous tunnel and over to one of the buildings fronting the Square. There Duncan was greeted by a young officer and taken straight up to the meeting room, which was full of men standing around in small groups talking quietly.

As Duncan walked in, his friend from Brigade stepped forward, shook his hand and led him towards a tall man in battle dress and kilt who was introduced as the Commanding Officer, and therefore their host. Duncan thanked him for his hospitality and hoped they had not caused too much trouble.

'Not a bit,' said the CO, whose name was Mackenzie, 'pleased to have you here. Anything you need, just ask. Jimmy here knows the ropes,' he added pointing to the Brigade Major. 'Now, if you will excuse me, I have other duties to attend to.'

As soon as the Colonel left, they all moved over to the table in the centre of the room and Duncan suggested that before getting down to business, they should introduce themselves. As well as the Brigade Major, who was also representing Highland District, the army contingent consisted of a Brigadier from Scottish Command in Edinburgh and a slightly built officer who, rather surprisingly, turned out to be a Major in the SAS.

The police presence consisted of the Deputy Chief Constable and Inspector Nicholson. In addition there were two naval officers: one from the Fleet Air Arm at Lossiemouth and a US Commander from the NATO fleet. Lossiemouth had also sent two WRNS to give secretarial and communication support.

Introductions being complete, Duncan got to his feet and, with the aid of his charts, gave a brief history of Unicorn and its American connections and how the organisation had come to the notice of MI6. He then went on to describe their present activities and why it was felt that they could pose a threat to public order; a threat that had increased considerably since the discovery that Unicorn, with American and French help, had obtained an *Hirondelle* guided missile system.

So, having obtained their missile, what were they going to do with it? Duncan then explained how his investigations, his knowledge of the people involved and information in the possession of MI6, had led him to conclude that, however improbable it might seem, Unicorn were proposing to assassinate the US Secretary of Defense by shooting down his helicopter while he was en route to the parade in Inverness.

'They are certainly aware of his journey plan,' broke in the man from Scottish Command, 'you said that Paddy Jenkinson, the Scottish Secretary's PPS, was at the Drumcairn place in Argyll and you thought that he had been somewhat indiscreet. Well, I understand that he has confessed all to his boss. His night with the girl and just what he told her. But I still don't see what they hope to achieve by this manoeuvre.'

'I think their plan is something like this,' Forsyth replied. 'The helicopter is ambushed by a team disguised as SAS. This is duly filmed and reported. Everyone knows that Jacobsen has strong anti-colonial and pro-independence views, which he is prone to air at the most inappropriate moments. Indeed, the Government advised against his coming. We also know – and this may be news to you – that there is a strong faction in the USA who would not be sorry to see the end of Jacobsen. One of the leaders of this faction is connected with Unicorn.'

'You are saying, therefore,' said the Brigadier, 'that up goes the missile, down comes the helicopter. Jacobsen's body found, filmed by the tame journalists, then the next morning, or even the same evening, there are banner headlines all over the world: "US Statesman Murdered by SAS. Government Implicated in Plot to Suppress pro-independence Speech." This incidentally is reinforced by something else Jenkinson told his boss. Apart from his indiscretions to the lady, he apparently made some rather silly remarks in an interview, and the tape of this has gone missing. But will this help them with their intention of bringing forward the day of Scottish independence?'

'Frankly I doubt it,' Duncan replied, 'for one thing it is naive to think that the deception will work. Then, once it is discovered that the Army is not involved and that the whole thing is a plot by a lot of amateur gangsters, the Government will be left with several nasty decisions. First, how do they restore relations with the USA and NATO, and secondly what do they do with the plotters? The penalty for treason is death. But to string them up might result in them achieving their objective rather quicker than by relying on their silly little plot!'

At this point Maclay looked up and said 'Aye, that all hangs together and is probably a correct assessment of the situation. I understand your Chief has already told the Prime Minister something along the same lines. But now, Mr Forsyth, what are we going to do about it? My information is that the Prime Minister has demanded a detailed plan to resolve the matter by tomorrow evening. He has no intention of allowing an American politician to be assassinated on British soil.'

'Right, gentlemen,' said Duncan, 'you heard what Mr Maclay said. So now, what do the military propose?'

'The first thing will be to send Jacobsen by a different route. I am presuming he will not want his appearance at the parade cancelled,' said the Brigadier. 'Then we will need to find out their firing position.' And he turned and addressed the SAS man. 'What then, Sam?'

'I presume they have small arms, Mr Forsyth,' the SAS man replied, 'and that they are likely to have taken some precautions against surprise, such as posting sentries. Do you think they are likely to resist if attacked?'

'We know they have rifles and we'd better assume they have light automatics,' replied Duncan. 'As to whether they resist? I really don't know, but I suspect they would. If they see the operation failing, I think they might try to salvage something by turning themselves into martyrs.'

'In that case,' said the Major, whose name was Porterfield, 'you will want them captured rather than killed and minimal casualties all round. We'll have to go in by helicopter, I think, and we'll need to have some form of diversion.'

'My orders are that, if at all possible, they are to be arrested and treated as common conspirators,' Maclay said, 'and obviously I need help from you boys to do this, but we certainly do not want casualties if they can be avoided.'

'Well now, gentlemen, I guess we may be able to help there,' broke in the USN officer. 'Suppose we send over a helicopter at just the right time, but without Mr Jacobsen on board. Instead of him, we will have on board some very clever toys which are still strictly classified information. All I can say is that once a missile is fired, the crew will be able to track and destroy it. Then I guess, if the terrain allows it, a bit of smoke and some fancy flying will give the impression that the helicopter has been destroyed.'

'I wonder,' mused the Brigadier, 'would it be an idea if we added a fly past to the parade? Suppose immediately after the helicopter appears to crash, several jets fly low over the site then peel off to Inverness. This would have two advantages. First the noise of the jets and the element of surprise would cause confusion in the *Hirondelle* team; secondly it would minimise the chance of any other diversion – grenades and LMG for example – being heard in Inverness. Again it would depend on the terrain at the missile site.'

'I'm sure that could be arranged,' said the man from Lossiemouth, 'but to be effective, it would have to be kept secret and sprung on the parade at the last minute. Would such a surprise cause too much confusion? Also we'd need pretty high-level authorisation.'

'Such things have been done before,' said Maclay. 'Ye'll ken that there's always a man responsible for running such an event. Aye, well this man just makes an announcement about an addition to the celebration. And he does it almost as the planes arrive.'

'If that can all be arranged,' said Porterfield, 'and provided the site they choose proves amenable to our operation, we can, I believe, land a helicopter close enough for an attack group to go in and get them without casualties; unless of course someone decides to be a hero. It would help if there could be a further diversion of some sort, and in the opposite direction to that from which we'll come in.'

'That will be no problem,' said the Brigadier. Then after a pause he added, 'I imagine all this will have to be presented to someone pretty high up, and no later than tomorrow morning. We therefore have rather a lot of planning to do. I suggest, Forsyth, that the military adjourn to some other place and get down to details.'

'Yes, I think that's an excellent idea,' Duncan agreed. Then he turned to Maclay and said, 'I would like to go back to police HQ. I think we should report to your Chief and there are several things on the non-military side to be organised. Also I will try and find out what is required of us tomorrow. So gentlemen, I suggest that we get on with these various tasks and then meet again this afternoon to pool our ideas.'

Leaving the military to their planning, the others returned to police HQ in Inverness. As soon as they got there, Maclay went off to report to the Chief Constable and Nicholson took Duncan up to his office. There, while the Inspector sorted through the papers in his in-tray, Duncan looked at his notes of the previous meeting.

'Well now, this will surely interest you,' said Nicholson, suddenly looking up and waving a flimsy sheet of paper. 'It's a telex from Superintendent Davidson at Fort William. Early this morning Customs and Excise, with the aid of the Fishery Protection people, arrested a French trawler off Mull. On board was a Frenchman called Alain Lefevre who fitted the description of the man you saw at the quarry. There was also a considerable sum of money, all in dollars. The Customs people are in touch with both the Treasury and the Foreign Office about the affair.'

'One up to us, I think. No doubt we'll hear more when I speak to my Chief.'

Any further discussion was cut short by a telephone call summoning them both to the Chief Constable's office. In the room with Marshall and Maclay there was a short grey haired man in the black jacket and stiff collar that are the hallmark of the Civil Service. He was introduced as Mr Cummings from the Scottish Office in Edinburgh.

Mr Cummings expressed himself delighted to meet Forsyth, of whom he said he had heard great things, and who seemed to have achieved quite a lot in the last few days.

'Aye, young Duncan Forsyth,' said the Chief Constable, 'your doings have stirred up a fair amount of activity in high places. We've heard the general gist of your plan from Jock here. Just fill us in a bit more. I have already given Mr Cummings the background of the operation so far.'

While the others found chairs, Duncan once again took up a position in the window and, after watching the brown waters of the Ness for a moment, turned to face his audience.

'It now seems quite certain,' he said, 'that we have a plot to assassinate the US Secretary of Defense. This must be prevented and my orders are to do just that, to prevent it.'

Duncan then went on to explain about the missile and how he believed Unicorn intended to use it. To prevent this happening, it was obviously necessary to mount a quite complex military operation, particularly if loss of life was to be avoided.

The outline of such an operation had been planned that morning at the Fort George meeting and the military were now working on the details. There were, however, a number of non-military matters to be considered.

'First, have we bugged the Urquhart house and if so, have we heard anything of interest?' asked Duncan.

The Chief Constable looked at Inspector Nicholson and asked what had been done.

'Yes sir,' Nicholson replied, 'the house is bugged and so far nothing of interest has been heard. But then, as far as we know, Mrs Parsons is not yet there.'

'Well, keep watching and listening. Let me know if anything interesting happens and particularly if and when Jane Parsons returns,' Duncan said. Then after a quick glance at his notes, he continued, 'Chief Constable, I wonder if I could be briefed about the parade. The people at the Fort gave us the general outline of the military side. What about VIPs and other invited guests? How are they getting there and what are the security arrangements? And what about the general public? What size crowds are expected and where will they be?'

Marshall looked towards Maclay and said, 'Jock, I think you'd better answer that one. I take it everything is now in place.'

'Aye, just about. There's mebbe a few small details to be sorted. Of course we don't know what the new plans may entail,' replied Maclay, 'but the current arrangements are as follows: You will know that the parade takes place in the park behind the Cathedral and that the troops will march there from the barracks. Guests with chauffeurs will be dropped at the gates and their cars driven off. Other invited guests will park locally and walk. All these people will have seats in the stand. As things are at present, Mr Jacobsen's helicopter will land on the green at the back of the park. He will then be taken to the front of the stand in an army Land Rover with police outriders. There he will be met and escorted to his place by the Provost and the Colonel of the Regiment.'

At this point Maclay paused and looked across at Duncan, who took the hint. Turning to Marshall he said, 'Chief Constable, one of the things we decided this morning was that Jacobsen must come to Inverness by car. We would like the car journey to be as inconspicuous as possible, but I think the last part, Land Rover and outriders, could stay.'

Maclay nodded and said 'Aye, I think that's right and I'll be talking to the army about the details. Now about crowds and security. There will be people all along the route from the barracks. They should be no bother, but there will be policemen along the way. Aye, we'll have enough men. We're getting help from the neighbours. The parade ground will be roped off, and I would expect there to be big crowds round the outside. We'll have plenty men there to keep them back inside the ropes.'

Both Marshall and Duncan Forsyth asked again about numbers and Maclay replied that it was very difficult to guess.

'It's early for the tourists, but there will be a lot of regimental people from further north and also from Elgin and, I would imagine, quite a few from the west and down Fort William way. The best estimate we have is five, maybe six thousand. Under normal circumstances that should present no problem, but maybe the circumstances are not normal. Tell me, Mr Forsyth, do you think there will be any other sort of demonstration?'

'No, I don't. Remember the assassination is supposed to be the work of the Government, so the Nationalists will have been told to keep a low profile. Has Mr Cummings heard anything on the political grapevine?'

The man from the Scottish Office agreed with Duncan's analysis and said they had no other information. What he did want though, was confirmation of the arrangements for the arrival of the Scottish Secretary.

'He's coming from Edinburgh by train and I will be with him,' he said, 'and I understand we will be met at the station by the local Member.'

'That's right, isn't it Jock?' said Marshall.

'Yes sir,' answered Maclay, 'then you'll be taken to the park gate in Lord Darrochy's car – he's the Minister's brother, you'll mind. There will be a police escort. At the gate you will be met by the Provost and Lord Darrochy and escorted to your seats. Then if all goes right, Jacobsen should arrive exactly five minutes after you are seated. One thing I still have to decide with Mr Cummings is how we introduce Mr Jacobsen to the Minister.'

'What about the speeches?' asked Marshall, and Maclay indicated that the Inspector should reply.

'Well sir,' Nicholson said, 'there is a small platform at the front of the stand where the mike will be. The Provost will welcome Mr Jacobsen, who will deliver his speech and there will be a short reply by the Colonel of the Regiment. Mr Jacobsen will then take the salute as the parade marches off. The Provost and the rest of the civic party will drive to the front of the Town Hall to receive the troops, who will have lunch there before returning to barracks. Cars will then come to the front of the stand and take the VIPs to the reception at the Castle.'

'Chief Constable, I think that sounds fine,' said Duncan, 'but what will actually happen when they find their plan has gone wrong, I just don't know. We'll have to play it by ear. I suspect they will have a fall-back plan, but I have no idea what form that will take. Maybe we'll get a hint from the bug. One thing I'm sure of, and that is we must have plenty of plain clothes men around the park. What about the US bodyguards?'

'I'm liaising with them,' Nicholson said, 'and with the Edinburgh boys who cover St Andrew's House.'

'Now, if I may, I'd like to use the secure line again,' said Duncan. 'I need to talk to my HQ and probably the Chief. I must also find out about tomorrow.

'Jock will look after you then, and I expect that he and Nicholson have things to discuss with Cummings.' Marshall rose, with a gesture of dismissal, and as they left the room he said: 'Duncan Forsyth, before you leave, let me know what's been decided. I'll need to give some sort of report to Lord Darrochy.'

Duncan was taken to an office and once again a blue telephone with the red lable was produced. 'There you are,' Maclay said, 'and from here the number for central is 6NS. And now I'll leave you to it. Come across to my room when you've finished.'

As soon as he got his HQ on the line, Duncan was put through to the Chief of Operations.

'Good morning, DF,' he said, 'we've been waiting for you. There's been a lot of activity here, which the Chief will tell you about; and I hope you have a solution to the problem or there are going to be a lot of very unhappy people around. But now, before you speak to the Chief, you'd better put me in the picture.'

As concisely and clearly as he could, Duncan explained that all his suspicions were proving to be true. Unicorn had plans in place to murder a member of the United States Government and to put the blame on the British Army. All this to try and further the cause of Scottish independence.

Subject to learning a few more details, they now had a very good idea of how the crime was to be committed and, more important, how it could be prevented. That morning, at a meeting with the police and military, a plan to accomplish this had been proposed. The military were now working on the detailed implementation and he, Duncan, was working with the police on security at the parade. Two matters were still outstanding. The first was what might be the reaction of Unicorn when they discovered that things had gone wrong. This could only be played by ear. The second was what to do with Unicorn. This was a political matter which the Government would have to address.

Duncan finished his summary with this statement: 'We hope to be in a position to present our plans tomorrow morning. We will need to get agreement to them from both the UK and US Governments, so whenever we do present them, there will need to be some high level politicians present.'

'You will certainly get them,' the Chief of Operations replied, 'but I'd better let the Chief tell you that himself. Hold on a moment.'

After a pause and some clicking and buzzing on the line, Duncan heard again the well known voice of the Chief of the SIS.

'Well, DF, what have you got for me?' the Chief said, 'and be quick, for there are a lot of people waiting to hear from me.'

Duncan reiterated to the great man what he had already told the Chief of Operations. When the Chief asked for more information on what they were proposing, Duncan summarised the ideas of the Fort George meeting and got a grunt from the other end of the line.

'Well, I just hope it works. Chances of success, DF? They'd better be good, for failure does not bear thinking about.'

'Pretty good, sir,' was Duncan's reply, 'provided that the political will is there, and that will need some real heavyweights to give the go ahead.'

'You'll get them, DF. Probably more than you bargained for,' the Chief said, 'and now listen to me for I shall not repeat this. You and your military and police teams will report to Scottish Command at nine o'clock tomorrow morning. There you will present your plans at a meeting, at which there will be present the Foreign Secretary, the Scottish Secretary, the American Ambassador and the Chief of the Imperial General Staff and possibly others. You will fly from Inverness to Edinburgh. Check the details with the army. This meeting will be empowered to give all the agreements you need. Good luck, DF.'

Before Duncan could say anything, there was another click on the line and he was speaking again to the Chief of Operations.

'I hope you got all that, young man,' the voice said, 'and I too will add my good wishes. One last thing. A rather worried PPS told me that a certain lady has some photographs and tapes that could do him no good. As a reward for coming clean, we have said we will try to recover them. Can do?'

'Will try, but no guarantee,' Duncan said and the line went dead.

Duncan immediately sought out Maclay and explained the plans for the next day. He then rang the Scottish Command Brigadier at the Fort and arranged that they would all meet there at eight that evening, hear the detailed plans and agree the procedure for the next day's meeting. He also asked him to tie up travel arrangements with all concerned. Finally he asked Maclay if he could have a police car to take him to Dalbeg and then back to Fort George.

'I must tell General Forsyth and Miss Drumcairn what is happening,' he said. Then having given a quick report to the Chief Constable and promised another after the Edinburgh meeting, he got in the car and was driven to Dalbeg.

When he arrived at the house he found Daphne and his Cousin Geoffrey just finishing a tour of the garden.

'Not much to see yet, I'm afraid,' the General said as he shook Duncan's hand, 'it's not been a bad winter, but March was cold and wet. Good for the rhodies and azaleas, but it will be three weeks yet before we see any daffodils. Well now, my boy, how have you got on today? Daphne has been telling me all about Unicorn. Knew a bit about it of course, but no idea that Torquhil had got himself so involved. I used to see him when he was a young man in India. If you'll forgive me, my dear, I always thought he had more ambition than sense.'

'He still has, Sir Geoffrey,' the girl replied, 'but he feels very strongly that Scotland has been let down by its leaders.'

'He's probably right, but what he's doing seems to me unlikely to help. Now it's getting cold. Let's go in and see if Mrs Mack can produce some tea.'

Mrs Mack could indeed produce tea, and was in fact just bringing it in. The housekeeper, who had taken a strong liking to Daphne, looked at Sir Geoffrey and asked if she should put the tray in front of Miss Drumcairn.

'Would you mind pouring for us?' he said, nodding to Mrs Mack, 'as you saw earlier, the arthritis is getting at my hands.' Then, turning to Duncan he said, 'now you'd better give us some idea of your plans.'

'Before I say anything, could I ask Mrs Mack to look after my driver. He must have some tea, for he's got to take me back to the Fort in about forty-five minutes' time.'

'Aye, I've already taken care of him. He's one of the Bisset boys from up the glen. You'll mind the father, Sir Geoffrey. Charlie the carter he was, that worked for the forestry.' With which pronouncement she turned and left the room.

'Must you go so soon?' said Daphne with disappointment in her voice, 'surely he could stay for dinner, Sir Geoffrey?'

'I'm afraid not, my dear. We've a very high-powered meeting in Edinburgh at nine to morrow. And I've arranged a briefing and rehearsal at eight tonight at the Fort. Anyway, listen and I'll give you a rough idea of what's happening.'

Then, without giving away too much, he told them what was being planned. He suspected that his cousin, who was still well in with the higher echelons of the army, knew more about what was going on than he let on. But they both respected each other's confidence.

'I promise I'll keep in touch. And Daphne, I'll do my best to protect your father but I think you must steel yourself for unpleasant news. Now I must go. You will look after her Geoffrey, won't you, and thank you for everything.'

'Well good luck my boy, and don't worry about Daphne,' the General replied with a shrewd glance at them, as Duncan kissed her goodbye, got in the car and was driven off by Constable Bisset.

Chapter 20

When the bus from Fort William deposited her in Academy Street, Jane went straight to the Station Hotel, rang her sister and arranged to be picked up. Seeing a copy of the local daily on a table in the lounge, she took it over to a chair and read with considerable interest the details of the forthcoming parade and of the arrival of the United States Secretary of Defense.

It appeared that after arriving in the UK, Jacobsen had made a series of visits to US Air Force bases in England and was now believed to be visiting naval establishments in Scotland. Security, it appeared, was very tight and it was difficult to find out either schedules or itineraries; but as far as Jane could make out from her study of the paper, Jacobsen was expected to join the fleet in the Cromarty Firth that evening and spend the next thirty-six hours at sea. Then followed details of Saturday's parade and the expectation that the British Ministers, together with other VIPs and their American guest, would join the troops in the Park at about 10.30 am.

'Very interesting,' thought Jane, 'but it doesn't really tell us anything we don't already know. We must try to find out about timing and security. Perhaps Roddy's friend will be able to help.' However, at this point her musings were interrupted by the arrival of her sister.

As they drove out of the station yard, Mary asked what had happened since she left Fort William, but Jane told her that could wait. 'The most important thing,' she said, 'is have you contacted Roddy's policeman friend?'

'Yes,' replied Mary, 'and I have arranged for us to meet him. It was not easy for he was definitely unhappy about meeting any friend of Roddy's – even me. And when I said I wanted him to meet my sister, he got in one hell of a state. I think he guessed what we wanted to talk about, for he said everyone in the force was dead twitchy about Saturday. However he eventually agreed that we could meet this evening at the house of a mutual friend, but we must be careful that no one sees us with him.'

'The mutual friend – is he safe?' Jane asked.

'Yes, he's the local Nationalist Party Secretary,' Mary said. 'He's also a member of Unicorn and has the job of ensuring there is no other Home Rule type demonstration on Saturday. He was in the police and so there would be nothing suspicious about our man visiting him.'

'Is "our man" going to be any help, do you think?'

'We'll have to wait and see. He was far too nervous to say anything more on the telephone. We're meeting him at half seven, so there's plenty of time for a cup of tea.' And with that Mary pulled into a short driveway covered with granite chippings and stopped in front of a pink sandstone house with two high gabled windows.

Once they were settled in the front room with their tea, Jane described to her sister the happenings of the past few days at Altachonich: the shooting in the quarry, the arrival of the missile, the demonstration to the American and the eventual departure of the Frenchman with the money.

'Up to that point all had gone reasonably well, except for the raid on the quarry,' she continued, 'but then, just as I was leaving to drive down to the pier with the money, Simpson got a message from Vass – that's your friend who took the money to the castle – to say that the Drumcairn girl and a man had been spotted in Spean Bridge. This caused something of a stir and I thought the sooner we were away with the Frenchman and the money the better. So we didn't hear what happened until the next day, when we got back to the castle.'

Jane then went on to describe the meeting with the trawler, the handing over of the money and the eventual return to Fort William and Altachonich, where they heard of the failure of the Vass plan and the capture of Vass and Macneil by the police. 'I can tell you, Roddy was bloody furious with Simpson for sending Vass and Macneil after a top professional like Forsyth, for by then they'd guessed it was him.'

'And was it him?' her sister asked, 'and where is he now?'

'Of course it was him,' Jane replied. 'I asked what he was like and when they described him, I knew at once. When you've sat opposite a man at dinner and then had him between your legs, you don't make mistakes.' Mary looked at her sister with a certain distaste but let the remark pass and Jane went on. 'As to where they are now, that we don't know, but it's what we hope to find out from your friend. And on what we find out, depends what happens on Saturday At present they are inclined to go ahead. The old man more than any of them.'

When Jane paused, Mary glanced at the clock. 'We ought to be going shortly. You know where your room is. I'll just clear this away and see you downstairs in about five minutes.'

Their meeting was in a house on the other side of the river and when they got there Mary said, 'I think we'll park round the back. There's a gate into their garden off a little alley and we can go in by the back door without being seen.'

Their host had obviously hoped they would do this, for he was waiting there to let them in, and as Jane was introduced he said: 'Aye, I'm glad you came this way. Jim's here and he's gie nervous. No, he doesn't know of our plans; but he says there's terrible security everywhere, with people up from

London and Edinburgh. I'd say just get him to talk naturally and you'll mebbe get what you want. But dinna make it look like an interrogation.'

They were led through to the front of the house where they found Jim – Jane never did find out his full name – perched uneasily on the edge of an armchair. He jumped up when they entered, gave Mary a nervous smile and Jane a limp handshake.

When the introductions had been completed, their host begged to be excused as he said he had other things to do but that he would be back in about forty-five minutes. After he left the room, Jane smiled encouragingly at the policeman and suggested that they sit down. Then she leaned forward and said, 'I was reading in the *Journal* all about the parade on Saturday. I gather there are all sorts of distinguished visitors coming and that security is very tight. It must make a lot of extra work for you boys.'

'Aye, it does that,' he said, 'what with all the Ministers and other VIPs, we're fair overrun with the Special Branch and the Secret Service. And then there's this Yank. He's brought all his own people – a right rough lot they are too, more like a poacher's convention than a bodyguard.'

'Who is this American?' Jane asked. 'I couldn't quite make out from the papers.'

'He's the Secretary of Defense,' came the reply, 'and he's making a speech. They say the Government's dead worried, for this man is not always gie tactful. Aye, they've sent a special man up from Whitehall to keep an eye on him. He was in with the Chief Constable yesterday, and they say there was a big meeting over at Fort George.'

'Do you know this man's name? I think he might be a friend of mine.' Then turning to her sister, Jane said: 'You'll mind, Mary, I said that I thought Duncan might be in the north. You know I'd love to see him, if it is him.'

'No I can't say I heard his name. It could be Duncan but I don't really know. I can tell you though, you'll not find him today. They're all off at another meeting. Aye, this time in Edinburgh.' Jim paused and looked up, as if wondering why he had said as much as he had. 'Why do you want to know all this?' he asked Jane. Then with a worried look he added: 'Are you the Press? Roddy didna say anything about that. Just asked me if I'd talk to a friend. For God's sake dinna print anything about what I've told you. It would be as much as my job's worth.'

'No, I'm not really the Press,' Jane replied, 'I'm an author of sorts and a Scottish journal is interested in my writing an article on the parade, so I need some background information. Roddy said you might give me something on the security angle. What you've said is very helpful, and I promise nothing is going to appear for at least two months.'

'Aye, well I hope that's right,' said Jim getting to his feet, 'and now I must be away. Pleased to have met you.'

They heard the front door open and their host's voice saying goodbye to the visitor. Then the door closed and he came back into the room.

'Well, how did you get on?' he asked. 'He's not a bad wee man. But for a man o' his experience, he does stupid things and he's always owing people favours. Not right for a policeman, ye ken.'

'I got enough,' Jane replied, 'he didn't know that much. I told him I was writing an article, so I think he is reasonably confident I'm not going to drop him in it with his superiors. Now we must go home because I need to ring Roddy. Thankyou for your help.'

'It's a pleasure to help the cause. Aye, and good luck for Saturday.' Then to Mary he added: 'Grand to see you again, and tell that husband of yours that we must take a dram together when all this is over.'

At Altachonich Castle a meeting to decide whether or not to go ahead with the plan to assassinate Norman Jacobsen was about to start. Around the table in the library, in addition to Sir Torquhil and Cyrus P. Groat, were Davie Simpson, Fergus Crawford, Roddy Urquhart and two of the men from the quarry. One of the two was the man in charge of the *Hirondelle*, the other the man who was to be responsible for transporting the men and the rest of the equipment from Altachonich to the Black Isle.

The first person to speak was Simpson, who asked Sir Torquhil if the staff had been dealt with.

'All the house staff have gone into Fort William,' the laird replied. 'There's a big shinty match on and two lads from Glenlochan are playing. Those that aren't interested in shinty – and I doubt Charles is! – will probably go to the cinema. I believe there's a good film on. The keeper has gone to a meeting at an estate fifty miles north of here. He then has to collect and bring home a new pony. He will not be back until tomorrow evening.'

'Fine,' said Simpson, 'and I've got people watching all the entrances, so I don't think we'll be disturbed. Now all we want is to hear from Jane.'

'Say, I hope that girl will not be too long,' remarked the American. 'Torquhil, what time did you say I ought to leave for the train?'

'In about two hours,' answered the laird, looking at the clock above the fireplace, 'so you ought at least to know the decision before you leave.'

Sir Torquhil had hardly finished speaking when the telephone on the table beside him rang. He picked up the receiver and listened for a few moments, then said 'Yes, Mrs Parsons, we're all here in the library waiting for your call. Just hold on a moment, I think the best person for you to talk to is Urquhart.'

He handed the instrument to Roddy saying, 'You talk to her. What we need to know is, has she has found out anything that suggests the authorities are aware of our plans.'

Roddy listened to his sister-in-law for several minutes, saying nothing himself except for an occasional 'sure' and 'uh-huh'. Then came a pause at the other end of the line.

'But these meetings in Fort George and Edinburgh,' Roddy broke in, 'do they suggest that the authorities think that someone is planning something or are they just the Americans insisting on special security for their precious Secretary of Defense'

There was another long reply from Jane, then Urquhart turned to the others and said that he thought she had told them everything she could and she now wanted to know what else they wanted her to do.

'The most important thing she can do,' said Simpson, who had been unusually quiet, 'is to find out if Forsyth went to Edinburgh, if he has returned, what he is doing now and who he is seeing. Then you, Roddy, and also Fergus had better meet her tomorrow. You can tell her what we have decided and see whether she has any additional information that might affect our plans. We'll ring her later and tell her where.'

Sir Torquhil nodded his agreement with this and Roddy passed on the message. Then, after mutual good wishes, he rang off.

'Right,' said Roddy, who felt he should now take charge of the meeting, 'here is the gist of what she said.' He then told them of the meeting with his friend the Police Sergeant.

'She said he was very nervous and obviously was not privy to all that was going on. However he did say that there was more than usual concern for security for the Saturday parade, with people up from London and Edinburgh and non-police groups involved. In particular there was a man from London who was awfu' interested in the welfare of Jacobsen. He did not know his name, but Jane said it was obviously Forsyth. This man had spent time with the Chief Constable and had been to a meeting at Fort George and was now down in Edinburgh. What do we make of all that?'

'Hard to say,' said Sir Torquhil. 'I don't much like the mention of the Fort. Sounds as though the military are interested. Then again, extra security would be only natural with all those VIPs around.'

'I wish we knew more about Forsyth's doings,' said Simpson. 'I don't trust the man, and catching those two following him must confirm any suspicions he already had. That episode was a mistake, I have to admit.'

'I guess Forsyth is a problem, for he must know something is up,' remarked Groat, 'but we don't have any evidence that he knows what. If they had any suspicion of what we intend, I would expect to hear rumours of alterations and cancellations and that is not happening. You know, you British usually accuse us of undue caution, but in this case I'll stick my neck out and advise action. Nobody ever won freedom by sitting on their ass. Get up and go, I say. You may never have a better opportunity.'

This call to action stunned everyone and for the next few minutes they all remained staring at the table. Sir Torquhil was the first to recover, raising his head and looking out of the window at the grey waters of the loch. Then he turned and looked at each of his companions. Finally he said: 'You know, I think Cyrus is right. If Unicorn is going to achieve its purpose – independence for Scotland – then it must act and act now; if it doesn't, it will die. And we all know that Unicorns never die. I think we should make the "go" decision, and move into position on Thursday as planned.'

In saying this, Sir Torquhil was speaking from the heart, for his head told him that their whole operation was too amateur to succeed, a feeling he suspected might be shared by some of his colleagues, notably Jane. Furthermore all his experience suggested that Forsyth must have guessed what they were planning and have alerted the Government. All these meetings had to mean a major disaster-averting operation. But, like his Maclean ancestors, he was a proud man. He felt that, having raised the money, found the missile and recruited the leaders, he could not now draw back. To do so meant letting too many people down.

Cyrus P. Groat smiled with pleasure at this robust speech. Simpson, who was determined to go ahead whatever the cost, banged the table.

'That's right, man,' he said, forgetting himself in his enthusiasm, 'strike while the iron is hot, that's what I say.'

Fergus Crawford, ever the political firebrand, leaped to his feet. 'At last ye've all seen sense,' he shouted, 'I keep telling ye, Scotland only maintained her independence while she was prepared to shed blood. She'll only regain it by doing so again,' and here he raised his clenched fist and roared, 'Scotland the Brave she must be – and hound the Sassenach for ever from her shores.'

After this outburst Fergus sat back exhausted and Sir Torquhil looked round the company.

'Well it's pretty clear what most of you think,' he said, 'but what about you, Urquhart? You've got to lead the expedition, so what's your opinion?'

'I've heard what you've all said and I mostly know why you've said it,' Roddy replied. 'For myself I'm not so certain. I know of Forsyth and I know how those boys operate. I heard what Janie said and I find it hard to believe that they have not made a pretty accurate assessment of our intentions and prepared appropriate counter measures. Now one of those measures might be a raid on this place and we'd have no chance if they did that. Destroyer out in the Sound, helicopters on the hill. No, I'd not fancy that at all, and if we were caught here we would have achieved nothing. I'd sooner take my chance on the Black Isle – and we might just get Jacobsen before they could stop us. Might as well be hung for a sheep as a goat! But don't say I didn't warn you.'

The discussion went on for another half hour, at the end of which Sir Torquhil got to his feet. 'Well that's settled,' he said. 'On Saturday we go ahead with our plan to deal with Jacobsen. Now I suggest we have a short break while I see Mr Groat off to his train, then reconvene and discuss the final details of the operation. Come on Cyrus, there's a man downstairs ready to drive you to the station.'

The American rose and followed his host to the door, then turned and looked at the people round the table.

'I'm sorry to be leaving you all, but I guess there is nothing further I can do here,' he said. 'It sure is up to you now and I know that you will not fail. I shall report so to the Sons when I get home – and I guess I shall be telling them that the day when Scotland achieves independence is fast approaching. And now, may God be with you, and all of you remember this: at zero hour on Saturday morning there will be one American citizen saying a prayer for your success.'

Ten minutes later Sir Torquhil came back into the library and resumed his place at the table.

'Now let's hear from you, Simpson,' he said, 'and you, Urquhart, exactly what is going to happen over the next three days and what you want each of us to do.'

The plan that unfolded over the next two hours was a very simple one, which depended for its success on the fact that two farms on the Black Isle, close to the chosen missile launching site, were owned and occupied by Unicorn sympathisers. One belonged to the Urquhart family and the other to a man who had been a friend of Roddy's from childhood. By using the Altachonich Estate timber lorry and cattle float, the *Hirondelle* and other equipment could be moved north without arousing suspicion. This arrangement was facilitated by the fact that the quarrymen were not the only Unicorn members on the estate payroll. Unknown to their fellow workers, the drivers of both trucks and the head shepherd were also part of the plot.

'What will happen tomorrow,' explained Simpson, 'is that first thing some timber for the saw mill at Muir of Ord will be loaded and the lorry will then go down to the quarry. The estate foresters have been told that we are lending a piece of equipment to another quarry. This will of course be the missile launcher and Jack here,' nodding to the *Hirondelle* supervisor, 'will see to the loading. As soon as this is completed, they will set off for the Black Isle. I was going to send Roddy with them but we think it more important that he and Fergus go on ahead to make sure everything is OK, and also to confer with Jane. Jack and the driver both know the way.'

'Aye, I think that's essential,' said Roddy. 'We don't want them arriving and finding the farm surrounded by police.'

Simpson nodded and then continued: 'When they get to Muir of Ord they will unload the timber and if anyone asks where they are going next, they will say they are off to a quarry up beyond Brora. But of course they will go straight to the farm. So that's them organised.' Here Simpson paused for a moment for questions. But there were none, so he went on. 'Now for the other party. About nine o'clock the cattle truck will go out the Meall

Garbh track and the shepherd will load some sheep which are to go to a farm up north. They will then drive to a place where they are well in cover and will be met by the two Land Rovers. A special panel will be fitted in the float which will confine the sheep to the rear end. The rifles, uniforms and all the other gear will be loaded in the space in front of the panel. Three of the men will also be in there as guards. They will then set off with Pete, who knows the way, in charge. The rest of the men with myself will follow in the Land Rovers. Now let's hear Roddy's plans.'

'I suggest that Fergus and I meet Jane at that hotel near Culloden at ten tomorrow morning to get an update on anything new she has discovered. Unless something drastic has happened, in which case I will ring the castle, we will decide any further jobs for Jane and then go on to the Black Isle farms. Just before they get to Inverness, I suggest each of the vehicles rings me, and I'll give you a number before I leave, just to check that there are no problems. We will then decide on the dispersal of our force between the farms, and direct them to their places when they arrive. Davie and I will then give out the orders for the next twenty-four hours.'

'Fine Roddy,' said Simpson and then looked round the table. 'There's one other thing I should add. In the event of any sort of failure at the missile site, we have a fall-back plan. I'm not going to tell you about it now, but it will be put into operation by Roddy, Fergus and Jane and the final details will be decided on Friday. Now Sir Torquhil, have you any questions?'

'Just one,' said the laird. 'I think the plans are fine, but what part do I play?'

'Sir, we think you are too well known and too valuable to be with the forward troops,' Simpson replied, 'and anyway we need you here, in charge of the rear echelon. For if everything goes wrong, what happens at the castle is going to be very important, not least in allowing you to escape. We have a suggested plan which perhaps we can discuss in the morning.'

Here the laird gave one of his famous grunts and looked at his watch. 'Well it is getting late and all of us must be up early – and I don't suppose anyone will sleep much. So let's call it a day. I'll see you at eight, Simpson.' And with that he stumped out of the room.

'I'll just ring Janie,' said Roddy, 'and arrange about the meeting tomorrow. Then I'll see you all down at the quarry for the final briefing.'

Chapter 21

At six-thirty that morning, about an hour before Jane left Fort William on her way to Inverness, the operations group from Fort George assembled in the Officers' Mess at RAF Kinloss. They all looked somewhat exhausted, for they had been working until two o'clock perfecting the plan they were to present to the representatives of the British and United States Governments in Edinburgh.

Every part of the operation had been worked out in detail. Permission to use the units required had been obtained at the highest level and the Commanding Officers warned to prepare their teams under conditions of the utmost secrecy. All that was now required to put Operation Saviour into action was the agreement of the politicians.

The responsibility for presenting the plan and obtaining agreement to it now rested with Brigadier Robertson, who had been given overall command of the operation. His staff had been strengthened by the addition of the Captain of the RNAS Lossiemouth as second-in-command and co-ordinator of naval and flying operations, and an Air Force officer to liaise with Air Traffic Control. Now that the military were in control, Duncan Forsyth's responsibility was mainly the provision of intelligence information, although he had been charged by his Chief with ensuring that none of the principal conspirators managed to escape.

Such had been the speed with which this very complex plan had been put together, that even as the Station Commander came in and called for their attention, Duncan and the Brigadier were still discussing the details of their presentations.

'Gentlemen, your plane is ready,' he said, 'so would you please follow the Staff Sergeant out to the bus,' and then, as they walked towards the door, he added, 'and may I say that I and my colleagues offer you our best wishes for the success of your mission.'

A drab grey bus took them to the other side of the airfield, where a Viscount of Transport Command was waiting. There was none of the usual delay before take off, for as soon as they were seated, the plane taxied to the end of the runway and moments later they were on their way to Edinburgh.

When they landed at Turnhouse, the plane did not go anywhere near the main buildings, but was guided to a hardstanding where a bus was waiting, a rather more comfortable civilian bus this time, in which they made the fifteen-minute drive to Scottish Command Headquarters. There they were met by an ADC, who took them straight to a large, windowless conference room, the main floor space of which was occupied by a U-shaped table. At the far end of the room, facing the table, was a screen on which was projected a large scale map of the whole Moray Firth area.

As they entered the room, a tall man with piercing blue eyes and a bristling ginger moustache speckled with grey left a group who were studying the map and walked towards Brigadier Robertson.

'Good morning, Hugh. Good flight?' he said. 'Splendid! Now introduce me to your team.' Then seeing Duncan, he added with a gleam of recognition, 'Now here is someone I know of old. Duncan Forsyth and I always meet in unusual situations, and it seems we do so once again. The first time, I think, was outside Padua. I was about to set up my HQ in a farm across a vineyard from the railway, when this figure emerged from the vines and yelled "Get your men down! A train with a hundred tons of ammunition is just about to go up!" Never got down so quick in all my life!'

The two shook hands and Duncan acknowledged the truth of the Italian episode with a faint smile, then he left the Brigadier to introduce the others to the Army Commander in Scotland, General Sir Alexander Murray, and walked over to the group at the map. At his approach they turned and the officer in the middle looked him up and down. Duncan had been right in his surmise. One could never mistake the broad shoulders, short neck and massive head of the Chief of the Imperial General Staff.

'I know you, don't I, Forsyth?' he said, 'Your Chief told me you would be here. Well I hope you've got something to tell us. We can't have what sounds to me like a lot of amateurs creating international incidents. It's bad for Scotland, it's bad indeed for the whole United Kingdom. Much more serious though, would be if this ill-conceived act of terror were to succeed. It would put a question mark over the effectiveness of the security systems of both Britain and America – France too, if that's where the missile came from – and send a signal to terrorists world wide that they could act with impunity.' Then he turned to the rest of the group. 'Now, let me do some introductions. Gentlemen, this is Duncan Forsyth, who we have to thank for uncovering this plot – and whom, I hope, we are going to thank for preventing it happening.'

While Duncan was shaking hands and answering questions, the ADC came up and said something to the CIGS, who walked over to General Murray. After a few moments conversation the latter rapped the table for silence.

'I understand the plane from London has landed and that the Foreign Secretary and the others will be here in about fifteen minutes and are anxious to start the meeting as soon as they arrive,' he announced. 'I think if we could all take our places, I will just make sure I know who everybody is. Then when they arrive, we'll dispense with handshaking and I will introduce you en bloc to save time. Also Hugh, a quick word with you before they arrive, just to make sure I've got the agenda right.'

No sooner had he finished these discussions than the ADC appeared again and spoke briefly to him. He immediately rose and left the room with a brief nod to the CGS. Three minutes later he was back and everyone got to their feet as the Foreign Secretary, the Scottish Secretary and the US Ambassador, followed by their aides, trooped in. They shook hands with the CIGS and took their seats at the head of the table.

The seating had been arranged so that the politicians and the CIGS would be facing the map, with the senior officers, who now included the American Chief of Staff of the NATO fleet and the Flag Officer, Scotland, on their right and the operations team on their left. Brigadier Robertson and Duncan Forsyth were at the end of the right hand sprig nearest the map. There were also chairs behind each row for aides and notetakers.

General Murray went to a lectern on the right of the screen and opened the proceedings by welcoming everybody, identifying the players and giving a brief explanation of the purpose of the meeting, and was just about to introduce Duncan Forsyth when he was interrupted by the Foreign Secretary.

'Thank you, General, for that introduction,' he said, 'but before we proceed I must tell you something that is of great importance to us all. Last night the Prime Minister and the President had a long telephone call, after which it was made abundantly clear to me that there must be no possibility of this assassination attempt succeeding. Failure to stop it will result in an abrupt end to a number of promising careers, including, I suspect, my own and also those of a number of others round this table. So gentlemen, take heed.' With that he indicated to the General that the meeting should continue.

'Foreign Secretary,' General Murray continued, 'all concerned with this most unpleasant affair are well aware of the gravity of the situation, and your message has served to drive this home. However I hope that by the end of this meeting you will feel able to inform the Prime Minister and the President that we have an effective plan and we shall be successful. You all have agendas and at the end of the proceedings we shall provide each of you with a precis of the plan. Detailed copies will be sent via the usual channels to all the appropriate authorities. Now I am going to ask Colonel Forsyth from the SIS to give you the background to the affair.

Duncan moved to the lectern and gave a brief history of Unicorn and the people involved in it. Then, with the aid of a map of the west coast, he described the happenings at Altachonich and the discovery of the plot against the life of Norman Jacobsen.

He finished by saying: 'In conclusion, I would like to pay tribute to all those who had no need to become involved, but did so at some risk to themselves. Without their help we would not have got as far as we have. Their names will be included in my official report.'

When Duncan sat down, General Murray returned to the lectern and asked if there were any questions. The Foreign Secretary wanted to know how the missile could be transhipped to the yacht and then landed at the quarry without being intercepted. Maclay explained that the topography of the west coast was such that it was impossible to patrol every sea loch or to see, let alone stop, every boat flying a foreign flag. The Scottish Secretary asked about the activities in the quarry and was told that up to the arrival of the missile, there was no reason to suppose that anything odd was taking place there. In fact Sir Torquhil Drumcairn was receiving support from the Scottish Office for his attempts to revive old industries in an area of high unemployment.

The American Ambassador asked where Cyrus P. Groat was now. Again it was the policeman who answered.

'We have Altachonich Castle under observation, and as far as I know he is still there.'

'Well, watch him,' the Ambassador replied, 'I know Cyrus P. well, and he sure is a slippery customer.'

'Now gentlemen,' General Murray said, 'let me introduce Brigadier Robertson from my staff. He has been responsible for putting together the plan you are about to hear. He will also be responsible, together with the Chief Constable of Inverness-shire, for seeing that it is carried out successfully.'

Hugh Robertson put his papers on the lectern and walked over to the screen which now displayed the map of the Moray Firth. Pointing to the map, he explained that Jacobsen was at present on board the light fleet carrier *USS Boulder*, anchored about half a mile east of Invergordon.

The original plan for Saturday had been that his helicopter would take the direct route to Inverness, which entailed flying due south over the Black Isle. Tracing the route with his pointer, Robertson explained that it passed over a thickly wooded area between five hundred and a thousand feet in height. This provided ideal terrain for ambushing a helicopter, but also made it extremely difficult to identify and approach the firing point without arousing suspicion.

The missile party were still at Altachonich under observation. As soon as they moved, their progress would be monitored by the police. It was assumed that they would move initially to a hideout on the Black Isle close to the proposed launch site, and there were plans to follow them and identify their destination, although this would need to be done without arousing either their suspicion or that of the local population.

'And now I must tell you that the rest of our plan is based on a series of subterfuges and deceptions,' Robertson continued, 'and for obvious reasons

I do not want to go into them in too much detail. The first involves the Secretary of Defense, who will now travel to the parade by different means. The second involves his helicopter. A helicopter will indeed follow the expected route on Saturday morning and we hope that it will be fired on, as this will help pinpoint the missile site. If it is, the US Navy assure us that they will create the impression of a successful hit. Perhaps I could ask the Chief of Staff to confirm that these plans are all in place.'

The US Admiral looked up and nodded. 'Sure are,' he said. 'Secretary Jacobsen will appear at the parade ground as planned, but he won't have been near a helicopter. However, a specially equipped one will follow his proposed route, with results that I guess will surprise anyone who tries to destroy it.'

'We now come to the trickiest part of the operation, which involves the final subterfuge,' Robertson continued. 'We have added an additional item to the parade – a flypast by jets from Lossiemouth. As the helicopter flies down the Black Isle, three jets will be over the Dornoch Firth heading for their bombing range,' and here Robertson indicated two points on the map. 'This is a normal happening and should arouse no suspicion. The moment the missile is fired, simultaneous signals will be sent to the flight commander and to a commentator at the parade ground, who will make a suitable announcement. The jets will sweep in low, one at a time, over the place where the missile has been located; they will then turn east, reform in arrowhead, and make two ceremonial passes over the parade ground.'

He then explained that, taking advantage of the confusion caused by the jets and a feint by a platoon of infantry, two helicopters, coming from the opposite direction, would fly in the SAS attack squads. These troops would either abseil straight into the site, the preferred option, or else land as close as possible, force the occupants to surrender and then hold them until the police arrived. At that point Robertson stepped back from the map and said to General Murray:

'Assuming all goes well, that concludes the Black Isle part of the operation, sir, and before we go on to the next part, could I suggest we deal with any questions.'

And here Robertson returned to his seat, leaving the lectern to the General, who said, 'I think that's right. This is the most important part of the operation and we need to be quite sure that everyone is happy with it.'

The CIGS looked at the two senior politicians and said: 'I agree with that proposal and I have a rather important question.'

'Go ahead General,' said the Foreign Secretary.

'Brigadier Robertson, how do you propose to deal with the possibility of no missile being fired?'

'If our helicopter reaches the Firth without being fired on, it will turn and begin a detailed search of the whole area. At the same time road blocks will be set up on roads leading out of the Black Isle and mobile patrols will advance slowly down all the roads leading to Cromarty. There are then two possibilities. The first is that the missile site is discovered, in which case the capture plan will go ahead. This will happen well after the flypast is over so there will be no jet noise to cover any firing or explosions. The second is that they have lost their nerve and are still in their hideouts. These will have to be found and the occupants forced to surrender with, of course, an enhanced risk of casualties on both sides.'

The CIGS nodded, then turned to the two Ministers. 'This is a nasty one, but I think we have to accept that what has been described is the only course. However I would like to discuss it in more detail after the meeting.'

'General, what plans are there to reassure the local population?' the Scottish Secretary asked, 'and what will the press be told?'

General Murray looked across at Maclay, who got to his feet. 'As far as the farms and other houses in the immediate vicinity are concerned, I will have half a dozen motor cyclists ready to go round and tell them what is happening. Aye, I have enough men. We are well supported by neighbouring forces. Any calls that come via the 999 system will be routed to a special group at police HQ, who are briefed on what to say. A routine press conference has already been called for after the parade. This will give out some rather different information to that usually given on these occasions.'

'Do we have any feel for what Unicorn might do when they realise their plan has failed?' asked the Foreign Secretary. 'I imagine they will have some sort of fall-back plan, so Jacobsen could still be at risk.'

Here Duncan got to his feet and said to General Murray, 'Would you like me to answer that, sir?'

'Yes, go ahead Forsyth.'

'I'm afraid, Foreign Secretary, that I really don't know the answer to your question,' Duncan said, 'but yes, we must assume that they will realise the missile plan could fail for all sorts of reasons. I am sure they will have a fall-back plan and it could well include a further attempt on Jacobsen's life. What it might be I do not know. It is one of the things I am still trying to find out. What I can say is that Inspector Nicholson and myself will be at the parade ground and in touch with the assault group. We shall be close to Secretary Jacobsen and we both know the principal Unicorn players by sight.'

'Thank you, Mr Forsyth,' said the Foreign Secretary as Duncan resumed his seat, then looking up he added, 'I think, General Murray, that I would like to know what plans have been made concerning Altachonich Castle and anyone who may be left there, particularly if that includes Sir Torquhil Drumcairn.'

'I think, Brigadier Robertson, that you have that matter in hand,' said the General.

'Yes sir. As I said earlier, the castle is under observation at present and we expect the missile party to leave tomorrow. On Friday a group consisting of local police and Special Branch under a Superintendent, supported by an infantry platoon and an Ordnance Corps detachment, will be moved into the vicinity. As soon as the missile is fired or any other attempt is made on Jacobsen's life, they will be ordered in to take control of the castle and quarry. Anyone found there will be arrested for questioning.'

The meeting then moved on to hear from Robertson and Maclay about the security arrangements at the parade ground.

'These will be exactly as already published. Your party, sir,' said Maclay to the Scottish Secretary, 'will be met at the station and driven to the park with a police escort. There you will be met by the Provost and Lord Darrochy. If all goes well, five minutes later, you Mr Ambassador and Mr Jacobsen will arrive in a Land Rover and be met by the Colonel of the Regiment, who will introduce you to the Secretary of State and you will take your seats. The only difference between this and the published plan is that instead of arriving by helicopter and transferring to the Land Rover, you will come by car from where you will have spent the night, and the Land Rover will meet you just outside the town.'

After hearing further details concerning security for the troops on parade and the crowds, the procedure for the Defense Secretary's speech and the arrangements for the receptions after the parade, and after a further period of questions, the Foreign Secretary suggested an adjournment. The Ministers, the Ambassador and the two Generals retired to General Murray's office leaving the others to consider what had come out of the meeting.

'Hugh, the thing that worries me,' Duncan commented, 'is if abseiling proves impossible and the helicopters have to land at a distance, will the attack group be able to achieve their objectives without casualties or, more important, some of the Unicorn people escaping?'

'What about it, Porterfield?' asked Robertson.

'I don't think it's that bad a problem,' answered the SAS man. 'We have been practising in what we believe is similar country and we think that if we can't go directly into their position, we can still abseil. Whatever we do will be preceded by smoke and stun grenades. If we can't go straight in on the site, we will go as near as possible and we should still reach them before the effect of the grenades has worn off. If we have to land at a distance, we will probably use tear gas. Risky, but we should still be successful.'

'OK. But remember, no escapers, especially anyone using any sort of camera. And Jock, your boys will strip them of their uniforms as soon as they are under arrest, won't they? It must not come out that Unicorn used SAS uniforms.'

'Aye, you can be sure of that,' replied Maclay, 'that is, if we get a chance. I don't think Major Porterfield's men will be too pleased to see their uniforms on the enemy!' Then, glancing at his watch, he added, 'Man, I hope they'll not be too long. You and I, Duncan, are on the normal afternoon flight to Inverness and so is Nicholson. And I've an unmarked car waiting there to take you wherever you want.'

Any further discussion was halted by the return of the ministerial party. When they had all resumed their seats, the Foreign Secretary looked down the table, took off his glasses and leaned forward with his fingertips together.

'Gentlemen, we have considered your plan,' he said, 'and we agree that it is the best way to proceed. In fact, it is probably the only way. We have been in touch with Downing Street and I have spoken personally to the Prime Minister. He has agreed that you should go ahead. One thing he has made clear, and that is that under no circumstances must it come out that Unicorn was intending to blame the outrage on the British Government.'

'We have just been discussing that point, sir,' said Robertson, 'and plans are in place to ensure that this cannot happen.'

'Good. Whatever happens on Saturday will, of course, be all over the Sunday papers. The Prime Minister therefore intends to make a short broadcast on Sunday evening. The Scottish Secretary will coordinate the content of this and his Press Officer will attend the post-parade press conference. General Murray will be in overall control of the operation and confirmation of all this will be sent from Downing Street to Scottish Command and to the Chief Constable of Inverness-shire.'

Then, after a pause, he continued, 'I think that is all. So it just remains for me to thank you all for completing a very complex plan on a very testing time scale; and finally to wish you good luck on Saturday. We simply cannot afford a failure. And now, are we all ready to leave?'

'Yes indeed, the car and the plane are waiting,' said General Murray, 'and the helicopter is ready to take the fleet party to Invergordon.'

With goodbyes all round, the General escorted his senior guests to their cars. A few minutes later he returned accompanied by the CIGS, who said that he wanted a meeting with the soldiers and the two naval officers.

'I would really like you there, Forsyth,' he added, 'but I understand you must get back to Inverness.'

'I must, sir,' replied Duncan. 'I must see if our bugging operations have produced any information. I don't want to be caught by a sudden change of plan by Unicorn.'

A somewhat agitated ADC then appeared and announced that the car for Messrs Forsyth and Maclay was waiting, and if they did not leave at once they would miss their plane.

'Off you go then, and good luck,' said the CIGS, and the others echoed his sentiments.

When they arrived at Inverness Airport, a plain clothes man came up to Maclay. He was introduced to Duncan as his driver. He picked up the brief case and roll of charts and then asked where they wanted to go.

'First, I think, to the Urquhart house to see if the bug has produced anything, then to Fort George. We have a final briefing later tonight,' was Duncan's reply.

'Aye, well in that case I think Nick had better go with you to the house. He can then come back to HQ and report anything interesting. When will we see you again?'

'I'll ring this evening from the Fort and I'll come in sometime tomorrow. I'll need to let you know when. OK? Good. Then come on Nick, let's get going.'

While this conversation had been taking place, Duncan, out of the corner of his eye, had noticed Jane Parsons by the news stand, idly turning the pages of a magazine and, as they moved towards the door, she slipped out ahead of them. Hoping that she did not realise he had seen her, Duncan followed Nicholson to the car. As soon as they moved off, Duncan asked the driver if he thought they were being followed.

'Aye,' the man said, 'there's a wee blue car pulled in right behind us. I think the driver is the lassie who went out just ahead of us.'

Duncan turned to Nicholson and explained the problem. 'Jane Parsons is following us,' he said, 'so we obviously cannot go to her house. What to do?'

Nicholson leaned forward and told the driver to go to the Ness Bank Hotel. 'It's a big hotel the other side of the river,' he explained to Duncan, 'and they have a lot of functions there. When we stop, the driver will open the door and we will march in as though we were important guests. I know the manager, so leave the rest to me.'

As soon as they were in the hotel, Nicholson asked if the manager was in and was told he was in his office.

'Quick. In there,' and Duncan found himself bundled unceremoniously through the office door. With a hurried 'I'll explain in a moment, Donnie,' Nicholson went back to Reception and told the girl that if anyone was asking for them to say they were guests arriving for some party.

'Fine, Mr Nicholson,' the girl replied, 'we have a Distillers' Dinner this evening. I'm thinking you will be the privileged guests!'

When Nicholson got back to the manager's office and explained the situation, the manager suggested that they should go out the back way to where his car was parked.

'I'll get one of the porters to drive you wherever you want,' he said, 'and I'll have someone tell your driver to go – where? police HQ – fine. Cathy will deal with the woman, don't worry.'

The manager's car took them to a street round the corner from the Urquhart house, where they found an unmarked police car. When they got in, Nicholson asked the driver if he had heard anything. Apparently there had been a call earlier in the day, but the person they wanted was out. Here the constable looked at his watch.

'They'll be ringing back any moment, sir,' he said, 'and just before you arrived, a young woman drove up to the house. Here, put these headphones on.'

No sooner had Duncan done so, than he heard a telephone ring and Jane's voice answered.'

'Listen now,' a man's voice said, 'meet us tomorrow morning, ten o'clock, at the Clava Hotel. Know it?' When Jane answered that she knew it fine, the man's voice said 'OK, see you there,' and rang off.

Duncan took off the headphones and turned to Nicholson. 'Jane is meeting them at the Clava Hotel at ten tomorrow morning. Can we bug it? Now I must go. Can you send a car to the Fort at eight-thirty? I'd better meet you at HQ and we can go out to Clava together.'

'Do what I can,' he replied, 'and now I think we'd best walk to HQ and I'll have a car take you to Fort George.'

Chapter 22

Duncan arrived at the police HQ the next morning to be greeted by Nicholson with the news that there had been no further activity on the Urquhart bug.

'Do you want to keep that bug going?' he asked, 'I'm not terrible keen on leaving these things in place too long, so think about it. But now listen for a minute. At the Clava Hotel we've managed to get one of our young woman Detective Constables taken on as a temporary cleaner. So when our friends are nicely settled, she'll just happen to be putting out clean ashtrays and she'll put a special one as near them as possible. It's a nice wee device. Just an ordinary ashtray but with a built-in bug.'

'Excellent!' said Duncan. 'Now, as far as the bug in the house is concerned – yes, I think we should keep it there. It just might tell us something more and that, I think, is worth the risk of it being found.'

'OK – now, are you ready to move? If so, I think we should get out to the hotel. We have a small problem there which I will explain to you on the way out.'

When they got outside they found the same car and driver as on the previous night and, as they drove towards Culloden Moor, Nicholson explained that the remote location of the hotel made it difficult to position a vehicle within range of the bug without it being obvious.

'We canna put it in the car park or at the roadside without somebody wondering what men with earphones are doing,' he said, 'so what we've done is to borrow a Post Office Telephones van and park it in a field, with a ladder up the nearest pole. You and I, with our headsets, will be safely out of sight in the van.'

'Sounds fine,' commented Duncan, 'but how will we know that they have arrived and how many of them there are?'

'Constable Gunn here. He will be in the car in the car park,' replied Nicholson, 'and he will be in touch with us by radio and will let us know of all arrivals. He will appear to be a salesman checking his papers before calling on the hotel, and we'll just have to hope no one notices the extra aerial.'

Five minutes later they emerged from a wood and saw the hotel half a mile ahead. They drove on past it for two hundred yards and then pulled into a gateway. As Nicholson had said, there they found a van parked beside a telephone pole. The back was open and a man was unloading a reel of cable. As they drew up, he walked over to the car.

'We're all set up,' he said, 'although I dinna think anyone's arrived yet; but you'd best get in and let the car get away to the car park so we can test the link. I'll just go on fiddling with bits of cable and going up and down the ladder.'

The interior of the van had the usual shelves filled with the paraphernalia required to repair telephone lines. However one of the shelves had been cleared and a police radio, equipped to listen to the bug, had been installed. Nicholson picked up a headset and fiddled with the dials.

Duncan meanwhile took a small pair of binoculars from his pocket and found that by looking out of the van's rear window he could just see the road in front of the hotel where, a few moments later, their car came into view and turned left round the side of the building.

'That's good,' he said to Nicholson, 'I can just see the front of the hotel – and wait – yes, there's a car arriving. It has a woman driver. I think it is Jane Parsons but I can't be sure.'

'Aye, well it is,' replied the Inspector, 'Gunn has just said a woman has gone into the hotel. The same one as was at the airport last evening.'

During the next twenty minutes a number of vehicles drove past the hotel. Most went on down the road but two vans and a car turned into the hotel. Gunn reported that the vans were local firms making deliveries, and that there was just one man in the car, whom he recognised as a well known Inverness solicitor.

'Probably acts for the hotel,' Duncan thought to himself. Then out loud he added, 'I hope, Nick, that nothing untoward has happened. Just our luck if everything's cocked up by them crashing on the way here.'

'No, no. Never fear, they'll turn up all right,' Nicholson answered; then a minute or two later, holding up his hand for silence, he listened intently on the headphones. Eventually he looked up and said, 'I told you so. That was Gunn to say that two men have just walked in by the back way. One is a redhead and the other is an Inverness man who he thinks he's seen before. Sounds like Urquhart and Crawford, doesn't it? Wait now – he's saying something else. Aye, he thinks they've left their car down the road. Here, you'd better put on the other headset. Things could happen gie quick now.'

No sooner had Duncan done so than he heard Gunn's voice saying that the girl had signalled that the bug was in place. Nicholson immediately switched to another channel and the next thing they heard was Roddy Urquhart.

'Sorry we're late, Janie,' he said, 'but there was a lot of traffic which made it difficult to tell if we were being followed. Just in case we were, I thought it best to leave the car at the farm down the road. I know the people there well. So we went in the front and out the back, then down the track to here.

Now what have you got to say?'

'Not a lot,' Jane replied, 'I saw Forsyth at the airport and followed him to a hotel. Somehow though, he tricked me. The hotel said he was some important distiller there for a dinner. While they were telling me this, he must have got out the back door to another car. I never saw him again. I think he was with a policeman. So what's happened down at the castle?'

'Right. Three things to tell you. First we move up today. In fact they should be on their way now. As soon as we've finished here, I'll be away to the Black Isle to see all is ready. Fergus can go back to the town with you and stay there, for he has a job at the parade ground on Saturday. That's the second thing to tell you about – what will happen if everything goes wrong.'

'I was going to ask if we had a plan to deal with that happening,' said Jane. Then, after a pause, 'Have we any reason – any new reason – to think it will?'

'Aye, we have that,' Roddy answered, 'for we don't know what those bloody fools Vass and Macneil may have told the police – not that they knew much. However, as they were chasing Forsyth, someone must have guessed that there's something up. Anyway, here's what we have planned.'

'Hold on a moment,' came Jane's voice, interrupting her brother-in-law, 'before you tell me that, just tell me the next step if we are successful.'

'Och that will just happen,' and here Fergus took up the story. 'It will be all over the evening papers and the Sundays will make a right meal of it. On Sunday afternoon and Monday there will be rallies in Edinburgh, Glasgow and other big towns. Aye, and then on Monday questions in Parliament and we're well on our way.'

'That's roughly true,' said Roddy, 'but leave it for now and I'll fill in the details later. It's the fall-back plan that's more important, for you have a part to play in that. If things go wrong at the missile site, we will get a message to you and Fergus at the parade ground. You will wait to see if Jacobsen arrives and the parade goes ahead. If there's no sign of him and there are announcements, then you scatter and follow the instructions I will give in a moment. If things appear to be going ahead, here's the plan and I'll let Fergus tell you about the first part of it.'

'I have a friend,' said Fergus, 'a sympathiser, and he has the contract for the loudspeaker system at the park. I will be the man on duty and early on Saturday I will fit a wee device to the mike, with a radio link to another gadget in my pocket. It was provided by our French friends. If I get the word, as soon as the American gets up to speak, I shall press a button and he'll get his head blown off.'

'OK Jane?' said Roddy breaking in, 'so now here's your part. Suppose things go wrong due to what I would call enemy action. They, the enemy, will have people at the park who will also have been alerted. My guess is that one of them will be Forsyth, and that he will be on the lookout for Unicorn members – remember he knows most of us by sight. Now it is vital for our success that neither Fergus nor yourself are arrested. As soon as you see Jacobsen collapse, you must create a diversion. I'll tell you how later, and in the confusion you must both get away.'

'That's all very well,' Jane's voice came on again, 'but what good is all this going to do? It sounds like plain murder to me – an act of revenge. And just tell me how that advances the cause of independence.'

'That's all taken care of,' was Urquhart's reply. 'Our press people will still release the story implicating the Government in a failed attempt to shoot down the helicopter and showing how, finally, they resorted to murder to try and stop Jacobsen speaking.'

'I don't like it a bit,' came Jane's voice.

'Well, you'll just have to do it. It's all agreed, so don't you argue, my girl.' Urquhart had raised his voice and the sound was becoming distorted. Duncan thought he heard someone say 'and now to what happens at the castle . . .' and then the headset went quiet.

'Damn and blast,' he said, 'we seem to have lost them. I don't mind about the castle bit, although I do hope they are not going to harm the old man. But I did want to hear their escape plans.'

Nicholson meanwhile was fiddling with the set and getting nowhere. Finally he switched back to Gunn in the car and found that link still working. He explained to the constable what had happened and told him that when the three left the hotel, he was to try to find out where they went.

'But for God's sake, go careful. They must not know they are under observation. Keep in touch with us. We'll pack up the van and be ready to follow.'

It was some twenty minutes before the message came from Gunn that all three had left the hotel in Jane's car and driven off towards the main road. Now it happened that Gunn was a local man and the next word they got from him was that he was following the car, but on another road.

'I can see them fine,' he reported, 'but they canna see me. Aye, now wait a bit, sir, they've just stopped at Logie farm. The two men have got out – they are having a word wi' the farmer – now they've got into another car and both cars are off on the Inverness road. I'll follow . . . no, they'll not see me.'

'Right,' said Nicholson to the van driver, 'drive slowly on down the road towards the town.'

Then followed a long period of silence, broken eventually by Gunn's voice on the radio saying that both cars had turned into the driveway of a house.

'It's the same house as you were at last night. What will I do – sit and watch? They'll not notice me for I'm quite a way back.'

'Yes, tell him to stay there,' Duncan said to Nicholson. 'My guess is that

Urquhart will leave the others there and go out to the Black Isle by himself. At least I think that's what I heard him say. I'd dearly like to follow him, but I'll need a car. An unofficial and unrecognisable car.'

'You can have my own car,' said Nicholson. 'It's at HQ, so we'd best get down there quick.'

A short while later Duncan, in Nicholson's inconspicuous Ford, pulled in behind the police car, some hundred yards short of the Urquhart house. The constable walked over to him.

'You are just in time,' he said. 'One of the men, the dark one, he's the owner I think, has just come out and put something in the car. Aye, here he is again and it looks as though he's off this time.'

Sure enough, Urquhart walked out followed by his wife. She kissed him and said something. He nodded, got into his car, a black Rover 2000, and reversed out of the drive. With a hurried instruction to Gunn to report what was happening, Duncan got into the Ford and eased out from the kerb.

They went down the hill, over the river and, avoiding the ferry, took the main road to the north. Eventually, beyond Beauly, they turned off and headed for the centre of the Black Isle. Then, just after they had entered a thickly wooded area, Duncan, who was keeping well back, rounded a sharp bend to see the car ahead turn off the road and drive up a track towards the centre of a young plantation.

He drove slowly on past the entrance to the track, but could see no sign of the car. A hundred yards further on, at a point where a thick clump of whins gave some cover, he pulled off the road and got out a map. It appeared that the track led to a building of some sort. 'Probably was a croft back in the days before this was planted,' he thought, 'and I'll bet it's now a ruin and the surroundings all overgrown. An ideal firing site for the missile. What's more, it looks as though the path doesn't go on beyond the ruin, so presumably he'll have to come back down this way.'

Duncan made a note of the map reference and then, still under cover of the whins, got the car ready to follow Urquhart whichever way he went. He would dearly have liked to get out and try to get a closer look at the interior of the plantation, but he reckoned it was too risky. He might be seen and also Urquhart might get away and leave him stranded some way from his car.

His reasoning turned out to be correct, for Urquhart's reconnaissance took him no more than five minutes, and when he emerged from the trees he turned west on the main road and drove off in a great hurry. It was this speed that was Duncan's undoing for, on a winding stretch of road, he lost sight of the Rover and when he reached the next straight there was no sign of any car.

It was unusual for Duncan Forsyth to allow his concentration to lapse, but on this occasion he did, for instead of continuing at a steady pace and trusting to luck to catch up with his quarry, he increased his speed. Emerging fast from the woods, he nearly collided with a lorry which was grinding along at twenty miles an hour in the middle of the road. Throwing caution to the winds he decided to overtake, regardless of the fact that they were approaching the crest of the hill. He got away with it, just, and not without a furious blast on the lorry's ancient klaxon. As he breasted the rise, there, two hundred yards ahead, was Urquhart driving along quite normally and apparently untroubled by anything. Duncan immediately slowed, cursed himself for a fool, and for his pains got another blast on the klaxon.

'Where the hell had he got to?' he wondered, 'and does he know he is being followed? Probably yes; and does he know who by? Again probably yes.'

On the basis of this analysis, he decided there was no alternative but to proceed as though nothing had happened. Urquhart was now driving much slower, but as he knew the road, he was making it difficult for Duncan to keep him in sight without getting too close. This became even more difficult when they came down off the higher ground and crossed another main road, for here there were farms and houses everywhere and considerably more traffic. At one point, indeed, when the Rover was held up behind a tractor and trailer, Duncan found himself only fifty yards back with just one other car between them.

There he remained until, at the beginning of a short straight, Urquhart got past the tractor and raced ahead. 'He's trying to drop me, damn him.'

And with that thought, unaware that he was approaching a cross-roads, he pulled out to pass both car and tractor. There was a squeal of brakes, a great deal of hooting and, as he roared over the crossing, Duncan saw out of the corner of his eye a car sliding towards him from the right. He just squeezed past and as he raced on down the straight, he looked in the mirror. The car had just missed both him and the tractor and had stopped the other side of the cross-road. The tractor and trailer had jackknifed and the car behind it had its nose in the bank.

'A lot of bad temper, I think. But no damage or casualties. Best keep well out of it and continue in the line of duty,' was Duncan's reaction.

The decision was reinforced when he saw the Rover skid round to the right and vanish into a clump of trees. When he reached the spot, Duncan found what had once been the front entrance to a considerable demesne, with ruined stone pillars leading to a long weed-covered drive which ended in a slight rise.

Feeling he was better off away from the main road and the recent accident, he turned through the old gateway and drove briskly up the track. There was no sign of the Rover and there did not appear to be any turnings it could have taken. That is, until he neared the top of the rise. There the drive appeared to curve round to the left, and the way ahead to be blocked by a somewhat straggly hedge.

Perhaps he approached the crest too fast; perhaps he should not have taken it for granted that there was no way ahead. However, that is what he did and as he swung round to the left, Duncan realised too late that he was no longer on the track but in a narrow open space amongst the trees which appeared to end in nothing.

He braked violently but the tyres got no grip on the damp grass. The car spun round twice, plunged over the far edge of the clearing and landed on its roof half way down a steep bank before rolling over again and subsiding, nose first, into the muddy waters of what had once been an ornamental lake.

As happens on these occasions, the noise of the accident was followed by silence except for the scuttering of a family of ducks and the hiss and tinkle of cooling metal. Eventually, when even these noises had ceased, Roddy Urquhart emerged from the trees and clambered down the bank towards the wrecked car. The bonnet was now sunk deep in the mud, leaving only the top of the rear seat and the boot visible, the rest being obscured by the murky waters of the lake. Try as he would, Urquhart could not see inside the car, and short of getting a frogman's suit, could see no hope of doing so.

'He must be in there,' he concluded, 'for there's no way he could have got out.' But for all that he set about searching the immediate surroundings. Apart from a lack of boots and the vicious brambles, this was not difficult, for as yet the undergrowth had little leaf. But after twenty minutes of hard work and finding nothing, he decided his original conclusion was right and that Duncan Forsyth was lying drowned in the wreckage of his car. Furthermore it could be some time before he was discovered, for few people came by that way.

It was the slam of a car door and the sound of an engine fading into the distance that first impinged on Forsyth's consciousness and he cautiously opened his eyes. To start with all he could see was some very muddy water; but then, as feeling returned to his limbs, he realised that some heavy object was lying across the back of his right leg. The pain of this brought about a complete return of his senses and by twisting his head round, he could see that he was lying in the middle of a thick bush and that he was pinned there by a fallen branch. Moving cautiously, for he had no idea what other dangers there were, he managed to get on to his left knee and, with his shoulder, to lift the branch sufficiently to wriggle free.

With great care he raised his head and peered through the branches of the bush. He could see no one and he could hear nothing. Nevertheless he decided to remain a little longer under cover and during the wait his memory gradually returned. There had been a car, he thought, and a long gravel road. But how he got from the car to a clump of broom beside a muddy pond he had no idea.

Ten minutes or so later, having heard nothing, he decided it would be safe to move; so he rolled over and crawled towards the edge of the lake. The cold water he splashed over his head and neck served to complete his recovery, and he clambered up the bank and looked around.

As soon as he saw the end of the car sticking up from the water, he remembered exactly what had happened. He had been following Urquhart's car and had lost it after it turned into the old driveway. He had turned left at the top of the little hill and found himself no longer on the road, but in the clearing where he was now standing. He looked down at the grass and saw skid marks which showed only too clearly what had happened. As the car spun round, the weight of his body must have forced the door open. Then, as it pitched over the edge, he had been flung clear. He walked over and looking down the bank, saw that the bush which had saved him from injury had also saved him from discovery, for between it and where the car plunged into the lake was a deep, reed-fringed inlet.

'Speed sometimes pays and, come to that, so does having to deal with an amateur opponent,' he thought. 'For Urquhart must have come looking. So if I had not been thrown that far and he had not wanted to keep his feet dry, I would surely have been found. Pity about Nick's car,' he added with a wry smile, 'but I expect the Chief will pay!'

He scrambled up the bank again and walked across the clearing to the gravel track. Looking to the left, he realised that from the top of the rise the drive sloped sharply down, and that what he had taken for a hedge was the top of a line of tall trees some thirty yards away. At the bottom of the hill was a clearing and through his binoculars, which together with his map were still in his pocket, he could see traces of what had once been a considerable mansion, with shrubberies and woods behind. The map showed a track through these woods leading to a minor road which would take him, eventually, back to the main Beauly road.

Keeping in the cover of the trees, he made his way down the hill and through the shrubbery to the wood. The track, when he finally found it, was badly overgrown but just passable. After crossing an old railway bridge, however, it improved considerably and was obviously used by the locals for their Sunday afternoon walks and, apparently, other forms of recreation; for a couple of hundred yards ahead, just before it joined the road, leaning against the dyke were two bicycles.

Keeping below the level of the dyke, Duncan reached the bicycles. He could see no sign of anybody and was just about to stand up when from the undergrowth beyond came quickly suppressed laughter. He waited a moment but heard nothing more, so still moving quietly, he took the larger bike and pushed it cautiously towards the road. Across the handlebars was one of those thick woollen jackets in a vivid red and black tartan. For extra camouflage he put it on, and pedalled off towards the main road. He felt sorry for the bicycle owners and hoped their afternoon had been worth it, for they had a long walk before them.

His tartan jacket served him better than expected, for as he waited to turn on to the main road north of Beauly, the Rover, with Urquhart at the wheel, drew up beside him. The driver gave no more than a cursory glance in his direction before pulling out in front of him and heading south at speed. Duncan followed at a more sedate pace on his bicycle and ten minutes later arrived at Beauly Police Station. There, having identified himself to the Sergeant, he rang Inverness and was put straight through to Maclay.

'What the hell are you doing in Beauly?' he was asked, 'we need you here at once. We have just had word from the Argyll force that things are happening at the castle.'

He explained himself quickly and asked that a meeting at Fort George be arranged as soon as possible. He was just asking for a car to be sent for him when the Sergeant interrupted.

'Sir, the south train will be in in five minutes,' he said, 'and you're maybe quicker to take that.'

Duncan nodded and suggested the idea to Maclay, who was worried about security.

'I don't think we need worry about that. If what you say is true, they will all be far too occupied with the move to be watching stations. And anyway, Urquhart thinks I'm dead and you can bet he's wasted no time in telling them that. Have a car meet me at the station.' And before there could be any more argument he rang off, thanked the Sergeant, jumped on his bike and raced for the station, to hear whistles blowing and doors slamming. Leaving the bike against a wall, he ran through the ticket office and before anybody could stop him, he jumped into the last carriage as the train gathered speed.

Having finally been convinced that rail was the best way, Maclay was as good as his word. As the train pulled in, he and Nicholson were on the platform standing by a car, its blue light flashing. As Duncan jumped down, Nicholson hustled him into the car, Maclay said a word to the guard and they swept out through the cattle market. As they turned in the direction of Nairn, Duncan looked at Maclay and said, 'I don't know what you were telling the guard, but I might as well tell you that I had paid the fare!'

'Aye, but it's just as well to be sure of these things. And now what's all this about one of my officers' cars? Lost it in a lochan, have you, Duncan Forsyth?'

Nicholson, who was sitting in the front, turned round and Duncan looked across at him. 'Nick, I really am sorry,' he said, 'I simply missed the road, skidded, and the next thing I remember is coming to in the middle of a clump of broom – and later finding the car nose down in the mud of an old garden lake. But there are two good things about it. First, as far as I know, Unicorn now thinks I'm dead. This just might make them a bit careless. Secondly, from your point of view, you will get a brand new car, courtesy of my firm, and not a stain on your insurance! Oh yes, and tomorrow I'll arrange for a temporary hire. Incidentally I hope there was nothing important in the car, for I'd be happier if it was left where it was until after Saturday, although what we do if someone reports it, I don't know,'

'Not very likely, for very few people go that way, but we have warned the Ross-shire force and they will see it's kept quiet,' replied Nicholson. 'And don't you worry about it, it was all in the line of duty!'

'Och well, I'm not sure of that,' said Maclay with one of his rare grins. 'I can see we'll have every officer north of Perth offering their cars for special operations in the hope of getting a new one from the secret funds.'

At Fort George they found Brigadier Robertson, Porterfield the SAS man, and the two naval officers waiting for them in what was now the operational control centre. The middle of the room was occupied by a table on which was a large scale map of the whole Moray Firth area dotted with coloured pins, some joined by lengths of red and green tape. There was another long table with a battery of telephones and three chairs for the officers in charge, and at one end of the room two signallers were setting up the command wireless links.

Duncan walked over to the map and said: 'Let's have a full report on the current situation. The police first, please, on what is happening at Altachonich.'

In response to a nod from Maclay, Nicholson explained that they had been informed by the Oban police that a lorry with a load of timber and something covered by a tarpaulin had left the estate early that morning. It was now heading north from Fort William and was under observation by his men. Some time later they had another report that a cattle float had come down off the hill, apparently with a load of sheep. Its exact location was not known but they hoped to pick it up soon and any information would be passed to him at once.

'OK Nick, that's excellent,' said Duncan, 'but ring your HQ soon and get an update. And now I think you'd better hear what I have been doing. First we managed to listen in on a meeting between Urquhart and Jane Parsons and her brother and got some useful information. Notwithstanding all that has happened, they have decided to go ahead. Customs have done a great job in keeping secret the arrest of the trawler. If that had got out, it would have blown the whole thing. Then they confirmed that they intended to move today. Well, as we know, they have already started.'

He then went on to explain about the Unicorn fall-back plan and the booby-trapped microphone. He gave it as his opinion that they should be prepared to arrest Crawford and Parsons as soon as the decoy helicopter left the US carrier.

'It will only be a matter of minutes later that it will be over the launch site and we cannot risk any communication between the missile crew and the parade ground,' he said. 'Crawford is an unstable character and if he knows things have gone wrong, he's quite capable of firing that explosive device the moment he sees Jacobsen. In that case God knows what damage he might do. I'll give my detailed plans for dealing with this later – oh yes, and do we have a bomb disposal man handy? If so, I'll need him there. The other piece of information I had hoped to get from this bugging exercise was their dispersal plan in the event of failure, and what they proposed to do at the castle. Unfortunately as they started discussing that, our link went dead and we heard no more.'

He then turned to the map table and beckoned the others over. He took a crumpled paper from his pocket, checked the figures on it and then, picking up a pointer, he indicated a spot in the middle of the Black Isle.

'After our friends left the hotel where they were meeting, we had them followed back to Urquhart's house. I had a feeling that Urquhart might decide on a visit to the Black Isle to check preparations, so I borrowed Inspector Nicholson's car and prepared to follow Urquhart if he moved. Sure enough, it was not long before he emerged and drove out of the town and on to the main north road. Eventually we turned off on to one of the roads to Cromarty.' Here Duncan used the pointer to trace his route on the map. 'When Urquhart got to here – and I was rounding this corner, I was just in time to see him turn off the road to the left. Well, I drove on and it became obvious he had gone up this track – here. Now that was a bit of luck. As you see, there is a ruin there – in the middle of the wood – and no track on beyond. It seems unlikely that that would be an overnight parking place, so it's reasonable to assume that it is the missile firing position.'

Robertson bent over to get a closer look at the area that Forsyth had indicated, then looked up and turned to Porterfield.

'Looks OK for your operation doesn't it?' he said, 'but I would like to get a look at it to see how we can work the diversion and no-shot plans. And I expect you'd like a look too, Sam. Any chance of a chopper?'

The two naval officers looked at each other, walked away a few paces and held a short consultation.

'How many need to go on this recce?' the Lossiemouth man asked.

'Well myself and Major Porterfield and the Infantry Company Commander,' Robertson replied. 'What about you Duncan?' Forsyth shook his head. 'And what about your pilots, Sam?'

'No need,' replied the SAS man, 'I can brief them myself.'

'That's three then,' Robertson concluded.

A further consultation between the naval airmen resulted in the USN commander saying, 'I guess the other person who would like a look is the guy who will be flying the decoy on Saturday. Now we have a chopper goes over every morning to the airport and then on to the RAF at Kinloss. I guess you could call it the mail run, so it causes no interest. If you, Brigadier, can get yourself and your boys to the pier at Invergordon at eight-thirty tomorrow, we'll fly you over the site and back.'

'That's very good of you, Commander, eight-thirty it is. OK, Duncan, so you've found the firing point. Did you have a look for the harbouring locations, if so what luck?'

'I tried, but my luck ran out,' Duncan replied with a smile. 'When Urquhart returned to the main road, I followed him back for four or five miles. Eventually he turned into some sort of driveway where I missed the way and finished up with the car in a muddy lake and myself unconscious in a clump of broom! And I'm sure that's what he meant me to do.'

'Did he find you?' asked Robertson.

'I don't think so,' Duncan answered, 'but I think he came to look – or someone did – for I'm sure the thing that brought me round was the noise of a car driving off. He must have seen the car but failed to find me, for if he had, he'd hardly have left me. So presumably they think I'm dead.'

'What about the car? Won't there be questions if it's found?' asked Robertson.

'We've got the Ross-shire police keeping an eye on it. It's in the policies of the old House of Pitgairn. A great barracks of a place it was, that was pulled down some years ago. Not many folks go that way. It has a kinda queer reputation,' said Maclay.

'And now what about you, Hugh?' enquired Forsyth, looking round and addressing Robertson, 'have the SAS and the other army units arrived and are they ready to move?'

'One SAS troop will be at Fort George by midday tomorrow. The other troop will move independently to Invergordon, where it will be taken on board a British aircraft carrier and be ready for action by 1600 hours,' replied Robertson. 'Then as far as the rest are concerned, there are two infantry companies at Fort George. One will provide the diversion, the other will support the police at the road blocks. We also have all the necessary support available.'

'What about the road blocks? Where will they be and how will you account for them to the local population?' Duncan asked.

'Thirty minutes before the helicopter leaves Invergordon, all the main exits from the Black Isle will be blocked by cones and patrol cars,' replied Maclay. 'They will be supported by armed troops. In the event of our plan failing and Unicorn attempting a mass escape, the roads will be blocked with wire barricades and the troops deployed to prevent these being crashed or by-passed. Anyone asking about the presence of the police and army will be told it's all part of the NATO exercises. It always works!'

'By the way, I have arranged for all the road block sites to be under observation from tonight,' Robertson said. 'And no, nobody will see the observers – they will be snipers and are used to that sort of operation.'

After another hour of discussion the meeting broke up and agreed to reconvene for a final briefing the next morning, after the return of the helicopter reconnaissance party.

Chapter 23

It was a cold damp morning when the timber lorry drove out of the estate yard and down the steep track towards the quarry. The heavy cloud cover meant it was still dark and the driver had to use his lights to negotiate the sharp corners. With the missile launcher not yet loaded, the stack of pine trunks at the rear of the platform was making the lorry unstable and he was worried about pitching off the narrow roadway and crashing to the shore below. He equally knew that Simpson would be unhappy that he had used his lights, but he reckoned that that was the lesser evil.

The quarry was in complete darkness and he had to keep his lights on to avoid hitting the piles of rock and bits of old machinery with which the floor was littered. As he pulled up beside the building where the missile was stored, a furious Simpson appeared in the big double doorway.

'Put those bloody lights out,' he roared, 'I thought I told you not to use them. Do you want the whole neighbourhood to know what we're at?'

'Ay, and do you want the truck wrecked on the shore before we even start?' the driver shouted back. 'Look, boy, you're going to have to put the lights on for us to load unless you want an accident. I canna operate the crane in the dark and I must get this thing of yours properly fixed. It's a gie heavy load and I canna tak' any risks.'

'Oh all right,' Simpson growled and, looking up at the sky, added, 'it's getting lighter anyway. Come on Jack, let's have the launcher out and on the lorry double quick, for I want you on your way without delay '

At a nod from Simpson the two men turned and walked into the building. Moments later the lights came on and there was the sound of an engine starting. The driver walked slowly round to the controls of the hoist and swung the jib out towards the doors just as the fork-lift with the launcher drove out. Chains were already in position, the hook was attached and the heavy device was swung gently into place immediately in front of the timber. The fork-lift was driven back into the store and minutes later returned with the missiles. These were in a wooden cradle and held in place by thin metal straps. The chains were placed under the cradle and the missiles lifted into position in front of the launcher.

The driver picked up two tarpaulins and flung one over the launcher and the other over the missiles. Both were then expertly roped, the hoist was returned to its rest position and, after a quick final check, Jack turned to Simpson.

'Aye man, that's everything,' he said, 'and if ye've nothing else to say, we'll get going. See you on the Black Isle.'

'You've got all the papers for the timber and the machinery?' asked Simpson and when the driver said they had, he added, 'Right then, away wi' you, but for God's sake go careful. We don't want you stopped for some minor driving offence.'

With that Simpson turned on his heel and walked away towards the office. The two men climbed into the cab, the engine started and the lorry, with its deadly load, lurched off down the shore road and ground its way slowly up the track towards the cliff top.

About the same time as they were loading the missile equipment, the head shepherd was driving his pick-up out to the fank below Meall Garbh. He parked there and, whistling for his two dogs, set off across the shoulder of the hill. Two hours and a great deal of hard work later he returned, driving a flock of some fifty ewes. Having got these safely into the fank, he proceeded to sort out the thirty that were to go up north.

While he was doing this, the cattle truck appeared and backed up to the gate of the fank. The driver got out, lowered the ramp and then walked round to help the shepherd. Another half hour saw the sorting finished and the required thirty ewes safely loaded. The shepherd walked over to the pick-up and came back with a flask and the two men sat down for an early piece.

'When yon panel's been fitted, thirty ewes will look about right in the back of the float,' the shepherd said.

'Aye, it should be fine.' The driver was a man of few words. 'And now I'd best be off. You staying here?'

'Uh uh. Jim'll be out soon,' replied the shepherd; then nodding towards the sheep, 'we'll do their feet then. But now, good luck to you,' adding under his breath, 'ye'll surely need it,' as the truck drove off in the direction of a small plantation about a mile down the hill and on the edge of the lower track.

The plantation was in the shape of a U, and such was the lie of the land that anything in the centre of the U was pretty well invisible. So good a place of concealment was it, that it was not until the cattle truck turned off the track that the driver realised that the two Land Rovers had already arrived.

The parts of the wooden partition had been unloaded and, as soon as the truck stopped, two men opened the small side door, jumped in and urged the sheep to the rear. Ten minutes later the partition was in place and the floor of the compartment swept. In another twenty minutes all the equipment had been loaded and secured. Then the men who were to accompany it climbed in and seated themselves as comfortably as possible on the various packing cases.

The foreman, Peter, after a final look to see that everything was correctly loaded, jumped down, closed the door and turned to Simpson.

'That's it then,' he said, 'will we be off now?'

'Yeah,' Simpson replied, 'and the second Land Rover can go with you, so all of you on board except you, Findlay; you can come with me. We'll follow on as soon as I've had a word with the laird. All ready now? OK then – let's get moving.'

As soon as he saw the two vehicles safely out on the track and driving off in the direction of the castle, Simpson climbed into the other Land Rover and followed them down to the Glenlochan road. At the castle gates he stopped and watched them until they turned in the direction of Fort William, then he drove round to the stable yard and walked across to the back door of the castle.

Unknown to Simpson, all the morning's comings and goings had been watched by Dougie Fletcher and Constable Cameron from a well concealed hide in the trees above the road. When the Land Rover disappeared in the direction of the stables, the stalker lowered his glass.

'Well now, what do you make of that?' he said to the policeman.

'They're on the move, as Mr Forsyth said they'd be. That stuff under the tarpaulins on the timber lorry, that'll likely be the weapon or whatever it is. But what about the cattle float?'

'That was queer enough,' the keeper said. 'Did you see that the sheep were all penned at the back end, so they must have a separate compartment up the front and what's the reason for that? They'll mebbe have other equipment, and possibly even some of the men, in there. Aye, that'll be it. And those two drivers – and the shepherd forbye – they'll all be in the plot. Bastards!'

'You're likely right,' Cameron replied, 'so I'd best get back to the car and report what's happening. Will you keep watch, Dougie? I wonder why Simpson's gone down to the castle?'

'He'll be wanting to tell the laird they've gone, I expect. Anyway I'll go down later and see that the old man's all right. Now boy, you get that report off soonest.'

Simpson, meanwhile made his way through the castle to Sir Torquhil's study, where he found the laird sitting at his desk and staring out across the loch, his shoulders drooped and wearing an expression of the utmost gloom. He waved the manager to a chair.

'Did you see that, Simpson?' he said without moving, his voice heavy with doom.

'Did I see what?' Simpson asked, somewhat taken aback.

'No, you wouldn't have done,' Sir Torquhil said, almost to himself, 'and if you had, you would not have known the meaning.' Then he continued barely above a whisper. 'Well, I'll tell you. I've just seen an eagle sail down from the crags of Meall Buidhe, and there was a pair of ravens after it. It was coming down all the time so that when it reached the loch it was almost on the water. Then the ravens left it. But the eagle, it went on out to sea getting lower and lower all the time, until it vanished beneath the waves. And that's what the rhymer says in the Curse of Altachonich.

> The chastened eagle leaves the sky
> To tell Maclean 'Prepare to die'.
> And should it fly beneath the waves,
> 'Thy cause is lost. Prepare the graves.'

It's never failed. After the rising of 1715 Maclean of Altachonich was executed and in 1746 his son fell at Culloden. In both cases an eagle vanished over the loch and there are many earlier stories. My name does not matter. I am the laird of Altachonich and what will be will be. We're fated, Simpson, and the eagle tells us all is lost.'

For once the manager found himself not knowing what to say. He was not a superstitious man and his life had made him contemptuous of fate, but there was enough Highland blood in his veins for him to feel a shiver run down the back of his neck.

One thing, though, he knew for certain; not a word of this must get out, certainly not before Saturday. If it did, curse or no curse, they were lost. He got up and walked over to Sir Torquhil.

'Man, we can't have this sort of talk, you know,' he said, 'everything's in place and going well. The missile and the crew, the uniforms, weapons and other stuff are all on their way to the Black Isle, and don't forget what I told you earlier. Forsyth and your daughter have gone their separate ways. She apparently to wherever she intended to go originally. As for Forsyth, well, you remember that Urquhart reported that his car crashed and he is presumed dead. So he no longer poses a threat and we're going to win – no question – and you'll be at our head when we achieve our goal of Scottish nationhood! Come sir, maybe it was just a dream. Here, let me get you a drink.'

He poured a stiff dram and gave it to the man slumped at the desk. Sir Torquhil looked up and took a sip from the glass. Then he straightened up, swallowed the rest of the whisky and put the glass down.

'You could be right. Perhaps it was just a dream,' he said, though there was doubt in his voice, 'but if you have been brought up with a family curse, and you see the doom – or think you do – it is something of a shock.' He paused – and then, straightening his shoulders, he continued: 'but now, if you say that everything is in train, I'll try and put it to one side. Anyway is there something you want to see me about?'

'Yes, indeed there is,' Simpson answered, 'I want your final agreement to the suggestions I made last night about what happens here at the castle once I've left. First, there is what happens if we are successful. As soon as the helicopter crashes, all the gear at the launch site will be removed to a hiding place only Roddy and a couple of others know about. There should be no question of immediate search or pursuit, for we hope to achieve complete surprise.'

'That's all very well, but once it is realised what has happened and with all the troops and police about, the authorities are not going to sit around and do nothing. How are the men going to get away?'

'Look sir,' Simpson went on, 'with all the chaos there will be in Inverness, in Edinburgh – aye, and in London too – it's going to be a while before proper orders are issued. By that time we will have released our photographs and copies of Jacobsen's speech. The evening papers will have the story all over the front pages and that will cause more confusion. No, there should be no problem in getting the lorries back here and the men will all make their way – singly – to Glasgow, ready for the rallies tomorrow and Monday.'

Simpson walked towards the seated man, his voice rising with excitement. 'You, Sir Torquhil, will make your way to Edinburgh, ready for our great Unicorn press conference and rally. A rally at which we will show that Jacobsen's death was no accident, but a deliberate act of murder! Murder, moreover, of a visitor from a friendly power, undertaken by Government agents to prevent him speaking in favour of freedom for Scotland!'

Overcome with emotion, he paused and leant against the desk before continuing. 'Aye,' he said, his voice now much calmer, 'by the time we've finished our revelations, the Government will find itself with two problems: in Scotland, Unicorn and an outraged Scottish population; in America, a furious US President and Congress.'

'I still don't like it,' said Sir Torquhil, 'suppose we fail; or suppose we are only partially successful? In either case we must assume that it is because we have been discovered by Forsyth and company. There will be troops and police and God knows what waiting for us.'

'If that happens, you know fine what the plan is,' Simpson replied. 'Fergus will do his bit at the parade ground; all the equipment will be left where it is, and everyone who is able will try to get to Glasgow and lie low until told to board a ship for the continent.'

'As for what happens here, Sir Torquhil,' he said, 'you know what you have to do. The store and office are mined. You just fire the charges and then, when the police arrive, you tell a story about the wholesale dismissal of an incompetent work force, some disgruntled members of which appear to have taken revenge on your property.'

Sir Torquhil rose to his feet and stood for a moment staring out of the window. Then he walked over to the fireplace and looked straight at the manager.

'Very well,' he said in his chairman's voice, 'that's it. But just let me tell you that, success or failure, it is my opinion that the aftermath will not be as easy as you are supposing. Now you had better get going, Simpson. There's no time to waste.' With that he turned and walked quickly from the room. What the manager did not see was the curiously distant look in his eyes.

'That's an odd one. We cannot do without him now, but by God I hope he's not going out of his mind,' was Simpson's thought as he made his way back to the Land Rover and drove off towards Fort William.

Minutes after he had watched the Land Rover leave, Dougie was joined again by Cameron, who said that when he gave his report he was told that the timber lorry had already passed Fort William.

'They also want to know if the man Simpson has gone yet,' Cameron added, 'and we are to let them know if Sir Torquhil is still there and is he OK.'

'Simpson and another man have just this minute left,' the keeper said. 'I'll give them fifteen minutes, just to be sure the coast's clear, and then I'll go down and see the laird. He thinks I've taken a pony up north, so I'll have to explain that I couldna' go – a bit problem with the horse box, ye ken,' he added with a grin. 'Just you go and report that and I'll wait till you come back.'

Meanwhile Sir Torquhil had left the castle and walked down towards the pier. It was there that Dougie found him some fifteen minutes later, seated on a bollard and gazing out to sea. He had apparently forgotten that the keeper should be away up north, for when he heard Dougie's footsteps he just looked at him.

'Dougie,' he said, 'you know about the Curse of Altachonich, don't you?'

'Aye, I ken it weel,' the keeper replied.

'Half an hour ago an eagle came down from Meall Buidhe. I saw it plainly, and the two ravens. When they reached the shore, the eagle alone flew out to sea and I watched it till it vanished.' And he resumed his staring out to sea as though he hoped the eagle might reappear. Dougie, not knowing what to say, followed his gaze until finally Sir Torquhil stood up and turned to face him. 'Dougie, I sometimes think Miss Daphne tells you more than she tells me. Do you know where she is? I need to talk to her.'

'No, Sir Torquhil, but I could mebbe find out.'

'Do that and let me know,' he said and walked back towards the castle.

'The laird's in a gie queer mood and I'm no' happy about him,' the keeper said when he got back to Cameron, 'he seems to have aged ten years in these last few hours, and now he's asking for his daughter. Do you think the police can find her and get her to ring me at the cottage?'

Some forty minutes after the others had left the meeting at Fort George, Duncan Forsyth and Brigadier Robertson were discussing with Nick Nicholson how to deal with the members of Unicorn once they had been arrested, and also how they would deal with possible happenings at the parade ground, when there was a call for Duncan from the Deputy Chief Constable.

'Look, there seems to have been a breakdown in communication. Aye, and I apologise for it. Earlier this afternoon there was a message from the Argyll police,' he said, 'telling us that the watchers at Altachonich are very worried about Sir Torquhil. The keeper, Fletcher, has been down to see him and says he's in a kinda fey mood and wants to talk to his daughter. Fletcher asked if the girl could ring him before she talks to her father. The message has only just reached me and obviously needs immediate action, so what do we do?'

Duncan thought for a moment and then said, 'I'd better ring Fletcher. Where is he? . . . at his house, have you the number? . . . good. I'll ring at once and get back to you.'

He hurriedly explained his problem to the others. 'Look, I won't be long,' he said, 'just give me fifteen minutes. I must sort something out. We don't want Sir T doing anything stupid. Equally I must support Daphne. And I must do it all in the context of this infernal operation. What a bloody awful mess!'

It was a very worried Dougie that Duncan finally managed to contact and after apologising for the delay, asked what was the problem. When the keeper explained about the Curse and his doubts over Sir Torquhil's mental health, Duncan realised that somehow they had to deal with the situation without Daphne also becoming over emotional.

'Dougie, I will ring Miss Drumcairn now. When she has talked to her father, we will decide what to do and come back to you. Meanwhile keep an eye on things and if you see Sir Torquhil behaving in any way suspiciously, go down and stay with him.'

When he got through to Dalbeg, Duncan spoke first to General Forsyth. He explained the situation and asked his cousin to make sure Daphne stayed in the house.

'Whatever happens, she must not try to go down to Altachonich,' he said.

'Leave that to me,' the General said, 'and now hang on while I fetch her.'

Daphne listened while Duncan explained, as gently as he could, what Dougie had told him, but she made no immediate reply.

'I'm sorry darling,' she said after a long pause, 'yes, I'm still here and I'm OK. It's just it was a bit of a shock and I was trying to think of the best thing to do. You see, we've had this problem before. I'll tell you about our family curse one day, but father's always had a bee in his bonnet about it. I suppose the worry of Unicorn has brought it on this time, and of course he must be comforted and got under control . . . yes, I'll ring him now . . . and no, I won't go and try to see him but I'll do my best to calm him on the telephone . . . yes, I'll ring you back. Goodbye and I love you.'

By the time all this was finished, the others had returned, bringing with them a rather embarrassed Maclay newly arrived from Inverness. After more apologies, he said:

'I thought you'd like to know how the tracking of the Unicorn vehicles has gone. We followed their progress the whole way up. No, I don't think they had any suspicion that they were under observation,' and he walked over to the map table and pointed. 'The lorry with what we believe to be the missile equipment stopped at the saw mill in Muir of Ord. Then it crossed the main road here and turned off up this road. That was about three hours ago.'

'What about the others?' Duncan asked.

'The cattle float drove straight through together with one of the Land Rovers and they took this road,' Maclay answered. 'The other Land Rover, now that's interesting. It went to the Urquhart house in Inverness, and it's still there.'

'That'll be Simpson gone to collect Urquhart,' said Duncan, and before he could continue, the telephone rang and Daphne came on the line.

'I've spoken to Father, she said, 'and he's not at all good. He's seen the wretched eagle – that's all part of the Curse of Altachonich – and he thinks the Unicorn enterprise is doomed to failure and it's all his fault. He thinks he's going to die and wants to see me . . . no, don't get excited, I've said I can't possibly get there before Saturday evening, implying that I was at the other end of the country. I told him he certainly wasn't going to die and I'd see him soon and meanwhile to get Dougie down and have a nice talk about stalking or something. Oh dear, it's very hard to stay calm.' And for the first time there was a catch in her voice.

'I know, darling, but you've done exactly right,' said Duncan, 'and now listen. We can't risk him ringing the Black Isle in a panic, assuming he has a number. We need to do something to distract him. Provided my colleagues agree, I'm going to have the police visit him and tell him a little bit of what is happening. It means we'll have to cut off the castle telephone, but there will still be Dougie's phone and the police wireless. And listen, tell Geoffrey I'll try to get over for dinner and let you know what we have arranged; and I promise you, everyone realises how awful this is for you, and we'll all do what we can for your father.'

'Yes, all right,' the girl replied, 'but don't let Father come to any harm, he's the only father I have! And you too, look after yourself,' and without any further remark she rang off.

'Can we do that?' Duncan asked. 'What I suggest is that Gray goes to see him and tells him about the capture of the French trawler and that the authorities know something's up but they are not sure what. I'll take the responsibility as we've no time to lose, and I'll brief Gray. How do you all feel about it?'

Maclay and Robertson agreed that something had to be done or Sir Torquhil might panic Unicorn into taking some drastic action before it could be stopped, and that Duncan's proposal offered the best hope. Robertson said he was prepared to authorise that they go ahead and do it now, but he would have to inform Scottish Command in the morning. Maclay said he too would have to inform the Chief Constable, who in turn would need to square his opposite number in Argyll.

They were fortunate to discover that Inspector Gray was in fact at Altachonich, and agreed without demur to do what Duncan asked.

'I was told to give you any support you asked for, so I will,' he said. 'I know the old man well, so it can all be done in a fine friendly manner. Aye, he'll take it well from me and I'll mix it up with other gossip.'

When the Inspector had rung off, Duncan looked round at the others. 'Well I hope that really is all for today. We meet tomorrow here, as soon as the recce party gets back. Jock, I hate to ask, but can the car take me out to Dalbeg and bring me back later? I must see Miss Drumcairn and talk to her about her father's predicament and it can't be done on the telephone.'

Chapter 24

It was late evening and just starting to rain when Roddy Urquhart and Simpson left Inverness in the Land Rover and drove slowly round to the Black Isle. As they crossed the main road from the ferry to Conon, their passage was noted by one of Brigadier Robertson's observation posts, who immediately passed the information to Operation Control at Fort George.

They had intended to leave earlier but their departure had been delayed by the need to consider the significance of Forsyth's appearance on the Black Isle. Was he, as seemed probable, aware that something was to happen there? In which case how much information had he passed on before his car plunged into the lake? And finally had he died there? Deciding that he had, and that a major obstacle to their plans had been removed, they agreed to proceed.

Now, unaware that their arrival on the Black Isle had been seen, Urquhart and Simpson were heading towards Cromarty on one of the many minor roads that seam the area. After about a mile they turned into a farm entrance and stopped outside a large barn-like building. Urquhart got out, and telling Simpson to switch off his lights and wait in the vehicle, walked through a gate in a low wall and round to the back door of the farm house. In answer to his knock, the door was opened by a tall man with a broad weather-beaten face and prominent nose. He took Roddy's hand and still shaking it, pulled him quickly into the house and led him through to the kitchen.

'Best not hang about outside,' he said, 'there's no knowing who may be around.' Then in answer to the other's enquiring glance, added, 'aye, Pete's arrived – and no, they had no trouble but I'd rather you all kept under cover. We're just a bit close to the road here.'

'Sure,' Roddy agreed, 'now where's Pete and the others? I've got Davie Simpson in a Land Rover outside and we'd like to check that everything is OK. Then we'll take Pete on to the other place for a final briefing. By the way, where are the vehicles?'

'The Land Rover, the cattle truck and the men are all in the potato shed. They are quite safe in there; it's reasonably comfortable and there are washing facilities in the byre next door.'

'Good. So if it's OK by you, here's what we'll do. The lorry with the sheep is no longer needed so it can go on north, deliver the sheep and then return to Altachonich. The Land Rover and the men will have to spend

187

tonight and tomorrow where they are and Davie and Pete can come back here later and take charge. I'll stay up at the other place. They've said they can provide a car if I need one. I'll take the equipment up to the wood tomorrow evening as soon as it's dark. The two Land Rovers with the men can leave here a bit later, say at about nine-thirty,' Here Urquhart paused as an attractive young woman entered the room.

'I'm certainly glad to hear that, Roddy,' she said. 'I'm not minding helping you as far as we've gone, but I don't want Geordie mixed up in any violence. So the sooner that lot are away, the better.'

'Aye Sheila, I know your feelings and what I said just now is true. We'll be away from here tomorrow evening and you and Geordie need know nothing of any further happenings.' Then with a smile he added, 'and we're all very grateful to you for your help; Scotland will be greatly in your debt.' Then, looking down at his watch, he turned and added, 'now I must leave you. No, don't come out. I'll manage fine.'

He shook hands with them both, and walked quickly out of the house and back to the Land Rover, where he repeated to Simpson what he had just told the farmer.

'Why the rush about the sheep?' asked Simpson, 'surely it's rather late to move them now?'

'Not a bit,' Urquhart replied, 'I'll give the farm a ring, say they've been held up and will be there about midnight and sorry, but the lorry must return home as soon as they are unloaded. I want them out of here and the lorry back at Altachonich as soon as possible. Someone might just begin to wonder if it's away too long. Geordie has agreed to the men and vehicles staying here until tomorrow evening. Sheila's a bit twitchy, so you'll need to move up to Milton Mains tomorrow as soon as it's dark. Now come on. We'd best tell the boys what's happening. Move the vehicle round to that wee door over there and we'll go in by that.'

The building which they entered had, in its time, had many uses, and at present was used for storing and sorting potatoes and anything else that needed protection from the weather. At one end, in front of big sliding doors, the cattle float was parked and behind it the Land Rover. At the other end a dozen men, having just finished a meal, were sitting around talking. Urquhart greeted the foreman and accepted a mug of tea. Then, having got the attention of the men, he went through the plans for the next twenty-four hours and finished by emphasising the need for security.

'Aye, I know it's boring, but no one is to leave this building except to go to the washroom in the byre. No fires – cooking only on the gas stove – and no singing or other noise. Davie, Pete and I are off to the other place now. I shall remain there but the other two will be back later and will give you your final orders.'

Then he turned to the driver of the cattle float. 'Have you finished your meal? Right, then you leave now, deliver the sheep and start back to the castle as soon as that's done. You'd better stop somewhere for a bit rest. We don't want you ending up in a ditch. If you are stopped, you know what to say, don't you?'

The man nodded and got up. He collected his belongings, climbed into the cab and started the engine. Two of the men opened the sliding doors and he drove off into the night. Urquhart nodded to the rest of the men, then, beckoning to Simpson and the foreman to follow, walked out to the Land Rover.

The drive to Milton Mains took little more than ten minutes but when they got there, they found it a very different place to the previous farm. Whereas that was barely a hundred yards from the road, the steading at Milton was at the end of a mile-long farm road which passed through a considerable wood, with the house a further three hundred yards beyond. To the north and east the ground climbed steeply, the lower slopes being covered with stunted beech and oak interspersed with birch and alder and an undergrowth of whins and bracken. Beyond this scrub, the higher slopes were covered by endless plantations of pine and spruce.

Urquhart indicated that they should drive straight to the house, where they were met at the front door by the farmer, a cousin of Roddy's. After the introductions he led them through to the back of the house saying:

'I think you'd be best in the study. The other two are there already. Now we've all eaten, but the wife has something left for you, so what do you want to do?'

'Peter here has had his dinner, but Davie and I are starving so a bite of something would be fine. We can eat as we talk to save time.'

Their host left them at the door of the study saying he would organize the food and then leave them to it. 'The less I know of what you're doing the better,' was his comment.

'Just one thing before you go,' said Roddy. 'OK if we go out later and look at the tunnel?'

'Sure. Whenever you want,' was the reply. 'but go easy with the lights.'

In the study they found Jack, the man in charge of the *Hirondelle*, and the driver of the timber lorry. When they had all got themselves chairs, Roddy looked across at Simpson and said:

'Shall I just tell you a bit about the geography of the area, so everyone knows what we are talking about. Then you can give out the orders.'

'Aye, that'll be fine,' replied Simpson. Further conversation however was cut short by the entry of a large cheerful woman carrying a tray. She put it down on a table and then bent over and kissed Roddy.

'There,' she said, 'I've brought you mince and a bit cheese. I hope it's enough.'

'I'm sure it'll be fine,' said Roddy, 'anything you do always is.'

'Och away wi' ye and yer flattery! aye, and mind you be good.' With that she blew them a kiss and bounced out of the room.

While he ate, Roddy described the area around Milton. 'From our point of view this farm has two advantages – no, perhaps three. First it is almost completely hidden from the road and from anyone else; for the nearest neighbours, other than the farm workers, are over a mile away. Secondly, the hill just behind the house was an ammunition dump during the War and is a mass of tunnels. They were mostly sealed up, but one was overlooked and some years ago we found an entrance – it's very well hidden. That, I hope, is where the launcher now is.' Jack nodded and Roddy went on, 'the third advantage is that it is only three miles from the launch site and only one mile of that is on a public road.'

He pushed his plate aside and pulled a one-inch map from his pocket. 'Just look here,' he said, and when they crowded round, he pointed out the main features he had been describing.

Then, as soon as Urquhart had finished, Simpson got to his feet, took a sheaf of papers from a folder and perched himself on the edge of a desk facing the others.

'Now listen carefully,' he said, 'and take notes where necessary, for we won't have another chance to talk before Saturday. First, when this meeting ends, Peter and I will return to the other farm; the rest of you will remain here. Then there will be no more moving until tomorrow evening and during that time everyone remains under cover. As soon as it's dark tomorrow, that's about seven-thirty, Roddy will move the launcher up to the firing place, camouflage it and put the truck in the old shed there. At nine-thirty the two Land Rovers will leave the farm with the rest of the team. The men will be in civilian clothes; their uniforms and rifles will be in the special compartments under the seats. One vehicle will go straight to the site, the other will park for an hour in the wood at the end of this drive. We don't want a procession to be seen going to the plantation. At the site the men will change into uniform and then get what rest they can in the shed and the remains of the croft. There's to be no moving about. Roddy will give instructions for the parking of the vehicles. Is everyone quite clear so far?'

'What about food?' Peter asked, 'and bedding? It'll be gie cold.'

'Everyone should take a piece – and a thermos of tea, as there will be no cooking at the site. There's no room for bedding, so everyone should have a coat.'

'And now for Saturday,' Simpson continued. 'We don't know the exact time the helicopter leaves Invergordon, so by first light everybody will need to be in position and under cover. From then on we play it by ear. You all know the drill, so listen for my orders.'

'Just confirm the dispersal plans,' Roddy said.

'Right. First, if we are successful. As soon as the helicopter is hit and the photographs have been taken, all change into civvies. Then launcher, rockets and all other equipment on to the truck and Roddy takes it back here to the tunnel. Everyone else will be taken to Inverness, and from there they will make their own way to Glasgow ready for the rallies. Roddy and I will pick up Jane and Fergus and drive on to Edinburgh.'

'And if we fail?' someone asked.

'We won't,' Simpson replied, 'however if we do, then we play it by ear. In Inverness Fergus and Jane will, I hope, deal with Jacobsen; here it will be every man for himself. Make your way to Glasgow and lie up there until you get further orders. Now, one piece of good news. We believe that Duncan Forsyth is dead. So, with him out of the way, let's take a dram to the success of our mission,' and Simpson produced a bottle from his brief case, filled glasses and raising his cried, 'Slàinte mhath!' then added, 'and now let's go about our business. Roddy, can we see the tunnel and check the launcher and rockets?'

When Duncan Forsyth arrived at Dalbeg, he told his driver to go round the back where Mrs Mack would look after him. The General, who was standing at the top of the steps, beckoned to him to follow and led him to the little panelled ante-room off the Great Hall.

'I don't like the situation at Altachonich at all,' he said. 'The keeper and a police officer have been down to see Torquhil and found him in a very strange mood. The keeper – Dougie, that's his name I think – rang Daphne an hour ago and said they were having trouble getting any sense out of him. Keeps rambling on about some curse and they – whoever they are, Unicorn presumably – will never be able to save Scotland now. They've just rung back again and Daphne is talking to the policeman. She's in the drawing room.'

As they came into the room they heard her say, 'Yes, I'll get him to ring you.' And then she put down the telephone and turned to face them. Despite her outward show of calm, Duncan could see that she was deeply troubled and not far off tears.

'That was Inspector Gray,' she said. 'I expect Geoffrey has told you that Dougie and Gray went down to the castle earlier to see father and to try and take his mind off things, but all he would talk about was the curse, and after an hour they had to leave. I said he shouldn't be alone, but until Charles gets back, there's nobody else.'

'Does he suspect that we know all about Unicorn's plans?' Duncan asked.

'I don't know,' she replied, 'for when they went back to see him, he'd been drinking and was making even less sense. I knew this would happen if he was left on his own. Fortunately Charles is now back and they are going to get someone over from Glenlochan. Anyway, Gray says will you ring him at Dougie's as soon as possible. Oh darling, what can we do for him?'

'I promise we'll find something, but first let's hear what Gray has to say,' said Duncan picking up the phone.

The Inspector had a sorry tale to tell. Sir Torquhil had been drinking heavily and had become steadily more incoherent. He kept muttering about failure, and more worrying, his own death. Furthermore a combination of the whisky and his own uncertain mental state had made him careless of what he said.

'Ye ken how a man in his cups becomes all kind of confidential,' Gray said, 'well, Sir Torquhil staggers up to me and puts his hand on my shoulder. 'You know, Gray,' he says, 'that helicopter will be like the eagle, down from the sky it'll come and the American, like me, will die.' I, of course, did not let on I knew what he was talking about.'

Apparently Sir Torquhil then launched into a long rambling story about blowing up the quarry. 'They'll fail, so it will have to be done and I will have to do it,' he said. 'Daphne was right, as she always is. Scotland's not ready yet, but one day she will be and then she'll take her rightful place in the community of nations.' With that he'd slumped in his chair and fallen fast asleep.

'We got him up to his bed, and I'm thinking he'll sleep for a long time and wake wi' a terrible head,' was Gray's opinion. 'Dougie or the butler will stay with him and I'll come back again tomorrow. But I think the sooner Miss Daphne can come here the better. Aye, and you realise, sir, that I will have to report all he's said.'

'Of course,' Duncan replied, 'and I shall have to too. And I don't like that mention of explosives. It sounds as if they've mined the quarry and Sir Torquhil's to blow it if they fail. For God's sake don't leave him alone for a second until we can get it cleared. I'll send the bomb disposal people down as soon as possible. Good night and ring me at Fort George tomorrow.'

Putting down the telephone, Duncan walked over to the sofa and sitting down beside Daphne, told her as gently as he could what Gray had said. Then, as she turned a tear-stained face to him, he took her hand and let her bury her face in his shoulder.

'Look, my darling,' he said after a few minutes, 'I know your father's not at all well, but you do see that we cannot let you go to the castle till we know what happens on Saturday.' She lifted her head and nodded, and he continued, 'it would be too dangerous for you both. We'll just have to rely on Dougie and the others to look after him. I can't even let you ring him, for he must continue to believe the phone's out of order. But why don't you ring Dougie every now and then? Do you agree, Geoffrey?'

'Absolutely,' the General assented. 'Poor old Torquhil. You know Daphne, he always was a man for wild ideas. Maybe that was the secret of his success. The trouble is when wild ideas go wrong, that sort of person takes it hard.'

Then he thought for a moment. 'You know, Duncan, I think that as well as Daphne ringing Dougie, we should find a way of getting Torquhil a message from her. It might help to calm him. Leave it to me. And now Daphne, I think you need a drink, and then let's have dinner because Duncan will be wanting to get back to the Fort.'

After dinner, leaving their host to finish his coffee, Daphne went with Duncan to the car. 'Listen, darling,' he said, 'I'm sorry about your father, but I dare not let you away from this place. If anyone from Unicorn saw you, despite their other preoccupations, they'd get you without doubt. You see, you would be a very valuable bargaining counter. But I promise that if everything goes according to plan, I'll take you to Altachonich on Saturday evening, even if I have to come straight back.'

'Oh Duncan, I know,' and she looked up into his eyes, 'I understand, but I can't bear to think of him all alone in that great house, just sitting and brooding. I know I can't go to him – but oh dear . . .' and she gave a sigh, then putting her arms round his neck said, 'it's so very hard to have both you and father in danger. Oh darling, please look after yourself, and – and good luck.' And she kissed him and fled before the tears came again.

When Duncan got back to Fort George, he found Brigadier Robertson in the Operations Room. 'All well?' he asked Duncan, who then told him of the problems with Sir Torquhil. 'I'm just worried that when he comes to, he may guess that we are on to them, and despite our precautions get a message through.'

'We'll just have to deal with that if it happens, which I don't think it will. Now just come and look at this,' Robertson said, walking over to the map table. 'A local policeman on the Black Isle stopped one of the patrol cars and mentioned to the crew something he thought a bit odd. While cycling past this farm here – Lamington its called – he noticed lights on and a lot of noise coming from a big barn, one that's used for storing potatoes, he thought. Then he added as an afterthought that the farmer there is an ardent Nationalist. The patrol car thought it worth reporting. We'll fly over it tomorrow morning.'

'I guess that could easily be one of their harbour areas,' said Duncan. 'Any other news?'

'Yes, one of the observation posts reported that the Altachonich cattle lorry has left the Black Isle, still with sheep on board. One of the men on duty is a west coast lad and recognised it. Anyway I've an early start in the morning, so I'm for my bed. See you when we get back from the recce.'

'One final thing,' said Duncan, 'I'll need to get a bomb disposal squad down to Altachonich. They've mined the quarry – and, now I come to think of it, possibly the castle itself.'

Chapter 25

At about twenty past eight the next morning a rather cold reconnaissance party was waiting on the pontoon at Invergordon. Sharp at eight-thirty a launch came alongside and ferried them out to the US carrier. There they were welcomed on board by the American Commander and escorted to the helicopter. Moments later they were airborne and heading south towards the Black Isle.

Robertson, who was sitting up front with a map case on his knee, turned to the pilot and pointing to a marked spot, asked:

'Can we fly over that place – slowly, if possible?' The pilot nodded and adjusted his course slightly west.

Soon they were flying over an area of solid pine plantations when suddenly Robertson spotted a small clearing and several ruined buildings with, just to the north, another opening, the result of felling or windblow.

'There you are, gentlemen,' he said, 'take a good look, for you may not get another chance.' Then to the pilot he asked: 'Now can we have a look at this farm? Not too close for I don't want to arouse suspicion.'

As they approached Lamington, the Brigadier got his glasses on the farm, but although he had a good look at what he guessed was the potato store, he could see nothing untoward. However the pilot nodded towards the ground and said:

'Say General, I guess there's been a big truck in that barn recently. See the tracks?'

'I agree, Hugh,' said Porterfield, who also had his glasses on the barn, 'the main tracks are those of a lorry – but look there – there to the right. See those other tracks? That's a Land Rover for sure. OK, all what you'd expect on a farm, but makes you think nevertheless.'

Shortly after that they landed at Inverness Airport, picked up some packages and then flew on to Kinloss. There, as well as a further pick-up, they went into a hanger for a cup of coffee. It was while they were there that Robertson, who had an old WD version of the one-inch map, noticed something that interested him greatly.

'Do you think,' he said to the pilot, 'on the way back we could fly past this farm – again not too close?' And he pointed to Milton Mains.

'Sure, General, anything you say. And I also have a request to fly over that bit of woodland again on the way back.'

'Yes, Hugh,' said Porterfield, nodding towards the Major from the infantry battalion, 'both Dick Carmichael and I are very interested in that cleared ground to the north of the croft.'

As they approached Milton, Robertson directed his binoculars at the rough field between the farmhouse and hill behind, and told the two soldiers to do the same. Then as they flew on, he looked down at his map, grunted, and then nodded his head with satisfaction.

Some ten minutes later they landed safely on the aircraft carrier, where the Commander introduced them to the Captain of the ship.

'Pleased to have been of help to you, gentlemen,' he said. 'I hope you saw all you wanted?'

'We certainly did,' replied Brigadier Robertson, 'in fact we learned more than I expected. A most successful exercise. Our grateful thanks to you, Captain, and to your crew.'

Back in the Operation Control Room at Fort George they found Duncan Forsyth on the telephone to Inspector Nicholson. 'OK, Nick,' he said, 'they've just arrived back. They'll need to get their breath back, so that'll give you time to get over here. Let's say we'll meet in forty minutes.' Then he put the telephone down and turning to the others explained, 'that was Nicholson to say that Fergus Crawford and the Parsons woman are at the Urquhart house and have neither moved nor used the telephone. I guess they are all keeping very quiet for today. Anyway tell me, have you boys had a successful trip?'

'Yes, very good. Just give us half an hour and I'll tell you all about it,' said Robertson, then turning to his batman, a splendid ex-poacher who was always ready with whatever he thought might be needed, he added, 'do you think, Mackay, you could find us coffee and sandwiches?'

'Aye sir, they're on their way. I just thought they might be needed.'

Forty-five minutes later they were all gathered round the map table, and Robertson was describing to Forsyth and Nicholson what they had seen from the helicopter. He finished by saying that after they landed, he had had a word with the pilot who was to fly the decoy helicopter and who had said that he foresaw no difficulty in his part of the plan, a fact which the USN Commander confirmed.

'We can sure give a convincing impression that the machine has crashed just over the crest of the hill.'

'Right. Now what about your part, Sam, and also yours, Dick? Let's hear your plans.'

Porterfield asked them to look at the map again and explained that the lie of the land made his task easier than he had expected. The reason, he said, was the area of cleared ground to the north of the croft. This would make abseiling unnecessary.

'We are going to come in very close behind the decoy,' he said. 'Unicorn are going to be so busy dealing with it that they are not going to take in what two other helicopters are doing, and even if they do wonder, they will be distracted by the fly-past planes and by the time they've gone we shall be down and out of their sight.'

'Are both your planes going in that way?' asked Duncan.

'Yes. I have already arranged for the one that's here at the Fort to move over to Invergordon. Now the troop in that one, as soon as it lands, will use a handy little device we've just acquired. It's a bomb we fire from a small mortar. It explodes harmlessly about twelve feet above the ground, but the shock waves stun and disorientate. Coming immediately after the jets, it should leave the enemy more than a little confused. This troop will then assume a back-up role, and be ready for unforeseen eventualities.'

'And the other troop?'

'They will go straight in. Two men each will swing left and right, and we hope the missile and its crew will be surrounded before they know what's happening.'

'That's fine so far,' said the Brigadier, 'and we'll come back to you in a moment. Now what about your lot, Dick?'

'Your orders to us are to create a diversion that will increase the confusion in the Unicorn ranks, and also to bring up the police to effect the arrests,' Carmichael replied. 'Well, Sam and I have worked out a plan which will meet your requirements, and without our getting in each other's way. We'll move from the Fort tomorrow afternoon and spend the night here,' and he pointed to a place on the map.

'It's a recognised training area so should not arouse undue interest. At 0500 hrs we take the transport out to here,' and again he pointed at the map, 'arriving at 0600 hrs. The route is well clear of anywhere Unicorn are likely to be. We de-bus and then two platoons go up this track – to here, and deploy, taking the police with them. One will create the diversion, the other will await Sam's success signal and then advance with the police. The other platoon will remain with the transport, ready to move if and when required. The two advanced platoon commanders will be doing a little recce in plain clothes this afternoon – keen bird watchers, they are!'

'Now Sam, let's come back to you. What happens if the assault troops are fired on?'

'We stop; then two minutes covering fire from the second troop and the assault goes in, right flanking. Success signal will be two red Vereys.'

'Dick, you must make sure your chaps are in cover in case of any firing and I think you should start earlier. My guess is that the enemy will start moving around six. Rules of engagement normal – no firing unless fired on. Then as soon as police and infantry take over, your men, Sam, straight back to the helicopters and away. We don't want an identified SAS presence.

Final orders 1700 hrs. These to include communication plan, evacuation of casualties and disaster and pursuit plans.'

Robertson then turned to Nicholson and said, 'Now Inspector, let's have your comments. And then Duncan, I'd like to know what you'll be doing.'

'Well sir, everything I've heard so far is just what we have agreed with the military,' Nicholson reported. 'The police party to effect the arrests will be an Inspector, a Sergeant and four Constables. They will go out with the supporting troops in the army transport. As soon as the success signal is seen, they will go forward supported by one of the platoons and make the arrests. In the event of problems, they will remain under cover and await further orders.'

'What arrangements have been made to remove the prisoners?' asked Duncan.

'Two vans and a patrol car will be waiting here,' and Nicholson pointed to a track leading to a small wood. 'It's not much used and the cover's good. Aye, the laird has been warned and has agreed. They will be called up by the army, the prisoners will be handcuffed and loaded, and the vans will proceed to Inverness with motor cycle and patrol car escort.'

'Where will you be?' asked the Brigadier.

'In Inverness with Mr Forsyth. I will have a patrol car outside the park which will be on the army wireless net, so I can keep everybody at the parade informed.'

'OK. Now Duncan, what about you?'

'I shall be at the park very early, but no one will see me. Don't ask me any more about that, just accept it,' Forsyth replied. 'The moment I know that Crawford has booby-trapped the mike, he'll be arrested. A bomb disposal expert will then remove the mike as evidence and it will be replaced with a harmless one. I shall then be around on the look-out for Jane Parsons. Whether she will realise her brother is under arrest, I can't know. Nor do I know if she has any means of communication, but she's nothing if not resourceful, and could make her own attempt at assassination.'

'Well, that seems to complete the present meeting,' said Robertson, 'except for one other thing. Some of you will remember that yesterday we had a report of unusual goings on at a farm called Lamington. Well, when we flew over it today, there were clear indications of both large and small vehicles using a barn-like building. Not absolute proof I know, but tends to confirm that it is one of Unicorn's hideouts. Then I noticed that on my map there is an old wartime ammunition dump marked behind this farm, here, Milton Mains. Probably tunnels in the hillside, and they must still be accessible. Because, as we flew over, I noticed tracks on the field below going nowhere other than up to the edge of this wood. So we seem to have located their two harbours. We can't make use of this knowledge, but it does tend to confirm that we are right in our location of the firing site. I am arranging for both farms to be kept under observation. Now if there is nothing further, we'll break off and meet again at 1700 hrs. So see you then.'

'Not me, Hugh,' said Duncan, 'I have other things to do. and I must find out what is happening at Altachonich. But I will try and be with you later.'

As soon as the meeting broke up, Duncan got Nicholson to take him back to Police Headquarters in Inverness. There, in the Inspector's office, he made certain requests concerned with meeting the Superintendent of the local parks. Nicholson said he would see what could be done but it might take a wee while, so Duncan then asked if, in the meantime, he could use both an ordinary telephone and the secure line.

'I must find out what's happening at the castle,' he said, 'and then tell Miss Drumcairn. I must also report to my Chief. The army will already have updated the Cabinet Office on the situation and my HQ will not want to get information second-hand.'

So once again he was taken to the room with the locked cupboard and the blue telephone was produced. 'There's an ordinary telephone on the desk. Do you remember the secure line code?' When Duncan nodded, Nicholson said he'd be back in an hour and went out, closing the door behind him.

The first call he made was to Dougie Fletcher's cottage. Mrs Dougie, who answered the phone, said her husband had just come up from the castle and would be with him in a moment.

The keeper's report was not encouraging. It appeared that Sir Torquhil had slept until late in the morning and was now in a state of black depression. He was refusing food and drink and just lay staring out of the window. Fortunately the doctor had looked in a short while since – Inspector Gray had met him in Glenlochan and had taken the opportunity to explain the laird's condition. He had administered a sedative, with the result that Sir Torquhil was again sleeping peacefully.

Dougie ended by saying that a man on a motor cycle had just delivered a letter from Miss Daphne, which might help the situation, but the doctor had said that the sooner she could be got to visit her father the better.

Having finished with Dougie, Duncan then rang Dalbeg and reported to Daphne what Dougie had told him.

'I'm afraid it's not good news,' he said, 'and I got the feeling that the doctor was genuinely worried. Perhaps the letter will help. Incidentally, how did you organise that?'

'Oh that was all Geoffrey. He told me to say that I'd heard Father was very worried; that I'd tried to telephone, but to no avail; so I'd got a friend, who was going to Glasgow on the late train and then on to Oban, to take this letter and he'd see it was delivered. I then wrote a good comforting letter and Geoffrey got one of the estate staff to take it down to Altachonich on his motor bike. Darling, you will take me to him as soon as you can, won't you?'

When he'd finished talking to Daphne and had had a word with his cousin, Duncan moved to the blue telephone and got through to his friend the Head of Operations, who told him the Chief was not available. 'Gone to Downing Street. So what can I do for you?'

'You can give him an update on the final plans for tomorrow,' Duncan said, 'and what I'm going to tell you is probably more up to date than anything you've heard via the army.'

'Splendid!' was the reply, 'I'll get it straight down to the PM's office and our revered leader will score any amount of Brownie points, which will please him no end. Go right ahead – Janet's here and she'll take it down as you talk.'

Duncan gave a resumé of all that had happened over the previous two days, followed by an outline of the final orders. He finished by saying that all units were ready and would be moving up to their start positions in the next few hours. Finally he summarised the problems at Altachonich and the action he had taken.

'You'd better tell the Chief, and he may want to inform the PM. They both know Sir Torquhil, so they'd better be told that tomorrow, in all probability, the Argyll police are going to have to arrest him; though between ourselves, I doubt he'll survive that long. I just hope I can get his daughter there before anything drastic happens. Now I have things to do, so I'll ring off. My salaams to the great man.'

He put the telephone back in its cupboard and minutes later Nicholson walked into the room with a broad smile on his face.

'Well, I hope I've done what you want,' he said. 'I saw Joe Rapson – he's the head park keeper. Now if you'll go down and see him at about half five at the Council Offices, he'll fix you up. He's a good lad, but I'm afraid he thinks you are mad. I told him it was some secret government business and his reply was "aye, well then he's bound to be mad!"'

'He could be right. Anyway, thanks Nick and I'll go along and see him, then I'll go back to the Fort and spend the night there. Tomorrow I'll be down at the park early. You'll not see me – at least not till I want you to – and that will be when I gave you the signal to arrest Fergus Crawford, so have men ready in the stand.'

It was three hours later when he got back to Fort George. The five o'clock meeting was over and he found Hugh Robertson in the mess. Duncan beckoned him over to a corner where they were out of earshot of anyone else and explained what he'd been doing.

'So that's my plan for tomorrow up to the arrival of Jacobsen and party, that is. After that I'll have to play it by ear. I have a communication plan with the police, so you can get in touch with me via Nicholson's patrol car. The vital thing is to let me know what happens on the Black Isle the moment it happens. We must not forget, you see, that Jane Parsons will almost certainly still be on the loose. You, I assume, will remain here all day.'

'I think it's the best plan,' Robertson answered, 'but if I do move I'll let you know. Now I'm for my bed, although I don't suppose I'll get much sleep.' He picked up his glass and with a final 'Good luck to us all,' he left the room.

Chapter 26

On Saturday the people of Inverness awoke to a mild, clear morning, with the forecast of a fine day to come. This improvement in the weather came as a relief to all concerned with the parade. Many of them were already about their business, and were the cause of an unusual amount of activity in both the town and the surrounding countryside.

In the barracks the troops taking part, having had an early breakfast, were engaged in the final cleaning of uniform and equipment. 'Rather them than me,' thought an elderly man on a moped as he puttered along the road below, on his way to work at the parade ground.

On arrival there, he parked his machine behind a shed and joined a number of others who were loading posts and coils of white rope on to a trailer. It took them just over an hour to cordon off the parade ground and when this was done, the elderly man was detailed to sweep out and generally tidy the grandstand.

It must be admitted that in doing this he spent an inordinate amount of time sweeping the stairs and entrance area, possibly because this allowed him to see what was going on in the street outside. In fact at one moment he actually moved down to sweep the pavement and collect the litter in a shovel. Then, as he emptied the shovel into a bucket, he deftly pocketed a piece of paper. Back in the stand he glanced at the paper, replaced it in his pocket and returned to sweeping the stairs.

Just before eight he noticed a van bearing the legend 'Highland Sound Amplifiers' draw up beside the entrance. A man got out, opened the back of the van and took out a tool box and a cardboard package; he then went up the stairs and out to the front of the stand. He did not notice the man standing on the back row of seats and busily sweeping cobwebs from the roof. Nor did he notice the two men painting white marks on the grass in front of the stand, for he was engrossed in his own business.

From a corner he took a microphone and stand and placed it in front of the first row of seats. This he connected to a cable which led to a junction box. He then took up four other cables and plugged them into the same box. Having done that, he got up and walked round the field inspecting the loudspeakers, which were already in position. Apparently satisfied, he returned to the stand, flicked a switch and proceeded to test the system. After several tries, the results of which were not at all satisfactory, he disconnected the mike, and from the package he had brought with him, produced and fitted a replacement.

He still appeared oblivious of the cleaner, who was now working along the front row of seats and who, just after he passed the microphone position, seemed to trip and drop his bucket. At the noise of the fall the sound engineer looked round, and while he was still distracted, the two men painting the white marks leapt on to the platform, grabbed his arms and in a second had him handcuffed. While one of the men held his arm, the other stepped back and said:

'I believe you to be Fergus Crawford and I must ask you to come to the station with us as we wish to question you about a conspiracy to endanger the public.'

As Crawford was led to a police car and driven off, the elderly cleaner, having first checked that the street was clear, began showing surprising agility for one of his age. He climbed over a wall and disappeared into the back of a waiting van.

After some twenty minutes he emerged from the van, and after once again checking that the coast was clear, made his way through the stand and out on to the field. There he had a brief conversation with the man in charge, after which he finished the marking, which had been interrupted by the arrest of Crawford. That completed, he vanished through a door in the base of the stand, where he remained for the next hour.

Even before the troops were stirring in the barracks or the elderly man was mounting his moped outside a cottage on the Nairn road, two three-tonners had left the army's overnight area and driven towards the Black Isle. They were followed ten minutes later by a third lorry and fifteen minutes after that by two Land Rovers, one stopping on the way to pick up the police party.

By the time Major Carmichael and the policemen arrived at the rendezvous, the other vehicles had all been parked off the road and camouflaged and it would have taken a very observant passer by to notice them. Two of his three platoon commanders, who were sitting under the trees by the side of the road, got up as Carmichael approached.

'What's the form, John?' he asked one of them, 'and where's Sandy?'

'My men and Sandy's are under cover on either side of the track,' was the reply, 'the other platoon is back there and their truck and one of the Land Rovers are parked ready for a quick move. Should you need 3 platoon, they can be moved quickly to wherever you want, either on foot or by transport. Now about Sandy – he has taken two men forward to do a recce. When we came up here yesterday we found another path, one which should allow us to move up without alerting anyone at the croft, but we thought it best to check that it's clear.'

'OK. Now, did you meet anyone – man or vehicle – on the way over?' When they shook their heads, Carmichael looked at his watch before continuing. 'No, nor did I once we left the main road. Now it's just after six, so as soon as Sandy gets back, the diversion party can move up. You, John, will take your platoon and the rest of us up to our positions at six-thirty. I will report our situation at that time. After that, complete silence until the helicopters arrive.'

At that moment the missing Sandy appeared from the trees and reported that he'd been to the diversion position and then right up to the start line and everything was quiet.

'I even crawled forward and had a look over that bank I told you about. They are there all right and sure, they've got a SAM. They were just setting it up; but they had also put out sentries and as it's getting light, I thought it prudent to retire. I've left Corporal Taylor up there to guide my party and Sinclair is watching John's position. Will you be with him, Dick?'

'Yes, but probably a bit back. I'll just have a runner and signaller with me,' replied Carmichael, then with another look at his watch he said, 'OK Sandy, you can move off now. John, your chaps had better load their weapons, just in case of the unexpected. I'll report back to HQ and we'll move in – yes, in twelve minutes exactly.'

The move up was accomplished without any problem, and by six fifty-five all the troops were in position; a fact which Major Carmichael was able to report to Brigadier Robertson at Fort George. He was also able to confirm that Unicorn had set up their missile at the croft and appeared to be behaving exactly as forecast. All this information was passed by Robertson to his superiors in Edinburgh, and also to the police in Inverness, who undertook to inform Forsyth, if they could find him.

The Unicorn move the previous evening had gone exactly according to plan and by eleven o'clock they were all at the croft. The launcher had been unloaded, the vehicles parked and sentries posted. The rest of the men had then dispersed to find what shelter they could. Roddy Urquhart, using his local knowledge, had done a patrol of the whole area and reported to Simpson that all seemed quiet and it looked as though they would achieve complete surprise. Unfortunately for them this was not true, for the departure of both the launcher party from Milton Mains and the Land Rovers from Lamington, had been noted and reported by Robertson's observation teams.

Now, at five-thirty on Saturday morning, Simpson and Urquhart were going round waking the men, none of whom were in the best of tempers after a cold and uncomfortable night.

'Tea and a piece now,' they were told, 'but save some for later for it may be a long wait. Then everyone report to duty stations.'

Fifteen minutes later Simpson was supervising the final positioning of the *Hirondelle* and Urquhart was posting the riflemen in positions which would give observation and defence from all directions. Having looked at the lie of the land to the north, the direction from which the helicopter was expected to come, he moved two men over the crest, right on the edge of the growing timber, from where they should be able to give early warning of the plane's approach. While Roddy was explaining what he wanted them to do, one of the men who was looking down to the west thought he saw movement.

'Wheest! what's yon down there?' he said, pointing in the direction of the edge of the clearing, 'Aye, look there's someone moving down there in the trees.' Roddy raised his binoculars and had a long look at the cleared ground and all the surrounding woods.

'I can't see anything. Maybe it was a deer – plenty of them about,' he said. Then giving the glasses to the man, he added, 'here have a look yourself. Now can you see anything?'

'No, I canna say that I can,' he replied after a long scan of the countryside, 'but I'm sure of one thing, it wasna a deer I saw, it was a man. But he's no' there now.'

'Well, both of you keep your eyes open and if you see anything, one of you come back to the croft and report. Here, you'd better have these glasses, I've another pair in the Land Rover.' And after another quick look down the hill, he left them and walked back to the croft. There he found Simpson standing in the ruins of the byre and pointing to the edge of the trees.

'All ready here,' he said, 'the launcher's set up and well camouflaged. We haven't loaded yet – too risky – and it only takes a moment to do. How much warning will we get?'

'If all goes according to plan and the lads down there do their stuff,' Urquhart replied, 'about thirty seconds to a minute.'

'Aye, that'll be plenty. Are all the sentries out?' and when the other nodded, Simpson went on, 'That's it then, we're all ready. Now all we have to do is to keep everyone awake for two or three hours.'

'Just one thing,' said Roddy. 'When I was putting those two boys out, the ones over the top there, one of them thought he saw movement in the plantation further down. I had a good look but saw nothing. Will I do a bit recce?'

Simpson thought for a moment and then said, 'I'd like to have a look myself. Let's go up to the edge of the trees again.' There, despite a prolonged search with the glasses, they saw nothing further and finally Simpson said, 'Let's leave it. We can't afford to lose you if there are enemy there. Even if there's not, you might be seen by a farm or forestry worker who just might get suspicious. Now, we're here and ready. Let's stay like that.'

While all this was going on, the officer called John had found himself an observation post in a clump of taller trees. From this position he had been able to watch both Urquhart's positioning of the lookouts and his conversation with Simpson.

'Look, Dick,' he said to Carmichael when he came down from his perch, 'There's one of their leaders there who I think is suspicious and just might decide to come looking.'

'More than likely, John; so just keep an eye on him and make sure your men are well concealed and remain absolutely quiet. I'll send a runner to warn Sandy. You have a snatch squad ready and if he or anyone else gets too close, silence them and secure them but no weapons and least physical injury.'

Some two hours later, over in the Cromarty Firth, three helicopters stood ready on the flight deck of the USS *Boulder*. One was the decoy and the other two were the SAS machines, which had been moved from the RN to the US carrier for ease of control and communication. Down below, the SAS men and the helicopter crew were getting their final orders from Sam Porterfield and the USN Commander. Also present were the Captain of the carrier and an American Admiral, the fleet Chief of Staff.

'Now are we all quite clear on these orders?' Porterfield was saying, 'We will only be one minute behind the decoy. This means that the moment it appears to the launcher crew that they have shot it down, we will be landing right behind them. Almost immediately then, the jets will fly over and the military will be creating their diversion. No 2 Troop, as soon as they are out, will fire stun bombs from the mortar and No 1 Troop will go in. The noise will be appalling and there should be considerable confusion amongst the enemy, so absolute adherence to orders is essential. Non-lethal weapons only, even if fired on. Return fire only if things get right out of control. Signal for this will be my green Verey. Any questions?'

There being none, Porterfield concluded his orders. 'Loading will be at 0945 hrs, that is in twenty-five minutes. Take off 1010 hrs and good luck to you all!'

With that he turned to the senior American officers, saluted and said, 'that is all I have to say, sir. We are ready to go.'

The Chief of Staff stepped forward, acknowledged the salute and said, 'Well you sure seem to have everything buttoned up, Major, and I just hope our boys' performance comes up to your expectations.' Then he turned to the carrier's Captain and asked, 'is there anything further I should add, Captain Gess? – No? Well then I guess we all wish you good hunting and safe landing.'

Both officers then shook hands with the men as they filed up to the flight deck. Ten minutes later the decoy was airborne and heading south over the Black Isle and a couple of minutes later it was followed by the SAS.

At about the same time Norman Jacobsen and the US ambassador, after a comfortable night as guests of the Lord Lieutenant, had been taken in their host's somewhat ordinary looking car to the outskirts of Inverness. There, at the rear of a large warehouse, they transferred to a very smart military Land Rover, and with motor cyclists in front and a police car behind, set off towards the town centre.

At exactly ten-twenty, one of the two Unicorn men watching the northern approach saw a helicopter coming from the direction of the Cromarty Firth and heading straight towards them. Without waiting to see any more, the man got to his feet and ran back towards the croft. The other man, not wanting to miss any of the action, turned to watch him.

'Get down and under cover quick, you damn fool,' Simpson bellowed as the man came panting into the clearing in front of the croft, 'what the hell do you think you're doing?'

'There's a helicopter coming from the direction of Invergordon. So I, no I mean we – we thought you'd want to know,' the man stammered.

'Aye, I can hear it, and in a moment I'll see it without your help. You're supposed to be looking out for interference from the ground. Stay where you are now; and I only hope your friend's doing better than you.'

Then turning to the crew of the launcher, he shouted to them to load and prepare to fire. He looked up at the sky just as the helicopter came, quite low, over the crest behind them.

'Aye it's a Yank all right,' he said and then, much louder, he shouted to the man at the controls, 'fire when you're ready.'

Seconds later there was a loud explosion, followed by a high pitched hissing noise as the rocket streaked towards it's target. Simpson, watching it's track, saw a brilliant flash just behind the helicopter which lurched violently and disappeared behind the trees trailing black smoke. A loud thud, followed by another explosion, seemed to indicate it had crashed just out of their sight.

'Aye that's him down,' Simpson was jumping up and down with excitement. 'Quick now, load another rocket just in case.'

At that moment more explosions and a burst of machine gun fire came from the wood to the right. 'Christ, what's happening?' he yelled at Urquhart, who was running towards him. But before he could answer, they heard the beat of another helicopter coming up behind them.

'Where the hell's that bloody lookout? No, don't fire unless I tell you, you idiot!' Simpson was shouting and cursing everyone in sight.

So much so that he did not hear Roddy shout that they were surrounded and there were men in uniform at the edge of the wood. 'We must leave everything and run for it,' he bellowed, 'quick everybody – come on, scatter! They canna follow all of us.'

'God, it's too late,' he said, looking back, 'there's two helicopters landing.'

Then he shouted to the sentries and riflemen, 'we're under attack. Shoot when you see a target.'

At that moment there came the scream of jet planes flying low. Three of them there were, and they banked steeply right over the croft as they turned in the direction of Inverness.

'Not you!' Simpson yelled at the man at the launcher, as he saw his hand go to the firing lever – but too late. The man had obviously taken Urquhart's last order to refer to him, and the third plane, unable to avoid the missile, plummeted into the trees and burst into flames.

Simpson looked at the man, drew his pistol, and without saying a word, shot him in the head at point blank range. As the man fell backwards, Simpson flung himself to the ground.

'Well, that's done for him,' he said to Urquhart who was lying beside him, 'and serve him right. If they catch us now, we'll surely swing. No story, no photographs, no army uniforms will excuse shooting down a British aircraft. Aye, we'd better run for it.' And he got to his feet.

But before he could take a step, there were two sharp explosions in the air above them, and Simpson found himself thrown to the ground with a force that left him winded and unable to move. Roddy, who had been lying on the ground, was less affected. Despite a ringing in the ears and a bruised shoulder, he was able to wriggle into cover and then take a cautious look at the situation.

From over the crest to the north men were advancing towards the croft, men with camouflage scarves across their faces and wearing sand-coloured berets. A few shots came from his men and one of the attackers fell while the rest took cover. But then two more stun grenades exploded and he heard no more shooting. Just a voice using a loud hailer.

'We have you surrounded. Drop your weapons and stand up with your hands above your heads. Any further firing and you will be killed.'

'Do as he says,' Urquhart shouted, but doubted whether anyone heard him. Then he wriggled away into the thickest part of the young plantation and lay absolutely still.

Chapter 27

Carmichael's troops had been lying in their position for over two hours and were getting distinctly cold and stiff, when they were alerted by the sound of an approaching helicopter. The leading platoon commander, with one of his sections, crawled to the edge of the wood. He could not see the launcher as the croft was hidden by a small ridge, but as the helicopter came into sight and flew low over the clearing in front, he heard the crack as the rocket was fired. The next thing he saw was a flash, and then a plane, engulfed in a cloud of black smoke, disappeared behind the trees and moments later they heard a crump as it apparently hit the ground.

'Christ sir, what went wrong?' said the corporal next to him, 'they've surely hit him.'

'Well, if you think that, I hope the launcher crew feel the same,' John Munro replied, 'but don't worry, as he vanished I could see the rotor and the whole thing looked quite stable.'

Further explanation was abandoned as at that moment all hell broke loose. Behind them, back in the wood, came a series of explosions and the sound of machine gun fire as Sandy's diversion went into operation. From the north there was the sound of an approaching helicopter, and then from the east the jets roared in, barely above the tops of the trees. As they passed over the croft, there was the roar and flash of another rocket and the third plane turned on it's port side, cartwheeled into the trees and burst into flames.

There were more loud explosions, this time from the direction of the croft, followed by a burst of small arms fire, and then Carmichael came on the wireless ordering them forward to the cover of the ridge.

'Be ready to support the helicopters. Not one man must escape. Shoot if necessary – that's orders from HQ. I'm sending a section from 2 platoon to see what can be done for the pilot and 3 platoon are moving to block all roads and tracks. I'm sending you another of your sections to join you, and I'll bring up the third with the police as soon as we get the success signal.'

Warning his men that both sides would be wearing SAS uniforms, and that there was to be no firing without his express order, Munro led the two sections forward on hands and knees. As soon as they got into cover behind the ridge, he crawled forward and peered through the bracken just in time to hear Porterfield's warning on the loud hailer. At first nothing happened.

Then he saw a man, crouched by the side of the ruin, raise his arm to throw. A shot rang out, the man clutched at his throat and fell forwards dropping the grenade, which rolled down the slope and exploded amongst the trees.

Again the loud hailer rang out: 'Drop your weapons and stand up with your hands above your heads. This is a final warning. My men are right in amongst you. If you don't believe me, look to your right.' And one of the SAS troopers materialised from nowhere, holding a man in dishevelled battle dress in a ferocious arm lock.

That was too much for the Unicorn team. From all round the croft and the surrounding trees men appeared, their hands aloft. Silently the SAS men herded them into the remains of an old byre, where they were made to sit with their hands on their heads. Then two red Verey lights soared into the sky. As soon as he saw them, Munro moved his men down to take over from the SAS, when suddenly from a patch of undergrowth behind and to his right a man in civilian clothes burst out clutching a satchel and making for the road.

'Get him! It's a photographer,' some shouted, 'alive if possible!'

The man had a head start, but John Munro was a centre three-quarter of some note and was soon overhauling him. What he hadn't reckoned on, however, was the motor bike. The man dragged it from behind a tree, jumped astride and was pushing off down the hill when, with a leap that would have done credit to a kangaroo, Munro brought down both man and bike in a flying tackle that left them both severely winded.

As Munro struggled to his feet, still gasping for breath, two of his men appeared and stood over the photographer, rifles at the ready.

'Can you stand?' he asked the man and when he nodded, Munro turned to his corporal and said, 'take him over to join the others. Here, I'll take the satchel – and you, Reid,' (this to the other soldier) 'you stand the bike against that tree. Quick man, can't you see it's leaking petrol and we don't want another disaster. We'll leave it there for the moment. I must report to Major Carmichael and the area will have to be searched.' Leaving the bike was a decision he would come to regret.

At the croft he found that Carmichael had arrived with the police, and also the third section of his platoon, and that they had started taking over the prisoners from Porterfield and his men.

'The police say they believe there should be fourteen prisoners,' the SAS man was saying, 'well, I'm handing you those eight over there plus the man in civvies. I'm afraid two had to be shot, both for offering armed resistance, so that leaves four more somewhere.'

'Yeah, I've organised a search,' Carmichael said, 'and two of those missing are the ringleaders, Simpson and Urquhart; I've got photos of them and they are not amongst that lot.' Then he turned to Munro and added, 'Here John, you take over the search now – and get'em all rounded up. I must deal with the police, and I've just had a message to say that the fire and rescue people are on their way to the crashed plane.'

As soon as Munro left to organise the search, Porterfield, who felt the place was getting altogether too populous, said, 'OK then Dick, I'll be off. The men are already on board and the sooner we're out of the way the better. Thanks for your help.' Then with a half wave, half salute he ran back to the clearing and climbed into one of the helicopters, which took off immediately, closely followed by the other.

'Here, Dick, come and look at this,' someone shouted, and looking round, Carmichael saw they were waving to him from a clump of trees on the edge of the open ground. When he reached the place, he found Munro standing by the *Hirondelle* launcher and looking down at two bodies. One had been shot through the head, the other had no head to speak of and what was left of him was lying in a shallow hole.

'That grenade must have rolled down literally on to his head as he lay there. He probably never even felt it before it went off,' said Munro, 'but I don't know about the other. The SAS said they only shot two and this is not one of them. They are both over there.'

'Better leave it to the police to see if they can find any identification,' Carmichael was saying, when he was interrupted by the sound of a helicopter approaching from the south. He looked round in the direction of the noise and said, 'That'll be the RAF fire team. I'd better get down there and see what's happening. You take charge here. Ambulances for the bodies and the police vans should arrive shortly.'

Munro immediately set about carrying out these orders. Leaving two of his men to guard the launcher and the bodies, he ordered his Sergeant to organise a further search of the woods and then walked over to the croft and found the Inspector in charge of the police.

'We've found two more bodies, Inspector,' he said, 'and we'd like you to look at them. I'd better warn you one has no face and very little head, but we need to know if he has any means of identification on him.'

As one of the police Sergeants went off to perform this unpleasant task, the officer called Sandy appeared, followed by two of his men dragging between them a frightened looking man in a crumpled battle dress.

'We found him creeping away through the plantation,' he said handing the man over to the police.

'If fourteen was correct, that just leaves one unaccounted for, so where the hell can he be?' commented Munro.

'Aye, that'll be right,' said the Inspector, 'and it'll be the other leader, Urquhart – isn't that his name? For they've just told me the body with no face has the driving licence of a certain David James Simpson in its pocket.'

'Well, that's something; and now, dammit, we've got to find Urquhart,' exclaimed Munro and then added, 'incidentally, Inspector, what about the man who was shot in the head?'

But before the Inspector could answer, the sound of sirens heralded the approach of the police convoy and also fire engines from Dingwall.

'Sandy, get your boys helping the police, while we go on searching,' Munro said and then, 'God, what's that?' he yelled as the sound of a motor bike engine came from the trees below them, and there was shouting from the direction of the road. The engine noise rose to a scream and then faded, as the rider accelerated away towards Cromarty.

Meanwhile across in Inverness, as the time neared ten-thirty, the spectators at the parade ground heard the approaching pipes and drums as the troops arrived at the assembly area.

By a quarter to eleven the last of the special guests with seats in the stand had taken their places and were looking round expectantly at the steps up from the main gate when a sharp word of command and a stamping of feet indicated that something was happening outside.

What this was and what the crowd round the gate saw was a Rolls Royce, preceded by two police motor cyclists, draw up at the entrance. A soldier stepped forward and opened the door and, to some desultory clapping, the Secretary of State for Scotland got out and shook hands with the Provost and with Lord Darrochy, the Convenor of the County Council. After a few minutes' chat the Secretary of State and his retinue were escorted to their seats by an officer of the regiment.

Five minutes later another motor cycle escort and a very smart military Land Rover with an estate car body drew up at the entrance. The soldier again stepped forward and opened the door, the sentries on either side of the gate presented arms, the crowds cheered and the small figure of the United States Secretary of Defense stepped out to be greeted by the Provost and Lord Darrochy. Then, preceded by the stout figure of the Provost, and followed by the hawklike Lord Darrochy with the Ambassador, Norman Jacobsen was led to his seat at the front of the stand. The Colonel of the Regiment, an immensely tall thin man, saluted and then bent down to shake hands with his guest. As he saluted, the military band, which was already on the park, struck up a rousing Sousa march and everyone in the stand and round the ground cheered.

Whilst all this was going on, the cleaner had emerged from his lair under the stand and made a circuit of the ground, ostensibly picking up rubbish but also having a good look at the spectators.

Having completed his circuit, he returned to the stand, picked up a brush and swept and straightened the VIP carpet along its entire length and out into the street. There, after looking round, he leaned on his broom and proceeded to exchange pleasantries with one of the policemen controlling the crowd. Whilst they were thus engaged, another constable, who had been talking to a van driver on the other side of the road, came across and said something to his colleague, at the same time surreptitiously slipping an envelope into the pocket of the older man's overalls. He, after a moment's pause, nodded to the others, then walked back to the stand and through a door beside the main gate.

Once inside his storeroom, the cleaner took the envelope from his pocket, opened it and read the contents, which appeared to cause him considerable concern. So much so that he immediately left his lair and once more resumed his scrutiny of the spectators. He was just in time to hear the announcer telling the crowd that in honour of the longstanding relationship between the regiment and Fleet Air Arm, the parade would be preceded by a fly-past; and almost as he finished speaking the jets could be heard approaching. Two planes screamed low over the field, peeled off left and right and turned and made a further pass, and as they roared off into the distance the crowds clapped and cheered.

The cleaner, now looking decidedly worried, wondered whether anyone would think it odd that there were only two planes taking part, when a man just in front of him turned to his friend saying, 'Man, d'yer no think it's a wee thing odd they can spare only two planes for such an occasion?'

'Ach well,' his friend replied, 'it'll be all this economy business.' And the other nodded knowingly.

Then, as the noise of the planes died away and a clock in the town struck the hour, to the sound of the pipes and to the cheers of the assembled company, the Regiment marched on, formed up in front of the stand, and the Commanding Officer gave the order for the General Salute. Then the announcer called for silence for the Provost, who stepped forward to the microphone.

The Provost of Inverness was a keen supporter of the local armed services and a good friend of America, where he had business connections. Fortunately he was also a competent speaker. He congratulated the troops on the success of their recent tour of duty in the East and on their splendid bearing and discipline. He gave a very brief biography of the Secretary of Defense, said what a pleasure it was to have him with them today, and invited him to inspect the leading company and then to address the parade.

It was while the inspection was taking place that the cleaner, who had completed another circuit, suddenly became interested in a tall fair haired woman who had made her way to the front of a crowd of spectators near the stand. Keeping her in sight, he hurried along the back of the crowd until he reached the side of the building, where one of the men who had made the earlier arrest came up to him. After a quick whispered conversation the other slipped away through a gate in the wall, leaving the cleaner leaning against the stand and still watching the blonde.

As she pushed her way nearer a point where she could see the front row of guests, he edged forward and transferred his right hand from his trouser to his overall pocket.

The inspection over, the Commanding Officer raised his claymore in salute and Jacobsen, with the Colonel on his left and the Provost just behind, turned to walk back to the stand. When he was about two paces from the steps, the woman darted forward raising her right arm. He turned in astonishment, a look of fear on his face, and made as if to push her away. She appeared to say something. Then, before the Colonel or anyone else could move, a shot rang out.

Jacobsen recoiled but remained on his feet. The Colonel grabbed his left arm, and with the Provost on his right, they hurried him up the steps to the stand. Once there, and after a brief argument with his hosts, he resumed his seat.

His assailant, her eyes wide with surprise, half turned to her right, her arm dropping slowly. Then she clutched at her breast with her left hand, gave a rasping cough and sank to her knees. The cleaner, his hand still in his overall pocket, walked forward and stood over her. She looked up at him and those near heard her say: 'Oh God, not you! How did you know?' Then her voice died as she gasped for breath. She tried again to speak, but there was no time left to her and she fell back, a small trickle of blood coming from her mouth, her wig awry and her dark hair spread over the grass.

Someone in the crowd started to scream, and for a moment there was a real danger of panic. But the troops stood fast and this appeared to have a calming effect. Then, with great presence of mind, the Bandmaster lifted his baton and the Military Band struck up the National Anthem. Everyone stood and, apparently without command, the parade presented arms.

So effective was this procedure that hardly anyone noticed a small party of men, including two stretcher bearers, enter the ground through the gate in the wall. The body was placed on the stretcher and escorted by a uniformed Inspector and Sergeant, was carried out to a waiting ambulance. The cleaner, accompanied by the Deputy Chief Constable and Inspector Nicholson, followed and was pushed into a police car, which drove off rapidly up a side street. After a couple of turns, it drew up in a deserted piece of road with playing fields on either side.

'Now what?' said Maclay. 'The girl's dead and Crawford is safely locked up, so they are out of the way. But as I said in my note, there's one hell of a mess on the Black Isle. Aye, and it's worse now. Simpson's dead and all but one of the others are under arrest; but that one is Urquhart. He's escaped on a motor bike. He's bound to make for here and when he finds out what has happened, he'll be hell bent on revenge.'

Forsyth, who had removed the wig and other bits of make-up that comprised his disguise, said that the first thing was to take care of Jacobsen and the next was to watch for Urquhart.

'Though God knows how we do that!' he remarked. 'However, lets deal with the American first. What's happening to him now?'

'I've arranged with the Colonel for some sort of announcement to be made and then, if Jacobsen's willing, for the march past to take place,' said Maclay, 'but what then? I suggest it's announced that the Castle reception will go ahead. Then, if he is willing, I think that Jacobsen should attend it for a short while. We've plenty protection there and afterwards he can be spirited away back to Invergordon.'

'I agree,' said Duncan, 'can you organise that?'

'Aye, I can that,' replied Maclay, 'but I'll need to go straight back to the park and that means taking this car, so you and Nick will need another car for whatever you plan to do. Nick, just get on the blower and arrange it.'

While the Inspector was speaking on the wireless, Maclay continued talking to Forsyth. 'One thing you need not worry about is the Black Isle. Brigadier Robertson is dealing with that; but you will both be required at a meeting in the Chief Constable's office at two o'clock and then there will be a press conference at three-thirty. Oh aye, and I nearly forgot; the ferry and the road from the north are under observation, and so is Urquhart's house, but of course he could get a boat across to anywhere.'

'Sure,' said Forsyth, 'but it's me he'll be after, so I'll need to make myself conspicuous. You see, after the failure of their plan he must realise that I'm alive.' Then he and Nicholson got out of the car and watched it drive off in the direction of the park.

As they waited for another car, Duncan turned to the officer and said, 'Tell me Nick, what would you do if you were Urquhart?'

'Well, I think I would hope to get to Kessock without being seen,' the Inspector replied. 'Aye, ye see, he'll have friends there with boats that'll not arouse suspicion. I'd get them to put me across to the mouth of the canal.' Then he looked over his shoulder and said, 'here's the car, so let's get on the radio and see if there's any more news of Urquhart's whereabouts.'

Even as he spoke, the radio crackled and the driver leant out and said, 'Sir, the army's wanting to speak to you from the Black Isle.' Duncan, not being that familiar with the wireless procedure involved, left the talking to Nicholson, who, after five minutes of exchanges, beckoned him into the car.

'Now this is just a bit of luck. My guess was right, for Urquhart's been spotted by one of the army road blocks,' said Nicholson. 'It seems someone saw a motor bike on a farm track some half mile from the main road. Five minutes later a pick-up, with what looked like sheep in the back, left the farm in the direction of the ferry. Apparently the truck was waved through one road block, but was picked up in Kessock. The police there saw two men leave the truck and row over to a boat belonging to one of the two, a local fisherman. The other man has been identified as Roddy Urquhart.'

Duncan looked at his watch. 'We've hardly time to go after him ourselves. It's twenty to two now, so we need to get back for the meeting. Can you get them found and have Urquhart followed and us kept informed?'

Nicholson nodded and again came the crackle of the wireless. 'Right, that's fixed. There will be a watcher on the main north road and the car at the ferry is moving to the area of the canal bridge.'

When they got to police headquarters, they were told the meeting had been moved from the Chief Constable's office to a larger room. There they found the Chief Constable with Maclay and a uniformed Superintendent, also the Secretary of State and two civil servants from the Scottish Office. Then, shortly after they arrived, they were joined by Brigadier Robertson and a tired looking Major Carmichael.

'The purpose of this meeting,' the Scottish Secretary said, 'is to hear exactly what happened this morning on the Black Isle and at the parade ground, then to decide how much information should be given to the press and to have that agreed by Downing Street. I have already spoken to the Prime Minister and you, I believe, Brigadier, have been in touch with Scottish Command.'

'Yes, sir, and General Murray has spoken to the CIGS,' replied Robertson.

'Right,' continued the Minister, 'so now perhaps you can tell us exactly what happened on the Black Isle. Then after that I shall want to hear from you, Mr Forsyth. I also want detailed minutes kept. These, together with the naval and SAS reports, will go to the Cabinet and also, I expect, to Washington.'

'I think, sir, you should hear what happened from Major Carmichael himself,' Robertson said and the Minister nodded his agreement.

Despite his hectic morning and the fact that he had been up since before five, Carmichael still had a sharp mind and was a clear and concise speaker. He described the identification of the Unicorn site, the deployment of his troops and the successful use of the decoy helicopter and the SAS.

'It was then that trouble started,' he said, 'for as the SAS came in, the jets flew overhead and another missile was fired, bringing down the last plane. One of my subalterns saw it all and says it was a huge cock up – a complete misunderstanding of orders by inexperienced people in a state of panic.'

'What happened then?'

'The SAS went straight in supported by my men. All the Unicorn people, including a press photographer, were rounded up. Unfortunately two of them decided to resist and were killed. One other was shot, apparently by his own side, and one of the ringleaders was blown up by one of their own grenades. One SAS man was wounded.'

'And the plane?'

'I'm afraid it crashed in flames and the pilot is dead. The other unfortunate thing is that another of the ringleaders, Urquhart I believe is his name, escaped by taking the photographer's motorbike.'

'Thank you, Major Carmichael,' said the Minister, 'now let's hear from you, Forsyth.'

Duncan described the arrest of Crawford and the dismantling of the booby-trapped microphone.

'That was the easy bit,' he said. 'The difficulties came when the police told me of the success of the Black Isle operation and the capture of the Unicorn gang. I knew then that I had to find Jane Parsons. I was sure that she was somewhere in the grounds and that she knew of Crawford's arrest, but I had no idea whether she knew what had happened on the Black Isle. But the only safe assumption was that she did know and would make a further attempt at assassination. She is a resourceful and ruthless woman.'

'How did you find her?'

'Well, I very nearly didn't. I made two circuits of the ground without seeing her, and then I saw this blonde. There was something not quite right about her hair. Then I remembered that Parsons had used a blonde disguise in London, and I realised the woman I was watching was wearing a wig; so I got a bit closer and was able to make a definite identification. Even then she nearly won, and if I had not been standing where I was, she would have got Jacobsen before I could have stopped her. As it was, I bitterly regret that I had to shoot – but it was the only way.'

'I'm sure,' rejoined the Minister, adding, 'this whole affair is very unfortunate, and we can only be grateful that your quick thinking averted the ultimate tragedy. Indeed we must be grateful to you for everything connected with foiling this ill conceived Unicorn plan. Now can we just have an update from the police, Chief Constable?'

'Certainly. Superintendent Graham, can you tell us the situation in the town and what you believe the people think has happened?'

Such had been the speed of events in the park, the quick thinking of the Bandmaster and Commanding Officer and the steadiness of the troops, that most people only knew there had been an incident of some sort but had no idea what had actually happened. The crowds had all dispersed quietly. The troops had marched off to the Town Hall and the invited guests were making their way to the Castle.

'Mind you, sir, when the Castle lot get talking they'll be putting two and two together,' the Superintendent said, 'aye, and once the rumours from the Black Isle start flying round, and they mebbe have already, then we've got trouble. And of course they'll know all about the plane in Lossiemouth. They'll be pretty angry about it too and so won't be inclined to keep quiet.'

At that point the Colonel and the local MP, who had accompanied Jacobsen to the Castle reception, joined the meeting. The Minister asked what was happening there and was told that things were still under control.

No one seemed to know exactly what had occurred, but that couldn't last much longer.

'I suggested to Jacobsen and the Ambassador,' the Colonel said, 'that if he was asked what had happened – and he obviously would be – the best answer would be to say that everything took place so quickly he wasn't really sure, but some crazy woman . . . and so on. He was marvellous, for of course the Yanks are good at that sort of thing. I heard him say to Lady Darrochy, "Yes, ma'am, some crazy dame came rushing at me brandishing a toy pop gun. But your guys were real quick and hustled her away . . . No, I didn't hear any shooting. You say there was a shot? Well, ma'am, it was sure not at me." Anyway he eventually said he was feeling a bit tired, so he made his farewells and we put him and the Ambassador in old Darrochy's Rolls and returned them to the bosom of their countrymen on board the ships of the NATO fleet.'

'Well at least he's now safely out of the way,' the Minister said with a sigh of relief. Then he added rather more briskly, 'We've only got about forty-five minutes before we face the Press. What are we going to say?'

'Surely the best thing would be to keep as near as possible to the truth,' suggested Duncan, 'so why don't we say something like this: "For some time it has been known that a gang of anarchists, whose avowed intention is the overthrow of the existing union between England and Scotland and the setting up of a separate state, has been planning a spectacular terrorist outrage. The exact nature of their plans was unknown until the last few days, when it was discovered that an attempt was to be made on the life of a leading member of the Government of a friendly country. Steps were taken to prevent such an event happening, but such was the scale of the terrorists' activities that the Armed Forces had to be involved. The action taken was successful and a major incident was averted. Unfortunately, however, a number of the terrorists lost their lives and a Fleet Air Arm jet crashed. The remaining terrorists are now in police custody and the gang no longer exists."'

The Minister turned to one of the civil servants and asked if he'd got that, and the man tapped his notebook and nodded.

'It's not perfect but it'll do, I think,' he said. 'Do we all agree?'

'The part about the action taken needs expanding a bit and you'll have to say something about the girl,' suggested the more senior civil servant. 'Some press man is sure to have seen what actually happened.'

'Aye Minister, and you'd better say something to the effect that the police have the matter under control and the Armed Forces are no longer involved,' added the Chief Constable.

'Agreed,' the Minister said, and then to the two civil servants, 'can you put that into a speech and have it ready for me to check with the PM in fifteen minutes? And we'll also need a handout.' As they left, he turned to the local MP. 'Jamie, we ought to make clear that the actions of this gang had nothing to do with the Scottish National Party. Can you see that they include something to that effect? And do you know someone high up in the party you can check it with?'

'Yes I do, Minister. Leave that to me,' the MP said.

'Minister, if you don't mind, I'd better check what we're going to say with Scottish Command,' Robertson said, 'for they will need to brief the CIGS before Downing Street gets on to him.'

'Yes indeed, Brigadier. Good point. Now, the press conference. I'll want you there, Brigadier Robertson, and you, Chief Constable, and my two Scottish Office boys. What about you, Forsyth?'

'I don't think my Chief would want me there, sir. And anyway I must find Urquhart. Don't forget he's still on the run – but please don't mention that, I want it kept quiet. He's after me, but I think he's also after Sir Torquhil Drumcairn and his daughter and he'll certainly want to see that all traces of Unicorn are removed from Altachonich. I think, if you and Mr Marshall agree, Inspector Nicholson and I ought to leave now and get after Urquhart.'

'Yes, all right – and that reminds me, what about Sir Torquhil? What are we going to do about him?'

'I'm afraid that he's not at all well; so what I propose to do now is to take Miss Drumcairn to Altachonich. After she's seen him, the police will interview him and report to the Chief Constables.'

'Just to me, Duncan, just to me. I've already agreed that with Argyll,' interposed Marshall.

'And, of course, I will have to report to my Chief on what is happening about Sir Torquhil and Altachonich,' said Forsyth. Then he turned to the Scottish Secretary and added, 'I have a request to make, Minister. A tape of a speech by your PPS was obtained by Unicorn and edited to show that the Government was involved in the plan to shoot down Jacobsen's helicopter. I do not know if these tapes have been found, but I think they should be – and then destroyed.'

'Thank you, Colonel. Perhaps the police would look into the matter. And now let's hope you can find Urquhart,' the Minister said, shaking hands with him. 'We already owe you a great deal. I wish you luck in this one outstanding item.'

Chapter 28

After they left the meeting, the Inspector took Duncan to his office and rang the bell for tea and biscuits.

'You realise, man, that we've had nothing to eat since dawn and there's still a long day ahead,' he said, 'and just tell me, Duncan, how are you going to fill that time?'

'The first thing I'm going to do,' Duncan replied, 'is to hire another car. Incidentally, on that subject I understand my people have come up trumps over your car.' The other man grinned and said that they had indeed.

'Good – I'm glad to hear it. Even my old boss can be generous at times! Although I've no doubt I shall get a lecture about care of government money. Now I'd better just ring Dalbeg to see how things are there and to warn Miss Drumcairn to be ready to go to Altachonich; then I'll see about the car. While I'm doing all that, can you find out if we know where Urquhart is and what he's doing? Also can you find out what the situation is at Altachonich Castle? What happens after that depends on what you find out about Urquhart.'

An hour later Duncan drove into the car park at police HQ in a splendid light grey two year-old Alvis coupé and went up to Nicholson's office.

'Now just how did you get hold of that?' asked Nick, who had been looking out of the window.

'I have good friends in the trade,' was the reply. 'I just said I wanted something conspicuous and fairly grand – and also fast. So they came up with the Alvis. It belongs to the boss's brother, who is abroad for six months. I have promised faithfully that it will come to no harm. And you know me – I always keep my promises! Now what did we find out at the various fronts?'

'From Altachonich it's not good,' Nicholson replied. 'I managed to get Dougie Fletcher, who told me that when the butler called Sir Torquhil this morning, he found him sitting up in bed looking deathly pale and complaining of a terrible headache. When he tried to get up, apparently he couldn't. He just gave a gasp, fell back and lay there.'

'What happened then? And how is he now?'

'Aye well, the doctor came over from Glenlochan and he said the laird had had a stroke. They decided it was best not to move him, but he got up a retired nurse from the village. Dougie hadn't seen the old man; however the nurse told him the laird was paralysed down one side and, although conscious, his speech was poorly.'

'And what about Urquhart?'

'My men watched him off the boat and followed him into town, where he went to his office. They thought that a bit odd – but he had a good reason, and because of it they very near lost him. Then, just in time, someone remembered that the building has a back door into one of those wee closes. They got round there in time to see him running towards the station. They went after him, but he beat them to a train that was just leaving – first stop Aviemore.'

'Then what?'

'Then came a real bit of luck,' Nicholson said. 'He must have persuaded the guard to slow down at Culloden, for he jumped off there. Now by chance our local man was in the ticket office. Urquhart didn't see him, but he knows Urquhart and knew there was a call out to find him.' At this point Nicholson picked up a map and spread it on the desk.

'Look now,' he continued, 'Urquhart walked off in this direction. Our man guessed where he was heading, so gave him a bit start and then followed on his bike. Sure enough, he went to this farm here. The laddie was just wondering what to do when the vet came by and took a message to the police house at Inshes. They telephoned us and a car is now watching the farm from this point here, and they believe Urquhart is still there.'

Duncan studied the map with great interest and ran his finger along the course of a couple of roads, then looked up at Nicholson and smiled.

'Now that's very interesting,' he said. 'Urquhart being where he is has given me an idea which might just work. Here's what I suggest we do.' Then with the aid of the map, Duncan explained his idea, at the end of which the Inspector said, 'Aye, I believe you're right, it just might work.'

Half an hour later Urquhart and his wife, who had arrived at the farm just before him, were discussing with the farmer what his next step should be. Suddenly he jumped up and crossed to the window.

'Come here and look,' he said pointing towards the road. 'Do you see yon car? Aye, the big grey one. That's Forsyth, I'm sure. I thought it was him I saw near the station, and driving a car like that, he was. Ach, I was a fool to think he died in that lochan. I should have made sure.' He gazed out of the window for several minutes, lost in thought. 'And that fool Simpson – he should have got them somehow. God, what an opportunity and look what a mess we've made of it!' And he turned and faced the room.

'Bastard!' he screamed, 'it was all his doing, that ambush this morning. By Christ I'm going to get him!' Shaking his clenched fists, he turned back to the window, paused for a moment, and then pointed. 'Just look there,' he said, his voice now much calmer. 'He's stopped – aye, and he's out looking at a map.' Then he turned to the farmer and said, 'I'm going after him. Can I borrow the car?'

'For God's sake think for a moment,' said his wife. 'It must be a trap. Why else would he suddenly appear up there?'

'Aye man,' the farmer said, 'Mary's right. He could only be on this road if he knew you were here. The police will be watching.'

But Roddy was deaf to their entreaties, intent on his own idea. 'No, you're wrong,' he snapped, 'I know why he's here and just where he's going. He's going to pick up the Drumcairn lassie. She'll be at that big house by Nairn. It belongs to the old man's cousin.' Then he turned to the farmer: 'quick now, he's back in the car. Come on man, give me the keys and I'll follow him,' and as the farmer moved to join him, he held up his hand saying, 'No, I'd best go alone. I don't want to involve any of you any more.'

With that he ran to the car and drove off in the direction Forsyth had taken; but instead of following him, after half a mile he turned left. 'The way he's gone, he's got to come out on the main road,' he said to himself, 'so I'll just cut down here and wait for him a bit back. Less chance of being seen.'

The Alvis, with Duncan at the wheel, dropped down the hill, through the woods and turned east on to the main road. Half a mile and some three or four cars behind, a nondescript black saloon pulled out from a lay-by and followed the Alvis towards Nairn. After about five miles the grey car turned to the right up a narrow road, then almost immediately left through some gates into a long tree-lined avenue. The nondescript car drove on beyond the side road and, at a convenient spot, turned to face the way it had come and stopped by a heap of gravel.

'Just as I thought – that's old Cuthbertson's place; so he has gone to collect the girl,' Roddy said to himself, shaking the steering wheel with excitement. 'Now I only hope they are not too long. I don't want to have to follow in the dark.'

He need not have worried, for after about ten minutes the grey car emerged from the turning and drove off towards Inverness, and sitting beside the driver was a woman in a high collared coat with a beret pulled well down over her hair.

At first Duncan drove fairly slowly with one eye on the mirror. There was only one car behind him but then, after he'd gone about half a mile, he saw another car pull out from the verge and follow in his direction. 'That's him, I think,' he muttered and increased his speed.

After about three miles they rounded a bend and saw the lights of a level crossing ahead. As soon as he saw them, Duncan put his foot down and went over the rails at a considerable speed. He glanced in the mirror and saw the car behind them just make it as the gates began to close, leaving the next car skidding to a stop. Then they were round another corner and he saw no more.

As he came in sight of the crossing and saw that the Alvis was already beyond it and heading west at a good speed, Urquhart swore loudly for he realised what was going to happen. His somewhat elderly car was slow to respond to the throttle and the gates began to close when he was still some fifty yards short of them. He jammed on the brakes and slid to a stop with the bonnet almost touching the red warning lamp.

As he did so, a police car appeared from nowhere and pulled up immediately behind him. Two men jumped out, and before he could move, he found his door opened and a revolver covering him. Then someone leant over from the back seat, handcuffs were slipped over his wrists and a voice said, 'Roderick Urquhart, I am arresting you on suspicion of complicity in events which took place on the Black Isle earlier today.' And he found himself hauled from the car, marched over the crossing and into another police car, which immediately drove off towards Inverness.

When, some twenty minutes later, they reached the outskirts of the town, Duncan turned to the woman in the passenger seat of the Alvis and asked her where he should take her.

'The Town Police Station will be fine,' the young policewoman said, removing her beret and turning down the collar of her coat, 'and I hope the operation was successful.'

'I'm afraid we'll have to wait to discover that,' he said as he pulled up outside the station to let her out. 'What I do know is that you played your part perfectly and I shall report that to your superiors. Goodbye – and thanks for your help.' As he drove off, she turned and smiled wistfully before vanishing into the building.

Deciding there was no point in calling at police HQ and risking a prolonged delay, he drove straight out of the town in the direction of Dalbeg, where, some forty-five minutes later, he found Daphne and his cousin listening to the end of the six o'clock news.

'Well, young Duncan,' said Sir Geoffrey, 'you seem to have had quite a day. As far as I can make out from the news, a Fleet Air Arm plane has been shot down, several bandits of some sort have been killed and an American politician has been saved from assassination. Well done! I couldn't have done better myself; but it does all sound more like the Balkans than Scotland!'

'If that's your impression, Geoffrey, then they must have done a good job at the press conference,' Duncan replied, 'but did they say anything about it being in aid of Scottish independence?'

'Not really. They just said that a gang of anarchists had planned to assassinate the American Secretary of Defense, that their plans had gone wrong and that the police, with the aid of the army, had foiled the plot. Some of the gang had resisted and they had been dealt with, but the majority were now in police custody. Then they mentioned the loss of the plane. I think they said it crashed while preparing to take part in a fly-past.'

'Did they mention anything about the parade?'

'Just that there had been an incident and the event had been cut short to ensure the safety of the American. What did happen there?'

'Let's just say that a direct attempt was made on Jacobsen's life which fortunately failed. I would like to leave it at that for the moment.' Then he put a hand to his head and said, 'God I'm tired, I must sit down for a moment,' and he looked vaguely round the room.

Daphne was at his side in an instant and with the General's help, got him over to the sofa where he lay back and closed his eyes. She bent over and loosened his collar, then beckoned to Geoffrey.

'Let's leave him for a bit. He's completely exhausted,' she said, leaving the room and gently closing the door.

It was half an hour later when she looked in again and found Duncan standing in front of the fireplace. He glanced in the mirror, smoothed his hair and straightened his tie before taking her in his arms.

'I'm sorry if I gave you a fright. I'm sorry too, if I didn't greet you properly.' And he bent down and kissed her lips. 'I've been up since about half-past four and I suddenly felt I could not go on any longer.'

'But darling, are you all right now? Shouldn't you lie down a bit longer?'

'Definitely not,' he replied with a smile, 'that would only make me feel worse. There's nothing the matter with me that a drink and something to eat won't cure. I've had hardly anything all day.'

Then he led her back to the sofa and said in a gentle voice, 'Look darling, I'm afraid the news from Altachonich is not good. Your father has had a mild stroke and the local doctor is with him. Yes, he's still at the castle, so I suggest we go there as soon as I've had something to eat, but I think it would be an idea if you rang Dougie first.'

'Do it in the study. It will be more peaceful,' said Sir Geoffrey appearing in the doorway, 'meanwhile I'll give Duncan a drink and we'll get Mrs Mack to produce sandwiches or something.'

Mrs Mack was having nothing to do with sandwiches and when Daphne came back she found Duncan drinking whisky and soda and preparing to attack cold ham and salad.

'What news?' he asked.

'Poor father,' Daphne said, dabbing her eyes with her handkerchief, 'he can hardly move and now the nurse says he's lost his speech. I spoke to Dougie first and he said I could now ring the castle and he thought the doctor was there. When I got through, the doctor had just left so I spoke to the nurse. I know her well. "Oh Miss Daphne," she said, "will ye no come quick. Your father canna speak now, but after I was reading your letter, he asked for you. That was the last time he spoke." My dear, I hate to ask you this when you're so tired, but can we go straight away? I'll even drive if you like.'

'That won't be necessary,' he said, 'just get your things and I'll be ready.'

'Are you sure this is wise?' asked his cousin when Daphne had left the room.

Duncan, having finished his meal, pushed the plate aside and got to his feet. He looked out of the window, then turned to his cousin.

'Probably not, but needs must when the devil drives,' he said, 'and we'd better get straight off. It's obvious the old man is not going to last long and I must get Daphne there before he goes. Also I don't like the look of the weather. There's a storm coming, and with the way the wind is, it'll be worse over on the west coast. If we go now we should be OK; so thanks for the drink and for looking after Daphne and I'll be in touch.'

They found Daphne in the hall talking to Mrs Mack. 'Yes dearie,' the housekeeper was saying, 'I'll mind your things and I hope your father gets better.'

'Thank you, Mrs Mack,' she said and then walked over to Sir Geoffrey and took his hand, 'and thank you Geoffrey for looking after me so well and for your help in getting the letter to father. I hope it's all right leaving my things here. I promise I'll come back for them.' And she looked up and kissed him on both cheeks.

'Of course, my dear,' he said, 'and now come on both of you, off you go.'

Daphne picked up her hat and coat and got into the car. Sir Geoffrey shut the door and stepped back; Duncan let in the clutch and the Alvis swept silently down the drive.

They drove for several miles in silence, but when they turned on to the main road to the west and driving became easier, Daphne, who had been deep in thought, looked up.

'Tell me what really happened at the parade ground this morning,' she asked. 'Who tried to kill Jacobsen? Was it Jane Parsons?'

'Yes.'

'And what happened to her?'

'Do you really want to know?' When she nodded, he said, 'OK, then I'll tell you. As soon as I got the message about what had happened on the Black Isle, I set out to find Jane. I guessed she was somewhere on the field. I also made two assumptions: first that she knew her brother had been arrested and then that she would have received a message telling her things had gone wrong.'

'And did you find her?'

'Eventually, but I had a major problem,' he replied, and told her about the wig. 'When I finally realised it was Jane, I followed her towards the grandstand. I had just reached it when she darted towards the American, who was walking back from inspecting the troops. She had a gun and she was only two yards from him when I shot her. I had no alternative.'

'You mean you killed her. Was the gun loaded and was she really going to use it?'

'It was loaded. Whether she was going to use it – well, we shall never know.' There was an uncomfortable silence, broken only when Duncan said, 'but in those circumstances you can never take the risk.'

'I know, darling. I shan't think the worse of you for doing it. I realise you had to, for if she had succeeded, the consequences don't bear thinking about – but I still wish you hadn't.' Then she put her hand on his knee and said, almost in a whisper, 'Did you sleep with her on that train journey?'

He looked down at her for a brief moment. 'Let's just say that though she was a ruthless and utterly amoral woman, she was also a very intelligent and charming woman.' As he was saying this, he still had half an eye on the road. Then as he returned his full concentration to the way ahead, something in the rear view mirror caught his attention.

They were on a hill and what caught his eye was not the lorry following him, but the motor cycle overtaking it, for this was the second time in as many miles that he had noticed a motor cycle closing on him but never passing.

Over the next few miles he tried alternately speeding up and slowing down and the motor cyclist followed him exactly, and when two cars got between them on a twisting section of road, he just followed on behind. Then, on a long straight, both cars overtook Duncan and he noticed the motor cycle close right up. The rider put a hand up and took something from the front of his leather jacket.

Duncan changed down to third, and at the same time pushed Daphne to the floor. 'Get down and stay down,' he shouted.

Then, as the man on the motor cycle drew level with the back of the car and raised his arm, Duncan dropped to second and put his foot flat down. The six-cylinder, three-litre engine responded at once and the car surged forward. The motor cyclist, taken by surprise and having only one hand on the handlebars, almost lost control. He hurled whatever was in his hand at the fast disappearing car but missed, and the object rolled to the nearside verge. With the machine back under control, he opened the throttle wide and was just round the next corner when the grenade exploded harmlessly amongst the trees.

They were now into another dangerous bit of the road and some three miles from the next village, when on a short uphill straight, and with no other vehicle in sight, the motor cyclist again closed right up. Again Duncan used the power of the Alvis to pull ahead, but this time his adversary would have none of it, and regardless of the approaching corner, he pulled out to overtake and his hand went to the front of his jacket.

Whether he did not see the lorry or whether he thought there was room for all three of them, it was not until it was almost abreast of them that the rider appeared to realise he could not get through between the two vehicles. He swung across the front of the lorry, just missed it, and raced up the verge between it and the rock face. It was not a feasible manoeuvre, for the lorry was braking violently and its rear end was swinging wildly from side to side.

Nevertheless he was almost clear when he had to swerve to avoid being pushed into the cliff, and the nearside handlebar clipped the tail of the lorry. Machine and rider slid across the road, missed the rear of the Alvis, and disappeared down the slope on the opposite side. Seconds later came an explosion and a sheet of flame.

Duncan pulled on to the verge and found himself shaking at the thought of what might have happened.

'That was far too close for comfort,' he said.

'What was?' asked Daphne in a whisper, then pulling herself together added, 'What on earth's going on?'

'It's all right, darling, you can come up now,' said Duncan, and as she struggled up from the floor, he went on, 'I'm afraid Roddy Urquhart has had a nasty accident,' he said, 'although how he came to be following us, God knows.'

He got out of the car and turned to the girl. 'Will you be all right if I leave you for a minute or two?' She nodded.

'I must go back and comfort the lorry driver and get hold of the police. There was a cottage about half a mile back and with any luck it'll have a phone. If I were you, I would stay here, for I think the scene back there will be pretty unpleasant.'

When he got to the lorry, he found the driver standing by his cab in a state of shock.

'What happened man?' he asked. 'It wasna' my fault. Yon motor bike shot across my front – then next thing, I see in the mirror him skidding over the edge there and then a big explosion. You saw it sir, didn't you? You'll tell the polis it wasna' my fault?'

'Yes I'll do that, and don't you worry,' Duncan said. 'I'm afraid you got tied up in the end of a rather nasty story which you'll read about in the papers tomorrow. We'll have to get hold of the police and when they arrive, just tell them what you saw and what you did. Leave the rest of the explaining to me.' He was just about to ask if the driver felt able to drive to the nearest telephone, when he heard the sirens and saw the flashing lights of two police cars.

The front one pulled up alongside them and Inspector Nicholson jumped out and walked over. A Sergeant and two Constables, one carrying a fire extinguisher, got out of the second car and ran straight down the bank to where a fire was still burning. Another man, notebook in hand, got into the lorry cab with the driver.

'Aye then, he caught up with you,' Nicholson said, looking down the bank. 'That'll be him down there, I take it. How the hell did he get that bike, I wonder?'

'That's him all right,' Duncan replied, 'but what I want to know is – how the hell did he escape?'

'That's a sorry story, I'm afraid. I sent him back to Inverness straight away while I arranged for the car to be moved and thanked the crossing keeper. It should have been fine. He was handcuffed and with experienced officers. Well, just as they came to the town he had an attack of sneezing – how he did it I don't know – but he was gie short of breath and so they unlocked the handcuffs. He put his hand in his pocket as though for a handkerchief. What he pulled out I don't know, but he verra near knocked out the officer beside him. Then, as the driver slowed to see what was going on, he jumped out and vanished behind the distillery buildings. Where he went, I dinna ken, for they could find him nowhere.'

'And how do you come to be here?'

'I caught up with them while they were still searching and when they told me what had happened, I sent them off to look at some of the places where he might be. I then went back to my office, rang Dalbeg and found you'd left. So I warned General Forsyth and also sent a car round that way and came straight down here hoping to catch you and warn you, but it seems he beat me to it. What happened?'

Duncan explained, adding, 'I'm afraid there'll not be much left of him. It was a bad crash, then he went down the bank – I don't know how far – then there was the grenade and the fire.'

Duncan paused for a moment before saying, 'Nick, I must take Daphne on to the castle. The old man is near death and if we don't go now, she'll not see him alive. I'll probably have to stay the night but I'll be back at your office by half-ten tomorrow.'

The Inspector agreed to this and said that it looked as though he'd be there for some time yet, and then he'd have to go and see Mrs Urquhart, assuming the body was that of Urquhart.

'Aye, it's him all right,' a voice said, and the Sergeant climbed back up the bank and on to the road, 'and he's no' a pretty sight, Sir, there's still another grenade lying there. God knows what the heat will have done to it, so we'd best get the bomb disposal people and we'll mebbe need to close the road.'

Leaving Duncan to go back to his car, Inspector Nicholson accompanied his Sergeant back down the bank to inspect the body and assess the situation.

Chapter 29

After leaving the scene of the accident, they drove for some miles in silence, each busy with their own thoughts, until eventually Daphne looked up and asked what had happened.

'I was sitting there wondering why you thought Jane Parsons was charming. I thought she was an absolute bitch!' she said. 'Then suddenly you started driving in the most extraordinary way and pushed me down on the floor. Why?'

'Because Roddy Urquhart was chasing us on a very powerful motor cycle, with a pocket full of hand grenades which he intended to throw at us. He was so busy with this that he failed to notice he was heading straight for a lorry. In his effort to avoid it, he skidded down the bank and the grenades and petrol tank exploded. The police say it looks a very nasty mess. No one except the lorry driver saw anything, so we may be able to pass it off as an unfortunate accident.'

Daphne shuddered but made no further comment. This suited Duncan very well for it was now dark, and in the deteriorating weather it required all his skill to make any sort of speed on the main road, and he knew it would be far worse once they reached the open hill.

'How much do you suppose Father can understand?' asked Daphne suddenly, 'and what am I going to tell him if he asks about Inverness?'

'I don't think he will ask – remember his speech is badly affected. And I'm sure they won't have let him hear any news, even if he could understand it. My advice would be to say as little as possible. But I think it's a question of take the doctor's advice and play it by ear.'

Daphne nodded, and then for the first time appeared to notice the rapidly worsening weather. The rain was now lashing down and the twin-speed wipers were having a hard job keeping the windscreen clear; the wind too had increased to a full gale, making any sort of conversation difficult. Then the lights of a village came into view but so poor was the visibility that even with her local knowledge, she could not identify it.

'Where are we?' she asked peering into the gloom, 'and how soon will we get to the castle?'

'We're just coming into Fort William,' replied Duncan, 'so I guess we'll be there in about forty-five minutes. But I don't like the weather at all; I just hope we don't meet any floods or landslides, and there's that dodgy bridge you told me about the other day. How will that like a flash flood?'

'Inversallachy?' Daphne thought for a moment and then said, 'Yes, we could have a problem there, but only if it's been raining all afternoon higher up. Wind and tide are wrong for the loch to be over the road, but we will need to watch the bridge.'

As they climbed the pass they got some shelter from the wind but all the burns were in full spate and water was coursing down the road. Once over the top, though, it was a different story. On the west side of the watershed they met the full force of the wind, and at one point Duncan had to negotiate a small rock fall, not easy in the low-slung Alvis. However they reached the lochside road safely, but when the Sallachy River loomed out of the darkness, it was all tumbling white water and even above the howling of the gale, they could hear the roar of the spate.

Minutes later the headlights picked out the bridge, and they could see there was water up to the top of the arch and could hear the boulders crashing into the supports.

'Go on darling, go over quickly,' Daphne shouted, her voice barely audible above the voice of the storm. 'If those rocks go on smashing into the bridge, it'll give. And then we're stuck.'

Duncan accelerated and, as they came on to the bridge, they could feel it shaking with the force of the water. On the other side he had to slow abruptly, for the road was flooded to a depth of several inches. While they were negotiating this, there was a grinding crash from behind and a further great mass of water surged down the road. Throwing caution to the winds, Duncan put his foot down and preceded by a massive bow wave, they emerged from the flood and on to higher ground.

'We were lucky to get away with that,' said Duncan with relief. 'From the sound of it, the bridge has gone, and more than likely taken a good bit of the road with it. Let's just hope I haven't drowned the engine! It seems all right at the moment.'

Twenty minutes later, and without any further hazards, they reached the gates of the castle. As they drew up at the front door, it opened and Charles came down the steps with a large golf umbrella.

'Oh Miss Daphne,' he said as he opened the passenger door, 'we thought you'd never get here. The doctor and Nurse Fraser are up with your father. I think you should go straight up. They said he was speaking again, but it's very hard to understand what he's saying.' He escorted Daphne up the steps and when she vanished into the hall, he came back to the car and bent down to speak to Duncan.

'I do hope, sir,' he said, 'that she's in time to speak to Sir Torquhil. They say he's very near death. It's been a terrible twenty-four hours, sir. And then hearing the news from Inverness . . . oh no sir,' he said shaking his head, 'Sir Torquhil knows nothing. He seems to have lost interest in his friends that went off there. When he can speak he just mutters about the eagle and how it has all come true.'

'I think I'll leave Miss Daphne for the present,' Duncan said when at last he managed to stem the butler's flow. 'Is Dougie here or up at the cottage?'

'Mr Fletcher and Inspector Gray are in the gun room and I think they are anxious to talk to you, sir,' the butler replied.

'Right Charles, hop in and I'll drive round to the back and then you can take me to them. Oh, and let me know if there's any news of Sir Torquhil.'

In the gun room he found Inspector Gray, who was studying pictures of the Boer War in an old copy of the *Illustrated London News* while Dougie was pretending to sort out some boxes of flies.

The Inspector looked up. 'Thank God you're here, sir,' he said, 'tell us what has been happening in Inverness. The wireless is no' verra precise. Poor Sir Torquhil, I'm almost thinking it'll be best if he doesna' last much longer.'

'I'll tell you about Inverness later,' replied Duncan, 'but first we must deal with the bridge at Inversallachy. Is there a telephone in the gun room?'

'Is the bridge away then?' Dougie asked. 'I tell you, I've been waiting two years for it to happen.'

'Yes it's away,' Duncan replied, 'at least I think it is. As we reached it there were boulders and every sort of thing coming down. "Make a run for it," Daphne shouted, "or we'll be stuck here for ever." So I did; then just as we got clear there was an almighty crash, the flood water rose alarmingly and we just about made the higher ground.'

'Aye, it'll be gone all right,' said Gray, 'but we'll not bother with the telephone. I'll get the laddie in the car outside to report it on the wireless.'

While Gray went to organise this, Duncan asked the keeper if the bomb disposal people had been over to check the castle and the quarry and what, if anything, they'd found.

'Aye, they found things all right,' Dougie replied, 'more like a minefield than a quarry it was. Every hut and shed had a charge -and a hefty one at that. They also found two caves which had been fitted with well concealed steel doors. There were more weapons and explosives in them. And in one there was a corpse, pretty far gone it was. Simpson must have imprisoned some poor sod in there and just left him. I told you he wasna' a very nice person. Man, I'm sure the poor laird didna' really understand what likes he was consorting with. Anyway they said the whole thing was wired to one wee switch that's right here in the castle . . . Aye, they've disconnected it all and taken it away. Good thing they did it before the storm.'

'And what about the castle?'

'They didna' find anything. Mebbe the idea was for the laird to say he knew nothing, and he could only think that some fools must have got at the explosives in the quarry and . . . well, dangerous thing, dynamite.'

'Right,' said Gray coming back into the room, 'Oban says they'll report it to the roads people but they doubt very much can be done while the storm lasts. God, man, it's a terrible night.'

'Can we get out by the Brackla track?' asked Duncan, 'I've got to be back in Inverness tomorrow morning.'

'I'm no' that sure,' Dougie said, 'it'll likely be all right for a Land Rover. What sort of car have you got?'

'Mr Forsyth has a right fancy sports model and he'll no' be getting out in that – not by Brackla, he won't!' and Gray gave a great guffaw. 'But not to worry, sir. If Dougie can get you out to the main road, I'm sure we can fix with the police in Fort William to take you to Inverness. Aye, I can talk to them. What a blessing this wireless is, for I'm not sure how long we'll have the telephone if this wind keeps up. And it's as well you still make your own electricity. The Hydro will be having a hard time of it tonight.'

After further talk on the wireless, it was arranged that the next morning Dougie, in the Land Rover, would take Duncan to the main road at Brackla, where a car from Fort William would meet them and drive him to Inverness. Then, having got his departure fixed, Duncan gave them a fairly heavily edited account of all that had happened earlier in the day.

'So you see,' he ended, 'all the main conspirators are accounted for. I imagine the survivors will be tried, whether for capital offences or something less, I don't know. What will happen to Mary Urquhart I also don't know. And then there is Sir Torquhil. I have to say that I hope we will not have to make a decision in that case. Let the verdict on him be between himself and his Maker. Oh yes, I knew there was one other thing. What happened to the cattle truck driver? He should have returned here this morning?'

'Aye, he did, and he should now be in the cells in Inverness.'

There was a knock on the door and Charles entered. 'Would Mr Forsyth please go to Miss Daphne in the morning room?' he said.

'Of course,' said Duncan, adding, 'will you excuse me, gentlemen? I'll let you know what happens.'

In the morning room Duncan found a tearful Daphne standing by the fire. As he walked over to her, she flung her arms round his neck and buried her face in his jacket. She stood there sobbing for two or three minutes while he stroked her hair; finally he raised her head and wiped her eyes with his handkerchief.

'Tell me about it,' he said, 'you'll feel better if you talk. Did your father recognise you and were you able to speak to him?'

She moved away and sitting on the sofa, made a visible effort to get her emotions under control.

'When I got upstairs I found Dr Ford, and he suggested that we had a chat before I went in. So we sat on a sofa in the passage, and he told me father was conscious and could just speak, though he couldn't move. "I don't know whether he knows what's happened to him," he said, "he's conscious but seems to be living in a world of his own." I then steeled myself to ask if this was the end. "Aye, when you see him now, I'm afraid it'll be your last meeting. He'll no' last the night."'

After a pause, during which Duncan moved across to the sofa, she continued, 'I went in and, oh darling, I could hardly bear to look. He was propped up in bed and his face was ashen. He obviously heard the door for his eyes moved in my direction.

'Nurse Fraser said: "Look, here's Miss Daphne." Then she whispered to me that he had been saying my name and that she'd leave us for a wee while. I pulled a chair up to the bed and took his hand. It was ice cold and I could sense that he couldn't feel. I said: "It's Daphne Father, your daughter Daphne." He turned his head very slightly and looked at me. Then he said my name a couple of times as though it meant something to him; I think he smiled, but he said nothing more, just closed his eyes as though he were thinking. I tiptoed out, told Nurse Fraser I'd be back in five minutes and came down here.'

'Do you think he knew who you were?'

'Yes I'm sure he did and I think he wanted to say something. If he does say whatever it is, I want you to hear it. So will you come with me when I go back to him?'

Duncan nodded, then stood up and gave her his hand. When she got to her feet, he put his arm round her shoulder as they walked towards the door. Outside the partially closed door of Sir Torquhil's bedroom they found Nurse Fraser.

'He's conscious, Miss Daphne,' she said, 'and he's asking for you again. It's a wee thing hard to understand him, but his mind is clear. Dr Ford said this might happen. He's gone down to the telephone but he said he'd come at once if you need him. I ken the laird feels these may be his last conscious moments.'

'We'll go in – this is Mr Forsyth and I want him to hear what father says. Will you be outside if we need you?'

'Aye, I will that,' the nurse replied, and as they went into the bedroom her gaze followed them and she nodded in a knowing manner.

Daphne went straight over to the bed and sat down. In the few minutes that she had been away a remarkable change had come over her father. When she took his hand, he did not move except for the same slight inclination of the head. But his eyes were now bright, almost intense, as he looked at her.

'I'm glad you've come,' he said. His speech was a little above a whisper and very slightly slurred, but perfectly understandable.

'I'm sorry I've been so long,' she replied, 'but it's been difficult to get here. It's a terrible night of wind and rain. This is Duncan Forsyth, who very kindly drove me up.' The eyes wandered towards Duncan, but whether they took him in he could not tell.

'Daphne my dear,' Sir Torquhil's eyes turned again towards her and his voice strengthened, 'I've been a fool. You were right, I should never have got mixed up with that independence stuff. It's too early; the people are not ready for it yet.' He paused and the eyes turned inwards again. Then he looked at his daughter.

'It'll come though, but not through violence.' Then his voice rose, and took on an almost prophetic quality. 'I see a time,' he said in the traditional manner of the Highland seer, 'when there will be a Scottish Parliament. It will be a parliament of a country within a federal union – the Federal Union of Great Britain. Separate but yet united. There will be many problems to overcome, many false starts perhaps. There must be no violence, however, and everything must be acceptable to all the people of Scotland, not just to a few hotheads or to an ignorant and nervous English Government.'

The fire went out of the eyes, the voice dropped and became difficult to understand. 'I'm glad those men went away,' he said almost to himself. 'I'm glad they gave it up when I told them it would fail.' Here Daphne looked round at Duncan, who was standing by the foot of the bed.

'I told them it would fail,' the faltering voice went on, 'it had to once the eagle came. So I'm glad they gave it up. Listen! I hear the waves. Soon they will engulf me and I'll be safe from the storm.' Then, almost to himself, he added these dying words: 'Remember the Unicorn is for Scotland and Unicorns never die.'

His eyes turned to Duncan, and in a final moment of lucidity, the voice strengthened and said: 'I give Daphne into your safe keeping.'

And Duncan walked slowly from the room to look for the doctor, leaving Daphne alone with her father.

Epilogue

The aftermath of Operation Saviour – or what came to be called the Battle of the Black Isle – was rather less than a seven-day wonder.

The information given out at the press conference on the Saturday afternoon missed all but the late editions of the Sunday papers, and these only carried brief items about an attempt on the life of a prominent foreign statesman.

The lunchtime and evening news bulletins on both radio and television had accounts of a plot by extreme Scottish Nationalists, thought to be associated with other international terrorist groups, to assassinate the American Secretary of Defense. The plot had been discovered by British intelligence services, and swift action by police, assisted by the armed forces, had avoided a major international incident occurring. Resistance by the terrorists had resulted in the death of the ringleaders and two other members of the group. All the rest were now in police custody and the organisation, which, it appeared, was known as Unicorn, had ceased to exist.

By the time the press reached the Black Isle site, the army and police had removed the SAS uniforms used by the gang, and also the photographs and other papers found in the photographer's satchel, and the *Hirondelle* had been taken to Fort George. Brigadier Robertson and Deputy Chief Constable Maclay, who met the press at the croft, informed the assembled reporters that it was unclear at present what the Unicorn gang had intended to do. An investigation was proceeding and as soon as there was anything significant to report, a further briefing would be held.

On the Sunday there was considerable diplomatic activity between London and Washington, the result of which was a personal and confidential letter, signed jointly by the President and the Prime Minister, to the owners and editors of the principal newspapers in both countries. This letter, which has never been made public, is believed to have indicated that the Black Isle incident was an attempt by a group of inexperienced agitators to involve the United States in a plot to change the constitution of the United Kingdom by force. As the plot had been foiled, it was suggested that the less said about it the better.

Surprisingly, this view was accepted by the majority of the media leadership. This, and the fact that the people of the Black Isle mostly kept their own counsel, meant that interest in the affair died rapidly, helped, in the following week, by a number of important political events around the world and a couple of interesting high society scandals.

The local papers carried stories of the success of the parade in Inverness but regretted that it had to be cut short due to the temporary indisposition of Mr Jacobsen. Some expressed pleasure that he had eventually recovered sufficiently to meet some of the local dignitaries at the Castle. Few of the nationals showed any interest in this local happening and by the time information on the use of a guided missile was released, interest had died and it was barely mentioned.

The surviving members of Unicorn who took part in the attempt appeared before the Sheriff in Glasgow on a variety of charges, including illegal possession of firearms and conspiracy to cause explosions, and received fines or short terms of imprisonment. It must be assumed that it was made clear to them that disclosure of the nature of the plot and their part in it could result in a substantial increase in their penalties, for none of them subsequently talked about it, even, it is believed, to their families.

On the political front these events caused no interest in the United States, although shortly afterwards Norman Jacobsen retired from his position in the Administration. Cyrus P. Groat also found it expedient to give up most of his business and public appointments and to retire to his ranch in Wyoming.

In Parliament the Prime Minister made a brief statement about a plot to try and change the constitution by force. In the foiling of this plot the police had had the support of certain army units and they, because of armed resistance, had been forced to open fire, resulting in the death of four of the terrorists. The Prime Minister also deeply regretted the loss of a Fleet Air Arm plane which had become accidentally involved. He finished his announcement by assuring the House that whatever they may have heard to the contrary, the official Scottish National Party was in no way involved in any of these events. Then, in a rare show of unity, the Leader of the Opposition congratulated the Government on the successful outcome of what could have been a major disaster.

Paradoxically, the death of Sir Torquhil Drumcairn caused more press interest than the events on the Black Isle, of which he, to some extent, had been the instigator. The Scottish papers had headings such as 'Death of Noted Businessman and Patriot', while the English press favoured 'Death of Former MP and Eastern Shipping Tycoon'. All the serious papers had obituaries extolling his contribution to British commerce and his support, while an MP, of many Scottish causes, particularly the creation of employment opportunities in the Highlands. The Scottish papers added paragraphs on his interest in the cause of independence.

For all that, it was felt best by the Government that there should be only a small semi-private funeral and no memorial service, a view supported by his family, who explained that this was his express wish. Nevertheless the funeral was well attended by local people of all walks, and by many friends and colleagues from all over Scotland. The Secretary of State was represented by his PPS, still Paddy Jenkinson, now happily reunited with all the copies of Jane Parson's mementos.

Because Sir Torquhil died when he did, his involvement and that of the Altachonich Estate with Unicorn never became public. The estate now belongs to his daughter, who has revitalised the farm, which now has well known herds of both Highland Cattle and Garrons, the hardy Highland ponies. The quarry is also working again and produces limited quantities of very high-class stone, something that would have delighted the former laird.

To his intense surprise, shortly after the events related here, Duncan Forsyth's wife announced her intention of getting married again and asked him for a divorce. This should become absolute in the near future, and those in the know confidently predict that the Lady of Altachonich will not long be remaining single.

Thus ended one of the strangest and least known episodes in the recent history of Scotland's struggle to achieve, if not independence, at least a greater recognition of its individual nationhood. This particular plan was ill conceived and poorly executed and resulted in inevitable failure. But one day, who knows, Scotland may achieve its goal. If it does, it will surely not be by violence. Perhaps, as Sir Torquhil prophesied, it will be as part of a federal grouping of the British Islands.